Dyed In The Green

a novel by George Mercer

Library and Archives Canada Cataloguing in Publication

Mercer, George, 1957-, author
    Dyed in the green / George Mercer.

Issued in print and electronic formats.
ISBN 978-0-9879754-0-9 (pbk.).--ISBN 978-0-9879754-1-6 (pdf)

    I. Title.

PS8626.E743D84 2014   C813'.6
C2014-905828-4   C2014-905829-2

Permission to quote lyrics from Kenzie MacNeil's composition,
"The Island", was provided by Kenzie MacNeil.

Cover art and design: Dan Stiles
Editing: Kate Scallion
Typeset in *Bembo* at SpicaBookDesign

Printed in Canada on 100% recycled FSC certified paper.

FSC
www.fsc.org
MIX
Paper from
responsible sources
FSC® C016245

For the protectors of wild places.

ACKNOWLEDGEMENT

THIS FIRST BOOK has been in the works for a long time, aging, hopefully improving with age, as it fermented in storage. Whatever it lacks may be attributed solely to me, and at the end of the day, I take full responsibility for any flaws that may be rendered within these pages.

The book has benefitted, though, from the input of numerous people, including my editor, Kate Scallion, and a small army of volunteer readers who agreed to tackle the draft manuscript and provide feedback. Rundi, Gord, Rick, Todd, Granville, Roger, Jordie, Harry, Lorna, Jason, Brenda and last but definitely not least of all, my most ardent supporter and objective reviewer, Jan – thanks so much.

To our writing group – Amanda, Christine, Mark, Mary and Susan – your continued commitment to the craft inspires me daily and to Robert, who really started it off for me, thanks for helping to point the way.

To a great extent, this book and the series that follows has been inspired by the men and women of Canada's national parks, who share a "green" ethic and who truly are, in every sense of the expression, "dyed in the green".

Many of these men and women nurtured my passion for parks and protected areas and the species that live there. Many were mentors who led by example and walked the talk.

My fervent wish is that *Dyed In The Green* and the other books that follow in the series do justice to their stories.

EGM
September 2014

PROLOGUE

Gulf of Saint Lawrence, off Cape Breton Island

THE AUTUMN STORMS struck early along the shores of northern Cape Breton Island. As darkness settled over the coast, a low-pressure system released its energy. Blasts of wind hitting speeds of one hundred kilometres an hour funnelled down through the crevices and outwash valleys toward the Gulf of Saint Lawrence, picking up speed as the cold air fell to the sea.

Most of the fishing boats based in the numerous small communities along the northwest shore had made their way home, but a medium-sized crab boat, the *Highlander*, was still twenty kilometres back from its berth at Pleasant Bay. The sturdy Cape Islander continued to plow through the chop, sending spray up and over its small cabin. The southeaster screamed overhead, ripping foam and spray into the blackness.

Gerald Moores had a stranglehold on the steering wheel, his knuckles white as he peered into the pitch black, trying to distinguish open water from rocky headland. On the back deck, Gerald's cousin, John Donald, was encased in heavy raingear and struggling to shift the fishing gear forward.

Gerald reckoned they were almost through the worst of it, having to stay well offshore to avoid the sunkers along this stretch of the coast. Soon they would be past Fishing Cove and able to hug the cliffs, staying in the lee of MacKenzie Mountain.

Suddenly the wheelhouse door burst open.

"Shut her down," John Donald yelled.

Gerald hesitated, not wanting to stop while they were still vulnerable, then reconsidered and pulled the throttle back, easing the diesel engine into neutral. He steered toward shore, seeking protection on the leeward side of Mackenzie Mountain.

1

John Donald stormed through the door, pushing Gerald away from the wheel.

"Shut the fucking thing down, I told you," he yelled, turning off the ignition.

As the *Highlander*'s bow dropped into the calmer waters off Fishing Cove, John Donald let go of the wheel, allowing it to spin aimlessly as the boat lost momentum and drifted toward shore.

"Take it easy," Gerald shouted. He moved toward John Donald but the wild look in John Donald's eyes told him to lay back. They had recently gone head to head and he was not keen on repeating the ordeal.

"Go and get him," said John Donald, motioning to the forecastle.

"What are you going to do?" said Gerald.

"Never fucking mind," said John Donald. "Just bring him up here."

Reluctantly Gerald made his way down the ladder into the forward sleeping quarters, returning moments later pushing a small man back up the steps into the main cabin, where John Donald was seated at the table, appearing to ponder the intricate detail of the soundings marked on the navigation chart spread out in front of him.

Wearing a dark leather jacket and torn jeans, the man's face was swollen and bruised with a smear of dried blood creasing down his right cheek. A small coin dangled from a gold chain around his neck.

"What are you going to do with me?" he stammered, barely able to raise his head to meet John Donald's steely eyes.

The dim light over the chart table aggravated the scowl brewing on John Donald's face but for the moment he was silent.

"I'm not sure Jimmy. I'm not sure," said John Donald. "You're almost like family to us but you kind of fucked up this time."

"No more than you guys," said Jimmy. "Gerald said as much ..."

"Shut the fuck up Jimmy," said Gerald. "If you know what's good for you."

Jimmy lowered his head slightly, glanced at Gerald and heaved a sigh.

"That's your problem Jimmy," said John Donald. "You just never know when to keep your mouth shut."

"No more than ..."

"Shut the fuck up," said John Donald, the veins in his neck bulging, a cold sweat beading down his brow. Without warning he pushed the pencil and dividers to the side of the table and made a wild swing at Jimmy, striking him on the bridge of the nose. Getting up from the table, he swung again, striking Jimmy on the temple. Jimmy crumpled to the cabin floor.

Gerald was leaning back against the opposite wall, off balance. He started to right himself, but before he could intervene, John Donald shoved him to the floor and towered over him.

"Don't move your fucking lips," he screamed at Gerald, who was starting to shake uncontrollably. "Jimmy has had it coming so let's finish this thing off."

"What do you mean?" Gerald questioned.

"I mean finish him off. He's done," John Donald scowled.

"But we need him," Gerald pleaded.

"Fuck him. We're better off without him. Now give me a hand!"

"But what are we going to do with him? Everyone will know something's up when we take him back to town."

"He isn't going back to town."

John Donald glared into Gerald's eyes, challenging him to suggest otherwise, but Gerald fell silent.

Jimmy's breathing was heavy as crimson blood pooled around his head.

"Pick up his feet," John Donald commanded.

Gerald obeyed as John Donald reached under Jimmy's

shoulders and lifted. Straining under the deadweight, they half-dragged Jimmy onto the afterdeck, his blood staining the grey paint on the floorboards. They propped Jimmy up against the hull as he started to regain consciousness. Quickly, John Donald retrieved a piece of heavy cable from the rope locker and began to wrap it tightly around Jimmy's upper body.

Sensing what was happening, Jimmy began to panic and desperately tried to free himself, the focused power welling up inside like a drowning victim's last efforts. As John Donald towered over him, he lashed out with a powerful kick, catching John Donald in the shins and sending him crashing against the side of the boat. The force almost catapulted John Donald into the sea, but at the last second he managed to thrust out his hand, grab a stanchion and hang on.

For an instant, Gerald contemplated making a move but hesitated long enough for John Donald to cross the boat and send a pulverizing kick into Jimmy's face.

"Give me a fucking hand," John Donald screamed at Gerald as Jimmy's eyes rolled back in his head.

Gerald obeyed, pulling Jimmy's shoulders away from the hull as John Donald completed wrapping the cable.

"Up and over," John Donald shouted at Gerald, not wanting to lose the momentum, not wanting rationality to cast the hate aside long enough to cause some hesitation, some rethinking of what he was about to do.

Gerald was stunned.

How could this be happening? He had been John Donald's right-hand man for so long, but wanted no complicity in a man's murder. Jimmy was like a brother to them for Christ's sake. What had brought all this about?

Without warning, John Donald suddenly smacked Gerald across the face, bringing him back to the job at hand.

"Up and over," John Donald yelled, the echo resounding against the distant shoreline.

Together they lifted Jimmy onto the side of the boat.

With one last fleeting effort, Jimmy's eyes met John Donald's. His stare fixed, mumbling almost incoherently, he pleaded, "Please don't, John, I didn't ... tell ...! Please, John, we're like brothers. Flesh...and blood. And blood is...blood is thicker...than water."

John Donald stopped and stared into Jimmy's face. Only a few years separated them in age, yet Jimmy looked so much younger. He had been like a brother. They had shared most of their early childhood until Jimmy dropped out of school, tired of taking his step-dad's beatings, left home and headed to the mainland. John Donald was left behind to do all the work and fend off his old man as best he could. He was glad to see Jimmy come back when things had turned sour for him on the mainland. But he was still a little jealous that Jimmy had managed to get away, at least for a while.

John Donald grabbed Jimmy as the boat rocked with the groundswell. He braced his knees against the hull of the *Highlander*, holding him tightly.

For a second, Gerald thought Jimmy had gotten through to John Donald, saw his cousin's grip relax and the force of his chest against Jimmy lighten.

John Donald stared coldly into Jimmy's eyes. "Not tonight," he said, "not tonight." Reaching for Jimmy's throat, John Donald ripped the gold chain from his neck and held the coin aloft for him to see.

"This is the only thing that kept you alive this long," he said. "You should have stayed on the mainland."

With that, John Donald tossed the coin into the ocean.

Gerald saw what was about to happen and stepped forward as Jimmy wrestled with the weight of cable ensnaring his body. Grabbing John Donald's arm with both hands, Gerald wrenched his cousin around to face him, leaving Jimmy balanced precariously on the side of the boat, still in John Donald's vise-like grip.

"No way," said Gerald, grimacing to keep John Donald from turning back to the task at hand. "If you do this, I'm finished. We're finished. If you do this, you're on your own."

John Donald's eyes seemed clouded as if life itself had drained from them.

"No shit," said Gerald. "Finished. I never signed up for this."

John Donald was unflinching, his stare almost hypnotic as he turned to Jimmy then back again to Gerald. Slowly, Gerald could see a faint glimmer of light in his cousin's face as John Donald reeled his other arm in, pulling Jimmy onto the deck of the boat.

"Tonight's your lucky fucking night Jimmy," said John Donald, prodding the smaller man with the toe of his boot. "Your lucky night."

Not missing a beat, John Donald picked up the mop and slop pail leaning against the wheelhouse and started to wash the blood from the floorboards as Gerald moved to help Jimmy.

John Donald stepped in front of Gerald and motioned towards the cabin.

"He's fine. Let's get out of here," he yelled, motioning to Gerald to get the *Highlander* running.

Gerald stood still, his eyes closed to hold back the tears.

"Let's get the fuck out of here," John Donald reiterated.

Gerald turned quickly, staring coldly at his cousin, then went into the cabin and sat behind the wheel, his whole body shaking. He fumbled for the key, turned it, and the *Highlander* roared to life. Gripping the throttle and pushing forward with one hand, Gerald spun the wheel hard, turning the boat into open water.

Powerfully, the *Highlander* rose up and vanished into the storm.

CHAPTER 1

Cape Breton Highlands, Many Years Later

A HEAVY FOG hung over the Highlands as the beacon from the Chéticamp Island lighthouse sliced through the night air. The foghorn reverberated through the mist, sending most of its warning inland toward the mountains instead of seaward into the Gulf.

Ben Matthews lay in bed staring at the ceiling, his lean, barely six-foot frame stretched from headboard to footboard as he tried to find the most comfortable position on the old mattress.

The room was a clutter of moving boxes and paper. His uniform lay draped across a small wooden chair, topped by a new Stetson that proudly carried his park warden badge. The alarm clock, sitting temporarily on the cardboard wardrobe, posted its time: 2:07 a.m.

Ben looked at it, then groaned and buried his head in the pillows in an unsuccessful attempt to fight off insomnia. He had recently moved into a new position as Assistant Chief Park Warden for Cape Breton Highlands National Park, and had just taken up residence in one of the two government bungalows that sat sentry-like at the edge of the road leading into the park.

Both houses were barely visible in the thick fog that blanketed the collection of two-storey homes lining the road, their yards neatly organized with fishing nets and stacks of lobster pots.

Spring weather, for sure, Ben thought as he lay there. *Oh well, The Rock wasn't any better and the Bay of Fundy, well that was another story.*

His last job in Fundy National Park had been challenging. It was his first permanent position after putting in several years as a term and seasonal warden in Terra Nova National Park in eastern Newfoundland, and it was his first opportunity to work as a station warden. All of the other young wardens in Terra Nova had been offered jobs in Gros Morne National Park in western Newfoundland, but in many ways he was happy to get off the island to see what the mainland had to offer.

Fundy was tucked into a small corner of New Brunswick and named after the bay that was world-renowned for its high tides and unique rock formations. The warden station at Wolfe Lake was on a high plateau above the bay and had quite different weather than the office in Alma, twelve kilometres away. It could have been a world away.

The small village was invariably socked in with fog, which came in with the flood tide and only left with the ebbing tide. The monotonous regularity of it seemed to wash over the village, instilling a sombre mood that permeated the residents.

Ben was glad to get the promotion to Fundy, but leaving his friends and family behind in Newfoundland had been difficult. They had expected him to stay on the island forever and to some extent, he expected that as well. But he had joined Parks Canada and the Warden Service specifically to take advantage of the mobility it offered. He was intrigued by the opportunity to work in some of the country's most spectacular places and planned to move around as much as possible while he was still young and unattached.

Now he was happy to be in Cape Breton and keen to try his hand at managing an area: essentially the entire western side of the park extending from the Chéticamp River to Big Intervale, the midway point around the Cabot Trail that roughly split the park into two equal-sized management areas.

Although small by western standards, Cape Breton Highlands was one of the larger national parks in eastern Canada; in Parks Canada circles, size mattered. Larger parks were more likely to have larger, intact landscapes that epitomized the wilderness national parks were supposed to protect. They were also more likely to have the full complement of large mammals, including moose, caribou and deer, and predators such as bears, wolves and cougars.

For its part, Cape Breton had lost its caribou around the turn of the century, reputedly to poaching, and there had been no records of wolves or cougars, a.k.a. "eastern panthers," in decades. But the remote northern reaches of Cape Breton Island harboured a robust deer population, some of the largest moose in eastern North America and a healthy black bear population. The predator void was also being partially filled by the recent arrival of coyotes from mainland Nova Scotia.

So the move from Fundy to Cape Breton was a desirable option for a young park warden looking to gain experience across the national park system. But it didn't come without some reservations, which Ben had when he realized that the move had transformed from "talk" to "walk."

Now that Ben was here, he started to have second thoughts, questioning his ability to take on this new job at such a relatively young age. He would have a crew of wardens working with him but the word was that they needed work to get them back to the task of protecting the park. Over the past few years, things on the Chéticamp side had been pretty well left to run on their own and it showed.

That was often typical when a position was left unfilled, as was the case with his. Joe Deveau had been covering things off until Ben arrived, but there was little incentive to do any more than was necessary. A veteran of the Second World War, Joe and his wife Rose lived next to him in the other government bungalow. Joe had joined the Warden Service after the war, taking advantage of a hiring process referred to as "veteran's preference." He had jumped at the chance to join the outfit and soon found his niche as a senior warden. He had kept things running while waiting for Ben's arrival, but was not about to take on management of the area. No amount of money could entice him into that role. Now that Ben was here, Joe could take it easy again and work himself back into the quiet routine of the Chéticamp side.

But for some reason, Ben thought as he tossed and turned trying to avoid the light, which bounced strobe-like off his bedroom walls, *quiet didn't seem to describe the first night in his new home.* The excitement and anticipation of the move was making it tough to sleep and the lighthouse and foghorn would take some getting used to. To top it off, the roar of a truck out on the road beat through the open window as it rumbled past.

Christ, I might as well get up and go to work. It's just my luck living in the last house before the park gate. They might as well have put the office in the house like at my old warden station.

Moments later, the rumble of another vehicle could be heard. *Sounds like the last one.*

Ben held his breath, straining to tease the sounds apart.

Suddenly, the rumble was transformed into a fevered pitch. Tires screamed as the truck spun on asphalt, dirt and grass. Ben sprung from his bed, pulling on his pants and crashing into boxes as he stumbled into the kitchen. Tripping and slamming against the cupboards, he managed to catch himself on the countertop.

Peering through the kitchen window, Ben was able to catch a fleeting glimpse of a pickup truck as it spun wildly out of control, peeling off the front lawn and back onto the road. As it veered past a streetlight in front of a neighbouring house and disappeared into the fog, he could see the outline of two occupants.

Ben ran to the front door and onto the lawn. He hit the wet grass flying, slipped and landed hard on his side. His head smacked with a thud as his cheekbone broke the fall. Something warm ran down his face. He looked up and into the eyes of a dead whitetail deer, a stain of blood mottling the gunshot wound in the centre of its forehead.

Ben lay flat on his face in the wet grass catching his breath then pulled himself up onto his knees. His cheekbone throbbed with pain as he felt for blood and broken bones. A warm mist swirled around the streetlight.

In the small house across the road, an upstairs light came on and he could see the outline of somebody peering past the curtain.

Don't rush over and help.

Just as quickly, as if they were reading his thoughts, the light went out.

Ben struggled to his feet, his throbbing cheekbone oozing blood. Standing in the fog, he worked his head slowly back and forth, quelling the stiffness and stretching his tender neck.

Looking across the road, the person's outline was still visible behind the curtains. "Welcome to Cape Breton," he said as he walked back to the house and disappeared inside.

CHAPTER 2

MORNING CAME TOO quickly as Ben lay in bed, recovering from the night's events. Struggling to his feet, his head throbbed with a quiet ache that pounded to the rhythm of his heart. Still wearing his pants from last night, he navigated past the moving boxes and went to the bathroom to check things out in the mirror. Two days growth and bloodshot eyes reminded him of early mornings after some of the parties in Terra Nova, but this time he didn't have a night's imbibing as an excuse for his dishevelled looks. His blood-matted, short brown hair stuck out from the left side of his head like the quills of a porcupine. Green grass stains ran down one side of his smooth chest, causing him to wince as he thought about the crash landing.

Wetting a face cloth, he carefully patted the blood from his hair, rinsing it frequently in the sink before trying to erase the grass stains from his body. Satisfied that he had cleaned up the worst of the damage, he gently pulled a t-shirt over his head and made his way into the kitchen. Slumping down at the table, Ben was slow to notice Joe's large frame filling the doorway, his immaculate uniform and spit-shined black boots serving as a reminder of his war years.

"Heard you had some trouble last night," said the older warden as he turned to close the door behind him. "Don't worry about it, they're just having fun with you," Joe continued, stopping suddenly when he turned and saw Ben's swollen face, the left cheek black and blue and puffed out the size of a small egg.

"Jesus. You better get that looked at. I didn't realize you hurt yourself."

"Don't worry about it, Joe. Sorry I didn't hear you come in. Get yourself a coffee and have a seat."

"Nah," Joe responded, "I'm trying to break the caffeine

habit. It keeps me up all friggin' night." He sat at the table and pushed his Stetson back on his head, revealing a buzz cut of tightly cropped white hair.

"So, did it keep you up *last* night?" said Ben.

"Yah, but I guess I must've crashed before all the excitement. I don't have the stamina of you young fellows, you know. I think I lost it after those years in Kouch."

Ben remembered the stories of Kouchibouguac in New Brunswick.

"I heard it was pretty tough working there when the park started up," he said.

"Yah," Joe replied. "I spent one full year working nothing but nights after they burnt down the admin building. We were always paired up with a Mountie and ended up responding to a lot of calls out of the park."

"So was everyone against the park?" Ben asked. "It sure sounded like it from what I've heard."

"It was a mixed bag," said Joe. "Of course the squatters were against the park and they had their supporters but when the locals realized the job opportunities the park brought, most came on side. It's funny though how old habits die hard."

"Like poaching and leaving a dead deer on the new guy's lawn?"

"Pretty much," said Joe. "By the way, I winched the deer onto my truck and will dump it at the pit. No sense leaving it out front as a lawn ornament."

"Thanks, Joe. I was sort of hoping you might be able to tell me who I could return it to. The truck looked like a two-tone pickup but they didn't exactly stop and pose for a picture. Any idea who it might have been?"

"Dunno," said Joe. "There are more friggin' pickup trucks along the coast than you can shake a stick at. It could have been any one of a dozen people we've had run-ins with. To make matters worse, it probably came out of the park. Here," he added, pulling a map from an inside pocket and laying it out on the kitchen table, "I thought I'd show you the lay of the land."

Ben pulled the map towards him as Joe leaned over and pointed out its features.

"The stretch of coastline between the Chéticamp River and the base of French Mountain seems to have more deer every year," said Joe.

"And it's actively poached?" said Ben.

"Yah," said Joe. "The major spots are the Rigwash Valley, Presqu'ile and Trout Brook. They're all within the first few kilometres of the park before you start to make your way up French Mountain."

"Presqu'ile?" said Ben. "What does that mean in English?"

"Literally, it's almost an island," said Joe, pointing to a short piece of coastline on the map that was nearly completely surrounded by water.

"Interesting," said Ben. "And it's a good area for deer?"

"Really good," said Joe. "There are some openings in the forest there that deer seem to favour. And it's easy to jacklight from the highway. It's the same for the Rigwash Valley and Trout Brook. I'll show you when you have time."

Joe stood up and looked out the kitchen window as an RCMP cruiser pulled into the driveway, then abruptly turned for the door.

"Well, I should go and get rid of that deer," he said. "You better get that looked at," he added, forgetting to close the door behind him.

Joe waved at the RCMP officer getting out of the car and jumped behind the wheel of his warden truck. Driving quickly past the Mountie, he turned onto the road and headed toward the park.

Ben got up to greet his visitor as the RCMP officer knocked on the half-open door.

"Come on in," said Ben.

The Mountie extended his hand.

"Yvan Bouchard. Welcome to Chéticamp."

"Ben Matthews. Have a seat. I'll get you a coffee?"

"Sure," said Yvan, laughing as he watched Joe's truck head down the road and out of sight. "Joe can never get out of a place fast enough when I walk in. He's gonna give me a complex."

Ben smiled as he poured a coffee for his visitor.

Yvan was typical of most new constables, he thought as he sized him up: clean-cut, sharp, tall and straight. *Every bit of six foot four.* The rigour of depot had not yet worn off, but Yvan sported a broad smile and deep laugh, and was instantly likeable.

Despite the injury to Ben's face, Yvan had a similar first impression of the new warden.

"So I heard you had some trouble last night."

"Word travels fast along the coast," said Ben.

"Yah, it's something you'll have to get used to."

"Any idea who it might have been?" Ben asked.

"Not really," said Yvan, taking a seat at the table. "In these parts it could have been any number of people."

"Great," said Ben.

"You being a park warden and all, they probably felt a dead deer was an appropriate welcome. To top it off, it probably came out of the park."

"Yah, that's what Joe figured. Sounds pretty easy."

"Pretty much," said Yvan, not trying to make light of the situation. "But you'll have lots of time to get things figured out. You'll have enough to do just to sort out the park gang."

"Time is something I have plenty of," said Ben, letting the other comment go.

He had heard the rumours before he took the job about how his predecessor, John Haffcut, had apparently let things slide on the Cheticamp side of park, but he also knew that rumours in the outfit were usually just that. Too often a warden had to tear down a bad reputation built around rumours and half-truths before he or she could begin to build a reputation based on what they actually did on the job. It was one aspect of the outfit that Ben didn't care for.

Besides, by all accounts John Haffcut had been a passionate protector of the park and his wardens. He'd just run up against a superintendent who was able to use his connections to move John elsewhere, "promoting" him to Chief Park Warden in one of the remote northern parks on the other side of the country.

Yvan was quick to pick up on the deflection.

"I don't mean to be talking about your staff behind their backs," he said. "I know the rumours can be just as bad in the RCMP. Just figured I'd give you a head's up."

"No worries," said Ben. "I heard the rumours when I took the job. Of course, there are always some things they never tell you, but I need a few surprises to make life interesting anyway."

"I've got a feeling you won't find it dull here," Yvan said with a wink.

Ben smiled and leaned back in his chair. "So are you from these parts?" he asked.

Yvan laughed. "No, unfortunately I'm a city boy from Montreal," he said. "A Quebecois. The Acadians generally hate us but I love it here in Cape Breton. And I think you'll like it too. The people are down to earth and as friendly as you'll ever meet. They just like to poach, that's all."

"So it would seem," said Ben.

Yvan looked at his watch. "Oops, gotta go. I'll catch up to you later," he said getting up from the table. "When you get a chance, come by the detachment and I'll introduce you to our crew."

With that, Yvan tipped his hat to Ben and walked out, pulling the door closed behind him. Ben stood at the kitchen window and watched as Yvan got into the police cruiser and drove off.

He appreciated the fact that the young Mountie had taken the time to stop in.

In his relatively short career in the Warden Service, Ben had worked with a number of RCMP officers and enjoyed the benefits of having a good relationship with them. After all, they were the primary law enforcement agency in the small towns and rural areas where most of the country's national parks were located.

Along with provincial conservation officers and federal fisheries officers, the park wardens and RCMP were often called on to work together and most soon realized that whether they were dealing with a petty thief, poacher or wanton criminal, they were often all dealing with the same people, what some law enforcement officers referred to as "the underbelly of society."

Sometimes, you never really knew who they were, unless circumstances brought you into contact with them. So sharing information with other field officers often provided the heads-up of who to watch for, and who to watch out for. There was a difference.

And sometimes you just never knew where they would show up, who they would show up with, or who they were related to.

Ben was reflecting on these last thoughts when he noticed movement in the window of the little house across the road.

"Exactly," he said to himself as he turned and made his way back to the bedroom.

CHAPTER 3

IT WAS MONDAY morning and Ben was about to make his first appearance at work. He had taken the weekend to settle in and to let the swelling on his face go down. He knew his first impression was probably already tarnished by the war wound. And the rumour mill that was busy fine-tuning the events surrounding his first run-in with the locals probably wasn't helping.

He had taken a quick run through his new office with Joe and met some of the park staff, but he knew it was the work crew at the park compound that he would have to build a relationship with. Most were Acadians from the surrounding communities, former fishermen who had given up the seasonal fishery and winter months on the dole for the steady paycheque of a government job.

Like many of the Maritime national parks, Cape Breton Highlands had been created for employment reasons rather than any sanctimonious ideals of protecting natural and cultural heritage. In the midst of the 1930s when people were living in poverty, the chance to work and earn a wage building the Cabot Trail, or "the Trail" as it was known locally, attracted many men to the park. Most drifted back and forth between the fishery and other construction jobs, but a few of the more fortunate ones were offered full-time jobs and chose to make the park their life.

Ben knew his first day would be important so he had asked Joe to pick him up early. He was just coming out of the bedroom when Joe walked in the back door. Ben was adjusting his tie, centring the clip and tucking it in neatly under his chin. On top of freshly polished black boots, he wore his new dress pants, which he had carefully ironed, and a fresh shirt, equally well pressed.

His hair was cut shorter than normal, barely touching the tops of his ears and squared off across the back of his neck. He wore his newly acquired collar dogs on his shirt, the dual stars signifying his position as assistant to the Chief Park Warden. He checked to make sure there were no loose threads hanging from his shoulder patches, then he pulled on the green summer tunic, buttoned and adjusted it, and looked at Joe.

"So what do you think?" asked Ben.

Joe whistled, "Spiffy or what? Who are you trying to suck up to?"

"Give me a break, Joe. I should to try to set a bit of an example to make up for the eye."

"This is true." Joe laughed. "All the gang will be there so you should be on your best behaviour. The chief likes a sharp-looking crew."

"Let's go then," said Ben, pushing Joe out the door.

Joe drove them to the compound and pulled up in front of the park garage. "Let's go in here," he suggested. "The men usually start their shift from here so we'll catch most of them before they head out to their job sites."

Ben nodded for Joe to lead the way.

The crew, a dozen or more local Acadians, were having a coffee and finishing their smokes before starting the workday. They spoke in a mixture of French and English, laughing frequently.

"Good morning, Joe," said a burly, short brute of a man as he walked up to the wardens. Holding out his hand to Ben he said, "You must be the new warden. I'm Louis Aucoin. Michel is my nephew."

"Pleased to meet you," said Ben. "I haven't met Michel yet but I've heard lots of good things about him."

"Come here men, this is the new warden," said Louis as he turned to his crew.

Most of the men looked up from what they were doing and

strolled over to meet Ben. As Louis introduced the men, Ben was impressed with their camaraderie and friendliness. He felt accepted instantly.

A man who Louis introduced as Emile the carpenter grabbed Ben by the hand and shook firmly. He was weathered-looking but had a huge smile. Ben noted a cross, tattooed on the back of his hand between his thumb and forefinger. Ben had seen the mark before on the hand of a forest fire fighter he had worked with in northern Ontario. The owner, who had done time in a federal penitentiary, told him it was a mark inmates used to identify one another.

Accustomed to explaining the tattoo, Emile commented before Ben could let go.

"Yes, I was a bad boy many years ago," he said smiling. "But I have found Him, or should I say that He found me. Luckily he left me one good hand," he added, raising his right hand while simultaneously showing that his left hand was missing the middle and ring fingers.

"Anyway," said Emile, "Pierre Boudreau, everyone calls him P'tit Pierre, he's my brother-in-law and lives across from you. I'm sure he will make you welcome here. Drop over and see him. His daughter Marielle is my pride and joy, my favourite niece."

Ben nodded, appreciating Emile's friendliness. He had noticed the little house across the road and had caught a glimpse of the daughter hanging out clothes. She was petite and attractive, but he was also certain that she was the person watching him behind the darkened curtains when the deer was delivered to his house. He expected they would meet before too long.

"And my other niece Lucille is married to your young warden Michel Aucoin," Emile continued. "Yes we are all one big connected family," he said, releasing Ben's hand from his powerful grip.

"Okay, okay," Louis interjected, pulling Emile away. "Don't talk his ear off, man."

Emile laughed and moved back, allowing the other men to introduce themselves.

"Well it looks like you got here just in time," Louis laughed.

"Why is that?" Ben asked.

"I don't think Joe could handle the fast pace of management much longer," Louis roared, looking around at his crew, who laughed along.

Ben smiled, shaking his head. He noticed a tall, dark-haired man in coveralls standing away from the gathering, his back to the group. Louis followed Ben's gaze and shouted to the man without even turning around.

"Maurice, get over here," he called out.

All eyes turned toward Maurice.

"This is one of our mechanics," said Louis as Maurice walked across the garage, making no attempt to hide the resentment piercing through his fiery eyes. "He works seasonally during the summer."

"Gives him time to poach in the fall," Joe said with a mischievous smile.

Maurice held out his hand reluctantly. He was powerfully built and his arm rippled with muscle as he shook Ben's hand.

"Salut," he said to Ben in a gruff voice, unimpressed with Joe's comment.

"Salut," Ben replied, sensing the hostility.

"Maurice just loves wardens," Louis remarked sarcastically, reading Ben's mind. "But don't worry," he said, looking with a scowl at Maurice. "He'll get over it."

Ben forced a smile but all he got back was a blank stare.

"Okay, men, time to get on with your day," said Louis, ending the formalities.

Holding his hand out to Ben but talking to Joe, Louis spoke for all to hear with his strongly accented English.

"Keep him away from that young Kate, now Joe. We don't want these wardens breeding."

With the exception of Maurice, the whole crew laughed.

Ben turned red, his hand clasped firmly in Louis' grip.

Joe was about to add to the fun but caught a dirty look from Ben and thought it best to leave well enough alone.

Releasing his grip on Ben's hand, Louis waved them both away and they headed for the door. Walking out into the cool morning fog drifting in off the Gulf, Ben turned to Joe.

"That's quite the crew."

"They're harmless," Joe replied. "Even Maurice is okay. He just does his job and keeps to himself. There's no law against that."

"Not at all," said Ben. "Sometimes it's good to keep your mouth shut," he added, looking at Joe with raised eyebrows.

Ben had not wanted to say anything about Kate in front of the crew, or in front of anyone for that matter. Kate was a big part of the reason he had ended up in Cape Breton, but he didn't want it to factor in to how he did his job.

They had met several years before in Fundy and he was smitten with the bright young university student right from the start. Now they were both members of the Warden Service and working together for the first time in Cape Breton Highlands. Neither was certain how well it would work out.

Kate and Ben needed to keep their personal lives separate from work, especially now that Ben was the area manager, and both wanted to avoid the soap opera that Parks Canada could sometimes become. Parks people often referred to themselves as "one big family," and some people in the outfit liked to top up that description to "one big incestuous family." Neither Kate nor Ben needed the added baggage of their relationship muddling things up for them at work, something Ben would have to remind Joe of before it became a standing joke.

CHAPTER 4

CHIEF PARK WARDEN John Kerry sat in the meeting room encircled by his crew of seasonal and fulltime wardens, his gleaming, brass collar dogs and neatly coifed black hair setting the standard by which all of the others would be compared. John had a reputation for running a tight ship but his wardens also knew he had their backs.

John's battles with management, and park superintendents in particular, were almost legendary and he was known for reminding his superiors that while their positions offered them incredible power and leeway, the National Parks Act trumped all. He also didn't hesitate to let some of the outfit's rising stars know that while they might have their own agendas, the park's mandate was what counted and they should make sure it didn't play second fiddle to their personal aspirations.

As he sat with the others, thinking about what he needed to cover in today's meeting, John was anxious to meet his new assistant. It had been months since the interviews and he was keen to get Ben in the park. The young warden who seemed to be rising quickly through the ranks had seemed a little unorthodox, but he had a reputation for getting into the thick of things. The situation on the west side of the park was a little too lax and John wanted someone who could stir up the pot. He was concerned that his warden service had become the local joke and he wanted that changed.

Joe had been able to do the basics but John recognized his limitations. He was the veteran on the Chéticamp side in more ways than one. He had seen action in the Second World War and was only a few years from retirement. John had relied extensively on Joe to keep an eye on things before Ben arrived, but he knew that Joe would never address the more serious issues like the active poaching he knew occurred quite regularly along the coast.

Joe had put in his years in Kouchibouguac and had done his share of law enforcement work, but John knew that Joe was tired of the night work and he wasn't prepared to force the issue. But he was comfortable knowing Joe would keep an eye on the general operations and that left his other wardens to concentrate on resource management and enforcement work.

Michel Aucoin was another one of John's full-time wardens in the Chéticamp area. He was young and motivated. John knew he would make a good Chief Park Warden someday, but he was still inexperienced in many regards and needed time to mature in the position. He would likely never move from Cape Breton so John had decided that if he couldn't convince him to transfer to gain experience, he would try to move good people past him.

John knew that Michel was a little put out with not getting the assistant's position, but he also sensed that Michel was able to let go and would work well with Ben. Lucille, Michel's wife, was a solid woman and John knew she would not let him sit back and sulk over losing the job to Ben.

There were two other full-time wardens on the west side of the park.

Norm Miller was a native Nova Scotian and worked out of the Big Intervale warden station, midway along the Cabot Trail toward Ingonish. An active hunter and fisherman, Norm was a strong, square-chinned brute of a man who could still outwork any of the others—when he wanted to. John had been frustrated with Norm's lack of motivation and knew he had more to offer, but he had been unable to get it out of him. He was relying on Ben to pull Norm out of the rut he was in.

The other station warden, Cole Tucker, was based in the Grande Anse Valley next to Pleasant Bay. A Prairie boy who had all the characteristics of a cowboy from the Wild West,

Cole even kept a couple of his own horses in a corral he built at his station. Much to John's chagrin, Cole had a habit of shaping his warden Stetson like a western sheriff's and walked with a bow-legged gait that reminded him of someone who had spent years in the saddle. Despite his misgivings about Cole's wannabe cowboy persona, John knew Cole was an experienced warden, having worked in several parks, and was considered quite progressive when it came to doing resource work.

Kate Jones was the lead seasonal warden on the Chéticamp side and had a number of years under her belt doing stints in eastern national parks. Young, attractive and extremely fit, she was a university graduate and one of the new breed of recruits entering the Warden Service. Kate was known for her professionalism, winning the hearts and respect of many of the Chéticamp staff with her hard work and friendliness. She knew she was regarded as one of the new-age wardens, but she remained sensitive to the older wardens, especially Joe and Norm. She also knew that, as a woman, she was breaking new ground and would probably have to work twice as hard as the others to avoid the prejudices of the male-dominated Warden Service. So she never shied away from even the toughest assignments and in a short time had built a reputation for holding her own.

John strongly believed his Chéticamp crew needed to work as a team and he expected Ben to bring them around to that way of thinking. Alternatively, he was prepared to make some drastic changes, including some forced moves to shake things up and send the message that status quo would not cut it anymore. He had also been under pressure from the superintendent to change things on the Chéticamp side, but for completely different reasons.

Superintendent Dickson seemed to always be riding him about his wardens not being responsive to the local community and was constantly threatening to shut down one or more of the warden stations, and send the warden living there, packing. The Grande Anse Station was his latest target but in reality, John knew that the superintendent was just responding to the local politicians who were always criticizing the park, looking for more involvement in management issues. Since the park wardens were generally not from the community, they were easy to pick on. But John always suspected there was more to the superintendent's constant badgering and he wondered if Dickson wasn't under pressure from some other source.

Either way, fending off the superintendent seemed to be taking more of his time and he was keen to put an end to it. John had managed to deflect Dickson's rants for the most part but had been unable to avoid transferring John Haffcut out of the park. In the end, though, he knew that Haffcut would be better off by putting some distance between himself and Arnold Dickson. Ultimately, Haffcut would outlast Dickson and get the final laugh. But some battles just weren't worth fighting.

It was just the way things worked sometimes.

CHAPTER 5

LEADING THE WAY into the information building, Joe took his time climbing the stairs to the office, seemingly reluctant for the meeting to start. When he spotted John, his mood changed and he was all smiles.

"Well, well. You made it," said Joe. "What gives us this pleasure?"

John Kerry smiled and held out his hand. "You old bugger. The sooner we get you out of here the sooner I can rest easy," he joked, noticing Ben coming along behind. "Good to see you, Ben," he said, shaking Ben's hand with a powerful grip.

"Likewise, John," said Ben. "Glad to finally be in Chéticamp."

John sized up Ben's face and remarked, with some concern, "Did you get that looked at?"

"No, it'll be fine," said Ben. "My first slip."

John nodded. "Well, I'm sure it won't be your last encounter with the locals. Joe and the boys have been letting them have too many deer over in these parts. They're used to getting their way."

"So I hear," said Ben, winking at John. "We'll see what we can do about that, hey, Joe?"

Red-faced and appearing a little flustered, Joe just mumbled and was about to sit down at the table with the rest of the wardens when John interjected.

"Actually, before we get going, I need to speak to Joe for a few minutes," said John. "I'd like to borrow your office if you don't mind, Ben."

"No, go right ahead," said Ben as he introduced himself to the other park wardens.

Joe remained silent but followed John down the hall. The rest of the crew looked at each other, wondering what was up.

John and Joe were gone only a few minutes before returning to the meeting room and taking their places.

"So I guess everyone is here except Michel," said John.

"He'll be around later in the day," said Joe, regaining his composure. "He had to take Lucille and their son to see the doctor."

"I'd like to start things off by welcoming everyone to Cape Breton Highlands," said John. "I know it still seems like winter in the mountains but we all know summer is just around the corner. The salmon will soon be back in the rivers and we'll get a chance to see how the new counting fence works here on the Chéticamp River. Of course we know that salmon stocks are down on the east coast so the national parks have an important role to play with salmon conservation."

"Maybe we shouldn't be allowing any salmon fishing at all," said Cole, knowing it would get a rise from Norm. "After all, we are a protected area."

"I agree," said Joe, keen on getting his digs in as well. "People can't hunt in the park. I don't know why we let them fish?"

"Now don't go talking crazy talk," said Norm, rising to the bait, his deep blue eyes piercing into Cole and Joe. "Fishing is a time-honoured tradition in national parks. As long as it's managed right, it's fine."

"Spoken like a model conservationist," said Joe with a grin.

"Okay you guys," said John. "Listen up. You've probably all heard that the superintendent is keen on this project so it's a priority. And he's contracted the local salmon fishing group to run the fence."

"That's fine," said Norm. "The local group knows what they're doing."

"But the superintendent wants to take the lead on dealing with them," John continued.

A few of the wardens laughed at this suggestion.

"That's just fucking great," said Norm. "It's like putting the fox in charge of the henhouse."

His comment drew a frown from the chief.

"Let's see how it goes," said John. "I agree we'll have to keep an eye on things but, ultimately, our job is to ensure that the ecological integrity of the park is not affected."

Joe laughed. "What the hell is this ecological integrity thing anyway, the latest buzz word from Ottawa?"

"Well, Joe," said John, starting to explain. "It's like..."

"It's like having balls," Norm interrupted.

All eyes turned toward Norm.

"Oh?" said Joe.

"Yah," Norm continued, "You know, like when people say you have integrity, they really mean that you have balls."

Joe nodded. "So when does an ecosystem have balls, Norman?" he asked.

Norm started to laugh. "I can't tell you Joe. I'd have to kill ya."

Everyone laughed except John. "Thanks for that, Norm," he said.

"Nothing to it," said Norm.

"Anyway," said John, peering at Norm as if to tell him to keep his thoughts to himself, "I'll say it one more time. Let's just wait and see how it goes. We've got other concerns right now, like getting the salmon regulations sorted out so that we can be consistent with what's going on outside of the park."

Kate, who had been silent up to this point, spoke up. "I don't understand how Federal Fisheries can change the salmon regulations in the province to catch and release for adult salmon, and we think we can leave our regulations unchanged. If we don't switch, everyone will be coming into the park to fish for the larger salmon. The national park is supposed to be a protected area, but we'll have more liberal regulations than provincial rivers like the Margaree."

"You're right, Kate," said John, "but we still have time to get our regulations in line with the province. I've been dealing with the other parks and everyone is on side. The superintendent seems to be the only stumbling block and I'm not sure why."

Norm laughed again. "I'll tell you why," he said. "He's just trying to appease the locals and stick it to the wardens at the same time. There's no other reason. He's no dummy. He knows we need to get our regs amended and the regional director has even told him to get in line with the other Atlantic parks."

"You may be right, Norm," said John. "Or maybe the superintendent is dealing with other aspects of the issue that we aren't aware of," he added, drawing stares from everyone around the table.

"Right," Norm muttered, with more than a hint of sarcasm in his voice. "Maybe he does have bigger fish to fry."

CHAPTER 6

IT WAS LATE in the afternoon before everyone went their separate ways.

After John left, Ben sat with Joe alone in the meeting room. He had wanted to see if things were okay with Joe, who had not said much all afternoon.

"You alright?" Ben asked.

Joe looked down at his coffee cup for a moment before replying. "Yah."

"So what did John want to see you about?"

"Oh, he just wanted to remind me that if I was interested in packing it in, he could get me a pretty good retirement package."

Ben was caught off guard. "You mean he wants to buy you out?"

"In a manner of speaking," said Joe. "But I don't hold John responsible for this. The superintendent has been threatening us with cuts for a year and John sees me as a way of meeting a reduced budget, and giving me a chance to get a better payout. Dickson and John have been butting heads for a while. I think Dickson is just trying to keep us in line by threatening us."

"What's the supe got against us?" Ben asked.

"I'm not sure. Most days I find him to be a really good guy, but then he loses it over God knows what and comes down pretty hard on us. I think Dickson figures John is too hard on the locals. He wants him to back off, especially on any idea of cracking down on the poaching. For some reason he thinks it's all blown out of proportion, but you know, Ben, I can take you out any night and we'll see people jacklighting. I'll be the first to admit the locals have had a field day over here recently. John knows it and has been asking Dickson for more resources, but the supe goes ballistic whenever John raises the issue. John has been running interference for us for a year or more now. He's happy to finally get you here."

"Great," said Ben. "So what else are you not telling me?"

"That's pretty much it," said Joe. "Honest. Other than Dickson, we don't have many internal issues to deal with."

"I still don't understand where you come into this, Joe?"

Joe looked up at Ben. "I'm not sure," he said. "Dickson can only get at us in one of two ways. He either cuts our budget or he gets rid of staff. If he cuts our budget, it affects things like the counting fence, which is mostly local hire, so he doesn't want to do that and piss off the locals. And he knows the soft positions in the Warden Service are the terms and seasonals, which are mostly local, so he's screwed there as well. His only recourse is to put pressure on John to get rid of people like me. I think Dickson knows that John has a soft spot for my situation and he's trying to get at him by threatening to force me out of the outfit."

Ben could see that Joe was venting and getting flustered at the thought of having to leave. "So what do you plan to do?"

"I'm not sure. Rose and I haven't been able to put much away in the last twenty years. We don't own our own home and it would be nice to get this last year or two in to boost my pension."

Ben pondered the situation. No doubt Joe was concerned about how his new boss might swing on this issue. He could easily see that Joe wasn't the lazy type, but figured his good years were probably behind him. Still, Ben could tell that Joe was "Parks" to the core. Walking around the table he put his hand on Joe's shoulder.

"Don't worry, Joe. You and Rose will be here for as long as you want. I'm not going to screw you around."

Ben held out his hand to seal the deal.

"Excuse me," said a voice from downstairs. "Are you up there, Joe?"

Joe walked to the stairs and looked down. "Come on up

here, Michel," he said as a young warden made his way up the stairs. "Ben, this is Michel Aucoin, your other senior warden."

Michel was clean-cut, tall and lean, and looked smart in his warden uniform. His angular, dark features, high cheekbones and sharp nose gave him a distinctly French look that could almost be mistaken for being Native.

Ben held out his hand.

"Bienvenue à Chéticamp," said Michel, his dark eyes appearing resolute as he tested Ben's French.

"Merci," Ben replied, offering no more than necessary.

Michel sensed Ben's uneasiness with his second language. "Glad you are finally here," he said in perfect English. "It's good to be back to full strength."

"I'm sure it is," Ben answered, sensing that Michel was probably a little ticked with not getting the job. "Hopefully we don't lose you to Kouch," he said, referring to the fact that Michel had placed behind him on the competition, but was being considered for a bilingual position in Kouchibouguac.

"Oh, you won't lose me," said Michel. "My wife and I belong to this place and we don't intend to move for anyone." He made it sound more like a challenge than he intended.

Ben knew it was going to take time for Michel to let go of the fact that he had desperately wanted the Chéticamp position but lost it to an "anglais." Ben had completed language training to qualify for bilingual positions, but realized he certainly wasn't comfortable working in French. He also knew that he had more experience in more national parks than Michel and that's what had counted to John Kerry. Besides, the Warden Service tried to avoid promoting people in their home parks and certainly encouraged mobility so people gained experience and didn't end up getting too comfortable in one spot.

In any event, Ben was here now and he and Michel would have to work things out.

CHAPTER 7

IT WAS LATE and Ben was just clearing up the supper dishes. It had been a long day and after work he had decided to get out for some air. This was a routine he had established in both Terra Nova and Fundy, especially on those increasingly frequent occasions when work kept him behind a desk. It wasn't why he or any of the others had joined the Warden Service and like the others he thrived on his time in the park.

Late in the day provided a unique perspective on the landscape and he would often stay out well past sundown as the failing light forced him to rely on his full suite of senses, honing skills that would serve him well on the job. In Terra Nova, much of the night work had taken him out on the ocean as he navigated the park's fjord-like "sounds" stretching their tentacles into the farthest reaches of Newfoundland's east coast. On the water or on land, he was in his element, especially at night when poachers were more apt to net a river or stalk a deer.

Ben could never figure out what drove them but he was determined to beat them at their own game. He had made up his mind long ago to "work for wildlife," to help protect the few remaining places on the planet where wild species and wild spaces provided sanctuary from the onslaught of humanity that was carving away at wilderness. "Death by a thousand cuts" people termed it and it pretty much summed up how many park wardens felt.

Ben was happy to join forces with others who shared both his worldview and his passion to protect these special places from the poachers who regularly infiltrated parks like Cape Breton Highlands and other protected areas to kill wildlife. But to be good at the job, you needed a good knowledge of the park and if he couldn't get that during work, he would get it on his own time.

That evening Ben had followed a trail that led from behind his house to a small creek, which emptied into the Chéticamp River. He hadn't realized he lived so close to the river and decided this was a good way to access the river's estuary without anyone seeing him. The estuary had a narrow opening to the ocean and for any salmon or sea-run trout, it was a critical point they had to get past before they could make their way to the spawning habitat upstream.

Atlantic salmon in particular had to run the gauntlet of natural predators and fishermen's nets just to make it back to the rivers where they were born and once there had to contend with natural obstacles and fly fishermen to make it to the spawning grounds. Poachers added an extra level of threat to salmon populations that were already spiralling downward and Ben wanted to make sure that any salmon entering the rivers in the park had every opportunity to spawn successfully. It wouldn't be long before salmon were making their way into the Chéticamp and he wanted to be ready.

While winter still had a firm grip of the Highlands, the snow and ice was gradually disappearing in the woods along the river and Ben figured in high water he would be able to patrol the area easily by canoe. He worked his way down the Chéticamp then bushwhacked back home, making it back to his house well after dark. He liked exploring new areas and intended to get familiar with both the official trails and the plethora of game trails that criss-crossed the flood plain, winding their way through the ostrich fern and groves of birch.

Back in his house, Ben pulled out the map that Joe had left for him and pencilled in the routes he had checked out. He was busy getting everything down on paper when he heard a knock on the door and went to answer it.

"Kate!" They had agreed to lay low and keep their relationship on the back burner for the first little while, at least until Ben was settled in, but he was happy to see her.

"I just figured you were home alone waiting for another deer to be thrown on your lawn," she said as he opened the door.

Ben laughed. "No thanks, one is enough for me."

"Well, I thought I would come by and drag you over to the compound," said Kate. "The highways crew is having a bit of a ceilidh. You'd be surprised to see the same men you met today playing instruments and singing."

"I would be." Ben grinned. "Are you going to tell me that Maurice is the main event?"

Kate laughed. "Yes, and pigs fly."

Ben grabbed his jacket and locked up as he escorted Kate out the door.

"Are we driving or walking?" he asked, not seeing any vehicle.

"Walking," said Kate. "It's a beautiful night."

They strolled out across the lawn and along the road toward the park as Ben gazed skyward.

"Weather's coming," he said. "Probably more snow."

"How do you know?" Kate asked, looking at the sky.

"An old-timer back in Terra Nova used to say that when the stars looked farther away than normal, there was bad weather in store," Ben explained. "And the wind is swinging around to the northeast, so we'll be getting something before morning."

They continued toward the park and began to cross the Chéticamp River Bridge. They were just about across when a pickup roared around the corner.

Ben grabbed Kate by the arm and pulled her to the side of the road as the truck sped past with a distinctive rumble that Ben found oddly familiar.

"I've heard that sound before," said Ben. "I think that's the same truck that left the welcome gift on my lawn the other night."

"Are you sure?" Kate asked.

"I won't soon forget that sound. It's pretty distinctive," Ben replied. "Why? Do you know who it is?"

"Well, I'm not one hundred percent certain, but I think it's John Donald Moores."

"Who's he?" Ben wanted to find out everything Kate knew about his mystery guest.

"Well, let's just say he's a person of interest," said Kate.

"C'mon," said Ben. "What are you not telling me?"

"It can wait," said Kate. She grabbed his hand and walked quickly off the bridge, crossing the lawn of the information centre as they headed to the compound. Approaching the garage, they could hear a guitar and a lone voice crooning out a country-and-western song.

Kate opened the door and walked in.

Emile was perched on a stool, wearing a cowboy hat and boots.

A few of the men turned their heads, nodded and smiled. The rest listened intently as Emile finished the song.

He looked up from his seat and smiled at Kate and Ben.

"I was always closet country," he laughed.

"That's the best kind," said Kate, with a smile.

"Glad you two could make it," said Louis. "So, Kate, how about a tune?" he added, passing a fiddle along to the young warden. Turning to Ben he laughed, "We've been showing her the ropes so that she can give up her day job."

Kate blushed but took the fiddle and walked over to a chair where she took off her jacket.

"Are you going to accompany me, Gerard?" she asked a burly dark-haired man standing by one of the speed plows.

Gerard nodded, picked up his fiddle and walked over to Kate. Holding the fiddle across his chest, he slowly ran the rosined bow across the strings, producing a haunting melody that hung in the air. The audience of heavy equipment operators was silent as Gerard continued, seriously contemplating the piece. Kate stood at the ready, admiring the skill with which Gerard made the fiddle sing. He played solo for several minutes, ending the tune and instantaneously starting another. Gradually he picked up the pace and Kate readied her fiddle, holding the bow slightly above the strings. Suddenly she joined in as Gerard led them into a light-hearted reel. Louis and the others started to kick their feet and go through the motions of a jig.

Ben stood back and started to clap to the tune.

Gerard and Kate played together for several minutes, increasing the tempo to a fever pitch, at which point Kate stopped playing.

Gerard continued. Concentrating on the frets, he moved his fingers expeditiously across the strings. The tune peaked and then, just as suddenly, subsided to a slow waltz-like melody. At this point Kate joined in again as Gerard gradually eased out of the picture.

Kate continued to play, picking up the haunting melody that Gerard had started with. She closed her eyes and swayed slowly with the music, feeling her way through the complicated piece.

Ben was impressed. He loved fiddle music and appreciated how much skill it took to play the instrument.

As Kate slowed down the pace the highways crew started to clap. Ben joined in.

Kate ended the tune, opened her eyes and smiled.

"Bravo," shouted Louis, walking up to Kate and giving her a hug. Gerard looked at her and smiled.

Kate had barely finished when a couple of the plow drivers took up their guitars and started to sing a popular Acadian ballad, maintaining the momentum.

Kate walked over to Ben, who quietly complimented her. She smiled and took his arm, leaning against him as she swayed to the music. Ben was a little reserved, but started to let his hair down as he joined in the chorus.

They stayed for a couple of hours, joining the men for coffee before the midnight shift came on. Outside, a light snowfall had started to blanket the ground and it was time to go to work.

Taking their cue, Kate and Ben said goodnight and walked outside.

"I'll walk you to your cabin," Ben offered.

Kate took his arm and they strolled into the darkness. Neither one spoke until they had crossed the field and were at the door.

"Would you like to come in?" asked Kate.

"I better not tonight."

"Did you want me to give you a ride back to your house?" Kate asked.

"No, that's okay. It's a beautiful night for a walk, remember?"

"You're right. Go straight home and in the morning I can show you around the Highlands."

"That sounds like a good idea," said Ben. "Let's meet at the office around eight."

With that, Kate gave Ben a quick kiss and went inside, turning on the outside light for Ben, who headed back across the field toward home.

The snow was coming down quite heavily now and Ben could see the speed plows heading out onto the highway. This would probably be the last of the spring snows as the days were warming quickly. He made it to the Chéticamp River Bridge and started across just as a pickup drove out of the park and headed toward him. Ben stepped onto the shoulder and was showered by sloppy snow as the truck sped past, its now familiar rumble fading around the last curve in the road.

CHAPTER 8

BEN WAS IN his office bright and early the next day. He was surprised to find an older, white-haired gentleman perusing some paperwork on his desk when he walked in. Looking to be in his late fifties or early sixties, the man was short and barrel-chested and wore a dress shirt and tie along with a new suede bomber jacket that bulged at the seams.

The visitor was unmoved when Ben walked in the door, his balding head bent over an open file.

"Excuse me. Can I help you?" Ben asked.

The man looked up and nodded, but said nothing, sizing Ben up.

"Can I help you?" Ben repeated, moving around his desk and pulling his files away from the man's grasp.

"I certainly hope so," said the man. "My name is Arnold Dickson. I'm superintendent of Cape Breton Highlands."

Ben was surprised. He held out his hand. "I'm Ben Matthews."

"I know," said Dickson, quickly shaking Ben's hand and pulling back. "I wanted to get over here and talk to you before you got people worked up."

"I beg your pardon?"

The superintendent sat down on the edge of the desk and folded his arms across his chest, seemingly unable to maintain eye contact with Ben.

"Young man, this park has run quite well under my guidance for the last fifteen years," said the superintendent, sweeping his arms across the room as if to emphasize his point. "The Chéticamp side almost runs itself. The last thing I want over here is for you to turn things upside down on me."

"I wasn't planning to, Sir." Ben was caught off guard by Dickson's abrasiveness.

"Maybe not," Dickson continued. "But your boss seems to think that everyone and their dog is poaching in the park and that we have to put a stop to it."

"And you don't think so?" Ben feigned ignorance.

"No, I don't." The people here are simple rural folk. Poaching has been a way of life for them. Taking one or two deer out of the park is not going to kill us."

"Then what separates the park from areas outside the park?" said Ben, not willing to let the superintendent's statement go unchallenged. "If people can hunt anywhere they want, it might as well not be a park. It might as well be like most of the rest of the country and opened up to developers."

"I didn't say that," said the superintendent.

"So where do you draw the line?" said Ben.

"Now I didn't come all the way over here to argue with you, Ben. I want you to do your job. But I don't want you to embarrass me. We have a good rapport with the community and that's the way I want it to stay."

Dickson stood and started to leave.

"Excuse me," said Ben.

"What is it?"

"Well, I think part of the reason I was hired was to try to clean up the poaching."

Dickson stopped in his tracks, wheeling around to square off with Ben. "Don't screw around with me, young man," he said. "Park wardens come and park wardens go. The whole works of you can be replaced at the drop of a hat."

Ben nodded and smiled.

Dickson stormed out of the office, brushing past Kate as she walked in.

"Pleased to meet you, too," Ben said to no one in particular.

"What was that all about?" asked Kate, not quite catching what Ben had said.

"I'll tell you while we're driving," said Ben, not wanting to linger in the office any longer. "Let's get going," he said, as he grabbed his jacket and headed for the door. "John Donald's truck went by again last night as I was walking home from your place. He was just coming out of the park."

CHAPTER 9

AS BEN AND Kate headed toward the Highlands, they quickly realized the night's snowfall had obliterated any sign of tracks and the speed plows had disturbed most of the pull-offs, making it next to impossible to determine whether or not any vehicles had driven into them.

Finding nothing, they decided to continue on toward French Mountain.

Ben was surprised at the abrupt changes as they gained altitude. The plateau was a different world. Where there had been only fresh snow along the coast, the winter snowpack in the Highlands was still over six feet deep. Getting out of the vehicle in a couple of places to test the snow, they immediately sank up to their knees. Kate had pointed out that the snow would be rotten everywhere except on the trails that had been packed down, so they decided to check out a couple of the shorter routes on top of French Mountain.

As the pair walked down Benjie's Lake Trail, Kate used a long tree branch to demonstrate the depth of snow at the edge of the packed trail and pointed out the deep furrows left in the snow by moose trying to wade through the deep snowpack to find food in the thick forest of balsam fir.

"They usually end up moving downslope into one of the ravines," she said, pointing to a long trench that disappeared over an adjacent ridge.

"And how do they get out?" asked Ben.

"They don't," said Kate. "They usually starve to death and get washed downstream with the spring melt. Ever since the spruce budworm went through, the moose numbers have gone up because the regenerating forest is plugged with tasty young balsam fir. But for those moose unlucky enough to end up in the wrong spot, it's game over. And for those that wander out of the park, they are usually taken in the fall hunt."

"So would John Donald have been after moose?" Ben asked.

"Maybe," said Kate, "but I can't imagine him coming up here after a moose. Getting it out of the park is a lot tougher than if he had poached a deer, especially if he was alone."

Leaving Benjie's Lake, Kate and Ben worked their way back toward Chéticamp, stopping periodically to take a quick look at the occasional track along the side of the road. Rounding the curve at Presqu'ile, they drove to the crest of the hill overlooking the Chéticamp River estuary and pulled off onto the shoulder. There was still ice at the mouth of the river and the entire estuary appeared to be covered in snow. It was getting colder as the sun dipped below the hills.

Across from them, a gated road led up the hillside with what appeared to be footprints leading up the road. Driving up to the gate, Kate and Ben got out to check. The tracks only went in one direction and it was not obvious where anyone had come back down. Pulling their day packs from behind the seat, Ben and Kate followed the tracks to a small pit that was used to store sand and gravel for highway maintenance.

Two game trails led out of the pit.

"The tracks head down that lower trail," said Ben.

"But the trail probably swings around and comes back out here," Kate pointed out. "Why don't we split up?"

"Sure," said Ben. "You take the lower one and follow the tracks and I'll stay higher up. The tracks don't go back down the road so unless there's another way out of the pit, we should run into whoever it is."

"We can stay in touch by radio." Kate reached inside her jacket to turn on her portable radio.

"Sounds like a plan." Ben turned on his radio as he headed for the high trail, knocking snow from the alders that swung across the narrow opening in the trees as he broke a fresh trail in the knee-deep snow.

Shouldering her pack, Kate followed the footprints down the trail until she came to a small clearing. At the edge of the clearing, the footprints led a few feet off the trail. She checked the tracks and noticed a rabbit snare set at the base of a small alder along a well-worn rabbit lead.

Reaching in, Kate pulled the snare.

Suddenly, she heard a branch snap.

Kate looked across the small opening into the face of a man dressed in a windbreaker and snowmobile pants. He was of medium build and wore a fur hat that partially covered his face but Kate could tell that he was several years younger than her.

They looked at each other for a moment then, surprisingly, he started to make his way through the tangle of alders toward Kate.

"Park wardens," yelled Kate, fumbling for her radio. "Stay where you are."

Unfazed, the young man methodically pulled branches out of the way as he powered through the bush toward her.

Finally getting the radio out of her jacket, Kate yelled into the mike.

"Ben, the guy is down here. Get back here quick."

Ben could hear the urgency in Kate's voice as well as the commotion in the bushes not far downslope from where he was.

Yelling into the radio, his voice was easily carried downslope.

"I'm just above you, Kate. I'll be right there."

The man overheard the call and the breaking branches as Ben crashed through the bush. He took one last look at Kate, then turned and dove into the bushes, just as Ben came into view.

"Ben," Kate yelled. "He went that way." She pointed to the man as he disappeared into the thicket.

Kate and Ben pushed their way through behind him, stopping momentarily when they got back on the main trail.

The man had a head start and was out of sight by the time the wardens crossed the opening to where he had been standing.

Running headlong through the bush, they could not see their quarry. As they looked down, the two realized that all the tracks were coming towards them.

"Maybe he's doubled back," Ben suggested.

Backtracking, the pair found a break in the heavy bush where the man had jumped off the trail and tumbled down the slope. Ben picked his way carefully through the scrub spruce, its stiff branches tearing at his jacket. He followed the track to the edge of a high cliff, overlooking the highway. Peering out through the branches, he could see the man running across the road and over the bank towards the Chéticamp River estuary. For a moment, Ben considered trying to call someone on the radio to intercept him but figured it would take too long for anyone to get there. Sitting back in the bushes, he wiped the sweat from his brow then noticed a leather glove laying in the snow beside him.

"There's no way we'll catch him now," said Ben, pointing to the man as Kate made her way through the trees. "But he left this," he added, handing the glove to Kate.

"It's still warm," she said, putting her hand in the glove. Turning the glove inside out, she saw the letters "F.C." penned on the label. "Look," she showed them to Ben.

"Well, that's better than nothing," he said, as she sat down beside him to catch her breath. "Are you okay?"

"Yah. I'm fine," she said, leaning her head on Ben's shoulder. "But, I'm glad that guy didn't get to me."

"So am I," said Ben, putting his arm around Kate. "This is the part of the job I don't like you doing."

"Sometimes I don't like this either, but we're in this together. Agreed?"

"Agreed," said Ben. "But it'll take some getting used to."

"Well get used to it," said Kate. "Because it isn't going to change."

Ben shook his head and smiled. "So did you get a good look at him?"

"Not bad, but his face was pretty well covered by the hat and jacket collar. I don't know if I could identify him, but I don't think I'll ever forget the eyes. They were scary."

"It's good we checked this out together,' said Ben, pulling Kate closer to him.

Kate didn't reply but the look on her face suggested she felt the same way.

Ben put the glove in his pack and started to get up.

"Let's head back to the warden truck," he said. "It's getting too late to follow the trail. We can talk to the Mounties in the morning about who "F.C." might be. Yvan might have an idea."

"10-4 boss," said Kate with a smile, as Ben pulled her to her feet and they made their way back through the trees.

CHAPTER 10

THE CHÉTICAMP RCMP detachment was a small affair resembling a bungalow, with three extra-large covered bays for the detachment's two police cars and a four-by-four.

As Ben and Kate pulled up, they noticed a woman looking out the office window. She smiled and waved as they got out of the warden truck and made their way to the front door.

As they walked into the detachment, the woman got up from her desk and lifted the opening in the counter to let the wardens into the main office.

"Yvan, les gardes sont ici de t'voir," she yelled into the back room. "Hello," she said to Kate, "And this must be the new warden." She held out her hand to Ben. "I'm Giselle."

"Pleased to meet you, Giselle, I'm Ben Matthews."

"Yes, yes, I know your name. We've been waiting to see Kate's squeeze."

Ben blushed, uncomfortable with the idea that everyone seemed to know everyone else's business.

"But we're discrete with that information outside of this office," Giselle added as Yvan walked in.

"Sure we are," Yvan said with a laugh. "Good morning, you two, and good timing. This is one of those rare days when you've caught us all in the office. Hey, Luc, Steve, get out here."

A door leading to a smaller inside office opened and two RCMP officers came out.

"This is Luc Allard," Yvan pointed to a huge bear of a man who towered over the second officer.

"And this is the Sarge, Sergeant Day," said Yvan as Luc and the sergeant shook hands with Ben.

"We've heard a lot about you," said Luc. "You're smart to transfer here or else you would lose this young lady to one of Chéticamp's rich fishermen." He laughed, "You know, Chéticamp has more millionaires than any other town its size."

"I didn't know that," said Ben. "Obviously they don't work for the feds."

Luc laughed again. "You got that right."

Sergeant Day leaned against a desk, seemingly unimpressed with the banter. "So how can we help you fish cops today?"

"Park wardens, not fish cops," said Yvan.

"Fish cops, tree cops, park rangers, what's the difference?"

"You'll have to forgive the Sarge," said Luc, stepping into the fray. "He doesn't get out much. I think he's afraid *les suêtes*, one of those wicked winds we get around here, will snap his little pencil neck," he said, grinning at Day.

"I'll remember that comment when I'm scheduling night shifts," Day threatened.

"I think I have them all now anyway," Luc said with a more serious tone.

"Okay, okay, you two," interrupted Giselle. "I'm sure Ben and Kate don't need to hear this."

"I'm sure they don't," said Yvan. "How can we help you folks this morning, or did you just drop in to say hello?"

"Actually, our visit is work-related." Ben glanced at the sergeant. "We ran into someone snaring rabbits in the park yesterday and were wondering if you might be able to help us come up with a name."

"Rabbit poachers," the sergeant said sarcastically, "the worst kind."

"Can you give it a rest?" said Yvan as Day walked back into his office and closed the door.

Yvan shook his head. "Don't mind him."

"He's such a dick," Luc whispered.

"So what's up?" said Yvan. "Tell us what happened."

Ben and Kate recounted the details of the previous day's encounter, including a rough description of the suspect.

"We found this," said Kate, handing Yvan the glove. "There are initials marked on the label inside."

"F.C." said Yvan as he pulled out the label. "I can't think who that might be."

"Well, it's not surprising the last initial is a C," Luc said, smiling. "In Chéticamp, it would have to be either A, B, C or D."

"Seriously?" said Ben.

"Seriously," said Yvan. "If you are here long enough to experience an election, you will see that at the polling station, they have four polling booths set up for names that begin in A, B, C or D, and a fifth booth marked E-Z for everyone who isn't an Aucoin, Bourgeois, Chiasson or Deveau."

They all laughed.

"Anyway, from your description, it doesn't sound like anyone we've dealt with," said Luc. "But we can check around for you. It shouldn't be too hard to come up with a name."

"That would be great," said Ben. "If you do get a name, we'd appreciate it if you leave the questioning to us? We've got to show people here that the Warden Service means business."

"No sweat," Yvan replied. "Just let us know if we can help. When you want us to back off, that's fine too."

"Sounds good," said Ben. "We've got to head back to the park to pull the snares, but if you get any information, try getting in touch with us by radio."

With that, the park wardens said their goodbyes and headed back to the pit road to check the trail for other clues. The air was warmer and snow was melting off the trees, covering some of the tracks from the day before. Retracing their steps, Ben and Kate followed the trail until they came to the spot where the young man had detoured toward the cliff. At this point, the trail split and they could see by the tracks the man had made a loop and come back to the starting point.

Following the path, they found snares at every rabbit trail

and decided to pull them all, considering it unlikely the poacher would return. As they followed the trail, they also took note of the poacher's footprints, including the length and width of the stride. Whoever they were dealing with walked at a pretty good pace. Occasionally, in places where the track was not blown in, Ben tried to sketch the detail of each footprint in his notebook. For the most part, the pattern of the tread was not unique except for a cross-shaped impression left by the heel print.

Ben and Kate slowly worked their way around the trail, picking up twenty-five snares and one rabbit. They found nothing that would give them any idea who they were dealing with.

Back at the truck, they were surprised to get a call from Yvan. He had been able to come up with a name but didn't want to broadcast it over the park radio. He asked them to stop by the detachment instead so he could fill them in on the details.

"That was fast," Kate said to Yvan and Luc as they walked into the RCMP detachment.

"Easier than I thought," said Yvan. "But it was also a bit of a surprise to Luc and me whose name came up."

"What do you mean?" Ben asked.

"Well, the name we got was Francois Chiasson," said Luc. "He's just a kid, eighteen years old. We've never had any issues with him, but his old man is a different cat."

"How so?" asked Ben.

"His dad, Maurice Chiasson, has been linked to John Donald Moores, although it may only be rumour," said Luc. "We've never run into them together, but whenever John Donald's name comes up in association with anyone, we know it's worth checking into."

"Maurice Chiasson?" said Ben. "Not the same Maurice Chiasson who works at the park, I hope."

"The one and the same," said Luc. "Your mechanic. I take it you've been introduced?"

"Yup," said Ben. "I think that if looks could kill, I'd be a dead man."

"That good, eh?" said Yvan.

"That good," said Ben with a nod. "So what about his kid, Francois?"

"Well, snaring rabbits would be small potatoes for Moores or Maurice Chiasson," said Yvan, "but maybe it's Maurice's way of indoctrinating his kid into the whole poaching game."

"It didn't seem like a game when he was trying to get through the bush at me," said Kate. "He looked like a kid possessed."

"Like father, like son," said Luc. "The apple doesn't fall far from the tree, as they say."

"Well, I ran his name on CPIC," said Yvan, "and nothing came up so he either hasn't been caught or he plays pretty much by the rules."

"Give it time," said Luc. "Poaching is in their blood around here so don't be surprised if you run into this guy again."

CHAPTER 11

USING THE DIRECTIONS they got from the RCMP, Ben and Kate didn't waste any time before making their way to Chiasson's home, wanting to get onto this while the trail was still hot and before Francois could get his story together.

The large bungalow sat back in the trees, a short ways off the main road and, according to Yvan, was connected by ATV trails to several different access points into the park.

The wardens pulled into the driveway and parked in front of a large garage to the west of the house. There were several vehicles in the driveway, including a new blue Camaro, which still had a temporary licence stuck in the back window.

Knocking on the door, they could hear someone yell inside and feet shuffling as someone approached the door.

Looking at Ben, Kate heaved a sigh.

"It'll be fine," said Ben. "We'll let him paint himself into a corner."

Kate nodded as the door opened.

Dressed in a pair of dark-blue coveralls with the name Chiasson's Automotive embroidered in yellow across a chest pocket, Maurice Chiasson looked with disgust at the two park wardens.

"Yah?" he said coolly, the smell of alcohol wafting off him.

"Hello Maurice," said Kate trying to break the ice. "We're investigating a poaching incident and we were wondering if we could talk to your son?"

"My son hasn't been in the park," said Maurice.

"Well then, this shouldn't take long," said Kate.

Maurice looked at Kate then slowly lowered his guard and invited the two wardens into the house.

Ben and Kate followed Maurice into the kitchen.

"Have a seat," he said as he went to the counter and made a pot of coffee.

As Ben and Kate sat down at the kitchen table, Ben caught Kate's eye and motioned to a bottle of Ballantine's whiskey on the counter.

"Is Francois here today?" asked Ben.

"Yah, yah," Maurice stammered, his back to the wardens as he reached for the whiskey. "Francois," he yelled. "Get your ass out here."

There was no response.

"Fucking kid," said Maurice, turning around. "Wait here and I'll go get him," he said as he disappeared into the back of the house.

"Great father figure," Ben said to Kate as they waited.

Kate just raised her eyebrows.

Maurice returned moments later, leading his son into the kitchen.

"These people are wardens at the park," he said.

Francois nodded without saying a word.

Francois looked younger than eighteen but he was a physically solid kid. His face was scratched and Kate noticed he had a bandage wrapped around his left wrist. She hadn't seen much of his face yesterday, but she knew by the intensity in his eyes that he was the same person they had chased in the park.

Ben also noticed the injuries. He figured the kid had probably torn himself up pretty good on the spruce trees when he was trying to get over the bank and back to the highway.

"Francois, my name is Ben Matthews and this is Kate Jones. We are park wardens and we are investigating a poaching incident that happened yesterday in Cape Breton Highlands. We'd like to ask you a few questions."

Francois nodded.

"Have a seat," said Ben, making it sound more like an order than an offer.

Francois sat down across from Ben and Kate, but pulled

his chair back from the table. Ben wanted to pull around and sit right next to his suspect but figured his father might not like the intimidation. Ben was not keen on interviewing the kid with his father there, but couldn't figure out a way to get Maurice out of his own kitchen.

Ben pulled out his notebook and a statement form and began to read from his notes.

"Do you understand that you could be charged with an offence and you have the right to legal counsel?"

Francois looked at his father, who was standing back by the stove, a scowl brewing on his face.

"He doesn't need a lawyer," said Maurice, his voice slightly slurred.

"I don't need a lawyer," Francois repeated.

Ben noted the time and the responses. Gesturing to Francois, he asked, "Can you sign this form? It just acknowledges you've read and understand the cautions. Perhaps your dad can witness it?"

Maurice reluctantly scribbled his name on the form then passed the pen to his son. As Francois signed the form, Ben noted that he was left-handed.

"What were you doing in the park on Sunday?" Ben asked, jumping right in to the meat of the matter.

"I wasn't in the park," Francois started to explain but his father cut him off.

"He wasn't in the park. He was here at home," Maurice growled.

"What if I said I saw you at Presqu'ile?" Ben ignored Maurice and directed his question to Francois.

"He was here," Maurice repeated, sitting down at the table across from Ben and Kate with his coffee.

Kate tried to get Francois into the conversation.

"So how did you get your face all cut up?" she asked.

Francois looked at his father again.

"He was cleaning some brush out back and got whacked with a branch," said Maurice.

Ben knew this was not going to be easy and tried to figure out another approach.

"Not wearing safety gear, eh?" said Ben.

"Yah, I was," said Francois.

"Well that's good," said Kate. "What kind of gear do you wear when you're using a chainsaw?"

Maurice nodded for Francois to respond.

"This time of year I wear my Ski-doo jacket, chaps and gloves," said Francois.

"That would work, especially with the cold weather," said Kate. "Can you show me the jacket and chaps?"

Francois looked at his father.

"Go get the gear," said Maurice.

Already tired of the questioning, Francois got up and retrieved a snowmobile jacket and pants along with a pair of cutters chaps.

Kate recognized the torn jacket immediately.

"Looks like this was more than a branch?" Ben quizzed Francois.

"Yah, there were lots of dead branches," said Francois.

"Good-looking chaps," Ben said, inspecting them thoroughly. He opened one of the back pockets and pulled a glove out. It looked like the mate to the one he had found but he didn't let on. He checked for the other glove but couldn't find it.

"Where is the other glove?" Ben asked.

Francois looked concerned. "I'm not sure. It must be down in the basement."

Ben picked up the glove and looked it over. It was not as worn as the one he had found but turning it inside out he noticed the inside label was also marked with the letters F.C.

"Do you mark all of your gloves like this?" Ben challenged.

"Yah," said Francois.

"So where is your other glove?" Ben pressed.

"I don't know, I told you." Francois was starting to turn red.

"He said it must be down in the basement," Maurice insisted.

Leaning over, Kate pretended to pick something up from off the floor.

"Oh, here it is," she said, throwing a second glove on the table.

"Yah, that's," Maurice started but his son cut him off.

"No, that's not it," said Francois.

He reached for the glove, but Kate pulled it back.

"But it has your initials," said Kate, peeling back the glove to expose the inscribed label.

It was an exact mate to the other glove.

"I picked it up where you dropped it in the park," said Ben.

Maurice looked at his son and then turned to Ben.

"Are you fucking trying to trick my son?"

"Not at all," said Ben, putting his notebook away. "I'm just telling him where I found it."

"Well, how could you have found it in the fucking park, if he said he wasn't in the park?"

"Exactly," said Ben as he pocketed the glove and got up from the table.

"Thank you for your time," said Kate, following Ben to the door.

Turning to Francois, Ben said, "You'll be hearing from us."

Francois frowned and looked at his father. Maurice was brooding over his cup of coffee.

Ben and Kate closed the door behind them and walked to the truck as a shouting match erupted in the house. Ben smiled to Kate as they got in the truck and drove away.

"Good job," he said, high-fiving his partner.

Kate laughed. "That went better than expected," she said. "So what's next? Charges?"

"You know," said Ben, "he's young and pursuing charges with a young person is never easy. Let's just let him stew on this. It just might be enough to keep him out of the park.

Besides, having an old man like Maurice I expect he's going to regret us showing up at his house."

"True enough," said Kate. "Maurice didn't look too happy."

"Not at all," said Ben. "So maybe that will put an end to rabbit snaring for now."

"Hopefully," said Kate. "In any event, the snow won't last much longer and snaring won't be as good. Besides, we'll soon have our hands full doing salmon patrols and helping with the counting fence."

"Yah," said Ben. "I'm eager to see it in operation."

CHAPTER 12

IT WAS MID-MORNING and the Chéticamp River valley was bathed in sunlight as a light mist rose off the water. Maple, ash, yellow and white birch were all in leaf as the suite of hardwoods created a canopy that would blanket the Highlands in colour come fall. For the moment, spruce and fir added to the collage of green that dominated the river valley, but after October, when the hardwoods lost their foliage, the conifers would be the green sentinels that saw the forest through the winter.

The river itself was a steady current of meltwater from the last snow remaining in the mountains, washing a winter's detritus downstream towards the ocean and temporarily diluting the tannin-laced waters coming from the highland's peat bogs. As it moved through the lower reaches of the river valley, the current took advantage of braided channels, snaking around small islands of willow and alder that were barely clinging to the gravel bars that gave them a foothold on life.

"So this is it?" said Ben, standing with the counting fence crew and the other park wardens in front of the metal structure that spanned the river.

"Basically," said Cole, referring to the rebar and conduit "fence" angling downstream on either side of a large box trap. "The Chéticamp has a small salmon run, but an early run, so we expect fish any day now. As they move upstream they're directed into the box trap."

"You say a small run," said Ben. "How small, exactly?"

"Just a few hundred fish," said Cole.

"That is small," said Ben. "I'm kind of surprised we allow any fishing."

"Here we go again," said Norm. "Talking crazy talk."

"Maybe the boss is right," said Joe. "That's not a lot of fish. Maybe they should all be left to spawn."

"They are, for the most part," said Norm. "It's catch and release for any large fish so they can spawn. Fishermen can only keep the smaller grilse."

"Which are?" said Ben.

"Fish that have only spent one winter at sea and have come back into the river," said Cole. "They usually don't add much to the breeding population anyway. But adult or grilse, any fish going upstream end up in the trap."

"And these gentlemen release them each morning after they're counted, weighed and measured," said Kate, referring to the three young men wearing chest waders.

"We usually get them out as early as we can," said Darren, the oldest and most powerfully built of the three, his chest bulging against the tattered Gold's Gym t-shirt underneath his plaid jacket. "We release them on the upstream side of the fence and they're off like a shot."

"After a big rain we have to pull the pipes before the river comes up," said Cole. "Otherwise the fence would wash out, and it would take all of us at least a day to get it back in place."

"We don't know how many fish go up then," said Kate, "but we think they don't move much until the river drops again."

"I expect that's the case," said Norm, who was an avid fly fisherman. "The fish don't want to beat themselves up before they get to the falls above Second Pool."

"They usually hold up at Second Pool until they can jump the falls," said Darren.

"And that's really where they are most vulnerable to poachers," said Norm. "A couple of guys working a net could clean out a bunch of fish in one night. Twenty fish would probably be ten percent of the spawners."

"That's a pretty big hit," said Ben, taking it all in and

impressed with the way the counting fence crew and park wardens seemed to get along. "Sounds like you guys have it all under control," he said. "David, Marcel? Do you have anything to add?"

The other two young men shook their heads.

"That pretty much covers it," said David.

"We split up our shifts through the week," Marcel added, "so there's 24/7 coverage."

"And they do random patrols up the river at night," said Cole. "So they're our eyes and ears when we're not around."

"Yah, we'll have to talk about that," said Ben. "We might be doing a lot more night work than you've been used to."

"Well, these guys have it pretty well covered," said Michel. "We still have fishermen to check during the day."

Joe and the others nodded their agreement.

"I figure the fishermen can police themselves," said Ben. "They don't need us to babysit them."

"I don't see it as babysitting," said Michel, taking offence to the comment.

"That's fine," said Ben. "We'll talk about it later but I do want you guys to spend less time on the river during the day. That's not likely when the poachers are up here anyway, and we just heard what netting a few fish out of this run means to the salmon population."

Turning to the counting fence crew, Ben added, "You guys seem to have this well in hand. I'll try and schedule wardens to help out with releasing the fish but if there's no one here I want you to go ahead and do it yourselves. You can let us know if you have any problems with the fence and need our help or if you see any suspicious activities."

"Sounds good," said Darren as the other two young men nodded their agreement.

"And don't have your girlfriends up here," Norm added with a wink. "The shack isn't for screwin' or sleepin'."

The three counting fence attendants all smiled.

"Thanks for that Norm," said Ben, looking at Kate and the others and shaking his head.

"No worries," said Norm. "You know how horny these young Frenchmen can be."

"Right," said Ben, raising his eyebrows. "Let's go," he added, as he turned and directed Norm and the other park wardens to make their way back down the trail. "Before someone files harassment charges against you."

"I think you just pegged yourself for the first night shift, Norm," said Cole.

"First one for the summer," Joe smirked, rubbing it in.

"The first of many," said Ben, smiling at Joe and Kate.

CHAPTER 13
A few nights later

MOONLIGHT DANCED THROUGH the maze of hard-
woods; in the small openings along the trail, long shadows
disappeared amongst the alder and small spruce. Close to the
river it was difficult to hear Michel speak and Ben's impatience
was getting the better of him as they inched their way upriver.
It had been slow going, hiking without the aid of flashlights,
and was slower still where the route detoured into the forest,
forcing them to "guesstimate" the trail's location by looking
skyward to watch for breaks in the tree canopy and using their
feet to feel for the hardened gravel path.

Occasionally Ben would stop to ask Michel where they were
in relation to the salmon pools but as soon as Michel replied,
Ben was off again.

Anxious to stop for a smoke, Michel was tiring of the drill.

"Ease up there Ben, the river's running but it isn't going
anywhere," he joked.

Ben stopped and looked around. "Guess you're right. We've
got all night."

"Well, I wasn't exactly thinking that," said Michel. "But this
is supposed to be a tour, not a foot race. Besides, I thought
Norm was supposed to be doing this first shift with you?"

"He was," said Ben, "but he wormed his way out of it."

"Smart man," said Michel under his breath.

"Anyway, we're not turning back until I've seen the main
pools," Ben insisted. "The salmon run will be starting soon
and I want to know my way around the river before things
start happening."

"Oh, I don't know how much really happens," said Michel.
"We spend lots of time up here on patrol and never find much.

If you listen to the gang at the bar, you'd think they were cleaning the river out."

He knew the night shifts were largely due to the fact that Ben had heard rumours about people netting salmon from the pools and wanted to put his mark on things with increased effort patrolling the river. But Michel had heard all the rumours before and was getting tired of them. He knew this place like the back of his hand and spent his share of time on the river, day and night. He also knew the talk and the talkers in town. Most of them were too lazy to walk the river, much less drag a net full of salmon back to town. He told Ben the stories were the locals' way of trying to throw the new guy off but his boss would have none of it and Michel finally conceded.

"You're the boss," he said. "But I bet things will be back to normal after a few weeks."

"Maybe," said Ben. "But for now, let's just worry about getting upriver. Where the hell are we anyway? We must be getting close to First Pool."

"We're just about up to..." Michel started to reply but suddenly raised a finger to his lips.

"Hear that?" he whispered.

Ben strained to hear above the sound of the rapids. In the distance, barely audible, he could hear a motor running. "A truck?"

"ATV," said Michel.

"Where the hell is it?"

Michel pointed across the river.

"Look over there up on the hill."

Ben followed Michel's directions but shook his head. He could see nothing but the silhouette of the Highlands rising above the Chéticamp River on the other side of the park boundary.

"There," Michel pointed again.

Through the darkness, Ben could distinguish two lights

heading along the hillside, momentarily coming into view and then lost amongst the hardwoods. The sound of the machines gradually got louder but quickly faded again, disappearing into the night air.

"Are they on a trail?" Ben asked.

"The old quarry road," said Michel. "It goes up into the Highlands. It's the same road that comes out across from your place, next to P'tit Pierre's house."

"How tough would it be to access the river from the road?"

"Not hard at all. There's a trail down to the river just across from us."

"Can we get over there?" asked Ben, keen on checking out the other side.

"Cross the river?" said Michel. "Depends on the water. I'm not sure."

"Guess we're gonna find out," said Ben, starting into the bush.

"God, not tonight," Michel pleaded. "I can show you in the morning."

"There's no time like the present," Ben called over his shoulder. "The night is screwed anyway."

"You're right about that," Michel muttered as he hurried to catch up.

Ben headed straight for the sound of the river. It was dark in the undergrowth and a little further than he suspected. He crossed an old channel, choked with alder, kept his head low and pushed forward. He could hear Michel behind and to his left. Michel was calling out but he wasn't about to wait.

A few minutes later he crashed through an alder thicket and found himself back on the trail. Realizing he had taken them in a complete circle, he looked sheepishly at his partner as Michel pulled himself through the alders, muttering in French.

"Nice going," he said sarcastically. "How about going to the river next time?"

Ben swallowed his pride and apologized. "Sorry about that, I should have been using the moon as a reference point."

"No sweat," Michel remarked. "But let me go ahead this time."

Not waiting for Ben to respond, he turned and disappeared into the alders.

Ben followed along behind, keeping quiet, trying not to get ahead of Michel. He could see the Highlands every now and then and occasionally heard the river as it slid through the riffles. Finally they broke out of the forest, walking through the grass at the river's edge onto the cobble riverbank. The rocks were moist and treacherous and the moon was quickly disappearing behind the hills.

"Might as well go across and back down the road to my place," Ben suggested.

Michel knew it was pointless to argue. "Might as well," he replied. "Besides, by the time we get there it will be daylight and you can cook me breakfast."

"Sounds fine," Ben said over his shoulder as he started to wade into the river.

Standing back on shore, Michel decided against following his boss on this one and took his time to find an easier route a little further upstream. Picking up a long piece of driftwood, he carefully placed it on his upstream side and leaned against it for support as he picked his way along the river's slippery bottom.

He could see that Ben was almost across, but wading in knee-deep water as he navigated the last pool.

Finding a gravel bar where the water was only ankle-deep, Michel slowly made his own way to the other side and walked downstream as Ben struggled up the cobble at the edge of the pool and collapsed on the riverbank. He was untying his boots as Michel sat down beside him.

"Get a little wet?"

"Not too bad. I'll just wring these pants out and we'll be off."

"Should have stayed a little higher," Michel suggested. "It's usually better above the pools before the river funnels into a single channel again."

"Now you tell me," said Ben, grinning as he pulled off his pants and wrung them out. Michel smiled and sat back against a tree stump then pulled out his smokes.

"You want one?" he said, offering the pack to Ben.

"No thanks, that shit will kill you," said Ben as he struggled back into his pants.

"I'm not sure which one of you will kill me first," said Michel, as he lit his cigarette.

Ben laughed. "Bear with me Michel. I've got to figure my way around this place."

Michel nodded and took a long draw on his cigarette.

"I just want to get a feel for what's happening along the river," Ben explained. "I know the locals love nothing better than to get the new guy going."

Michel nodded. "Yes, they certainly do."

"Anyway," Ben added, "I want us to mix things up and do more night shifts on the river. It keeps people guessing. If we give it a good shot and find nothing, then we'll ease off. But if it stops even one poacher from netting salmon, it's worth it."

"Okay," said Michel. "Let's try it your way for the summer and see what comes out of it. The salmon fishing group is just going to have to accept that we don't have time to do day patrols and keep an eye on poaching activity at night. But if they go to the superintendent..."

"Screw the superintendent," said Ben, getting to his feet. "We'll deal with that if and when it happens. But right now my ass is freezing so show me that trail and let's get out of here."

"10-4 boss," Michel chuckled.

In a few minutes, they were on the quarry road and heading back to town. They walked the five kilometres to Ben's house in under an hour and were sipping coffee in Ben's kitchen as the sun was starting to break above the mountains.

Michel got up and looked at his watch. "Time to head home," he said. "I've got a shift to start in a couple of hours."

"You've already forgotten what I said last night," said Ben. "Don't worry about your day shift. We put in a good night so go home to your wife and kid. I expect you to work with me but I'm not asking for you to give your life to the government."

Michel was not about to protest. He'd been working lots of double shifts waiting for Ben to arrive and was eager to get home and see Lucille and Jean Marc. They'd been so patient with him the last few months, but he didn't want to take advantage of things.

"Thanks Ben," said Michel as he headed out the door. "By the way, you and Kate should come for a visit. Actually, plan to come over for supper on Saturday. Lucille and I were thinking about getting the crew together for a feed of lobster and it'll also be a chance for you to meet her folks and get to know some real Acadians."

"Sounds like a plan," said Ben. "It might be our last chance for a party before summer gets rolling."

"Especially with all the night shifts," said Michel, grinning.

CHAPTER 14

AS BEN AND Kate pulled in to Michel's driveway they were surprised to see so many vehicles.

"Looks like the Aucoins invited the whole Warden Service," said Kate, walking up to the house.

"And half the community," said Ben as they rounded the corner and walked into the middle of the crowded back yard.

Spotting them from his perch at the barbeque, Michel grabbed the hand of the woman standing next to him and walked their way, pulling a young boy away from a group of friends to come and meet their newest guests.

"Bienvenue," said Michel, extending his free hand. "Welcome to our home."

"Thanks for the invitation," said Ben, shaking hands.

"I'd like you to meet my son Jean Marc and my better half, Lucille," said Michel. "She wears the pants around here."

Ben laughed as Lucille gave Michel a stern look and smiled.

"I've heard a lot about you," she said as she stepped forward and embraced Ben. Turning to hug Kate she added, "A warden couple, eh? What is it about these guys and gals in green?"

"A very bad case of gangrene," said Yvan, overhearing the comment and stepping forward to offer an explanation.

"Better than scarlet fever," said Norm, joining the discussion. "You know what the women say, Yvan. If you can't get a man, get a Mountie."

Yvan howled with laughter as the throng of people gathered around the new arrivals.

"I never heard that one before," said Luc, "but touché."

Scanning the crowd, Ben noticed that besides the local RCMP, most of the wardens from the western side of the park were in attendance with their partners as were a number of the local fisheries and conservation officers. An older gentleman standing next to Lucille noticed Ben's wandering eyes.

"It would be a great time to go poach some salmon," he said, loud enough for everyone in the back yard to hear.

"Dad!" said Lucille, with a look of mock disdain. "You're bad." Grabbing her father by the arm and pulling him forward toward Ben and Kate she added, "Don't worry about him. My father still hasn't got over the fact that I married a park warden."

"Louis Gouthro," the old man said with a smile, extending his hand. "I'm just teasing. Since Lucille fell in love with Michel Aucoin, I have seen the light."

"More like a jacklight," said a rotund man with dark hair and beaming smile, wearing a white collar cinched around his broad neck.

"Father Camus," said Lucille's father, feigning surprise. "How could a man of the cloth say such a thing about one of his flock?"

Father Camus emitted a deep, rumbling laugh.

"After shepherding this flock for the past several years, I still can't tell the sheep from the wolves in sheep's clothing," he said.

Once again the crowd joined in the laughter.

Lucille introduced Father Camus to Ben and Kate.

"A warden couple?" said Father Camus. "It must be difficult working in the same job."

"It has its challenges," said Kate, looking at Ben.

"But you make it work," said Ben. "That's what's important."

"I think it has to be especially tough when you're from the area," said Father Camus, looking at Michel. "You know everyone."

Michel nodded.

"In my case," Father Camus continued, "I think it's an advantage. You see, my flock might be able to bullshit the Lord but they know I'm his eyes and ears, so they can't bullshit me."

Once again, Father Camus roared with laughter.

"This is better than a concert," Ben said to Kate with a smile. "I think I'm going to like this place."

"It grows on you," said Father Camus. "The Highlands really have a beauty all their own."

"That's for sure," said Michel, re-joining the conversation. "You know, I left here once to go to school but I ached for Cape Breton the whole time. I couldn't get back fast enough. I was counting the days until the term would be over and I could come home. I will never leave here again," he added emphatically, putting an arm around Lucille.

"I can see why," said Ben. "There's something about this place that grabs your soul and holds it hostage."

"I like that," said Father Camus. "God would like that," he added, but before he could continue Michel cut in.

"Enough talk of souls and God," said Michel, turning to the crowd and whistling to get everyone's attention. "The moose steaks are ready and the lobster is cooked so everyone can help themselves."

"Is this park moose?" said a voice from the back.

"No, it is not park moose," said Michel with a smile. "And the lobsters are legal. So dig in and for just this once, please give the park talk a rest. You may all be my friends and family but work is work and this is play."

"Beside, we have you surrounded," Norm added with a chuckle.

As Ben and Kate loaded their plates they looked around for a place to sit in the rows of picnic tables Michel had borrowed from the park for the occasion. Ben was about to sit with Cole, Norm, Joe and their wives when Kate tugged at his arm and led him to a table occupied by Michel and Lucille and some of their family and close friends.

"Let's sit here," said Kate. "Mix it up a bit."

As they settled in, Lucille's mother began interrogating

Ben about where he was from and how he had come to end up in Cape Breton, leaving no stone unturned as she queried Kate as well about how they had met. She ended with a comment about the park that had Ben wishing they might have chosen a better place to sit.

"I don't really understand the park," she said. "I think our parents did a good job of taking care of this place before the park was established. There was probably even more wildlife then."

Ben started to reply but Michel politely interjected to respond to his mother-in-law.

"There may have been as much wildlife when people just took what they needed for food," he said. "It was shared up and down the coast and fed a lot of people. And those were tough times so you could hardly begrudge someone feeding their family."

"But now it seems as if we aren't allowed to take anything anywhere," Lucille's father added.

"Not so," said Michel, getting frustrated that the conversation had immediately turned back to talking about the park. "There is a season outside of the park for everything you could possibly want to hunt or fish. But the real problem is that instead of people taking what they need, a few bad apples are slaughtering as many deer and salmon as they can and selling it offshore."

"What do you mean by offshore?" asked Ben.

"The Magdalen Islands for one," said Michel. "A few of the poachers from around here are making good money selling their meat to folks on the Magdalens."

"How do you know that?" asked Lucille's mother.

"I know. Everyone knows. People just turn a blind eye to it all," Michel said emphatically, raising his hands to signal he had had enough.

His mother-in-law was about to continue when Louis Gouthro spoke up.

"For God's sake, let it go," he said. "Lucille and Michel and their friends don't want to hear this."

"And neither does your grandson," said Michel, pulling Jean Marc closer to him at the table.

"Here, here," said Louis Gouthro, raising his glass of wine. "Now tell me Kate, what do you and this young man do for fun here on the coast?"

"Well, we like hiking and would like to do the trek across the park someday but we also have our diving certification so it would be great to get some dives in."

"You've come to the right place then," said Louis Gouthro. "Nova Scotia is a diver's paradise. I used to dive myself when I was younger. There aren't so many on this side of the island but Cape Breton has a lot of old wrecks to dive on as well. Some are quite famous."

"You're about to hear the story of the *Cape Enrage*," said Lucille.

"Yes you are," said her father. "In fact, your park superintendent was a diver himself and he found the wreck off Louisbourg but didn't know at the time how significant it was."

"What was it exactly?" asked Kate.

"A French pay ship," said Michel. "It was swept onto the rocks in a storm and all hands were lost."

"And the cargo was not recovered," said Louis Gouthro, "until almost two and half centuries later."

"Was Dickson involved in the salvage?" said Ben.

"In a manner of speaking," said Louis Gouthro, "but he always felt he deserved a bigger piece of the pie and the courts got involved. I don't know how it was resolved in the end."

"Another interesting tidbit about Cape Breton," said Father Camus. "Louisbourg is steeped in mystery."

"Ah yes, 'part of the mystery' as they would say," said Michel.

"Maybe we'll find some of that treasure when we go diving," Ben said, turning to Kate.

"You never know," she said. "Stranger things have happened."

CHAPTER 15

IT WAS DARK when Ben rolled out of bed and stumbled to the kitchen, his head still throbbing from the previous evening's festivities. The sun was still hidden behind the Highlands, an hour away from casting its light on the tiny village of Petit Étang. Ben poured a glass of juice and inhaled a piece of toast then quickly dressed and left the house. A slight frost coated the windshield of the truck.

He jumped in and started the engine, letting it idle for a moment before putting the truck in reverse and backing out from behind the garage. A light was on at Joe's place but he was not to be seen.

With the headlights off, Ben drove out onto the highway and headed for the park. As he crossed the Chéticamp River, a deer scrambled up out of the ditch and bounded across the road barely five feet in front of him. It was gone before he had a chance to react.

Turning off the highway, Ben sped past the fire shed and pulled up to the chain gate. Unlocking it, he drove into the campground, then pulled the chain across and locked it behind him. Parking at the trailhead, he grabbed a small day-pack from behind the seat and headed up the Salmon Pools Trail. A heavy mist hung in the river valley, swirling through the hardwoods.

As he approached the counting fence shack, Ben swung off the trail and made his way past, not wanting to let Darren know that he was on the river. The more they kept their schedule a secret, the better chance they would have of not only catching poachers, but also instilling a sense among fishermen and poachers alike that the park wardens could be on the river at any time of day or night.

Re-joining the trail, he made his way quickly upriver toward First Pool. He was almost there when he realized that someone was approaching. Quickly he got off the trail and crouched down in the bushes, his heart racing.

A lone figure appeared out of the mist, but it was still too dark to distinguish who it was. Ben wondered if he had stumbled onto someone poaching who was now trying to get off the river before the diehard fishermen made it upstream. He waited anxiously, poised to confront the intruder.

The figure moved quickly down the trail toward him, gliding through the trees as Ben strained to see past the cover of heavy bush that was dripping wet in the misty morning air. He was about to spring onto the trail but caught himself as he recognized Darren, his plaid jacket buttoned snugly to ward off the early morning dampness. Ben assumed he was just returning from a patrol upriver and was impressed that the counting fence attendants took their jobs seriously enough to leave the warmth of the cabin and check things out on their own.

Ben watched Darren slip by and disappear into the fog before crawling back onto the trail. Standing up, he brushed the water off his clothes and turned back upstream. He was a stone's throw away from First Pool and stopped there only a moment to scan the shoreline along the river below the chute.

Continuing on his way, he made quick time to Second Pool as the sunlight spilled over the hillside. Carefully, he picked his way through the bushes to an overhanging ledge next to the falls that provided an unobstructed view downstream.

Pulling a rain jacket from his pack, Ben laid it on the ground then sat down, waiting for the first fishermen to arrive. The mist was quickly burning off in the heat of the direct sunlight. The calm water, darkened by the tannin leaching from the highland bogs, was still clear enough to see the occasional flash of silver as the salmon fed on the emerging mayflies.

Second Pool provided a traditional resting place for salmon

before ascending the falls to access the upper reaches of the Chéticamp and its tributaries. A good rain would be needed to raise water levels high enough for the fish to make it over the falls. Until that happened, as many as a hundred fish could be sitting in Second Pool, where they were vulnerable to fishermen and poachers alike.

Ben sat back against a small tree, soaking in the sunlight. The early morning chill was gone as steam drifted off his wet pants. Inhaling the sweet smell of balsam, his thoughts wandered and for a moment he dozed off, only to be brought back to reality by a splash in the water below.

Ben opened his eyes to the bright sunlight and looked downstream, following the river through the valley.

Another splash.

Ben rolled onto his side and peered over the ledge.

Immediately below, a fisherman stood on a large boulder, his rod straining to hold the force of the hooked salmon ricocheting off the sides of the pool. Ben saw the top of the man's head and couldn't identify this early-morning fisher who now jumped to an adjacent boulder, closer to shore, playing out the line as he did so.

Figuring he could get a better look at the fisherman, Ben crawled closer to the edge but the man's face was still hidden from view as the fishing line sung, spinning off the reel as it sliced through the air.

Making one last leap toward shore, the fisherman landed lightly on the cobble beach. Despite his size, he was as agile as a young boy as he jumped from rock to rock, skillfully playing the big fish.

From his vantage point, Ben could clearly see the salmon as it rose from the murky depths of the pool only to turn at the surface and drive forcefully back down into the blackness.

As it manoeuvred through the water, the fisherman eased out the line then reeled it in again, making sure the fish did not have enough leeway to get to the boulders at the far end of the pool where it would be lost for sure. His control of the fish was firm but gentle, impressing Ben with his expertise.

The play continued for almost half an hour before the fish, summoning one last effort, rose out of the water and somersaulted in the air. Not to be outmanoeuvred, the fisherman let out more line then started to reel the big fish in, gradually overpowering it and pulling it toward the shallows.

Ben could see it was an adult salmon, at least twelve to fifteen pounds and almost a metre in length. Being larger than the sixty-three-centimetre size limit, this was a fish that could be legally caught, but had to be released. He waited anxiously to see if the fisherman would let the salmon go, quickly pulling his head back in over the ledge as the fisherman glanced around the pool.

Ben thought he recognized the face, partially hidden beneath the tattered ball cap, then realized that the fisherman was Norm Miller and smiled to himself.

What will he do, I wonder?

Ben peered back over the cliff as Norm reeled the fish into shallow water.

Stepping onto a small boulder, Norm held the rod high in one hand and grabbed the line with the other. Laying the rod down, he slowly hauled the fish in hand over hand. Reaching out, he gently wrapped his hand around the tail of the fish and gripped it firmly. Running his other hand along its belly and up around its jaw, he quickly removed the fly and inspected the salmon for injuries. Satisfied that the fish was not seriously hurt, he held it upright in the water and ran his hand underneath the fish's belly, simultaneously positioning the fish in the water so that its head was directed toward the pool.

Slowly, Norm moved the fish back and forth, allowing water to flow across its gills.

Ben was impressed by the care with which Norm handled the salmon. Leaning over the ledge, he could hear him talking to the fish.

As the salmon regained its strength, Ben could see the fish struggle against Norm's grip until finally, with a quick snap of its tail, it bolted into the middle of the pool. Norm watched as the fish hesitated on the surface then shot towards the bottom and out of sight.

For a moment, Norm stood motionless, looking out over the pool. Taking off his ball cap, he wiped the perspiration from his brow, his dark brown hair gleaming in the sunlight. Closing his eyes, he took a deep breath and exhaled.

Turning away from the river, he walked up onto shore, reeled in his line and carefully cut the salmon fly loose and placed it back in his fly box. Checking his watch, he started to break down his rod, carefully slipping the sections into a narrow tube. Packing his gear away, he scrambled up over the bank and headed down the trail.

Ben checked his watch. It was seven o'clock and Norm had already driven across the highlands to the Chéticamp River, hiked the trail to Second Pool and caught a fish. He knew that by eight o'clock, Norm would be at the office, in uniform, ready to work. In all likelihood, he would be back on the river right away checking fishermen.

Lying back against the tree, Ben soaked up the sun and waited for the first of the local fishermen to make their way up the river. It wasn't long before he could hear voices down the trail. Ben crawled onto the ledge just as three men came into view. Two of the men were unknown to him, but he immediately recognized Maurice Chiasson.

Pulling backing slightly from the edge, Ben lay down again, curious to see what would happen.

CHAPTER 16

THE THREE FISHERMEN had hesitated when they saw Norm coming down the trail towards them. There were a few words exchanged as Norm and Maurice barely acknowledged each other before continuing on their way.

As the trio of fishermen headed up the trail, Maurice motioned for them to stop for a moment until Norm disappeared around a turn in the trail.

Assured that he was continuing on his way downriver, Maurice and his companions walked on to Second Pool, where all three fishermen unpacked their rods and began fishing, crowded along the narrow stretch of shoreline. Maurice worked the uppermost portion of the pool while his two companions fought for space near the outlet where the smooth water flowed through a shallow riffle before exiting into the main river.

Pulling out his binoculars, Ben focused in on Maurice's friends, trying to get a good look at them as they bantered back and forth in French. One sported a dark beard, glasses and a braided ponytail that fell below his shoulders. Lean and well-muscled, he wore only a t-shirt and fishing vest along with camouflage pants.

The other fisherman was heavier-set but obviously fit, jumping easily from rock to rock, trying to gain the upper hand on his friend. He had short blond hair and a military look about him with multi-pocketed khaki pants and a sweatshirt sporting a US Army logo.

Ben lay face down in the bushes, focusing his binoculars on the trio.

As Maurice cast his line, accurately placing the fly in the small eddies which swirled behind protruding boulders, he looked with disdain at his companions as they constantly crossed lines and cursed at each other. Although Ben couldn't decipher the slang, he could tell by Maurice's tone that he was becoming frustrated with the pair. As his friends tangled lines one more time, Maurice turned and shouted at them, then cursed as a salmon rose to take his fly but pulled back when he inadvertently jerked the line across the pool.

Maurice quickly cast again, effortlessly making two or three forward and backward motions before letting the fly settle on the water and float down through the pool.

Ben could see the salmon circle in deeper water and turn for the surface. Once again it rose for the fly, grabbing it at the same time as Maurice pulled back forcefully, snapping the fishing line. The salmon turned and dove but Ben saw it resurface towards the falls, the red and silver fly stuck in the corner of its jaw.

Maurice's companions clambered over the rocks toward him as Maurice cursed aloud. They were jabbering away as he pulled out his fly box and selected another fly with similar markings. Quickly tying it to his line, he began to cast, motioning for the others to move out of the way. The two men scrambled back to the lower end of the pool where one of the men carefully picked his way across the river and pulled himself up onto a rocky ledge on the far side.

Ben was curious to see what they were up to when the fellow on the far side picked up some large rocks. Against Maurice's obvious protests, he started to toss the rocks into the deep part of Second Pool. Immediately, a number of salmon rose to the surface, darting sporadically around the pool as the rocks continued to hit the water.

The third fisherman, positioned near the outlet, cast his line and jerked it back and forth across the surface of the water, instantly hooking a large salmon in the side. The fish wheeled around and dove as the fisherman gripped the rod. Not letting out any slack, he tried to overpower the fish as Maurice yelled at him from the other end of the pool. Paying no heed, he continued to tug on the line as the large fish rose and dove, vigorously trying to escape.

Furious, Ben scrambled back through the bushes to the trail and made his way quickly down to the pool. As he broke out of the trees, he yelled at the fisherman, causing him to give one last jerk of the line. It snapped and the salmon swam off, the large yellow hook sticking from its back.

Maurice was surprised to see Ben coming out of the bush but knew they were in trouble as Ben glared at him before turning his attention back to the other two.

"What the hell do you think you are doing?" Ben yelled, losing his cool.

"Take it easy," the bearded fisherman replied. "We were only fooling around."

"I don't think so," said Ben, his blood boiling. "You were jigging salmon."

They started to deny the charge, but Ben cut them off.

"Don't bullshit me. I was up on that ledge and saw everything," he said, pointing to the overhang.

Realizing that they had been caught, the two men fell silent.

Reeling in his line, Maurice made his way over to the group. "What's the problem?" he asked.

Ben turned and stared him in the eyes.

"You know damn well what the problem is, Maurice. I've a good mind to charge you all with jigging. I saw that first salmon you snagged and you're lucky you never landed it."

Maurice started to protest but Ben waved him off and turned his attention back to the others.

"Give me your licences," he demanded.

Reluctantly the two men fumbled through their vests and pulled out their salmon licences.

"And your tags," Ben ordered.

They pulled the blue plastic salmon tags from their pockets and handed them over.

Ben took his notebook from his shirt pocket, wrote down the date and time, then started to take the information off the licences.

Looking at the bearded fisherman, he asked, "Are you Jean-Guy Boudreau?"

"Yes."

"From the Magdalen Islands?"

"Yes."

"And you are Brian Gaudet?" Ben turned to the other fisherman.

"Yes" he said.

"Also from the Magdalens?"

"Yes."

"Fine" said Ben as he recorded the information and pocketed his notebook. "I'll need your rods and fishing gear."

The two hesitated, looking at Maurice, who shook his head.

"You are both being charged with jigging salmon and I am seizing your rods," Ben insisted.

The bearded fisherman shook his head. "You're not taking my gear," he said, challenging Ben.

"You're not threatening me, are you?" said Ben.

Maurice stepped up to Ben, pushing his chest to within inches of Ben's.

"Why don't you just take the licences and go?" he growled.

"Mind your own business, Maurice," said Ben.

Maurice glared at Ben, his fists clenched by his side.

Turning to his companions, he spoke in French. Ben could not understand what they were saying, but sensed that they were going to resist. He knew he could never take on all three and would have to back down unless he could continue his bluff.

"Right now, you'll only be charged with jigging salmon," Ben started to explain to Maurice's friends. Turning to Maurice, he looked him in the eyes and said, "But if you don't pass over your rods, I'll charge you all with obstruction and you can kiss your park job goodbye."

Maurice raised a fist to Ben's face and was about to say something when Norm Miller walked out of the woods and strode up to Maurice. Norm was a foot shorter that the mechanic, but Maurice was no match for him.

"Got a problem here, Ben?" Norm asked, not taking his eyes off Maurice.

"I don't think so, Norm." Ben tried to hold back a smile. "Your rods and packs," he said, turning to Maurice's friends.

Both men handed over their gear, looking to Maurice for direction.

"I think you guys better head downriver," said Norm.

Reluctantly, Maurice grabbed his pack and started to walk towards the trail with his two friends in tow. Scrambling up over the bank, Maurice turned and said something in French before heading into the woods.

"I thought they were going to drown you," Norm said, turning to Ben, who nodded in agreement.

"So did I. Thanks for showing up. That was good timing."

Norm smiled. "I was watching for a while, but I thought I'd wait to see if you needed me. I figured there was no sense stepping in to help if you weren't having any problems."

Ben was surprised that Norm had made it back so fast but looked at his watch and realized it was after nine o'clock.

"Exactly how long were you watching?" asked Ben, a little annoyed that Norm had taken his time making his presence known.

"I got here when that fellow started to rock the pool. I stood back waiting to see what they were up to. I didn't figure you'd be up here so early," said Norm. "I thought you managers needed your rest," he laughed.

Ben pretended to laugh, mocking Norm.

"Come on, asshole, let's head back to the office," he said, passing some of the gear to Norm before starting down the trail.

Norm smiled and walked along behind.

"So you've got a few charges for yourself, lad," he said as they headed into the trees.

Ben nodded and picked up the pace, calling over his shoulder to Norm.

"And I thought I had you for an oversize fish too!"

Norm stopped on the trail and looked at his boss, who did not stop to wait for him.

Shaking his head and smiling, he started down the trail after Ben.

"Hey, wait up," he yelled as Ben disappeared around a turn.

CHAPTER 17

A few nights later

SILENTLY, THE TWO men pulled the nylon net out of the large pack, spreading it flat on the rocks at the edge of the pool as they untangled the bottom lead line from the float line. Taking the leading end of the float line and shining his flashlight across the pool, the first man picked his way through the shallows.

"Give me some slack," he said as he struggled to maintain his balance.

"Pull," said the second man as he fed the net into the water.

The first man hauled the net across the remaining stretch of open water and clambered onto the rocks on the far side while the second held the opposite end of the net firmly in his massive hands.

"Tie it off," said the first man.

As his partner tied the net to a small alder along the river's edge, the first man extracted a light rope attached to a small weighted ball and secured it to the leading edge of the float line.

"Are you ready?" he called out to the other man, who had made his way upstream and was standing in the shallows at the edge of the pool.

"Throw it," the second man replied.

The first man took careful aim and sent the ball hurtling through the air towards the opposite shoreline where his partner deftly grabbed it with his large paw. Pulling on the lighter line, he hauled the float line across the water towards him.

"Wait until I get there before you try hauling it in," said the first man as he scrambled back across the shallows and made his way upstream to where his partner was standing. Walking past him, he picked up several large rocks and tossed them into the upper end of the pool.

"That should get the salmon moving," he said as he walked back and untied the net from the small tree.

"Now, pull," said the second man as he held the lead line in one hand and the float line in the other, taking care not to tangle them together as the net billowed in the current, forming a large seine.

As the first man mirrored the actions of his partner, hauling the two lines towards him as he walked upstream, the surface of the river boiled as salmon caught in the seine fought to break past the barrier that was gradually drawing them closer to shore.

"Make sure you keep the lead line tight," said the first man, "so they don't get out of the net."

Struggling to maintain their balance, both men walked towards each other while simultaneously pulling the net ashore and letting the loose end of the net fall to the ground. As they dragged the net into the shallows, the salmon made one last desperate attempt to escape, but to no avail.

Taking a small wooden bat from his belt loop, the first man reached into the melee and began pulling the large fish out by their tails.

"Nice," said the second man, holding all four of the net lines while his partner dispatched each fish with a deft blow to the head and laid them on shore.

"A good night's work," said the other man as he killed the last salmon, the sand along the water's edge taking on a crimson hue in the moonlight. "How many is that altogether?"

"A dozen fish," said the second man as he separated the pile, putting the salmon into two large green garbage bags. "Not bad."

Pulling the net ashore, the men balled it up and shoved it into a third bag, which they dropped into their pack before sitting down on the rocks to rest.

"Want one of these?" said the first man, reaching into his jacket and pulling out a small plastic bag with four small joints of marijuana. "It's great stuff."

"Sure," said his partner, reaching into his own jacket and pulling out a small flask. "We can kick it back with this."

Lighting the joints, the two men lay back on the rocks and heaved heavy sighs as they recuperated from the short burst of activity that had netted them a dozen fish. Passing the flask back and forth between them, they soon consumed its contents and tossed the bottle into the shallows where it bobbed around for a few minutes before being caught in the current and washed downstream.

Stubbing his joint out on the rocks, the second man got up to leave.

"What's your rush?" said the first. "We've got all night."

"I'd rather get out of here," said his partner, slipping the large pack on his back and grabbing a bag of salmon. "In case anyone knows we're up here."

"Don't sweat it," said the first man. "The fucking wardens are probably all asleep in bed and David's too chicken-shit to come up here on his own at this time of night. If it was Darren, I'd be with you, but relax."

"I'd still rather get out of here and back across the river. I'm sure Boudreau saw us on the quarry road."

"P'tit Pierre? Don't worry about him. He hates the wardens as much as you do."

"Maybe, but his daughter might be another story."

"Relax," said the first man, flicking what was left of his joint into the river and getting to his feet. "But okay, if you want to go, let's go." With that he grabbed the second bag of salmon and led the way over the rocks to the trail.

CHAPTER 18

BEN LAY WITH Kate on the large sofa in the living room, a Stan Rogers album playing on the small turntable in the corner. They had been diving all afternoon and had just eaten a meal of lobster quiche. Both were exhausted and dozing in front of the crackling fireplace that was working hard to take the chill out of the night air.

"So how do you think things are going so far?" said Kate, nudging an elbow into Ben's chest.

"You mean with work?" said Ben, fighting off sleep and turning to face her on the crowded couch.

"With us and work," said Kate, curious to know Ben's response. "You seem to be scheduling your shifts with everyone else except me."

"Do we have to get into this now?" said Ben, trying to turn away.

"Now's as good a time as any," said Kate, holding his arm to prevent him from rolling over.

"Well, it's probably easier if we don't work that much together," he said, realizing she wasn't going to let go.

"Just don't leave me out of things," she said, releasing her grip and letting him roll his back towards her.

"I won't," Ben mumbled into the cushion, each word fading a little more than the previous. "I just don't like the idea of you dealing with some of the people we might run into.

"Like who?" said Kate.

"Maurice Chiasson, for example."

"I'm not keen on that either," said Kate, "but it's part of the job."

Realizing Ben was out like a light, Kate rolled onto her back and stared at the ceiling. She pondered their lives together and wondered if it had been a good move for Ben to come to Cape

Breton Highlands. Slowly closing her eyes, she finally succumbed to the fire's warmth, barely cognisant of the knocking in her brain.

Somewhere in her subconscious she locked on to it.

There's that sound again.

"Huh?" said Ben.

As the knocking got louder, Kate stirred and realized someone was at the back door. She rose to answer as Ben drifted back to sleep. A moment later she was leaning into him again.

"They saw him up there, Ben," said Kate. "I wonder what he's up to?"

Ben didn't stir.

"Ben, wake up. They saw him up at First Pool. Ben, for God's sake wake up."

Ben realized Kate was hovering over him, trying to wake him. He got to his feet as Darren and his girlfriend walked into the living room.

"What's up?" he asked, not realizing that Kate had been trying to tell him exactly that.

"This is Darren's girlfriend Janine," said Kate. "She and Darren just came off the river and they think they saw John Donald up there," Kate explained.

"I know I saw him," said Janine.

Ben rubbed his eyes. "What exactly did you see?" he asked, still confused and half asleep.

"Well, we were..." Darren started, but Janine cut in.

"I was fishing the chute right at First Pool," she said, looking over at Darren, who nodded to continue. "Darren was walking downriver, fishing as he went. I thought I saw something over my shoulder, moving quickly along the trail behind me. When I turned, John Donald Moores was standing in the bushes watching me. It was just starting to get dark and with the mist rising off the river, he kind of spooked me. I could barely make him out, but I know it was him. I looked down for a second to watch my footing and when I looked up again he was gone."

"Do you think he came back down after you guys left?" Ben asked.

"No, I think he's still up there," said Janine. "I didn't see where he went but I'm sure he was going upriver. I whistled to Darren and he came back up to meet me."

"And I was watching the trail pretty good on my way back up to meet Janine and no one went by," added Darren.

"Did you see anyone else with him?"

"No, and we came down right away and stopped at the counting fence cabin. David hadn't seen John Donald or anyone else go up. He seemed quite surprised to hear that anyone had gotten past without his noticing, but maybe he was checking the fence when John Donald went by."

"Okay, I'll go up and check it out," Ben said as he walked them to the door.

As Janine walked out, she looked at Kate and added, "I thought we should come in and tell you. It didn't look right."

"Thanks," said Kate. "You did the right thing. And if it comes up, we won't let anyone know who told us."

Darren nodded and held the door for Janine as they left the house.

When they were gone, Ben conferred with Kate.

"Well, what do you think?"

"Something's up," said Kate. "I think Darren was reluctant to come in here but Janine insisted. She's got a pretty cool head and doesn't fluster easy. Seeing John Donald behind her has got her a little upset."

"Okay, I'll head up to the counting fence and check with David. Why don't you..." He was about to finish but Kate would have none of that.

"Stay here?" she queried. "I don't think so. I'm coming with you."

"Let's get going then," said Ben. "We'll drive to the fence and walk from there."

Dyed In The Green

As they left the house, Ben noticed a light on in the upstairs window across the road. Pointing it out to Kate as he backed the warden truck out of the garage and turned onto the highway, she could just make out the silhouette of a person behind the drawn curtain.

CHAPTER 19

IT WAS GETTING dark as Ben carefully manoeuvred the warden truck past old washouts and slumps as it rumbled along the road leading to the counting fence.

David was expecting them after Darren and Janine's visit.

"We're headed upriver, David," said Ben. "We need you to stay here and keep your radio on in case we need to get ahold of back-up."

David nodded his head.

"There were several fishermen on the river this evening but they all came down," said David. "Darren and Janine were the last ones down and no one has come by since."

"Well, Janine seems pretty certain about what she saw," said Kate, "and I'm inclined to believe her."

"But John Donald hasn't been up here all spring," said David. "Why would he come up this late in the evening when he knows you can't fish after dark?"

"I guess we'll find out," said Ben. "How many fish have gone through so far this season?"

"A little over a hundred," said David, "and I bet they're all in Second Pool, waiting for the next high water to get over the falls."

"Well, there's your answer," said Ben.

The two wardens started quickly along the trail, running for the first kilometre above the counting fence where the trail was wider and the footing surer. As the trail wound its way into the forest along the river's edge, Ben would slow down, only to have Kate leapfrog past him.

As they approached First Pool, Ben motioned to Kate to stop.

"Take a breather," he puffed.

Kate nodded.

It was dark in the trees and they could only navigate by

looking skyward, following the break in the canopy that indicated the trail's path upriver.

Ben's heart pounded in his ears. He was sure that Kate could hear it above the murmur of the river.

Kate was quiet, going over in her mind what they would do if they ran into John Donald.

"What do you think we should do if we meet him?" she whispered.

"I don't know. If it's only John Donald, I'm not worried, but I can't imagine him up here on his own."

Ben hid the fact that he didn't care to have Kate in this situation with him.

This time, he knew she was concerned as well, but she did a better job of hiding it than he did.

"How should we approach this?" she probed.

Ben thought for a minute before speaking. "We'll have to play it by ear. If we meet John Donald alone, let me do the talking. If he's with someone else, we should step off the trail into the bush and let them get past us. Then we'll be able to see what they're carrying. We can follow them down the trail and call ahead to get someone to meet us."

"Good idea," Kate offered, not keen on trying to deal with poachers on the river at night by themselves.

It was at times like these that they both questioned the lack of protective equipment and poor radio communications their outfit was known for. It was no secret that most of the poachers that park wardens dealt with across Canada were usually armed and often better equipped than the wardens. Often they were known criminals with reputations that preceded them, and some had a penchant for violence.

Kate had met John Donald on a couple of occasions the previous year and questioned the rumours that swirled around his name. He had been nice enough, but his steely gaze suggested there was more to the man than met the eye.

For his part, Ben had only heard bits and pieces of the

rumours and previous experience suggested that these could often be blown out of proportion.

Or not.

"Let's keep going," said Ben as he continued up the trail. "But let's take it slow so they don't hear us."

Kate followed closely behind, as the narrow trail along this section of the river was difficult to navigate at night. Ben looked ahead, gazing skyward frequently to keep on course.

The trail widened gradually as it moved away from the river's edge and farther into the forest. Suddenly Ben stopped in his tracks. Kate almost knocked him over as she followed along tight to his heels, looking up more often than ahead.

"Lights," he whispered, pointing up the trail.

Kate looked ahead and could occasionally see two beams coming toward them.

"Let's get off the trail," Ben whispered.

Kate followed Ben into the bush, where they hid behind a large maple tree a short distance from the trail. The lights continued toward them but it was difficult to judge the distance accurately.

The two wardens were on edge as they mentally prepared for the encounter. Ben wondered what they would do if John Donald and his accomplice tried to resist. He didn't look forward to intercepting them with Kate as his partner. She could handle herself, but he was concerned she might get hurt. He weighed the options in his mind.

"We'll let them go by then follow them to the fence," he suggested, keeping an eye on the lights up ahead. "I'll try to call David and ask him to call the RCMP to meet us at the fence," he said, pulling his radio out of his pack. "He'll have to go down and open the gate to let them drive up. We'll have to try and coordinate this so that we have backup when we need it."

Kate nodded in agreement, nervously keeping an eye on the moving lights as they continued to get closer. Suddenly they stopped and appeared to move off the trail into the bush.

"What's up?" said Kate, breathing a noticeable sigh of relief.

They could hear men's voices but couldn't tell what they were saying.

Briefly, the lights moved away from the river, disappearing in the forest on the opposite side of the trail. Just as quickly they reappeared, continuing toward Kate and Ben, then without warning, the lights veered off toward the river and disappeared.

"Shit," exclaimed Ben.

"What?" said Kate.

Ben pointed to a light moving away from them.

"They're headed across the river," said Kate.

"They must have come down from the quarry road," said Ben. "That's why David didn't see them. Let's go." Ben headed back to the trail and turned downriver as Kate scrambled to catch up.

"What are we going to do?" she asked, grabbing Ben's arm to slow him down for a second.

"We'll have to get back to the truck and try and get around to the quarry before they're gone. If they head up into the Highlands, we've lost them."

They both started running down the trail and quickly made their way back to the fence.

Not certain who was coming, David had hidden in the bushes by the river and was holding a wrench, prepared to stop John Donald one way or another. "Stop!" he commanded, jumping onto the trail as Ben and Kate approached.

Ben quickly blurted out what had happened and asked David to radio the RCMP for assistance.

"I'll try them on the truck radio but we might be out of contact for a while. Monitor the radio until you hear from us," said Ben.

David was keen to leave his post to help the wardens, but Ben stuck to his plan, insisting David would be more help if he stayed put.

Kate and Ben jumped into the warden truck and drove back down the road, travelling with their lights out until they got to the gate at the trailhead. Racing through the campground and onto the highway, they sped across the Chéticamp River bridge and into Petit Étang.

Passing P'tit Pierre's house, they drove up the quarry road, bouncing along the gravel track, swerving to get past boulders and dodging potholes. At a sharp curve in the road, Ben stopped the truck and turned off the engine. Rolling their windows down, Ben and Kate listened intently.

Barely audible, but recognizable, they could hear the ATVs approaching from upriver. Ben looked at Kate and smiled. "This is better than tackling them on the river."

"I agree," said Kate.

"We'll stay here until they are almost on us. Then we'll turn on the lights and make our move. The road is narrow so they won't get past us," Ben suggested, not really certain what their next move would involve.

"Sounds good," said Kate.

Ben got on the radio and tried to raise the RCMP, but without luck. He tried David with the same result. "We're in under this hill and can't trip the repeater."

"So, what if they don't stop?" said Kate.

Ben hadn't considered the possibility. "We'll have to try and cut them off somehow," he replied, not exactly sure how.

As they waited, the sound of the ATVs grew louder and they soon picked up the headlights moving slowly toward them.

Ben was poised, his finger on the light switch. Kate was holding on to the door handle, waiting.

Two ATVs came into view, travelling side by side. They paused momentarily as their lights gave the wardens away. Ben quickly turned on the red and blue emergency lights and gave the siren a short blast. They were face to face with the two poachers, both of whom were dressed in dark clothes and wore knitted tuques.

"The one on the right is John Donald Moores," said Kate, immediately recognizing the man she had met on the river the previous summer.

"Are you sure?" said Ben.

"Yes, I'm certain."

"And the other one is Maurice Chiasson," said Ben, as the two men looked over their shoulders and tried unsuccessfully to turn their machines around in the narrow road.

"What are we going to do if they take off?" said Kate.

"Looks like we're going to find out," said Ben as John Donald roared his ATV toward the warden truck, brushing past Kate's door as she tried to hold it open. She jumped out of the truck as John Donald manoeuvred past the rear bumper and sped off into the darkness.

Watching John Donald disappear down the road, Maurice hesitated then gunned his ATV toward Ben's side of the warden truck, but not before Ben pushed his door open in an attempt to cut off the escape route. Slamming into the side of the truck, the ATV careened toward the edge of the bank but Maurice managed to keep the vehicle on the road and race past the truck in pursuit of John Donald.

"Jump in," Ben shouted to Kate. He tried to wheel the truck around in the narrow track, but the rear wheels slipped over the edge of the bank just enough to slow the truck down and give the two men time to put some distance between themselves and the wardens.

Finally, with Ben pressing the gas pedal to the floor, the truck climbed back onto the road and fishtailed down the track after the ATVs.

Ben grabbed the radio mike.

"RCMP Portable One, from 8-5-2, do you read me?"

Getting no response, Ben tried to raise David at the counting fence.

"Counting Fence from 8-5-2, come in David."

No response.

Cursing out loud, he slammed the mike into the dash and let it fall to the floor.

Flying down the quarry road, the veil of dust churned up by the ATVs made it difficult for Ben and Kate to see where they were going. From time to time they could see taillights in front of them, only to have them disappear at each turn in the road. When the air finally cleared, the wardens realized that the ATVs had turned off somewhere and they were no longer following them.

Turning around, they backtracked and found a narrow trail that appeared to head back up into the Highlands.

Ben slammed his fist against the steering wheel.

"We lost them."

"Looks like it," said Kate. "But let's go back to where we first met them on the road. I think something might have fallen off one of the ATVs when they went by."

As they made their way back along the quarry road, Kate pointed to something on the shoulder.

"Hold on a second, Ben," said Kate.

She jumped out of the truck and picked up a heavy green garbage bag. Ben got out of the truck to take a look. Opening the bag, Kate pulled out a salmon, its body lined with net marks.

"It looks like there are five more in here," said Kate.

"Fuck," said Ben.

"But at least now we have proof of what they were doing," said Kate.

"True," said Ben, resigned to the fact that this time around the poachers had eluded them. "That's better than nothing I guess."

As they drove back down the quarry road and turned back onto the main highway, Ben couldn't help but notice the upstairs light on at P'tit Pierre's.

Kate picked up on this immediately.

"Do you think they saw anything?" she asked.

"You never know," said Ben as he turned the warden truck into his driveway and parked. "It might be worth following up with them."

CHAPTER 20

THE TWO ALL-TERRAIN vehicles bounced along the narrow track through the backfields and woodlots along the base of the Highlands. As they approached a fork in the trail, John Donald stopped and turned around to speak to Maurice, who was slowly making his way toward him.

"I'll head this way." John Donald pointed to a narrow path that led to a two-storey house in the distance. "We both have fish so there's no need to split things up."

"Well, you do," said Maurice, a look of disgust brewing on his face. "Mine came off when we were trying to get away from those fucking wardens."

"I guess that's the luck of the draw," said John Donald, grinning.

Maurice glared at him.

"Okay, okay," said John Donald. "I'll bring you a couple of fish tomorrow and you can have the lion's share the next time. The main run has only just started and we can try again in a week or two when things have died down."

"Okay," said Maurice. "But before the next time I plan to pay a visit to that fucking Boudreau."

"I told you P'tit Pierre isn't going to rat us out," said John Donald.

"Maybe not, but I want to make sure that daughter of his is not telling her new neighbour when she sees us using the quarry road. How else would they have known we were up there?"

"I don't know," said John Donald, saying nothing about his close encounter with Janine and Darren earlier in the evening. "It's not a big deal. Just leave Marielle out of it."

"That's easy for you to say. You were always pretty tight with her," said Maurice.

John Donald got off the ATV and walked over to Maurice. "Drop it," he said.

"P'tit Pierre still scares the shit out of you, doesn't he?" goaded Maurice. "Or is it Emile, the crippled carpenter? You guys go back a ways."

"Give it a rest," said John Donald. "There's just too many people related to each other on this coast and it's important to remember who's who."

"Well, you certainly seem to think you know who to put the squeeze on, don't you."

"Fuck off, Maurice. I'm sure Marielle wouldn't say anything, so leave her out of it. And like I told you, P'tit Pierre would be the last guy to help the wardens. As for Emile, those days are long gone."

Turning around, John Donald walked back to his ATV.

"I'll see you later," he said, starting the machine and heading down the path toward the house while Maurice sat and stared as the taillights disappeared around a turn in the trail. He was pissed at running into the park wardens and losing his salmon in the bargain. He knew someone had to have tipped them off and he planned to find out who it was.

And he knew where to start.

CHAPTER 21

Next morning

BEN TURNED AWAY and pulled his arm out from underneath Kate's head and looked at the alarm clock. It was six o'clock in the morning and the sun had yet to make it above the Highlands. He quietly pulled his clothes off the foot of the bed and tiptoed out to the bathroom. Looking in the mirror, he shook his head.

Morning comes too early. I look like shit.

Pulling on his uniform pants and shirt, Ben realized he had forgotten his keys and crept quietly back into the bedroom, trying not to wake Kate. He picked up the keys from the dresser and started to leave when Kate mumbled.

"Where are you heading?"

He knelt on the bed and kissed her. "Go to sleep. It's only six o'clock. I just want to check something out."

She mumbled an incoherent response and slipped back to sleep.

Ben grabbed a granola bar from the cupboard and pulled his portable radio from the charger then walked out into the cool morning air. A light mist rolled down from the Highlands and hung over the village. He shivered and pulled on his fleece then fired up the truck.

Here we go again, he thought.

The village was still sleeping as he pulled onto the road and coasted across the Chéticamp River bridge. Shortcutting through the compound, he headed to the gated road that led to the counting fence.

David heard the warden truck coming and was out to meet him.

"I figured I'd let you know what happened last night," said Ben. "I also need you to come with me to First Pool to take a look around before you go off shift."

"Sure thing." David grabbed his jacket from the shack and locked the door.

They started up the trail as the sun was breaking over the hills, penetrating a canopy that was glistening with the early morning dew.

Ben explained the night's events to David as they made their way along the trail, hurrying to make it up and back before the local anglers got on the river.

"I tried to call you on the radio," said Ben. "But we must have been in a hollow and not able to transmit."

"I didn't hear a thing on the radio," said David. "The only thing I heard all night was something that sounded like a short blast of a siren."

"That was when we first met them on the quarry road," said Ben, walking off the path. "And this is roughly where we first saw their lights coming towards us down the trail," he added, pointing to the big maple where he and Kate had stopped to watch the poachers.

From this point, Ben got his bearings and tried to determine where they had seen the poachers' lights leave the trail. Walking a hundred metres farther up the trail, he turned off into the bush.

"What are we looking for?" David asked.

"I'm not sure," said Ben. "We'll know when we find it."

Walking farther away from the trail, Ben looked back toward the maple tree to get his bearings again, then walked up and over a slight knoll.

"Got it," he shouted, hauling a large plastic bag out of the bushes and holding it up in the air for David to see.

David helped Ben untie the bag and pull out a large net.

It was covered in salmon scales and stunk of fish.

"Looks like they were intending to come back."

"Absolutely." Ben looked around a little more. Deciding this was it, he pushed the net back into the bag.

"Well, this ties them to the park," said Ben. "There's no

way to get prints or anything like that, but it's pretty strong circumstantial evidence when you consider all the pieces."

"Does this mean it's an open and closed case?"

"You can never really say that, David. Anything can happen in court."

Ben left the net in the hiding spot and motioned for David to walk back to the trail. They headed upriver to check the pools for any other signs of the poachers' activities.

After taking a good look around First Pool, they continued upstream along the trail. As they approached Second Pool, the sound of water cascading over the falls competed with a cacophony of gurgles and croaks from a group of ravens gathered poolside. Walking into the flock and sending them skyward, Ben moved down to the water's edge and looked around as David stood back on the rocks. Several partially consumed salmon lay in the shallows.

"Fuck," said Ben, turning their bodies over with the toe of his boot. "Look at the net marks," he added, pointing to the scars left by the nylon net as the fish struggled to gain their freedom. "These salmon must have got out but were too beat up to survive. What a waste."

"See this," said David, who had come down to the edge of the pool and was pointing to a layer of fish scales embedded in the sand and gravel.

Ben walked over to him and knelt down.

"This is definitely where they dragged the net out," he said, pointing to a trough in the sand that glistened with scales. "That's probably ten percent of the run, gone in one night."

"Ouch," said David. "I guess that's a bigger deal than I thought. I figured most poachers only slipped away with a fish or two at most."

"I wish," said Ben. "That's why it's so critical to account for every fish. One night like this puts a serious dent into a small population. I wish people would understand the damage that guys like John Donald Moores and Maurice Chiasson do to fish and other wildlife."

"Maybe they would understand, if poaching resulted in the river being closed to fishing," said David. "People would see that a few assholes can spoil it for everyone."

"Good point," said Ben. "Maybe when it hits them where it hurts they'll figure it out."

As they continued to look around for other clues, Ben followed the current downstream a short distance, jumping from rock to rock along the river's edge. Bending down, he picked up an empty flask that was bobbing in an eddy behind a large boulder.

"Interesting," he said as he inspected the bottle.

"What is it?" said David, who had followed along behind.

"Ballantine's whiskey," said Ben, recalling the bottle he had seen at Maurice's house.

"Can you get fingerprints off of it?" said David.

"Not likely," said Ben, noting that there were some obvious markings on the glass. "Might happen if we were investigating a murder. It would never happen for a fish and wildlife charge."

"Seriously?" said David.

"Seriously," said Ben, putting the bottle in his backpack. "But it's still circumstantial evidence and every little piece helps."

"Then maybe this will help too," said David, handing Ben the remnants of a stubbed-out joint. "Smells like weed. I found it back on the rocks."

Ben took a sniff and popped the joint in a small plastic evidence bag before adding it to his pack.

"C'mon, let's see if there are any fish left in Second Pool," he said.

Ben and David walked back to the trail and made their way to the upper end of Second Pool, where Ben showed David how to get out to the cliff ledge.

"This is a great place to observe fishermen and fish," said Ben, donning his sunglasses. Leaning over the edge, he could see the outlines of a dozen salmon laying in the current.

"Well, they didn't get them all," he said as he passed the sunglasses to David.

"No, but it looks like a few others have net marks," said David, scanning the pool before handing the sunglasses back to Ben.

"Good eye, David. Those fish are probably lucky to still be alive," he said, pointing down at the ravens that were back to feeding on the dead salmon at the edge of the pool. "Anyway, let's head back before the real fishermen start showing up," Ben suggested.

On their way down the trail they retrieved the net from its hiding place and took turns packing it back to the counting fence. Kate was waiting for them at the shack.

"Figured you'd be here, so I hiked up," she said. "What did you find?"

Ben opened the bag and showed her the net.

"Where did you find that?" she asked.

"Where we saw their lights hesitate."

"So that explains why they went off the trail."

"Yah, they must have been planning to come back," said Ben.

"Maybe we should have left it and staked it out?" Kate suggested.

"I thought about it," said Ben, "but without the net, we only have our testimony and the salmon we picked up off the trail. If they came back and took the net without us knowing, it would be one less piece of circumstantial evidence for our case. Anyway, we've taken it and we aren't going back. Besides, we have to get rolling. We still have to put this all together."

"How about a coffee?" suggested David, trying to prolong the wardens' visit.

"Thanks, David, but we should be getting back," said Ben.

"Besides, Marcel should be up here any minute to switch with you. It's almost eight bells."

Kate and Ben jumped into the warden truck and headed back down the trail. Marcel was just arriving at the gate.

"Heard you had some trouble last night," said Marcel.

Kate and Ben looked at each other.

"Word sure gets around quick," said Ben.

"Well it is Chéticamp." Marcel winked. "You two look tired. I'll get the scoop from David."

"How the hell would he know about last night?" said Ben, as Marcel walked out of earshot.

"I expect folks are using police scanners to monitor our frequencies and can hear what's happening on the radios," said Kate.

"But the radios weren't working," said Ben.

"Well obviously someone can hear us," said Kate. "Word is getting out somehow."

Ben looked at Kate and shook his head. Deep down he continued to wonder about the house across the road and the possibility that they were somehow involved.

CHAPTER 22

AFTER DROPPING KATE off at her cabin, Ben drove back to his residence, taking note of the house across the road. There was an ATV sitting in front of the house and piles of freshly-made lobster pots dotted the yard.

Ben had seen Pierre Boudreau, or P'tit Pierre as he was called, working around his yard mending nets and fixing lobster pots, but they seldom spoke. P'tit Pierre was short and solid; his shoulders and forearms bulged from years of hauling nets and lobster pots. He had a crew cut, which made him look like a professional wrestler, and had the build to match. Often he would wear nothing more than bib pants and a t-shirt along with his knee-high rubber boots as he moved quickly about his business.

Ben sensed that, for whatever reason, the fisherman detested the park and wardens. He was polite enough, but had never managed a smile. Ben figured he would leave P'tit Pierre well enough alone. He had no reason to visit him other than to be neighbourly, but if P'tit Pierre wanted nothing to do with him that was fine.

Ben would see Pierre's daughter out and about from time to time. She was young and quite attractive, but kept to herself. He had never seen her around with any of the local boys and assumed that her father kept strict tabs on her. Apparently, P'tit Pierre's wife had died a few years earlier of cancer and his daughter had stayed around to help her father by keeping house for him. According to Joe, she was secretary to the manager of the local fish plant and her work varied as different fisheries opened and closed throughout the year.

As Ben pulled into his driveway and got out of the truck, he wondered about going across the road and asking P'tit Pierre and his daughter if they had seen anything the previous night. They might have some idea of who used the road to access the Highlands and may have even seen someone on the road last evening.

But they probably wouldn't want to get involved.

Ben walked up the step to his back door, then, changing his mind, threw his pack inside the house and walked across the road.

As Ben approached the Boudreau's house he began to have second thoughts but finally decided to push on.

"Is anybody home?" he said as he knocked on the door, wondering, almost hoping, that P'tit Pierre was out fishing. He was about to leave when he heard a sound from inside and the door opened.

P'tit Pierre's daughter was standing in front of him, wearing an apron covered in flour. She was even more attractive than he had thought, the lustre of her black curls emphasizing the profile of her face. Her deep blue eyes and high cheekbones accentuated her stunning features.

Surprised to see him, she quickly pulled her apron strings taut and adjusted her dress.

"Excuse me, miss. I'm sorry, I don't know your name," Ben stammered. "I live across..."

"Marielle," she interrupted him as she brushed her hair out of her face with a flour-covered hand. "I know who you are, Ben." She spoke with a slight French accent.

"Excuse me, Marielle." He hesitated with her name to make sure he got it right. "I was wondering if I could ask you a few questions? I'm investigating a poaching incident on the river last night."

Marielle nodded and asked Ben to come in, showing him to the kitchen.

Ben followed her into the back of the house, the air thick with the aroma of fresh baking.

"Have a seat," said Marielle. "Would you like some fresh bread?"

"No, thank you," said Ben, sitting at the table and noticing a single side-band radio and scanner on a shelf on the opposite wall.

"We use it to talk to the fishing boats," said Marielle, noticing Ben staring at the radio and scanner.

Ben nodded.

"I'll try not to take too much of your time. I just wanted to ask a few questions about last night."

As Ben spoke, Marielle cut a few slices of bread, put them on a plate and placed it on the table in front of him.

"Help yourself."

Ben conceded and buttered a slice.

"Were you home last night?" he asked, beginning the informal interview.

"Yes."

"Did you happen to see anyone driving up the quarry road by your house?"

"No, not really, I mean there are always people coming and going on the road."

"But I would expect there are not so many people using it at night."

"That's true. I did hear some ATVs going by last night, but I don't know who they were."

"Have you ever seen John Donald Moores using the road?"

"No, I don't think so," she said, her voice faltering slightly.

Ben noticed the hesitation but didn't push it. At the same time, a conversation in French crackled over the radio. Marielle looked away from Ben, listening intently.

"Marielle, I know a lot of people along the coast are intimidated by John Donald," said Ben, "but if you tell me, no one will know where I got the information."

Marielle turned away from the radio and looked back across the table at Ben.

"I'm sorry," she said. "You should probably leave. My father will be home soon."

"That's fine," said Ben. "I wanted to talk to him anyway."

Marielle stood up and straightened her dress and apron.

"I don't think that would be a good idea. He won't appreciate your being here with me."

Ben didn't want to push the issue.

Getting up from the table, he thanked Marielle and headed for the door. He opened it and turned to leave, then glanced back at Marielle. She looked pretty in her flowered dress and he wanted to say so, but thought better of it.

"Thanks again, and thanks for the bread."

Marielle smiled and nodded. "You're very welcome."

Closing the door behind Ben, she watched him cross the road to his house, at the same time catching a glimpse of a face in another neighbour's window.

As Ben walked into his house, he barely had his jacket off when he noticed P'tit Pierre drive home. Getting out of his truck, P'tit Pierre slammed the door and walked quickly into his house. Moments later, he came storming out and walked directly across the road. Ben knew something was up and went to his door. P'tit Pierre was already there, fuming.

Ben opened the door to a barrage of French.

"Mister, la prochaine fois…the next time you talk to my daughter, I don't care if you are a warden or not."

Ben tried to catch every word but didn't need a dictionary to figure out that he had just been threatened. P'tit Pierre was foaming at the mouth and making little sense, despite Ben's attempts to calm him down and piece together what he was saying.

"I was just asking your daughter about…" he started to explain.

"Je sais ce qu'… I know what you were talking to her about," said P'tit Pierre.

"I'd like to talk to you too."

"No goddamn way. I have nothing to tell you."

"But, I," Ben tried to reason with him.

P'tit Pierre held up his hand.

"Stay away from Marielle."

CHAPTER 23

BEN WASTED NO time going to the RCMP the next morning, arriving at the detachment as soon as it opened. Joe had told him they had relied heavily on the RCMP to deal with any charges the park wardens wanted to lay and usually asked Giselle to process the paperwork. Ben wanted to change that.

Giselle was not surprised when Ben knocked on the door and walked into the reception area.

"Good morning, Ben. I was expecting one of the wardens would show up today."

Ben shrugged. Looking around, he was disappointed to see Sergeant Day in the back office. Giselle noticed his concern.

"Don't worry about him," she said. "He's got his nose buried in his files."

"That's good," said Ben. "I still can't believe how word gets around here so fast."

"It's as simple as A,B,C and *D*," she said, emphasizing the last letter.

"I get that," said Ben. "Everyone is related and everyone knows everything."

Giselle nodded.

"But no one wants to tell us anything," said Ben, shaking his head.

"Oh, don't worry," Giselle smiled. "Before long, I expect people will be more than willing to tell you everything they know, and then some. You might wish you never turned that corner."

"I look forward to that day, but right now I need some information from you folks."

"Well, I hope you know that Yvan, Luc and I will help you however we can."

"I appreciate that," said Ben. "Is Yvan around? I wouldn't mind running something by him."

"He's probably grabbing a coffee in town, but I'll get him on the radio and ask him to make his way here." She reached for the desk radio. "Luc is off today but if we need him, he's around home."

"I hate to bug you guys and I know that in the past you've taken care of all the paperwork for the wardens, but I want to get our crew doing everything themselves. I appreciate what you've done, but the only way we'll build respect for the Warden Service in the eyes of the community is if we are seen doing the work ourselves."

"That's fair," said Giselle. "I don't mind helping, but I understand what you're trying to do."

"Thanks," said Ben. "I know it won't happen overnight, but we have to start moving in that direction. That being said, we have none of the proper forms in our office to even start the process."

"That's no problem. Tell me what you need and I can give you some supplies until you get your own."

"Well, to start with I need an Information to Obtain a Search Warrant."

Giselle's eyes lit up. "Where do you plan to search?" she asked, just as Yvan walked in the door.

"The residence of John Donald Moores." Ben acknowledged Yvan with a nod.

"Hey, Ben," said Yvan. "I heard you had some excitement in the park the night before last."

"Yah," said Ben. "We tried to call you guys for backup but the radios were pretty much useless."

"Figures. What happened?"

Ben related the details and was surprised by Yvan's and Giselle's responses.

"John Donald Moores and Maurice Chiasson?" Now that's

a combination we've heard about but haven't run into before," Yvan exclaimed.

"And not a good one," Giselle chimed in. "Being from around here I thought it was all just gossip."

Overhearing the discussion in the front office, Steve Day got up from his desk and stood in his office doorway.

"Good morning, Ben."

"Good morning, Steve."

"The park wardens had a run-in with John Donald Moores the other night," said Yvan, knowing that would get his sergeant's attention.

"Really," said Day. "What exactly was he up to?"

Ben related the story again, a bit surprised the sergeant was the only one who didn't seem to know anything about the incident.

"So you were outside of the park when you encountered them?" said Day.

"Yes," said Ben.

"So you were outside of your jurisdiction?"

"No," said Ben, tired of having to explain to people that park wardens were also "ex officio" federal fisheries officers and had every right to stop someone outside of the park.

"They could also argue that it was hot pursuit," said Yvan, referring to the fact that Ben and Kate had intercepted the poachers inside the park but circumstances beyond their control led them to pursue John Donald and Maurice on the quarry road.

"But they lost continuity," said Day.

"Whatever," said Yvan, frustrated with the sergeant's by-the-book attitude. "Right now they just want to get a search warrant."

"For John Donald's place?" said Day. "On what grounds?"

"We found salmon, which we think came off of Maurice's ATV, and we suspect John Donald would also have had fish," said Ben. "Right now, it's illegal in the province to have adult salmon in your possession."

"I don't think you'd get a warrant based on that," said Day.

"Are you kidding me?" Yvan challenged the sergeant's line of reasoning. "That's better grounds than we use for ninety percent of the warrants we execute. And to top it off, it's a chance to get inside John Donald's place to see what else that shitrat's up to."

"So you're going to use it to go fishing?" said Day.

"In a manner of speaking," said Yvan.

"You meant to say, 'damn right,'" said Day.

"Damn right, then," said Yvan. "We're all enforcement officers and we all deal with the same guys. Part of our job is to help each other, not obstruct each other."

"Are you suggesting I'm obstructing justice?" asked the sergeant.

"Not yet," said Yvan.

Sergeant Day didn't like the inference and went back into his office. "Do what you want," he said, as he closed the door behind him.

Turning back to Ben, Yvan contemplated the possibility of searching Maurice's house as well.

"Well, we think the salmon came off his ATV when he was trying to get away from us so it's unlikely we'd find fish. We did find some other evidence that might link him to this, but that might be construed as going fishing," Ben said, giving the sergeant's comment some thought.

"Fair enough," said Yvan. "Let's focus on getting a warrant to search John Donald's place. Giselle and I can show you the forms you need to obtain a warrant and you guys can take it from there."

"That would be great," said Ben. "We could probably also use your help executing the warrant."

"That would be our pleasure," said Yvan. "I've always wanted to get inside his house. And his head," he added with a grin.

Giselle pulled a file from her desk drawer and thumbed through its contents.

"Judge McIntosh is only in town on scheduled court days," she said to Ben, "so you'll have to see a Justice of the Peace to get the actual warrant signed."

"That's fine. Who should I go to?"

"Well, there are three JPs in Chéticamp to choose from," said Giselle.

"You can take it to Pierrete Camus, the post-mistress," Yvan offered, "but everyone in town will know what you're up to before you step foot on Moore's property."

"Or Ben Finch, the administrator at the hospital," said Giselle.

"But he likes putting you through the mill, asking questions that are totally irrelevant to the warrant," Yvan explained. "The guy thinks he's Perry Mason."

"Joseph LeBlanc is your best bet," said Giselle. "His office is next to the fish and chip restaurant on the main street."

"Is he good?" Ben asked, not defining what he meant by the term "good."

"Yes," Yvan and Giselle replied in unison.

"Joe will sign anything," Yvan grinned.

"So what do you do when Joe is not around?" said Ben.

"We wait for him to come back," said Yvan.

"JP shopping, eh?" said Ben.

"Welcome to the harsh reality of law enforcement in a small town," said Yvan with a smile.

Ben found the office easy enough, narrowing his search with the help of the acrid smell of deep fryers working overtime. Situated kitty-corner to the restaurant, its only identifying feature was a weathered sky-blue sign hanging on two pieces of light chain above the front door. The name and title, "Joseph P. LeBlanc, Justice of the Peace" were just barely legible to the unaided eye.

Ben tried the door but it was locked. Peering through the grime of dust on the front window, he was able to discern a small office with a vintage wooden desk and hardwood armchair. A light was on over the desk, so Ben decided to wait for a few minutes.

Standing outside the office in full view of the parade of vehicles wending their way through town, Ben watched as people pulled into the bank parking lot across the street and proceeded inside. As people met each other at the door there was a constant flurry of salutations in both French and English.

Ben noticed a small sedan pull into the parking lot and recognized Lucille Aucoin as she got out with Jean Marc in tow. Seeing Ben, she waved and pointed him out to her son. Jean Marc waved and called out to him, causing Lucille to howl with laughter. Unaware of what Jean Marc had said, Ben just smiled and waved back before Lucille escorted him into the bank.

After waiting for almost thirty minutes Ben decided to come back another time. Turning to go back to his truck, he heard a shout from across the street.

An elderly man in a dark grey suit was hobbling across the bank parking lot towards him. Approaching the roadway, the string of traffic suddenly stopped to allow the man to cross safely. He was out of breath as he walked up to Ben and held out his hand.

"Sorry to keep you waiting," he apologized, shaking Ben's hand lightly. "I had some business at the bank and the line-up was terribly long," he explained.

Opening the door with a small skeleton key, he showed Ben into his office and offered him a seat. Ben sat down and perused the surroundings.

The office was small, dark and well-endowed with the odours of deep-fried fish and potatoes. Besides the desk and armchair, there were two other wooden chairs and a small filing cabinet. A bookshelf on the back wall held a number of binders of outdated Acts and Regulations. A certificate hung on the wall behind the desk, designating Joseph Patrick LeBlanc as a Justice of the Peace and Commissioner of Oaths.

Joseph LeBlanc fussed about his desk, muttering under his breath. Clearing some papers to the side, he sat down and looked at Ben. Suddenly realizing that they had not been formally introduced, he jumped up and walked around his desk to face Ben.

"I apologize. I seem to be all out of sorts today. I'm Joe LeBlanc," he said, holding out his hand.

Ben stood up and shook hands again.

"Ben Matthews."

"I know," replied the JP, waving a hand in the air as if Ben's response was unnecessary. "Please sit down."

As Joseph LeBlanc slowly made his way back to his armchair, Ben wondered how much information he should divulge to the JP and decided to only give him enough to get the warrant and no more.

Considering how everyone seemed to know everything, the last thing he wanted was for word of their plans to get out before they were able to search John Donald's house.

CHAPTER 24

ALTHOUGH SHE HAD remained silent about what they had seen that night on the quarry road, Marielle knew she had taken a chance talking to Ben.

But she was tired of being locked away at home all the time and craved the attention of someone other than her father. Her life revolved around a forty-hour week as secretary at the fish plant and the extra duties at home, baking and cleaning for her dad. She was not opposed to helping him out since her mother died, but she felt he was smothering her.

She felt so alone and tried to keep herself busy with extra shifts at the plant. Often she worked until midnight, especially during the spring and fall fishery, catching up on the day's paperwork. During the summer she spent as much time as she could at the beach but it was still a few weeks before the holidays. Right now, she was working a lot of extra hours despite her father's reluctance to have her working late at night.

It had been a busy lobster season and the plant had been sending out a lot of orders. Marielle was doing double duty most days. But tomorrow she was off so she didn't mind working late. As she said goodbye to the other office staff who were heading home, she sat hunched over the books, carefully calculating the day's figures. It was midnight before she finished. She placed the papers in the file cabinet, put on her jacket and turned off the office lights.

Carefully Marielle made her way down the stairs to the back exit and opened the door. She closed it behind her and locked it, then put the keys in her purse. She turned to walk to her car.

Maurice Chiasson was standing in front of her.

Her heart jumped a beat.

She tried to scream but Maurice quickly grabbed her by the neck and put a hand over her mouth. He forced her back up against the door and stared into her terrified eyes. She knew he had a bad reputation and the rumours were rampant about his temper. She also knew why he was there and wondered what he would do to her.

"You're a smart girl, Marielle," he said coldly, tightening the grip on her neck as she struggled to move. He pushed her into the shadows, away from the small light above the back door.

"And a pretty one, too." He uncovered her mouth and moved his hand down her thigh.

Marielle wanted to scream but tried to hold back. The plant workers had all left hours earlier and the watchman was probably doing his rounds in the main plant and wouldn't hear anything above the noise of the ventilation system.

"What do you want with me?" Marielle managed to get the words out.

"What every man wants," said Maurice as moved his hand between her thighs. "But what I need," he whispered, smiling coldly, "is for you to keep your mouth shut."

"But I didn't say anything to anyone," she whimpered.

"Not even to your new neighbour across the road?"

"No, I…" Marielle started to reply but there was a noise from behind them and Maurice quickly put his hand back over her mouth. As the night watchman walked by shining his light, Maurice pushed Marielle deeper into the shadows.

"If I hear that you've been talking to the wardens again, I'll take what every man wants," he threatened her. He relaxed his grip and stood staring at her. "And the pleasure will be all mine," he added, then turned and walked away.

Marielle stood trembling and watched as Maurice walked through the shadows around the corner of the building.

When he was out of sight she ran to her car and unlocked the door. She jumped inside and laid her head against the wheel, sobbing uncontrollably.

She knew Maurice meant business.

CHAPTER 25

THE NEXT DAY Ben was up bright and early. This was the day they had planned to serve John Donald and conduct a search of his house. There was little chance he would have anything around that would implicate him, but Ben did not want to leave any stone unturned. Yvan had also been keen for the wardens to carry out the warrant. He wanted to see the inside of John Donald's house and this was a way to do it legally. The wardens would provide a front for him to check the place out for stolen goods, drugs and contraband.

Ben had organized the search as a joint operation among the park wardens and the RCMP but had decided not to involve everyone, asking Joe, Kate and Cole to hang back for the day. Ben was nervous with the prospects of conducting what essentially amounted to an early morning raid and immediately accepted Yvan's offer of assistance.

They were getting into position and synchronizing the operation just as the sun crested the Highlands.

John Kerry sat in the front of the police cruiser, eyes focused on John Donald's house about a kilometre away. Luc sat behind the wheel, stroking his moustache. Norm and Ben sat impatiently in the rear seat. They were waiting for Yvan and Michel to arrive on the scene before they served and executed the search warrant.

"Have you got the warrant, Ben?" John asked his assistant chief.

"Got it right here." Ben patted his breast pocket.

"Do you want to take the lead?" said John, not wanting to jump in on Ben's turf.

"Yeah, I might as well." Ben stared up into the Highlands as the sun rose above the ridgeline. "I figure John Donald and

I are going to have a long relationship so we might as well get through the formalities."

"We're just coming up to the house," the radio crackled as Yvan relayed his position to Luc.

"I see you," said Luc, pulling the car onto the road and heading toward the house as he spoke to Yvan on the radio. "You go to the back."

"10-4," Yvan replied, wheeling the car into the yard and around to the back of the property.

Luc drove the police car right to the front door and jumped out, opening the rear door for Ben. John did the same for Norm.

Ben walked to the front door with Luc looming over him. Norm and John stood at the bottom of the front step. Looking at his watch, Ben knocked on the door.

It was 7:00 a.m.

Ben did not know what to expect. He had developed a mental image of John Donald based on the stories floating around town and the other wardens' descriptions. Rose had painted a picture of "a nice man" who was always polite, but that image contrasted sharply with the rumours and was about to be challenged even further.

They could hear the sound of someone shuffling around inside then the door opened.

John Donald Moores stood in a t-shirt and sweat pants, unshaven and half awake.

"Yah," he snarled. "What the fuck do you guys want?"

"Are you John Donald Moores?" Ben asked nervously.

"Who wants to know?" said John Donald, turning his steely grey eyes contemptuously on the young warden.

"We have a warrant to search your house and outbuildings," Ben continued, pulling the document from his pocket. "You are suspected of having illegal salmon in your possession." Ben was staring at John Donald, trying to convince himself this was the same man they had met the night before on the ATV.

John Donald pulled the warrant out of Ben's hand and started to read, then threw it back at Ben.

"You read it," he ordered.

Ben began to read the warrant word for word, when Luc brushed past him and walked into the house, pushing John Donald out of the way.

"Where the fuck do you think you're going?" said John Donald.

Ben pocketed the warrant and walked into the house behind Luc, followed by John Kerry and Norm.

Luc turned to John Donald and smiled.

"We're executing a warrant. Call Irons if you don't like it."

Moores was silent for a moment as the wardens started to look through the house then went to the phone and dialled.

"Who's he calling?" Ben asked Luc, moving out of earshot.

"His lawyer," said Luc, motioning for the wardens to begin searching. "I'll stay here with him. You guys go ahead and search wherever you want."

Ben looked around the house, wondering where to begin. Like the outside, the interior of the house was unfinished, with curtains hanging in the doorways and blankets covering the untrimmed windows. The main floor was partitioned into a series of small rooms that had been framed out, wired and sheeted with drywall but not yet plastered or painted; the ply-wood floors, painted a dull grey, added to the gloomy early morning atmosphere.

Motioning for John to check out the main floor, Ben and Norm started up the makeshift stairs, which groaned under their weight. They quickly checked the top floor then made their way back down the stairs just as John Donald was finish-ing his phone call.

"You mean they can just walk in here and tear my place apart," he yelled into the receiver and slammed it down.

Luc walked over to him and suggested he let the wardens

do their job. John Donald sat down on the arm of the sofa, pulled a cigarette out of a pack on the coffee table, and lit it up.

The back door opened and Yvan and Michel walked into the living room.

"Nothing in the shed," Yvan said to Luc.

John Donald glared at Yvan and Michel, but said nothing.

John, Norm and Ben completed searching the main floor then went downstairs. The basement was unfinished: empty except for two large freezers. Carefully they sorted through the contents of both. They were packed with frozen meat and fish, but no salmon.

The three wardens went back upstairs.

Yvan looked inquiringly at Ben, who shook his head.

Turning to John Donald, he asked, "Well, John Donald, we haven't found anything but would you mind telling us where you were on Tuesday night?"

"We were up to the mother-in-law's house," John Donald replied. "We were playing cards all night."

Yvan returned the stare.

"We'll check it out," he said, walking past John Donald to the front door and motioning for the park wardens to come with him. As the wardens filed past, Luc turned to John Donald.

"You weren't with Maurice Chiasson that night?" he asked.

"No."

"He wasn't with you on the river?" said Luc.

"I told you I was at the mother-in-law's, playing cards," said John Donald.

"Sure," said Luc, as he headed out the door. "For your sake, I hope you played them right," he added as he pulled the door shut behind him.

CHAPTER 26

Marielle avoided her father's stare as she cleared away the supper dishes.

"Something is bothering you," said P'tit Pierre.

"It's nothing," she said, not able to meet his eyes.

"Goddamn, Marielle. I'm not stupid. It's this warden and the salmon poaching. Well, don't worry. We don't have to say anything. We didn't see anything."

"But we did. And we know who we saw on the quarry road."

"We don't have to say that."

"Then we are just as bad as everyone else here."

"How's that?"

"We know what we saw, Papa, and yet we let John Donald and Maurice intimidate us like they intimidate everyone."

"No one intimidates me," said P'tit Pierre.

"Then why won't you speak up? What are you afraid of? You know, Uncle Emile probably had the most to fear from them but he's not afraid anymore. Why can't you be more like him?"

"Emile got himself into trouble and paid the price. It's better if we keep our noses clean, Marielle. But I'm not afraid of anything."

"I believe that," said Marielle, "but I am. I am afraid of them."

P'tit Pierre could sense that there was something his daughter wasn't telling him. Getting up from the table, he walked over to the counter and put his arms around her.

"Marielle, I would not let anything happen to you. You know that."

"I know," she said, trying to hold back the tears, "but you're not always around."

"What are you not telling me?" he said, turning her around to face him. "Has Maurice done anything?"

"No," Marielle lied. "We just know they were up to no good."

"Maurice is no good," said P'tit Pierre. "But so help me Marielle, if he lays so much as a finger on you, it will be the last thing he will ever do."

CHAPTER 27

IT HAD BEEN a week since their run-in with John Donald Moores and Maurice Chiasson and Ben knew it was time to pay a visit to the Crown prosecutor. He had phoned Sean McIsaac earlier when he was looking for advice on processing the search warrant but now it was time for a face-to-face meeting to make sure that they didn't screw things up on a technicality.

On the phone, Ben initially found Sean to be distant and somewhat uninterested in their investigation, but he wrote it off to the young Crown prosecutor's inexperience in dealing with National Parks Act charges. In the two years he had been the designated Crown prosecutor for the park, the wardens had not taken any charges to him. John Kerry had advised Ben to involve Sean in the case as early as possible and Ben knew from experience that John was right.

In his own dealings with new prosecutors, Ben had found them to trivialize park charges. They had to be brought along to understand the significance of poaching in the context of national parks and it was sometimes difficult to impress upon them that this was the most serious charge under the Act. To many of the prosecutors based in rural areas, poaching was a common practice and was never addressed as a serious issue by the courts. Although not condoned, it was generally accepted as a way of life.

It was deeply frustrating for Ben to find that after all the hard work park wardens put into deterring poaching, the courts did not follow through with appropriate fines to send a message that poaching in a national park, or anywhere for that matter, was unacceptable.

Ben and Kate were up early to make the trek into Port Hood to visit McIsaac's office. As they drove into town, Kate pointed out the many contrasts between this community and those around Chéticamp. Where most homes in Chéticamp were prosperous and well-kept, Port Hood had a feeling of emptiness and abandonment. A number of shops along the main street were boarded up and the roadway itself was potholed and un-kept. Most of the people wandering the roads were elderly, appearing lost as they moved slowly around the town.

Ben and Kate found the government building easily, it being the largest and newest structure in Port Hood. The sprawling red brick edifice housed the post office, unemployment office, courthouse and legal offices. Sean McIsaac's office was on the second floor and had a commanding view over the ocean. His secretary, Mrs. Innis, sat in a brightly-lit front office that had a waiting area adorned with pictures of the Cape Breton coastline.

As the park wardens walked in, she got up to welcome them.

"Sean has been expecting you," Mrs. Innis said after the introductions. "Please have a seat. He'll be along soon."

Mrs. Innis silently busied herself with filing and typing, efficiently processing legal documents. She was middle-aged, with auburn hair and a pair of heavy plastic-rim glasses that hung from her neck on a gold chain. From time to time, she would don them to read the names typed on the manila folders in front of her. The glasses detracted from her appearance, giving the impression of a frumpy old school marm. Seeming to sense this, she would remove them immediately, obviously reluctant to keep them on her face any longer than absolutely necessary.

The two wardens sat back on a comfortable sofa and thumbed through old copies of magazines. Ben leaned back and closed his eyes, breathing in the smell of salt air wafting through an open window. Mrs. Innis notice him and smiled.

"It's great isn't it?" she commented, continuing with her work.

Ben opened his eyes and looked at her.

"The fresh air," she replied. "I love the smell of the ocean."

Ben nodded. "Yes," he said, smiling. "They should bottle and sell it."

Mrs. Innis laughed. "Don't say that too loud or someone will want a government grant to start up a new industry."

"Hah," Ben remarked, "It would equal some of the other make-work projects the government has funded."

Mrs. Innis started to describe some of the other projects she had seen start up in the area when her phone rang. She answered it, reverting back to Mrs. Innis the legal secretary long enough to take the call and place the receiver back down.

"Sean will see you now," she said, showing Ben and Kate the door to the back office.

As they entered the back room, Sean McIsaac got up from his seat and they made their introductions. Dressed in a light grey suit and white shirt, Sean had short curly brown hair, which was cleanly cut above the ears and straight across the back of his neck. His serious features and powerful brown eyes gave the impression of a quick study, a man who could cut through the chaff and focus on the essential elements of a case. When they shook hands, Ben noted that Sean's were tanned and calloused, those of a man who knew hard outdoor work.

Sean directed the wardens to sit down and took his own seat behind a large oak desk. A picture of Sean's family, his wife and two little girls, hung on the rear wall. Another picture of his children was prominent on the neat and organized desk. Ben was pleased to see a copy of the National Parks Act laying open to one side. The Crown prosecutor was obviously doing his homework.

Opening his briefcase, Ben handed Sean a copy of the court brief he and Kate had prepared. Sean scanned the document while the park wardens recounted the details of their encounter with John Donald Moores and Maurice Chiasson.

Ben was impressed with Sean's ability to review the file while listening to their version of the events, occasionally interrupting them to ask for clarification of a particular point.

Putting down the file, he listened intently, making notes from time to time on a large legal pad that he referred to when Ben and Kate had finished.

"So who were the people that reported John Donald Moores on the river that night?" he said, searching his notes for their names.

"The counting fence attendant and his girlfriend," said Kate.

"Yes," said Sean, laying the paperwork back on his desk. "Can we count on them to testify in court?"

"Not really," said Ben. "We've been trying to build a level of trust with the locals, promising that any information they provide would be confidential. If Janine and Darren testify that would probably put an end to any notion of getting help from others in the community. And besides, they're worried about what John Donald Moores and Maurice Chiasson might do if they find out who informed on them."

"Very well," said Sean. "I completely understand their concern, especially in a small community. But that means everything else in our case will have to be rock solid," he added, returning to his notes.

Ben and Kate nodded their understanding.

"So the two of you were outside the park when you tried to stop the suspects?" said Sean, directing the question to Kate.

"Yes, we were on a quarry road adjacent to the Chéticamp River," she said, as Ben laid out a map of the area and pointed out the location to Sean.

"But do you have jurisdiction outside the park?"

Ben and Kate had expected the question.

"Not directly under the National Parks Act," said Kate, "but we are sworn in as Fisheries Officers as well for these very circumstances. Besides," she added, "it could be argued that we were in 'hot pursuit.'"

"That's true, Kate, but we have to consider that these are elements of the case that Irons will go after."

"John Donald's lawyer?" Ben asked.

"Yes, Christopher Irons, from Halifax," Sean explained. "He is one of the top criminal lawyers in Nova Scotia. Moores and Chiasson have hired him to deal with this matter."

Ben was surprised to hear that John Donald and Maurice were connected well enough to bring in a top criminal lawyer for a relatively straightforward poaching charge.

"They obviously intend to fight this all the way," said Sean, reading Ben's mind.

Ben nodded and sat back in his chair.

"In cases like this, in which the suspects escape custody, a positive identification is critical. If Kate can positively identify Moores and you can both identify Chiasson, then we won't have any problems with Judge McIntosh in establishing jurisdiction," Sean said. "The critical element," he continued, "will be to prove unlawful possession of salmon. The fact that Chiasson had several will infer that Moores did as well. Even if he didn't physically have any, Moores was obviously with Chiasson and will be proven guilty by association. The circumstantial evidence is too strong to conclude there is reasonable doubt."

Turning to Kate, he added, "Remember, we have to prove the case beyond a reasonable doubt."

Kate nodded, impressed that Sean's strategy seemed straightforward.

"But we'll put him in his place in court," said Sean, smiling, a hint of mischievousness creeping across his face.

With that, Sean politely concluded the meeting, suggesting they meet again before the trial to deal with any final matters. He fully anticipated John Donald and Maurice to plead not guilty. Walking the park wardens to the door, he shook hands and wished them the best.

"I'm sorry if I sounded a little disinterested when you first contacted me," said Sean. "I haven't been called on to try National Parks Act cases since I came here two years ago."

"I understand," said Ben. "But you might see more of us from now on."

"That's great," said Sean. "Crown prosecutors deal with some pretty boring stuff. Until today, I never had a good feel for what you park wardens do, but I think this case is going to be very interesting."

"It will be important for us as well," said Kate. "The local community recognizes the value of salmon and salmon fishing but for one reason or another turn a blind eye to poaching. They really need to see that our work is helping salmon and ultimately helping them."

"Well, hopefully we can make them see that," said Sean. "But I should warn you, if Moores and Chiasson have hired a top criminal lawyer to represent them, you just never know how the chips might fall when we get to court."

"We understand that," said Ben. "But we're eager to get the matter dealt with. Whatever happens will directly affect how the locals view the Warden Service."

"We're hoping this will be the start of changing attitudes toward the park," said Kate.

"Well, if it's any consolation," said Sean, "I like our odds."

CHAPTER 28

THE OLD DANCEHALL was smoke-filled, a haze enshrouding the strobe light hanging in the centre of the ceiling.

The rows of metal chairs placed across the makeshift courtroom were packed with fishermen as a few of the town drifters jockeyed for ringside seats. There was a bustle of discussion as people passed on their versions of the facts to those not fortunate enough to know anything about the matters on the docket.

The charged persons themselves, normally relegated to seats in the front row, were nowhere to be seen.

Ben and Kate sat in the second row with Michel, along with the other Chéticamp wardens and several federal fisheries officers. John Kerry and a contingent of Ingonish wardens sat immediately behind them, reinforcing John's message that there would be strength in numbers.

Dressed in the Mountie's ceremonial red serge, Yvan loomed over a small table at the front of the hall. Today his role was that of court officer while Luc, dressed in the day-to-day uniform of the RCMP, oversaw the comings and goings at the main entrance. Sergeant Day, totally uninterested in the outcome of a fish poaching charge, had decided to stay back at the detachment, leaving today's court work to his constables.

As Yvan thumbed through the tattered manila folders piled on the table in front of him organizing the day's caseload, he would occasionally glance toward the door, waiting for Luc's signal that the judge was on his way.

Despite being consistently late, Judge McIntosh expected nothing but efficiency and expediency in his court and was notorious for reaming out the court officers if things went at all sideways.

Luckily, today Yvan looked up just in time to see Luc

frantically trying to get his attention as the court clerk and Judge McIntosh pushed past and made their way to the front of the hall. The clerk's slight build and light-coloured skirt and jacket contrasted sharply with the judge's dark suit, accentuating his large size. His slight limp gave the mistaken impression of being overweight.

From Ben's vantage point, the judge looked like a huge bear of a man. He was square- chinned with sharp features written across a broad face that seemed to only have a serious side.

"All rise," Yvan blurted out, scrambling to his feet. "Her Majesty's court is now in session, Judge Stewart McIntosh presiding."

Judge McIntosh strode to the front and took his seat then nodded to the court clerk to begin.

The clerk delivered a copy of the docket and legal papers to the judge, which he immediately began to peruse, carefully thumbing through the paper-clipped caseload, setting some of the papers aside in neat piles in front of him.

He was about to call the first case when John Donald pushed past Luc and strolled through the door followed by Christopher Irons. With his head held high, John Donald strutted up to the front of the hall and found a seat. Judge McIntosh peered over the top of his glasses, his expression one of complete disdain.

Sensing this, Irons quickly approached the front of the court.

"We apologize, Your Honour," he said before taking a seat with the other defence counsel. "I was just concluding discussions with my client and didn't notice when you arrived."

"Fine, Mr. Irons, but I should warn you that your client is no stranger to my court and if he continues to get off on the wrong foot with me, he will regret ever hearing my name."

Judge McIntosh glared at John Donald.

John Donald returned the stare, expressing little concern over the judge's comments. The stage was set. All eyes were on John Donald and there was a hum of whispered commentary, which fell silent as Judge McIntosh addressed the crowd jammed into the dancehall.

"Every other day of the month you may conduct yourselves in this building exactly as you wish. Today, however, you are guests in my court. I will not hesitate to expel anyone who interferes with the business at hand."

With that he continued with the first case, an impaired driving charge.

The accused man rose from his seat as the judge asked him to identify himself. He was a local fisherman who had been caught having one too many.

"Please come up here sir," Judge McIntosh ordered.

Red-faced and obviously embarrassed by the ordeal, the man moved slowly from his back row seat towards the front of the court. Others in the hall started whispering and staring at him as Judge McIntosh directed him to stand next to the defence counsel's table. A legal aid lawyer, dressed in sports jacket and dress pants, whispered to him to face the judge.

Yvan read the summary, providing only minor details but emphasizing that the accused had blown well over the legal limit of ".08" or "point zero eight" as everyone called it.

The judge, looking down at his notes, spoke to the accused without raising his head.

"How do you plead sir?"

"Guilty, your Honour."

"Do you have any information to provide, Mr. Mallory?" the judge asked the legal aid lawyer.

"Yes, your Honour. Mr. Bourgeois is a fisherman but also drives truck for the Fish Cooperative. He is married with five children and this is his first offence. I ask that your Honour take his personal situation into account in sentencing."

"Very well, Mr. Mallory. Constable Bouchard, did this man cooperate with officers when he was apprehended?"

Yvan reviewed the notes on file.

"Yes, your Honour. It would appear that Mr. Bourgeois in fact had to assist the member, he ah…" said Yvan, initially hesitating as he scanned the summary statement in the court brief for the first time.

Realizing he had committed himself, he continued reading out loud, "…he had to assist the member with getting the roadside sampling device working."

A round of laughter broke out in court but was quickly dispelled by Judge McIntosh.

Fighting back a smile, he looked harshly at the accused.

"Mr. Bourgeois, I am a fair man. I fine you the minimum $500. In addition, you must turn your licence over to the court but you may make application to have it returned, as it is a requirement of your work. I have no interest in adding to the unemployment lines."

The fisherman looked at the judge through red eyes.

"Thank you, your Honour. You will never see me back in front of you again."

"I hope not. I have little use for people who look a gift horse in the mouth and come back to my court," said the judge as he reached for another file.

Turning to Christopher Irons, he continued. "Speaking of which, the next case involves a frequent visitor to my courtroom. Calling John Donald Moores."

Irons stood to speak but Judge McIntosh cut him off.

"Mr. Irons, if there is one thing I despise more than people who have no respect for the law, it is a Halifax lawyer who has no respect for my court. Sit down and wait for your client to approach the court."

Irons slumped into his chair and motioned for John Donald to approach the judge.

John Donald glared at McIntosh as he stood in front of the court.

"Mr. Moores. I sense that you don't like my courtroom etiquette."

"I didn't say anything."

"Not in so many words," said the judge. "What brings you here this time, Mr. Moores?"

"Nothin', I didn't do nothin'."

"Then you must have done something, Mr. Moores," said Judge McIntosh.

Christopher Irons stood up, obviously frustrated with the judge's treatment of his client, something that would have never been tolerated in a Halifax courtroom.

"Your Honour, I can appreciate that you may not like my client, but I object to this treatment."

"Very well, Mr. Irons," Judge McIntosh conceded reluctantly. "Let's get on with the matter at hand."

Judge McIntosh motioned to the clerk for the paperwork and read the charges.

"John Donald Moores, you are charged with illegally fishing in a national park and possession of Atlantic salmon. How do you plead?"

"Not guilty," said John Donald.

Judge McIntosh stopped for a moment, reading from the sheaf of files in front of him. He looked momentarily confused.

"Is there a co-accused in this matter?"

The judge looked at Christopher Irons, who stood up to respond.

"There is, Your Honour," said Irons, motioning to Maurice Chiasson, seated behind him.

Judge McIntosh eyed the paperwork in front of him.

"Ah yes, Mr. Chiasson. Maurice Chiasson. Would you stand up sir and face the court?"

Maurice Chiasson hesitated then slowly got to his feet and faced the judge. A murmur went through the crowd, raising the hair on the back of Chiasson's neck. He looked around, staring coolly at the packed courtroom. As the crowd immediately fell silent, their eyes followed Maurice's cold stare as he locked his gaze on Marielle and her father sitting at the back of the courtroom.

Another murmur crept through the crowd.

"Mr. Chiasson," Judge McIntosh started, trying to re-establish order. "You are a newcomer to my courtroom."

Turning around and facing the judge, Maurice said nothing, barely acknowledging the judge's presence.

Judge McIntosh paused briefly then repeated the charges.

"Mr. Chiasson. How do you plead?"

"Not guilty."

"Very well. Mr. Irons, I assume you are representing both accused?"

"I am, Your Honour."

"Are you prepared to proceed with these matters?"

"We are, Your Honour."

"Is the prosecution ready, Mr. McIsaac?" Judge McIntosh asked the Crown prosecutor.

"We are, Your Honour," said Sean, who proceeded to take a seat next to Yvan, placing the court brief and his other papers on the table in front of him.

"Very well then, Mr. McIsaac. You may begin."

Sean walked around the table and stood facing the judge.

"I'd like to call Warden Jones to the stand," said Sean.

Kate stood up. She was smartly dressed in her ceremonial uniform, her shoulder-length hair neatly trimmed and pulled back around her ears. She walked up to the witness stand and turned to take the oath. At the same time, Sean excused Ben and Luc, who proceeded to the entrance where they sat behind the closed inner door, out of earshot of Kate's testimony.

Towering above Kate, Yvan held out a tattered Bible.

As Kate placed her right hand on the leather-bound tome, Yvan recited the oath.

"Do you swear to tell the truth, the whole truth and nothing but the truth, so help you God?"

"I do," said Kate, looking around the courtroom and catching the stares of John Donald and Maurice.

"You may sit down," said Judge McIntosh.

Kate stood motionless for a split second, her green eyes seemingly transfixed on the two accused as she stared across the courtroom.

"Warden Jones," said the judge. "Please sit down."

Kate regained her composure and sat in the witness chair as Sean approached the front of the court.

"Warden Jones, would you please identify yourself?" he said.

Kate cleared her throat. "My name is Kate Michelle Jones and I am a park warden and a peace officer in Cape Breton Highlands National Park, stationed in Chéticamp," she recited, quickly getting over her nervousness.

"Warden Jones, could you please describe the events of May 9th of this past year," said Sean as he started his questioning.

Kate hesitated as she organized her thoughts then looked up at the judge, who was waiting patiently for her to begin.

"I was at my residence in Petit Étang, Nova Scotia, around eight o'clock in the evening, when I received a report of unusual activity on the Chéticamp River in Cape Breton Highlands National Park," she said, remembering Sean's coaching to immediately establish the time and place.

"What type of information did you receive?" Sean continued.

"That John Donald Moores was seen heading upriver late in the evening," said Kate, taking care not to identify who had provided the information.

"And why was this unusual?"

"Because at that hour, most fishermen were off the river or heading downstream," she explained.

"And what did you do, based on this information?" Sean asked as he pursued the chronology of events.

"I informed Assistant Chief Park Warden Ben Matthews," Kate replied, avoiding the fact that Ben had been with her.

"And then what did you do?"

Kate recounted how they had proceeded up the river trail in the dark, attempting to locate John Donald. Judge McIntosh listened intently, occasionally taking notes. She recounted the observation of two suspects with lights heading through the bush toward the river and the details of backtracking along the Salmon Pools Trail to finally intercept two men along the quarry road.

"When and where exactly were you when you encountered the men?" said Sean, probing for details of this key event.

"It was now around one o'clock in the morning on May 10th and we were approximately two kilometres up the quarry road."

"And can you describe what happened next?"

"We had parked around a curve to surprise the two suspects and waited until they were within view before we activated the emergency lights."

"And how far were the men from you?"

"No more than five or ten metres," said Kate.

"Did you have a clear view of them?" Sean asked, wanting to establish in the judge's mind that they could easily see John Donald and Maurice.

"Yes," Kate replied, "they were in plain view as we had our headlights and takedown lights aimed right at them. In fact, they appeared to be momentarily blinded by the lights."

"Good," said Sean. "Warden Jones, did you recognize the men?"

"I immediately recognized John Donald Moores," she said. "I didn't recognize the other driver initially as he was turned away from me but then I did get a good look at him."

"And is that other suspect in the courtroom today?"

"He is," Kate replied. "It is the co-accused, Maurice Chiasson."

At the mention of Maurice's name, another murmur swept through the courtroom.

Kate looked at Chiasson, who stared coldly back at her. She looked away, catching the judge's eye. He nodded and smiled slightly, helping her regain her composure.

"Could you tell us what happened next?" Sean asked.

Kate recounted the night's events, concluding with finding the bag of salmon on the trail leading off the quarry road.

"Thank you, Warden Jones," said Sean, signalling the end of Kate's testimony.

"Your witness, Mr. Irons," said Judge Macintosh.

"Thank you, Your Honour," said Christopher Irons, rising dramatically, pulling his robe around his neck and brushing his long hair back with both hands. Slowly he approached the witness stand, his dark brown eyes penetrating Kate's calm appearance, intent on discrediting the park warden's testimony and building a reasonable doubt in the judge's mind.

"Warden Jones," he said. "How do you know that my clients were the same people that you observed in the park?"

"We didn't," Kate replied honestly.

"And were the two people you approached in the park doing anything wrong when you first approached them?"

"We didn't get a chance to find out," she answered.

"Well, did you follow them?"

"No."

"Why not?" said Irons.

Kate realized the defence lawyer was trying to get her rattled. Before answering, she took a deep breath and looked toward Sean. He nodded, encouraging her to proceed.

"Because it would have been difficult to catch them given the circumstances," she stated.

"So you lost sight of them?" Irons pressed. "Essentially you lost continuity?"

"Yes," Kate admitted.

"Then you proceeded back to the salmon fence and drove from there to the quarry road?" Irons continued.

"Yes."

"How long did all this take?" Irons demanded.

"Approximately thirty minutes," said Kate.

"Subsequently you proceeded to stop my clients, who you admit you could not identify as being the people you saw on the Salmon Pools trail?"

"We tried to stop them," Kate corrected Irons.

"So how did you justify this action?" said Irons. "You were out of the park and clearly out of jurisdiction."

"That's not correct," countered Kate. "We have fisheries officer status, which is intended for exactly this type of situation."

Judge McIntosh smiled to himself. Warden Jones was holding her own quite well.

"So you figure that it was okay to force my clients to stop when you really had no idea who they were or what they were doing and all the while being outside of your jurisdiction?"

"It seemed logical," said Kate, recounting the facts, "that the people we encountered on the quarry road were the same people from the park. We had information that John Donald Moores was on the river that evening. We subsequently observed two people on the river trail who departed the park before we could stop them. They headed across the river and when we intercepted them on the quarry road one of them was John Donald Moores and the other was Maurice Chiasson."

Kate paused for a moment before continuing. "We attempted to stop them, which they could easily have done. Instead they chose to elude us and we subsequently determined that they did indeed have salmon, which could only have come from the Chéticamp River," Kate stated confidently.

Judge McIntosh, barely able to keep back a huge grin, turned to Irons, who was busily flipping through his notes.

"Any further questions, Mr. Irons?"

"No, Your Honour." Christopher Irons mumbled as he flipped through his files then sat down.

"You may step down, Warden Jones," said the judge, turning back to Sean.

"Next witness, Mr. McIsaac."

"I'd like to call Warden Ben Matthews, Your Honour."

Yvan rose and walked to the back of the courtroom. Opening the inner door, he summonsed Ben. "You're up."

Luc gave Ben a pat on the back as he got up to enter the courtroom.

"It will go fine," he said.

Ben nodded and entered the courtroom, scanning the sea of faces in the crowd as he made his way to the front.

As he swore the oath and took the witness stand, Kate returned to her seat. She caught Maurice staring at her and she quickly looked away.

"Warden Matthews," said Sean. "We have already heard the testimony of Warden Jones regarding the night of May 9th and the early morning of May 10th. I would now like for you to recount your version of the events."

Ben nodded, and speaking directly to the judge and Crown prosecutor, recounted details similar to Kate's earlier testimony. Sean asked leading questions when he felt Ben had not stressed a key point, or to reinforce the details from Kate's testimony. Ben went on to explain finding the net the next day, and the search of John Donald's residence. When he concluded, Sean turned to the judge.

"No further questions, Your Honour."

Christopher Irons was already standing, preparing his attack.

Judge McIntosh looked at his watch.

"I assume you have questions for the warden?" he asked Irons.

"I do," Irons stated eagerly.

"Good," the judge replied. "I expect that this may take a while. It's now 10:45. I suggest we take a fifteen-minute break and resume at eleven o'clock."

Christopher Irons wasn't ready to have the wind knocked out of his sails.

"But Your Hon—," he began to protest.

Judge McIntosh cut him off. "Mr. Irons. It is going to be a long day. Take a break," he ordered. "And witnesses, please do not speak to one another."

The judge rose from his seat and proceeded to the rear door, where he pulled a cigarette pack from his breast pocket and lit up. He inhaled deeply, savouring the heady fumes. There was a babble of discussion in the court as the onlookers evaluated how things were proceeding and speculated on the outcome.

John Donald Moores was huddled against a far wall, a small group from Pleasant Bay pressed to his side. He looked unconcerned, occasionally casting a glance at Judge McIntosh and laughing.

Maurice Chiasson sat stone-faced in his seat, a cluster of empty chairs strewn around him. Christopher Irons regarded him from the front of the court but decided to leave him alone. Irons had dealt with Moores frequently, but Chiasson was an unknown and Irons had not quite figured him out. Chiasson had insisted that he testify in his own defence, but Irons had tried to dissuade him. He would not know until the moment of truth came whether or not he would take the stand. Christopher Irons would try to put the best case forward, but he could not prevent a client from testifying, despite that being considered a fatal move.

Judge McIntosh moved back to the front of the courtroom, signalling to Yvan to call people to order. Ben made his way back to the stand, where the judge reminded him that he was still under oath.

Christopher Irons resumed his position.

"You may proceed, Mr. Irons," Judge McIntosh said.

Irons began by getting Ben to recount his version of events again and tried to find discrepancies between his testimony and Kate's but made little headway. The park wardens had been well prepared and there were few holes available to build a reasonable doubt.

"Warden Matthews, when you first approached my clients on the quarry road, did you recognize them?" Irons began.

"I did not recognize John Donald Moores," Ben replied. "But I had met Maurice Chiasson previously and recognized him immediately."

"And where did you meet him?" Irons asked.

"When we interviewed his son as a suspect in a rabbit poaching incident in the park," said Ben.

Catching the judge's smile, Irons realized he had walked into that one, raising the inference that his client was implicated in other poaching incidents.

"But you didn't recognize Mr. Moores?" he said, returning to the attack.

"Not initially. I only met him and confirmed he was the same person we met that night when we searched his house two days later."

Despite not wanting to concede any points, Christopher Irons had been around long enough to know that the park wardens had done their homework.

"I have no further questions, Your Honour," he said, not wanting to irritate the judge with pointless questioning.

"Very well," said the judge. "Warden Matthews, you may step down. Mr. McIsaac, please call your next witness."

Sean scanned the court to see if he could locate his next witness.

"Your Honour," said Sean, "I would like to call Mr. Pierre Boudreau."

All eyes searched for P'tit Pierre, finally focusing on the far corner of the courtroom. P'tit Pierre stood up in the centre of a row of seats and moved slowly toward the aisle. Maurice Chiasson glared at the fisherman then turned again toward Marielle. She caught his stare and looked away.

P'tit Pierre was smartly dressed in a sports jacket and slacks. Turning to Kate, Ben remarked how different he looked without his fishing attire.

P'tit Pierre ground his way to the bench and was sworn in by Yvan.

Sean approached and asked if he was comfortable being questioned in English.

"Oui, monsieur," he started to reply then caught himself. "Yes, sir," he said, looking toward Marielle for support. He noticed she was staring, her eyes fixed as if in a trance, then noticed Maurice Chiasson turning and looking at her. P'tit Pierre sat tense and rigid, his fists clenched tightly by his side.

"Mr. Boudreau, I have only a few questions," Sean started, having decided not to keep P'tit Pierre on the stand for long. He knew that P'tit Pierre was uneasy about the whole ordeal and was also aware that he could turn into a hostile witness if mishandled.

P'tit Pierre nodded.

"Could you first identify yourself and tell the court where you live?"

"My name is Pierre Boudreau and I live in Petit Étang where the quarry road meets the main highway."

"And could you tell the court what you were doing on the evening of May 9th, and what you may have seen that evening?"

Maurice Chiasson stared at P'tit Pierre.

"Well," said P'tit Pierre. "I was at home, working on my lobster traps outside. It was getting late and as I was cleaning up, I saw two ATVs turn off the highway and go past my house, heading up the quarry road."

"And could you tell who was operating the ATVs?" Sean asked.

P'tit Pierre looked at Marielle. She was holding her hands in front of her mouth, as if she were praying. He knew that she had wanted him to testify, to tell the truth about that evening, but he sensed she was afraid of something. Glancing sideways, he caught Maurice glaring at his daughter.

"Yes, I could," he said.

A murmur slid through the courtroom and the judge raised his hand for silence.

"And are those two people in the court today?"

"Yes," said P'tit Pierre, pointing to Maurice and John Donald. "They are the defendants, Maurice Chiasson and John Donald Moores."

"I have no further questions," Sean stated.

Christopher Irons started to get up but Maurice Chiasson grabbed his arm and pulled him closer, whispering something to his lawyer. Christopher Irons looked at Chiasson then turned to face the Judge.

"No questions, Your Honour."

Judge McIntosh looked at P'tit Pierre and nodded.

"You are excused, Mr. Boudreau."

P'tit Pierre got down from the witness stand and made his way to the back of the courtroom.

Judge McIntosh looked to the Crown prosecutor to call his next witness.

Realizing the judge was waiting for him, Sean turned to face the court.

"I have no further witnesses, Your Honour," he said.

"Mr. Irons," said the judge. "Your turn."

Christopher Irons conferred with his clients for only a moment before addressing the court.

"I have no witnesses to call, Your Honour."

Judge McIntosh pondered his notes briefly then looked at the two lawyers.

"Very well," said the judge. "Concluding statements? Mr. McIsaac?"

The Crown prosecutor rose and succinctly summarized the evidence presented by the park wardens, pointing out that John Donald and Maurice were positively identified, that one of them was in possession of salmon, and that it could only have come from the Chéticamp River in the national park.

Sitting down, Sean felt confident that it was a strong case and considering the rapport John Donald had with the judge, was certain he would be found guilty.

"Closing arguments, Mr. Irons?" said the judge.

Realizing he was probably on the losing end of this case, Christopher Irons rose to counter Sean's points, to put his best foot forward.

"Your Honour. While the park wardens contend that my clients were the same people they met on the river trail, the fact is they never stopped them there. They lost continuity between seeing two people who they couldn't identify and finally stopping my clients some time later. They have also provided no proof the salmon they retrieved came from my clients or indeed, from the national park. I therefore strongly urge Your Honour to dismiss their testimony as conjecture and find my clients not guilty."

"Is that all, Mr. Irons?" said the judge.

"Yes, Your Honour," said the defence lawyer, taking his seat.

"Very well," said the judge, barely missing a beat. "We do not have to prolong this any further. I do not have to deliberate long in this matter to reach a conclusion as to the guilt or innocence of the co-accused. Mr. Irons, please ask your clients to stand and face the court."

John Donald and Maurice stood up and stared at the judge.

Ben, Kate and the other park wardens collectively held their breaths.

"John Donald Moores and Maurice Chiasson," Judge

McIntosh began, "I am satisfied with the Crown's evidence that you were involved in this incident. You may have run away, but you were positively identified and I have no doubt that had the park wardens or police been able to catch you, they would have found salmon in your possession."

John Donald and Maurice looked contemptuously at McIntosh but said nothing.

"I find you both guilty of the charges," said the judge.

John Donald and Maurice stood like statues as the courtroom buzzed around them.

As the park wardens began to congratulate themselves, John Kerry's stern look brought them back to order.

"Mr. Irons," Judge McIntosh began. "Do you have anything further to say before sentencing?"

"No, Your Honour," Irons said, conceding defeat. He knew he would gain more from his silence.

"Very well," said Judge McIntosh.

"John Donald Moores and Maurice Edward Chiasson. I fine you each fifteen hundred dollars. Please arrange payment with the clerk." The judge raised his gavel and struck the hardwood block.

"Court is adjourned."

CHAPTER 29

IT WAS AFTER dark when Marielle finally closed the books and got her jacket from the coat rack. She knew her father would be upset, but her boss had insisted she stay late to make sure all of the bookkeeping was in order before the audit.

She quickly gathered her things and locked up, making her way down the stairs and out the back door. As she closed the door and fumbled with her keys, the hair bristled on the back of her neck. She looked around but could see no one. Finally she got the door locked and turned to go to her car.

Maurice was watching her from the shadows.

He waited as she fought with the door, then slowly pulled a knife from inside his jacket as she started to move out of the light.

Marielle had not worked this late since her run-in with Maurice and had a momentary thought of his cold hands on her neck. Sweat beaded on her brow.

She quickly put the office keys in her purse and dug out the keys to her car. Much to her dismay, she had had to leave the car at the end of the parking lot, but at least she had managed to find a parking spot beneath a streetlight, that now hung mystically in the fog swirling in off the Gulf.

Maurice waited for her to walk by, planning to force her into the car with the knife. As Marielle moved quickly toward the corner of the building, Maurice gripped the knife firmly.

Marielle was mere inches away.

Silently, Maurice moved forward out of the shadows, about to pounce. Suddenly a figure appeared behind him and Maurice fell to the ground, hunched over in the dirt.

Marielle screamed and jumped away from the corner of the building.

149

Recognizing the man on the ground as Maurice Chiasson, she also noticed the other figure standing in the shadows, looming over her assailant.

Unable to tell who it was, she turned quickly and ran to her car.

Swiftly unlocking the car door, Marielle jumped inside and quickly locked it again.

Starting the car, she slowly pulled out of the parking lot, hesitating momentarily before pulling onto the road.

She glanced back towards the fish plant office, but Maurice was nowhere to be seen. As Marielle sped along the highway to Petit Étang, tears streamed down her face. Her tires squealed as she pulled off the road and into her driveway. Quickly she ran inside.

P'tit Pierre was in the kitchen and just getting up to greet her when she ran sobbing into his arms.

"Qu'est-ce qui s'est passé?" he asked. Then thinking the worst, he added "C'était Maurice?"

"Yes" she cried, nodding her head.

"Qu'est-ce qu'il a fait?" said P'tit Pierre, fuming.

"Nothing, he didn't have a chance to do anything."

P'tit Pierre sat Marielle down at the kitchen table and ran for his jacket.

"Je vais le tuer," he yelled.

Marielle jumped up and grabbed him as he went for the door.

"No," she cried, holding onto him tightly. She looked into his eyes, trying to get herself together.

"I think someone already did."

P'tit Pierre looked at her.

"I thought it was you," she sobbed.

CHAPTER 30

A FULL YEAR sped past as word of the wardens' success seemed to put a damper on all forms of poaching in the park. As autumn rolled around, the Highlands once again became a spectacle of colours: orange, red, purple and yellow hues, dappled with occasional hints of green. Tourist traffic on the Cabot Trail, drawn to the world-renowned drive through the mountains, had pretty much subsided for another year, leaving the highway to local traffic travelling between the small communities scattered along the northern Cape Breton coastline.

Ben started to wonder about all of the rumours of night hunting. His contacts in the province suggested that deer and moose were routinely being poached outside of the park but regular warden patrols inside the park boundary had turned up nothing of consequence.

John Donald and Maurice were apparently laying low, although the rumour mill suggested that Maurice was still recuperating from injuries sustained in a bar fight. He had not been seen around town for some time, although others speculated that he and John Donald were actively marketing deer meat around the island.

While Norm and the others felt it was only a matter of time before something happened, Ben was hoping their one big case had been enough to keep people from poaching in the park.

Ben and Michel were sitting in the warden office clearing up files from the summer when Norm walked in.

"Well, it's started," Norm exclaimed as he sat down at his desk.

"What's started?" Ben asked, not looking up from his work.

"They got two deer at Trout Brook last night."

Ben sat upright. "You're kidding?"

"Nope. I just came through and the drag marks were as plain as day. I checked it out and found two gut piles."

Ben got up from his desk and grabbed his patrol jacket.

"Let's go. I want to see this. Christ, Joe worked the late shift but he didn't leave any messages saying he had seen anything."

"Probably happened after he went off shift," said Norm. "They know when we're around so they just wait until later. They're always checking the houses to see if the warden trucks are in or not. We can't be out there all the time."

"Mind if I tag along?" said Michel. "I'll take another truck in case we need to split up."

"Sure," said Ben as they headed out the door. "The more eyes the better."

As they drove out of the parking lot and turned onto the highway, Norm provided Ben with a short history of his dealings with poachers on the Chéticamp side of the park.

"Pretty well everything happens between here and French Mountain," he said as he slowly made his way through the Rigwash Valley, pointing out clearings and small fields favoured by deer.

"Yah," said Ben. "That's pretty much what Joe told me when I started, but I could use a refresher."

"A lot of the lower valley used to be farmed by the Acadians," said Norm, "and there are apple trees scattered all over the place that deer like to home in on. If a poacher snags a deer here, it's pretty quick for them to get it out of the park before anyone is on to them."

"What if they run into a provincial Conservation Officer when they leave the park?" said Ben.

"If they think they might run into a CO outside of the park, they'll slap a tag on the deer to make it legal," said Norm. "If they don't think they'll get caught, they save the tag until they really have to use it. The COs have such a big area to cover, they rarely get out this way so if the poacher gets the deer across the Chéticamp River, they're home free."

"Unless we stop them first," said Ben.

"Exactly," said Norm as he steered the truck out of the Rigwash Valley, passing by the Grande Falaise. "Not much happens here," he added, pointing to the area below the massive cliff, "but it's a good location for stakeouts since there's a clear sight line right down the valley."

As they climbed the small hill past the Grande Falaise and rounded the curve, the coastline stretched out before them, extending all the way to the base of French Mountain.

"This piece of the highway from Presqu'ile Pond to Trout Brook seems to see most of the action," said Norm. "The large fields around Trout Brook are a hot spot for jackers because they can light them up pretty well right from the highway."

"Don't they worry about coming this far into the park?" said Ben.

"I don't know if they worry about anything," said Norm. "You've got to be bold as brass to come into the park in the first place. I don't think they give a fuck."

Norm drove to a spot overlooking the Trout Brook picnic area and stopped by the edge of the guardrail as Michel pulled in behind. They walked along the inside of the guardrail until they came to an obvious drag mark heading down into the bush toward the shore. Blood stained the top of the guardrail and a few strands of deer hair were stuck against the metal.

"How the hell did you see this?" Ben asked. "It's not that obvious from the road."

"I saw this first," said Norm, handing Ben a spent .303 casing.

"Good eye, Norm. This wouldn't have exactly jumped out at you."

"No, but I always take my time when I'm coming through here. Sometimes I just crawl along and you'd be surprised how you develop a bit of an eye for these things." He reached into his pocket and handed Ben three more casings. "I found these yesterday."

"Jesus, why didn't you tell us?" said Ben, a little irked by Norm's apparent complacency.

Michel just looked at Norm and raised his eyebrows.

"Well, I didn't find anything," said Norm, "so I figured they didn't get anything. Besides, I think John Donald throws these out every so often just to get our goat."

"Is everything a game with this guy?"

"Pretty much," said Michel.

Norm nodded in agreement and walked down over the bank, following the trail into the bush. The pair worked their way through the rose bushes and alder and came to a grassy patch a hundred yards from the highway. Norm pointed back to the road.

"They would have had a clear shot at this opening," he said.

"Still a pretty good shot," Ben suggested, following the drag marks through the grass until he came to the two gut piles guarded by a lone raven.

The large corvid flew into a nearby tree as the wardens approached, emitting a series of low cackles.

"It looks like they shot them both on the spot," said Michel.

"Would there have been two guns?" Ben wondered aloud.

"I don't think so," Norm replied. "They say John Donald is an awfully good shot."

"Before the other deer was spooked, he could have dropped him," Michel added.

Ben looked around the gut piles for a few more minutes before he retraced their steps back to the road. Norm and Michel followed along behind. At a muddy section of the trail, Ben bent down and pointed to a track in the mud.

"Hey, look at this," he said, pointing to a heel print. "What kind of a print do your boots make?" he asked.

Norm walked up to the spot and pressed his heel in the mud next to the print.

"Not mine," he said, noting the differences in shape and size.

Michel did the same.

"Or mine."

"Not mine either," said Ben, lining up his own foot and stepping in and out of the mud. "But it looks pretty distinctive," he added, pointing to a cross-style shape in the centre of the print.

Taking out his notebook and pencil, he sketched the outline of the boot print on a blank page.

As they proceeded along the trail, they came back to the thicket of alder and roses next to the ditch.

Ben walked into the thicket.

"Shit," he cried out. "These friggin' rose bushes are enough to tear the legs off you."

Bending down to pull a prickly branch away from his leg, he noticed a reddish tinge to the bush. Looking closer, he realized that a fine pink-coloured fibre was tangled in the upper branches.

Norm and Michel walked into the thicket.

"What'd you find?"

"Not sure. It looks like wool," said Ben as he pulled a long strand of red fibre out of the bush. "By the way this spot is trampled down, it looks like someone was standing here for a while."

"They were probably waiting to be picked up," said Michel. "Whoever it was wouldn't have wanted to leave their vehicle on the road so they must have been dropped off."

"Makes sense," said Ben as they walked back to the road and along the guardrail to the warden truck.

Michel took one last look along the shoulder of the road but there was no sign of any tire tracks. He was about to walk back to the warden truck when he noticed a piece of string in the gravel. He bent down and picked it up.

"What have you got there?" said Norm.

"Looks like a boot lace that's been cut in half." Michel passed the lace to Norm.

"I wonder where it came from?" said Ben.

"Not sure," said Norm as he put it in his pocket.

"I'll let you guys finish off here," said Michel as he headed for his truck. "I'm just going to do a patrol up the mountain and see if there is anyone else around."

"Sounds good," said Ben as he watched Michel jump in the other warden truck and drive off.

"They sure didn't leave much behind besides those gut piles," said Norm. "Half a boot lace, some wool fibres and a boot print."

"Well, it's not enough to nail anyone, but we might get some other leads," Ben suggested.

Norm shrugged and started to walk toward the truck as Ben just stood there looking at him.

Norm turned around, realizing that something was up. "What is it?"

"It's you," said Ben.

"What do you mean?" Norm asked defensively.

"I mean you don't seem to think this is a big deal."

"So what?" Norm was unapologetic. "It's only a deer. Not like they murdered someone."

Ben was turning red with frustration, trying unsuccessfully to hold back. "It's not about the deer. It's about John Donald and his cronies not giving a fuck that this is a park. It doesn't seem to bug you."

"You thought catching John Donald once was going to stop him?" said Norm. "Guys like him won't give up."

"Are you telling me that you are happy with that?" said Ben. "Are you telling me that you don't give a damn?"

"I don't give a damn about John Donald Moores and I certainly don't lose sleep over it."

"I don't buy it," said Ben. "I've seen you fishing and I've seen the care you take releasing a salmon."

"Take it easy," said Norm. "It's not that big a deal. These

guys just think they're playing a game of cat and mouse. Don't get your shorts in a knot."

"Bullshit, Norm. You never joined this outfit for any other reason than you believe in it. So smarten the fuck up."

Norm stood silent. "Are you finished?" he asked.

"With you? Not by a long shot."

They got into the truck and returned to the office, neither saying another word. Norm got out of the truck and closed the door, walking alone to the office.

Ben sat there and watched him walk away, frustrated with himself for losing it. He slammed his hand on the steering wheel and got out of the truck.

When he got into the office, he was about to suggest that Norm start an occurrence file and bag the evidence, but Norm had already begun. Silently, Norm took the strand of wool and the bootlace, borrowed Ben's notebook with the sketch and went downstairs.

Ben picked up the phone and dialled.

"Good morning, John," said Ben. "Thought I should let you know we had a couple of deer taken last night out around Trout Brook."

Ben hesitated, gauging the chief's response.

"Well, Joe was on, but Norm figures they would have taken them later in the night."

Ben continued to explain finding the casing and prints.

"I was figuring the same thing myself. I think we need to take the same approach as we did with the salmon poachers and forget regular patrols. From now on we'll be random and keep these guys thinking."

Ben finished his conversation with the chief as Joe walked into the office.

"Don't you ever go home?" Ben asked.

"Nah, I've got nothing to do there. Norm tells me they got two deer last night."

"Yah," said Ben. "Did you see anyone at all on the road?"

"Not a soul," said Joe. "It was a beautiful night with a full moon but there wasn't a frigging thing moving. I never saw one deer."

"Well," Ben continued, "I think we'll have to get into those random patrols again. And we'll probably pair up and put a person out in the valley."

Here we go again, thought Joe. "You know you might be right," he said, keeping his thoughts to himself. "Let's keep them guessing."

Norm walked back into the office, carrying his file.

"Hey, Norm, sorry about losing it back there," Ben said, swallowing some pride and trying to make amends. "We've been chatting about doing some stakeouts. What do you think?"

"Yah, we've got to break up the routine," said Norm. "I'm sure they know when Joe goes for a shit," he added with a grin.

"Or when you go for a nap," Joe shot back.

Norm laughed as the phone rang. "Hello," he answered. "Just one moment." He passed the phone to Ben. "It's John again."

"Hey, John," said Ben. "Did you forget something?"

Ben listened intently as Norm and Joe bantered about, then held up his hand for them to be quiet.

"Okay, John," he said, hanging up the phone and shaking his head.

"What's up?" Norm asked.

"The supe," said Ben. "He's already heard that we've had some animals poached and wants John to remind us of our priorities."

"Like turning a blind eye?" said Joe.

"Pretty much," said Ben. "I'm not sure what his issue is but I'm gonna have to find out otherwise he's going to drive me crazy," Ben added as he looked at Norm.

"Better him than me," said Norm with a sheepish grin. "So, about those random patrols?"

CHAPTER 31

BEN WATCHED LAZILY as Joe puttered around in his pack. They had parked on the top of the Trout Brook knoll and had a good view up and down the coastline.

This had been the routine for a week now, working the graveyard shift until first light, but they had seen little activity and tonight was no different. Ben had arranged for Joe to cover the day shifts and Joe was only too happy to oblige, but tonight Ben had asked him to take a nightshift with him.

Another new boss with a gut full of ambition, Joe thought.

He figured Ben and the others could take care of the night work if that's what they wanted.

"I know you're not keen on these night shifts," said Ben, reading Joe's mind.

"No, I'm not," Joe replied honestly. "I had my share of nights in Kouch when I first started in the Warden Service. By the time I got out of there, my nerves were racked up like at the end of the war."

"The war must have been tough," said Ben.

"You better believe it," said Joe. "I was this cocky young punk who thought he was invincible."

Ben grinned to himself.

"I lied about my age," Joe continued. "Enlisted at sixteen."

"You were just a kid," said Ben.

"Yah. Next thing I knew I landed in France, a tank driver barely old enough to drive a car. The Allies had just pushed the Germans back into Holland and we were part of the victory. The French were a beaten people but they showered us with hospitality. I was on top of the world...until Holland and my world came tumbling in on me. Literally."

"What happened?" said Ben.

"We were moving east through a small Dutch village and ran into resistance. Our division had split up as we moved through the countryside so we were working in pairs. We would take turns, leapfrogging ahead with one tank providing cover while the other checked the next block of buildings. As we approached a bombed out section of town we tried to work through the debris but had to turn back and retrace our steps to clear ground. As the first tank turned it was struck broadsides by a German armour piercing shell. The tank and its crew disintegrated in front of my eyes."

"Christ," said Ben.

"I knew we were sitting ducks," said Joe, his voice strained. "I screamed to the gunner to return fire while I turned the tank through the rubble, clambering up and over the remains of houses, trying to find cover. I could see a large building ahead , so I turned towards it. But a shell exploded to our left and I had to slow down to manoeuvre around a pile of brick. I could hear someone on the crew screaming to turn back and take on the Germans but we were in a bad spot. We had to make a run for it."

"What'd you do?" said Ben.

"Suddenly we were blocked off by more debris and houses reduced to rubble. I hesitated then drove the tank up and over an old cement foundation. We were almost across when I felt the floor give way beneath us. I tried to back out but one track spun freely, grabbing at the air. Another beam gave way and the tank settled in just as a German round connected with the gun turret. The gunner didn't have a chance."

"Shit," said Ben. "What happened then?"

"Fragments of shell ricocheted inside the tank. I couldn't tell the scream of metal from those of my mates. I knew we were done for. What was left of the tank shuddered as the building gave way under the weight and we crashed into the basement.

Debris rolled down on us, the air was choked with dust and

dirt. I felt a body next to me and ran my hands upward, stopping as the warm blood covered my fingers. When my eyes adjusted to the dark I felt around for an opening but could find no way out. I was imprisoned in an armoured coffin at the bottom of this oversized grave. All my mates were dead. I couldn't believe I was still alive! "

"Christ, Joe. Sounds like you were lucky to survive the war."

"Sometimes it doesn't seem like it's ended," said Joe. Sitting in the warden truck, he could feel the sweat running down his scalp. "I gotta get the hell out," he said, opening the truck door.

"Good idea," said Ben, also exiting the truck.

Joe walked to the back of the vehicle and stood by some bushes, relieving himself. Ben wandered to the front and leaned against the hood, gathering the warmth still rising from the engine. There was a chill in the air and he could see his breath. The sky was clear but there was no moon. His eyes soon adjusted to the darkness and he could see the outline of the highway winding up French Mountain. Looking toward Cheticamp, he followed the beam of rotating light pulsating across the water from the lighthouse.

Peering into the light as it swept across Trout Brook, he was momentarily blinded. He rubbed his eyes and looked around, only to see the silhouette of a revolver aimed into the darkness.

"Jesus Christ, Joe, what are you doing?"

Joe lowered the gun.

"Sorry, Ben, just sighting in," he replied.

Ben blew a heavy sigh.

"Sighting in? You nearly scared the shit out of me."

"Sorry, Ben, sorry." Joe fumbled with the gun.

"What the hell are you doing with that thing anyway?"

"Ah, shit, I've had this since Kouch. You don't think I'm working out here without some protection do you? Most of the guys are packing some kind of heat."

"Heat?" Ben queried. "What do you mean packing heat?"

"Hell, Ben, do you think the pony soldiers would be doing this type of work without handguns? Christ, the Fisheries boys have automatic weapons and even the provincial COs have been issued revolvers. Our outfit is the only one in the country that expects its law enforcement officers to go unarmed."

"Yah, but that's the way it is," said Ben. "If you use that thing and shoot someone, the outfit will never back you up in court."

"I know that," said Joe. "But I don't see them backing me up out here either if we get into trouble. And I'd rather be a live, ex-park warden than a dead one. You know pretty well everyone we deal with during hunting season is armed."

"I know," Ben conceded. "But, we've got our own protocols."

"Protocols?" said Joe. "What do you mean?"

"You know," said Ben. "Radios, back-up, self-defence training, personal protective equipment."

Joe laughed.

"You mean radios that never work so zero chance of back-up, a flashlight and a pair of handcuffs. That's about it."

"It's better than nothing," said Ben.

"Really?" said Joe, getting a little annoyed. He rolled the chamber of his gun against the palm of his hand, letting it spin freely for effect.

"Okay, I get the point," said Ben. "But if anyone asks, I didn't see it."

"Good answer," said Joe, unzipping his jacket and sliding the gun back into his shoulder holster.

"Come on," said Ben, jumping into the truck. "There's not much happening tonight. Let's get out of here."

CHAPTER 32

THE LIGHTS OF Chéticamp were obscured by the rise of land surrounding the Rigwash Valley. In the cool fall air, the sky was alive. The stars and moon illuminated the hillsides. A slight breeze off the water carried the sounds of waves rushing up the cobble beaches below the Grande Falaise. The monotonous regularity of the lighthouse on Chéticamp Island flashed across the face of the massive cliff.

Kate imagined herself in other places, but the cool ground beneath her sleeping bag and bivouac sack and the sprinkle of condensation falling on her face from the surrounding clump of small spruce trees prevented escape.

After a spate of deer poaching, the wardens had concocted a plan to spend the remainder of the year doing random patrols. Leaving their vehicles at home to give the impression that no one was on duty, they took turns dropping one another off, to spend the nights literally lying in wait.

The sleeping bags and bivouac sacks were a good idea but it was impossible to stay cocooned in them for long and also difficult to sit out on the open ground. After freezing their asses and temporarily breaking the monotony with a scramble around the hillsides, they were resigned to crawling back into the bags, regretting having left the solitary haven of warmth in the first place.

As Kate wormed around in the large winter sleeping bag, she tried to find the least uncomfortable position.

Hopefully tonight will be the night.

Ben had dropped her off earlier and was waiting at home by the radio for her call. Any call.

Staving off sleep was becoming a desperate cause and occasionally Kate would nod off only to jolt awake. But the warmth it offered tugged at her. She wondered how long she had drifted and checked her watch as the night slowly ground its way to dawn.

Only a few minutes. Oh well, I'll wake up when it happens. If it happens.

Ever so slowly Kate became aware of the headlights, alternately illuminating the sides of the valley as the vehicle worked its way along the winding road. It was taking its time coming into view.

This might be it.

Her stiff limbs retaliated as Kate sat upright, the icy air sweeping into her sleeping bag. She shivered as the combination of cold and adrenalin rushed through her body.

Pulling out binoculars, Kate squinted as the lights of a small car broke through the trees. The licence plate was obscured, but a cab light illuminated the interior. There were three men in the vehicle and as it passed by she thought she recognized the occupant of the back seat. Willing it to stop, the car nevertheless continued along the road and up around the curve beyond the Grande Falaise.

Kate settled back into the sleeping bag, pulling the drawstrings closed to prevent the remnants of warmth from escaping.

It was going to be a long night.

Closing her eyes, she traced the lyrics of a folk song across the inside of her eyelids, pulling her head further into the sleeping bag as she hummed along, impervious to the cold air sliding downslope across her covered body.

Suddenly Kate woke with a start. She sat up and looked out through the branches of her hiding place and was startled to see a pickup truck pulling back onto the highway, rumbling down the valley toward the Grande Falaise. Kate strained to distinguish the sound and was convinced it was John Donald's truck.

"Shit," she said to herself, scrambling for her binoculars. She was about to stand up to get a better look but caught a glimpse of something moving off to her left and lay back down.

Someone was coming up the bank toward her.

Kate pressed her body into her sleeping bag and reached for her flashlight. She could see the person moving slowly up the hillside but was unable to tell who it was.

Christ, he's coming right toward me.

Kate lay motionless, holding her breath, sure that whoever was coming would stumble upon her.

The man walked above her hiding spot, but Kate hesitated to turn and look. Straining to establish where the man was and what he was doing, Kate thought the footsteps were moving away from her when suddenly, a pair of feet brushed past her head, then stopped just as fast as they had appeared.

Christ, he's got to see me. He almost stepped on me.

Kate was prepared to move quickly if discovered. She could feel the man's eyes above her, searching the hillside, and could see the man's feet within an arm's length of her head. Slowly, the man walked around the clump of bush, circling Kate.

If it's John Donald, he's probably armed.

Kate didn't have time to dwell on the potential consequences as the man walked away from her hiding spot.

Breathing a sigh of relief, she turned to catch a glimpse of the man's back as he picked his way down the hill toward the highway. Obscured by the low bushes, Kate moved into a crouching position and peered through her binoculars, following the man down to the road. As the figure morphed into the dark shadows of the valley, Kate could still not tell who it was.

The man waited in the ditch until a set of headlights appeared around the corner of the Grande Falaise, speeding back down the valley. As the headlights approached, Kate stood up, determined to get one last look. She focused her binoculars as the man started to climb up out of the ditch, hoping he would be illuminated by the truck's headlights.

Suddenly the vehicle's lights went out as the man walked around the front of the truck and got into the passenger side. The cab light briefly illuminated the pair, but it was not long enough for Kate to identify either the driver or his passenger.

Still certain it was John Donald, Kate questioned whether or not she should radio Ben to stop the truck on its way back to Chéticamp, but decided against it.

There will be better opportunities. No need to let anyone know we are out here. There will be other nights.

CHAPTER 33

The next night

MICHEL CHECKED HIS watch and looked at Lucille. She had just put Jean Marc to bed and was sitting by the wood stove mending socks. Sensing Michel watching her, she looked up from her work.

"What are you thinking?" she asked, noticing his impatience.

"I was thinking about taking a run in toward French Mountain," he replied, guessing correctly that Lucille would not like the idea.

"What for?" she pleaded, a look of anguish on her face. "It's almost midnight."

"Don't worry. I'll be careful. I just want to see if there's anything up. We need to be a little more random in our patrols," he explained. "It keeps them guessing."

Lucille got up and walked to the kitchen counter. "God, you're starting to sound like Ben."

Michel got up and went to get his uniform, saying nothing.

Lucille turned to the counter and proceeded to put away the supper dishes that were drying in the rack.

Michel came back, buttoning his shirt and tucking it in. Sitting down in his chair, he pulled on his boots and tied them up.

Lucille continued with her work as Michel pulled on his fleece and patrol jacket. He walked up behind her and put his arms around her waist.

"I won't be long," he promised.

Lucille turned and looked into his eyes. She could tell that he was intent on going and there was no point arguing with him. He had his father's stubbornness. At times like this, she could see much of his father in him. There was the determination she admired but the streak of irrationality often frustrated her because he just would not listen. His mother had warned her about it before they got married.

"Don't do anything foolish," she said, kissing him on the cheek.

He pulled her closer and kissed her on the lips, lightly, sensuously. "I wouldn't think of it," he whispered, holding her close.

Lucille smiled and turned back to her work as Michel walked out the door, grabbing his daypack and Stetson. Jumping into the old truck, he backed out of the driveway and turned toward the park. He intended to travel the back road, passing John Donald's place as well as Gerald's.

A sliver of moon hung in the sky over the Highlands, passing in and out of the clouds moving in from the west.

It's on the wane, Michel thought. *Tomorrow night will be pitch black.*

The lights were out as he drove past John Donald's two-story. On the way he also passed the little bungalow belonging to Gerald Moores. He knew John Donald's cousin often accompanied the more infamous poacher but tonight there were cars parked at both houses along with an old pickup truck they used from time to time on their forays into the Highlands.

As he turned onto the main highway, he thought he passed John Donald's truck heading back toward Chéticamp, but again he couldn't be certain and didn't want to be too obvious.

Entering Petit Étang, Michel turned off at the government bungalows and pulled his truck behind the garage. Quickly he transferred his gear to the warden truck and drove back out onto the road, keeping the lights out until he got past the last houses before the Chéticamp River bridge.

It was a dark night; the moon was now lost altogether in the blanket of heavy cloud coating the mountains. Michel turned on his headlights and sped through the Rigwash Valley, stopping briefly at Raven's Rock to check for vehicles along the coast. Seeing nothing, he turned on his headlights again and proceeded toward French Mountain, where he pulled in to the parking lot, turned off his headlights and parked, positioning himself so he had a clear view of the coast but was well hidden from traffic coming down the mountain.

Michel rolled down his window, pushed a tape into the deck and waited.

Several hours passed before he saw anything. Checking his watch, he realized that it was after two in the morning. The lights worked their way along the coast, disappearing behind the rise of land at Corney Brook. Michel waited for them to reappear but they didn't. He was about to go and check the vehicle when he noticed taillights climbing the hill past Corney Brook, heading back toward Chéticamp. Through his binoculars, he could tell the vehicle was a pickup truck but nothing more. The vehicle moved steadily along the Trail, finally disappearing around the corner at Presqu'ile.

It wasn't long before another set of lights worked their way along the coast, moving steadily toward Michel. As the vehicle worked its way up French Mountain, slowly climbing around each curve, its headlights swept over the park warden truck.

It had been a slow night and Michel decided to see who was out at this ungodly hour. Although he was hesitant to stop the vehicle on his own, Michel's interest was piqued when he realized the vehicle was a cube van, something you didn't usually see on the highway, especially this late at night.

As the van went by, Michel pulled the warden truck out onto the highway and raced after it. Despite the steep grade, the van managed to stay well ahead of him. Michel geared down and put his foot to the floor, forcing the warden truck up French Mountain. He was almost to the top before he got close enough to turn on his red and blue emergency lights. The van continued until it was on the very top of the mountain, at which point the driver pulled over onto the narrow shoulder and stopped.

Michel pulled the warden truck in behind, positioning his vehicle out into the traffic lane far enough so the driver side headlight shone into the side mirror of the van. They had developed a protocol of calling in whenever they conducted a stop check and were in a location to make radio contact so Michel tried to raise the RCMP, realizing they would be the only ones out this late. He reached for the mike and tripped the repeater to see if he could make contact.

"Portable One, 8-5-3."

He waited a moment for the response.

"8-5-3, Portable One, what's up?" came the reply. Michel recognized the voice as Luc Allard.

"Hey Luc. Michel here. I just wanted to let you know I'm stopping a white cube van on French Mountain. Looks like a rental van. The licence number is Nova Scotia, Romeo 46392."

"10-4," came the reply. "Let me know when you are fin..." the radio crackled but Michel could not hear the last part of Luc's call.

"Will do, 8-5-3." He signed off and exited the warden truck.

It was cool on top of the mountain and Michel pulled his jacket collar up around his neck. Putting on his Stetson, he approached the driver-side window, standing slightly to the rear as he knocked on the glass.

The driver rolled down the window and stuck his head out.

Michel was surprised to see that it was Gerald Moores.

"Good evening," said Michel. "I'm just conducting a checkstop. Are there any guns in the vehicle?"

Gerald Moores looked at him and laughed. "No, sir," he said, mocking Michel's regimental tone.

"Do you mind if I take a look?" Michel asked, realizing he didn't have good grounds to search the truck.

"Yah, we do mind, don't we, JD?" Gerald responded.

Assuming Gerald was referring to John Donald, Michel moved forward to look across at the passenger seat. He wasn't comfortable with his predicament and especially didn't want to tangle with the Moores late at night, on top of French Mountain. He could feel the hair rising on the back of his neck, the cool night air creeping down his back.

Peering into the cab, Michel was somewhat surprised to see Jimmy Dickson sitting in the passenger seat. He had known the superintendent's nephew in school and although they weren't friends they recognized each other.

"Evening, Jimmy," he said.

Dickson nodded back but said nothing.

Gerald Moores stuck his face into Michel's.

"We ain't doin' nothin' so why don't you mosey on back to Chéticamp, Aucoin, and let us get home," Gerald said, a faint smell of alcohol on his breath.

Michel knew this was not the best time or place to tangle with Gerald so he backed off.

"You better head straight there," he said to Gerald. "The cops are doing late patrols tonight and right now they're making their way back toward us from Pleasant Bay," he lied, adding "and I bet they'd love an impaired charge."

Gerald scowled at Michel and started to roll up his window. "Fuck you, too," he sneered, pulling the stick shift into first gear and letting his foot off the clutch. The van jerked ahead as Gerald pressed the gas pedal to the floor and spun onto the highway, its tires screeching.

Michel was left standing in the road, watching as the taillights disappeared across the plateau.

He was getting chilled and jumped back into the warden truck.

Picking up the mike, he called the RCMP.

"Portable One, 8-5-3."

The radio hissed and spit but if Luc was responding, Michel couldn't make out any of the transmission.

"Portable One, 8-5-3," he tried again.

This time Luc's voice boomed in immediately. "You okay?" he asked.

Michel realized he had been out of contact for several minutes. "10-4. Thanks for standing by. I'm all clear of that check."

"10-4. I ran the plates while you were out of the truck and wanted to let you know that it was a rental," Luc replied. "Signed out to a guy by the name of Louis D..." Luc's voice faded away before booming in again. "I don't have any other particulars on him, but I can leave any info Telecom forwards to me with the ladies at your front desk tomorrow morning. I'll be on my way to Ingonish and can drop it off."

"You're breaking up," said Michel, "but I caught the last part of that transmission. Thanks for your help, 8-5-3 out."

CHAPTER 34

A few nights later

TIME TO GO, Kate thought as she peered out the window of her little cabin. *Michel should soon be here.*

At that moment, the warden truck pulled in and Kate grabbed her pack.

Closing the door behind her, she ran to the truck and jumped in as Michel wheeled the truck around and headed for the Rigwash Valley.

As they drove through the valley toward the Grande Falaise, Michel would periodically slow down and shine the alley lights into the fields, occasionally catching the glint of a pair of eyes from a deer bedded down for the night or feeding along the meadows.

They were at Presqu'ile before either said a word.

"It's a perfect night," said Michel. "There'll be deer all along the coast this evening. When it's cool they seem to keep mobile."

"I think you're right," said Kate. "So what's the plan?"

"We'll go up to French Mountain and park at the lookoff. If it looks like anyone coming from Chéticamp is going to continue on through we can get ahead of them and duck into the Skyline. Once they go by, we can come back here."

Kate was happy to see Michel taking the lead on things. She knew Ben expected more out of his senior wardens and sensed that Michel was rising to the challenge.

Michel leaned into the turns as he drove along the Trail. Winding along the coast, he kept his eyes on the ditches and forest edge. There would be no other traffic out tonight but he didn't want to hit a deer. They were always bolting across the road at the last minute. He enjoyed this stretch of highway. The adrenalin was pumping as he shot down the hill past Trout Brook.

Michel has driven this road a time or two, Kate thought, impressed with his driving.

Michel pressed the gas pedal to the floor as they rounded the first turn leading up French Mountain. Climbing higher and higher, the coastline fell away past the guardrail. The truck whined as it strained against the mountain.

Passing the lookoff, they continued to the Skyline trailhead then turned around and headed back down the mountain.

It was a protocol they had adopted to make sure there were no vehicles around before they set up for the stakeout.

Pulling in to the lookoff, Michel manoeuvred the truck to the back of the parking lot, reducing the likelihood of being spotted from the road but giving them a clear view of the Cabot Trail snaking along the coast.

"The waiting game begins," Michel said as he stretched out in the driver's seat.

Kate pulled binoculars from a leather case and laid them on the dash. "The waiting game begins," she echoed.

"You know," said Michel. "I came out myself the other night, just to show the flag, and happened to stop Gerald Moores. I forgot to mention that to Ben."

"What was he up to?" asked Kate.

"Not much," said Michel. "He was driving a rental van. But that reminds me, I was supposed to pick up some info about the rental from Luc and it completely slipped my mind."

"Losing your memory?" Kate said jokingly.

"I'll have to follow up on that," said Michel as a cool wind rocked the warden truck, moaning through the light bar.

The slow motion tugged at Michel, tempting him to sleep.

Kate poured a cup of tea from her thermos, the steam curling up and into her face as she savoured the aroma.

Out in the Gulf they could occasionally see the lights of freighters moving westward toward the Saint Lawrence River.

Michel concentrated on one that seemed distinctive,

appearing to have a flashing red light on its port side as opposed to a solid red. He watched it for a while longer then it disappeared.

Must be fog out there, he thought.

It was getting late now, past two in the morning, and a procession of fishing boats was making its way out of Chéticamp Harbour. The redfish fishery was in full swing and the Gulf would be full of boats for the next couple of weeks.

Kate watched as one boat sped out of the harbour, moving much faster than the others. Instead of following the string of boats moving along the coastline it headed straight out into the Gulf, moving very fast.

Kate motioned to Michel. "What do you make of that? It looks fast for a fishing boat."

Michel followed the lights for a few minutes until they disappeared into the fog bank shrouding the Gulf.

"I don't know," he said. "Maybe it's a Fisheries patrol vessel. I saw the *Port Hood* in at the wharf this morning."

"Is it a fast boat?" said Kate.

"I didn't think it was that fast," said Michel, barely able to keep his eyes open. "But it may be," he added, before drifting to sleep.

Kate looked at him and smiled. Turning on the tape deck, she kept the volume low and leaned back against the seat as she took in the familiar Cape Breton tune.

Closing her eyes, she couldn't get the thoughts of today's blowout with Ben out of her mind.

"I've told you again and again you don't have to be at my side every move I make. I can do the job as well as the rest of you men and better than some."

"I've never said otherwise."

"No, not with words, but your actions speak louder than words. It's always you and the boys."

"Take it easy, Kate. You've got yourself all worked up over nothing."

"It's something, Ben. You're afraid to schedule me for any of the night shifts."

"I just don't like the idea of you running into guys like Maurice or John Donald on your own."

"God, it's John Donald this and John Donald that. What is it with you and him anyway? You just can't let it go, can you? He's eating you up and you don't even realize it."

Kate had never been so mad with Ben and didn't know what had brought it on. Working together was taking its toll.

Why the hell did they always have to be trying to outdo each other?

She had stormed out of the house and took off back to the cabin. She was a little surprised when Michel called later to suggest they do a late night patrol.

They have it so easy, not working together, she thought as she looked over at Michel, who was starting to stir.

Lucille seemed to let him do his job and seemed equally content to do her own thing. It was all Kate ever wanted for herself but it wasn't so easy working at the same job, in the same park.

Michel stretched and sat upright.

"See anything?"

"No, it's been really quiet. Lots of boats coming and going but I never did see that fast one again. Maybe it was slower coming back in if it was loaded down with redfish."

"Well, it didn't look like a fishing boat to me but who knows," said Michel. "Anyway, I think we should pull the pin. The night's pretty well shot."

The words were no sooner out of his mouth when they spotted lights heading toward them from town.

Kate raised the binoculars to her eyes.

"The last of the drunks heading home to Pleasant Bay," Michel quipped.

"I'm not so sure," said Kate, passing the glasses to Michel. "Look at that, will you?"

The headlights had stopped moving and appeared to turn off the highway. The next instant, the hillside by Presqu'ile was lit up as a beam of light swayed back and forth across the slopes.

"Let's go," said Michel as he started the truck and drove onto the highway, keeping the headlights off to avoid giving themselves away.

As they crested the hill at Trout Brook, they had a clear view of the searchlight scouring the meadows. When they were close enough to prevent the jack lighters from turning tail and escaping, Michel switched on the headlights and the emergency red and blues and bore down on their target.

In an instant, a pickup truck sped out of a pulloff and tried to manoeuvre around the warden truck to make its getaway to town. As Kate held on for dear life, Michel veered toward them and sped past the truck. Easing up on the gas and slamming on the parking brake, he spun the warden truck around, blocking both lanes of the highway.

The pickup truck screeched to a halt, inches from the guardrail.

Michel turned on the alley lights, aiming them into the side windows of the pickup, just as Kate raced over to the truck.

"Park wardens," she yelled as she pulled open the door of the pickup, causing the driver, who was in the process of opening the door, to fall onto the ground at Kate's feet.

Michel rushed over, grabbed him by the shoulders and pulled him to his feet.

"You're under arrest, Francois," he said, recognizing Maurice Chiasson's son.

"Take it easy, man," said the teenager. "We weren't doin' anything."

"Right, then why the hell did you try to run for it?"

"Take it easy. I've got my old man's truck and he'd kill me if I got any tickets. We were just out looking around."

Michel pushed Francois up against the truck and leaned across to look into the cab. Another teenager sat wide-eyed in the passenger seat.

"Do you have a rifle in this vehicle?" said Kate as she opened his door.

"No, we don't have anything," said Francois, eyeing Kate.

Michel relaxed his grip on Francois as Kate started looking around inside the cab. It was empty except for a couple of bottles of pop and some snacks. Walking around to the other side of the truck, Kate opened the door.

"What's your name?" she said to the young man in the passenger seat.

"Jean," he replied, with some hesitation.

"Well, Jean, would you please get out?"

As the teenager exited the truck, Kate leaned inside and opened the glove compartment. She checked the contents but found nothing of significance. Moving the seat back and forth, she looked underneath but it was empty. Unlatching the quick release, she pulled the back of the seat forward as Michel looked in from the driver's side.

"Whoa, what do we have here?" said Michel, pulling out a pink blanket. It was tied into a roll with a piece of bootlace tied around the other end. "Looks familiar," he said as he inspected the blanket and pulled out a long, woollen fibre.

"What is it?" Kate inquired.

Michel looked at the teens.

"A lot of hunters don't pack their guns in a case to transport them through the park. The park regulations say they only have to be wrapped and tied. I'm thinking you guys had a gun wrapped in this blanket and I want to know where it is."

"I told you we don't have a gun," said Francois.

"You can stick to that story, but this is the same material we found by some gut piles a few days back and you boys have some explaining to do."

Michel faced the two youths, who casually looked at each other then back at Michel.

"What's the big deal?" said Francois. "There's no law against having a blanket."

"Kate, make a call to town and get a tow truck out here," said Michel.

The comment caught the two teens off guard.

"What the hell are you going to do?" said Francois.

Michel grabbed Francois by the jacket and pushed the teenager back up against the truck.

"You two have been out here jacklighting and your truck is being seized as evidence. We'll hold onto it until court," Michel bluffed.

"What the hell, you can't do that," said Francois. "My old man will kill me."

"Too fucking bad," Michel replied in French, loosening his grip on Francois and standing back. "We can and we will. We're tired of you bastards coming into the park and if you don't stop following in your old man's footsteps you'll lose more than a truck."

"Okay, okay. Whoa," said Francois, losing his confidence and not knowing if the wardens had the right to seize the truck or not. "Don't take the truck. What do you want to know?"

Michel knew they could only carry the bluff so far; he would be up the creek if he tried to pursue charges. There were no weapons and he had nothing to tie these two to the dead deer, only a strong suspicion that they were the ones who had been involved.

He looked Francois squarely in the eyes.

"You know, you can come in here every night and jack deer. It really doesn't matter to me," he lied. "But remember," he waved his finger menacingly. "We only have to catch you once," he said, hesitating for effect, "and I guarantee you that your old man's truck will be gone."

Francois looked at Kate, who nodded in agreement.

"Gone," Kate emphasized, looking at the other teenager.

Michel opened the truck door and threw the blanket back inside. When he did he noticed a boot sticking out from underneath the driver's seat. He reached in and pulled it out along with a second boot. Noticing the lace was missing from the second one, Michel eyed Francois.

Both teenagers were watching Michel and occasionally looked at each other.

Michel turned the boot over to look at the tread. It was worn, except for the heel, which had a cross shaped design stamped into the bottom. Michel smiled to himself and tossed the boots back into the truck then turned to face the teens.

"You boys had better smarten up."

"What do you mean?" said Francois.

Michel just smiled, and saying nothing, started walking back to the warden truck, leaving the two teenagers standing by their truck. As he opened the door he looked at Francois and repeated the warning.

"That truck will be gone, I guarantee it," he stared at the two menacingly.

"Come on, Kate, let's leave these two shitrats," he said for effect, getting in the truck and slamming the door.

As Kate jumped in, Michel started the truck and put the pedal to the floor. With tires squealing, the warden truck shot past the two teenagers and headed for Chéticamp.

CHAPTER 35

THE BULGARIAN FREIGHTER loomed out of the darkness, its size exaggerated in the fog enshrouding the massive ship. As the seiner *Le Magique* approached, a single spotlight exploded from the freighter's upper deck, lighting the way for the smaller craft to pull alongside.

As Gerald Moores positioned the orange fenders along the seiner's starboard side a voice called out in French, falling from the freighter's top deck. Gerald looked around for someone to answer.

"Jean-Guy, Brian," he called out. "What the fuck is that guy saying?"

But the two Magdalen Island fishermen were busy in the hold and didn't respond.

The voice from the freighter called out again.

Cursing as he emerged from the seiner's wheelhouse, Maurice Chiasson shouted up to the lone figure leaning over the freighter's railing.

Immediately, a rope ladder came hurtling through the inky blackness, the end landing in a pile on the seiner's deck within a hair's breadth of Gerald Moores.

Maurice grabbed the ladder and pulled himself up the side of the rusting hulk. Climbing over the railing, he stood face to face with a bearded brute of a man. He looked to be of Arab descent, but spoke fluently in French, confirming Maurice's identity through a series of passwords that Maurice recited from memory.

Maurice was led to the rear deck, where a crane was lifting huge bales from the bowels of the ship. Several men were breaking them down into smaller, tightly wrapped bales and tossing them onto a cargo net that lay outstretched on the deck.

Once loaded, the net was lowered over the side of the freighter onto the rear deck of the waiting seiner. Gerald Moores and the other two men hastily unhooked the net and stowed the bales into the fish hold while a second cargo net was loaded on the freighter.

Le Magique lay low in the water as the last load of bales was brought aboard. Packing them tightly into the hold, Gerald pulled the hatch over and tightened it down, waving up to Maurice, who was monitoring the process from the freighter.

Pulling a huge envelope from inside his jacket, Maurice passed it to the Arab. The man slowly opened it and thumbed through the stack of American money inside. Satisfied, he nodded to one of the crew, who led Maurice back to the ladder.

Clambering over the side, Maurice inched his way back down the ladder. Holding on with one hand, he readied himself and timed his jump with the rising swell that pushed the seiner up against the freighter's rusting hulk. Quickly, he made his way back to the wheelhouse as Gerald pulled the fenders over the gunwales and stored them in a sea locker.

As the powerful engines of the seiner roared to life, Maurice pulled the gearshift into reverse and slowly backed the boat away from the freighter. With less than a foot of freeboard in the back, the weight of the cargo caused the fishing boat to handle awkwardly, sending water churned up from the spinning propeller over the rear deck.

Bathed in the freighter's searchlight, Gerald stood by the cabin door, anxiously standing watch for Maurice, who gently shifted the boat into forward gear. As the diesel engines struggled against the weight, Gerald stood ready to abandon ship, sweat rolling off his stubbled face. Finally, shuddering noticeably, the seiner inched ahead as Maurice eased the throttle farther forward.

Picking up speed, he pushed the throttles full ahead, looking out the rear door to see if the seiner would respond. Slowly, almost imperceptibly, the fishing boat dropped its bow and moved forward as the stern rose with the force of the straining engines.

Breathing a sigh of relief, Maurice turned the boat toward Cape Breton as the spotlight from the freighter went out. Turning to look for the ship, he could just make out the silhouette of the huge boat as it faded into the fog-shrouded Gulf.

CHAPTER 36

YVAN SAT IN the coffee shop, listening intently as Philippe, the local Fisheries inspector, related his story. Yvan had just ended his own shift when he ran into Philippe, who was also finishing up for the night. He had been checking boats returning with their catch but appeared shaken, so Yvan offered to buy him a coffee.

"Goddamn it, Yvan, I don't know what the fuck I ran into tonight," said Philippe, as he settled into his seat. "It scared the shit out of me."

"Relax, my friend," said Yvan, trying to calm Philippe down. "Take it easy."

"At first I thought I had snagged Maurice with some illegal catch."

Philippe paused as he heaved a sigh and wiped the sweat from his brow.

"But that's no big deal. I mean we've had our run-ins before and he's been okay to deal with."

"So what did he have tonight?" Yvan asked.

"I don't know. I never found out. Tonight... tonight things were very different."

"How so?" asked Yvan, not wanting to get Philippe stirred up again but interested in getting to the bottom of the encounter with Maurice.

"Well, I went by the Co-op around three o'clock this morning and saw this boat, *Le Magique*, that I wasn't familiar with, just coming in to dock. That in itself was odd because everyone is usually out until daybreak. During the fall fishery, I usually work a split shift and I normally go back to meet the boats around seven in the morning."

As Philippe rushed ahead with the details Yvan motioned for him to slow down.

"Anyway, they had pulled into their own wharf instead of going to the plant with their catch," Philippe continued. "When I walked out to the wharf I was surprised to see Maurice and two other guys I didn't recognize just leaving the boat. That's not so unusual I guess. Guys often crew on different fish boats. But when I asked Maurice if he was going to offload he said they were going to wait until morning. It looked like they had an unusually good haul considering they were in four hours early so I asked what he had caught. He replied that it was mostly redfish so I asked to see the catch."

At this point Philippe started to sweat and turn red in the face as he continued with his story.

"Jesus Christ, Maurice walked up to me and pushed his face in mine and told me to go to hell. He said he was tired of being hassled and said if I wanted to get on the boat, I should go see the boat's owner, Pierre Lelievre. Maurice has never been like that with me before and I guess I backed off a bit. Maybe he was having a bad day. Anyway, I told him I would go see Pierre in the morning but in the meantime, I wasn't prepared to take any shit from him. At that point, the two other guys in his crew, who I've never seen before, backed up Maurice and suggested in no uncertain terms that this could wait until morning."

Philippe sipped his coffee and hesitated. "Oh yeah," he continued, "another weird thing was the two dogs they had with them. They were Dobermans I think. Scary looking bloods'o'bitches. I asked Maurice what he thought he was doing since dogs are not allowed on fish boats during a food fishery. He almost lost it at that point but the other two guys stepped in and told me they were going home and would come back in the morning. They suggested I do the same if I knew what was good for me."

"They walked off the dock and I took a good look over the boat then followed along behind them. Jesus Christ, Yvan, I'm pissed off with myself. I should never have let them get out of there without taking a look at that boat. Something was up and I let them walk away."

"You did the right thing by listening to your gut," said Yvan, looking Philippe straight in the eyes. "You guys with Fed Fish are crazy to be working alone like that anyway. They could have done you in so easy and gotten rid of you, it's scary."

Philippe acknowledged Yvan's comment with a shrug.

"And the next time you want to check out something like that, give me a call," said Yvan. "Maurice and I don't get along too well and I would be happy to make his day."

"Well, you're right about getting done in, Yvan," said Philippe. "It seems like the more we clamp down on the fishery, the more resistance we get from the fishermen, even though we are just trying to protect their livelihood. A few of our guys have had some bad run-ins this past year or so and just gotten out by the skin of their teeth. Helene wouldn't be too happy if I ran into trouble and didn't come home."

"No shit," Yvan said with a laugh. "If I had a woman like that at home I'd be working eight to four." He was about to continue but Philippe cut him off.

"Look there, will you?" he said, pointing out the window as Maurice's pickup truck slid past.

"What the hell is he up to?" Yvan wondered.

"Screw him anyway, Yvan," said Philippe, glancing at the clock above the counter. "I've got to get some shut-eye before the boats are back in. Christ, we've already whittled away two hours. It's hardly worth going home."

"You've already forgotten Helene again," said Yvan. "Go home and I'll see you in the morning."

Philippe started to head out of the shop then remembered something and turned to Yvan.

"You know, something else that was odd," he said. "Gerald Moores was with Maurice. He was standing back and not saying much but I recognized him."

Yvan scratched his head and repositioned his hat.

"There definitely is something odd about all of this," he said. "The Moores and Maurice Chiasson are not a good combination no matter what they're up to. Did you see John Donald as well?"

"No. Just Gerald," said Philippe as he turned to leave. "Anyway, I'll pay a visit to Pierre Lelievre in the morning and get to the dock before they offload. No one is going to pull the wool over my eyes."

CHAPTER 37

"C'EST LE DERNIER," said Maurice as Jimmy Dickson and the two fishermen from the Magdalens threw the last of the heavy bales into the back of the vans and jumped into the driver seats.

"Move 'em out of here," he ordered. "I don't want that Fisheries officer back snooping around. We'll follow along behind."

The three vans pulled away from *Le Magique*, proceeding slowly from the dock and turning onto the highway. The streets were quiet as they headed south, heading toward Margaree Forks, hoping to make their way through the coastal communities in the early-morning darkness without attracting attention.

On cue, one van turned off the main highway and took the back road. Gripping the steering wheel tightly, Jimmy Dickson manoeuvred quickly along the winding road, trying to make sure that when he reached the highway again, he would not be far behind. The two remaining vans would not split up until they reached the Forks, at which point all three would take different routes to Canso.

As he neared the intersection with the Cabot Trail, Jimmy hesitated to see if he could see the lights of the other vehicles. There was nothing approaching but a mile or so south along the coast he observed two sets of taillights. He quickly stepped on the gas in an attempt to catch up. The van spun out onto the highway and raced toward Margaree Harbour. Sweating profusely, Jimmy tried to gain some ground on the lead vehicles.

The van laboured under the weight of its load on the uphill climbs, but flew on the downhill stretches. Jimmy knew this road very well and took the turns on the inside, trying to lessen the gap. As he approached the small community of Saint-Joseph he slowed down slightly, cautious about not attracting attention, even at this early hour. A few vehicles were moving through town, no doubt fish plant workers heading in for the early shift.

Finally out of town, he hit the gas again and powered the van down a long grade. As he neared the bottom of the hill Jimmy pulled to the inside, then swerved suddenly as a transport truck came barrelling around the turn. He struggled to keep the van on the pavement but its wheels hit the shoulder and the van careened down into the ditch and rolled onto its side. Shaken but conscious, Jimmy scrambled out through the broken windshield and collapsed in the tall grass.

The transport pulled off the road and the truck driver scrambled out, running back toward the van to see if anyone had been hurt and to offer assistance. As he crossed the highway a pickup truck suddenly cut him off. Pulling onto the shoulder in front of him, two men with guns jumped out of the truck. The pickup's driver ordered the second man to go down to the van and see if the driver was okay.

Turning to the trucker, he yelled, "Get the hell out of here."

The trucker was twenty metres away, but could see that the man was wearing a hood of some kind over his face.

"I just wanted to see if that fellow is okay," he said pointing to the van. "I was coming around the turn and he came out of nowhere."

"Don't worry about him," the masked gunman said, "Just get the fuck out of here." He raised his gun to reinforce his point.

The trucker hesitated then turned and walked quickly back to his rig. Climbing up into the cab, he grabbed his mike and tried to raise someone on his CB radio. He released the hand brake, downshifted, and pulled the large truck back onto the highway.

Dragged along by the second gunman, Jimmy Dickson stumbled up out of the ditch and into the waiting pickup truck. He sat shaking between the two masked men.

"Jesus, I don't know what happened. That truck came out of nowhere," he stammered almost incoherently. "Christ, how are we going to get those bales back?"

The pickup driver shook his head as he pulled the truck back onto the highway.

"We won't be seeing those again," said John Donald as he pulled the hood over his head. "One third of the shipment down the tubes," he added, glaring at Jimmy.

"You really screwed up this time, JD," said Gerald Moores, also pulling off his hood.

"Big time," said John Donald, as the pickup truck rumbled down the highway.

CHAPTER 38
Two days later

ANOTHER DAY WENT by before Philippe and Yvan had a chance to talk again. Philippe had just opened the door to the Fisheries office when Yvan walked in.

"I just heard," said Philippe. "I'd bet a million bucks Maurice was in on this."

"Me too," said Yvan.

"I went to see Pierre Lelievre yesterday morning and he was surprised by my story," said Philippe. "I started to give him shit about the way Maurice screwed me around, but he insisted Maurice was not out fishing that night. He wasn't even aware the boat was gone because it had been in for repair. Some problem with the radar. I took off from his place and went to their dock, but you know what? The boat was unloaded and there wasn't a soul around. I couldn't believe it. They either went right back and unloaded after I left, or I was dreaming. And I know I wasn't dreaming. The way that boat was loaded down in the stern, they had to have been carrying something substantial."

"They had a load all right," said Yvan, "but I'll bet it wasn't fish. We just finished interviewing a trucker from Inverness who was almost in a head-on collision with the van that rolled over further down the coast. His story was like something out of the movies, a masked gunman with an automatic weapon, the works. Halifax called and told us to hold the trucker until the detectives got a chance to see him. They figured he might have been toast if any of the drug crowd were still around."

"So how much was there?" Philippe inquired.

"Well, the van was loaded with bales of hashish and everyone figures there was more than one van," said Yvan as a knock came on the door.

Before Philippe could get up to answer it, Ben walked into the office. Yvan could tell from the look on his face he knew something was up.

"Hello," Ben said and poured himself a coffee.

Yvan placed a finger to his lips, motioning to Philippe to not say anything.

Ben sat down and looked at the pair. "I just came in to ask you about something Kate and Michel saw two nights ago at Trout Brook," he said to Philippe.

"What'd they see?" Philippe asked, glancing at Yvan.

"Well, it was probably nothing, but Michel and Kate were staked out at the picnic grounds and sometime around midnight they saw the lights of a freighter out in the Gulf. They said she was ten or twenty kilometres off shore, but it was hard to tell. Anyway, they watched it for a while and then the lights went out, or at least they couldn't see them anymore, maybe there was a fogbank offshore or something."

Yvan and Philippe sat silently, waiting for Ben to continue.

"Anyway," said Ben. "That wasn't so peculiar, but less than an hour later they saw fishing boats heading out of Chéticamp Harbour. When they had all cleared the light, they saw another lone boat racing out of the harbour and couldn't believe how fast it was. They figured it was the *Port Hood* or another Fisheries patrol boat. It rounded Chéticamp Island and headed straight out into the Gulf toward the last place they had seen the lights of the freighter."

"What else did they see?" Yvan inquired, guessing that the park wardens had actually seen the boats involved in the drug shipment.

"Nothing," Ben replied. "They ended up stopping Francois Chiasson and another kid jacklighting around Presqu'ile and never made it back to Trout Brook. They called it a night about three in the morning."

"Very interesting, Ben," said Yvan, getting up and pouring himself another coffee. He realized Ben had not heard the news.

Ben could tell the two were holding something back. "So what's up? What did they see?"

Yvan sat back and explained what he knew about the drug shipment.

Ben sat back, stunned at the thought of Michel and Kate actually having witnessed part of the operation. When Yvan finished, Philippe recounted the episode with Maurice at the wharf.

"So who might be involved from around here, besides Maurice?" said Ben.

"We're not sure," said Yvan, "but I'd put money on it that John Donald is somehow connected."

"Oh, I don't know about that," said Philippe. "It's out of his league."

"I can't believe people buy into this idea of John Donald being some kind of a small-time criminal," said Ben. "Christ, this is just the sort of thing he'd be into."

"I don't disagree, but what makes you so sure, Ben?" said Yvan.

"Because they're all alike," ranted Ben. "It's an obsession with them. It isn't just poaching. Maybe that's the way it starts, but pretty soon the novelty wears off. When the chance comes along for them to get into bigger things, they go for it."

"It seems a little far-fetched for sleepy little Chéticamp," said Philippe.

"Listen," said Ben, "we were dealing with some guy in New Brunswick. We just happened to run into him, a total fluke. He was from the north shore but all of a sudden we started finding him down our way along the Fundy coast. I ended up in court one day talking to one of the RCMP officers who used to be a summer constable with us at the park. When I mentioned this fellow's name, he nearly choked. He said this guy was hooked up with a whole list of characters with long criminal records. They were involved in everything, smuggling drugs and even murder. This constable gave me a list of names and vehicle descriptions to keep an eye out for, so I distributed it amongst the wardens in Fundy, and the next thing you know we were finding them operating around the park. When they realized we were on to them, they fucked off, but not before we lost a few deer and God knows what else. John Donald and Maurice are no different."

"I still think those two are small-time hoods," said Philippe, continuing to be skeptical.

"I don't know," said Yvan, who was taking it all in and putting the pieces together. "There's more to John Donald than meets the eye and lately we've also had some run-ins with Maurice at the oddest times and in the most unusual spots. We could never figure out what he was up to, but we sure didn't trust him."

"Catching the two of them poaching salmon in the park together also raised a few eyebrows," Philippe conceded.

"Well, men," said Yvan. "Maybe we've got something here. I'll pass it on to the dicks from Halifax and see what they have to say."

CHAPTER 39

A WIRY-LOOKING DETECTIVE poured over the mountain of paperwork spilling onto the detachment floor.

Sitting huddled at her desk, Giselle was indignant at the snobbish nature of the detectives. She was disgusted that her space had been invaded and her normally tidy office had been demolished. The office files, once systematically ordered, were now strewn about the place as another detective transferred information from them to his notebook.

Yvan escorted Kate and Ben through the mayhem, grudgingly careful not to bother the Halifax-based investigators.

"This is Detective Squires," said Yvan, introducing the park wardens to the small man sitting behind a mound of papers.

The detective just nodded and turned back to his files.

"These are the park wardens I've been telling you about," Yvan continued, a little put out that the detectives seemed to be trivializing the importance of Ben and Kate's information. "I asked them to come in to let you guys know what they saw that night."

Squires finally looked up from the mess of paper and nodded for Ben and Kate to take a seat. His dark brown eyes studied the wardens from behind a pair of wire-rimmed reading glasses, pushed down the bridge of his nose to rest on flaring red nostrils.

Yvan leaned against the adjacent wall.

"So what exactly did you see?" Squires asked Ben.

"Well, actually it was myself and another warden," said Kate, interjecting.

"So what exactly did you see?"

Kate related the events of a few nights earlier, including the freighter in the Gulf and the boat from Chéticamp Harbour.

"What makes you think it was the mother ship?" Squires continued.

"Well, it was the timing," said Ben. "It all seems to line up and we don't believe it was a coincidence."

"Why not?" said Squires.

"We just don't think all of these separate events are coincidental," said Kate.

"Now that we've gotten to know some of the players around here," said Ben, "we think it makes complete sense that a number of them are involved."

Steve Day, who had been standing to the side and listening to the discussion, stepped in between Ben and the detective.

"C'mon, Ben. Are you going to tell me that folks from sleepy little Chéticamp are involved in an international drug-smuggling operation?"

"I don't know why you think that's so far-fetched?" said Ben.

"It's a perfect location to come ashore," Kate added. "In the middle of fishing season, no one would suspect one more boat showing up in the harbour."

"I think she's got a point," said Squires, opening up a file folder and spreading its contents of photographs on the desk. "The other two trucks believed to have been involved were found abandoned and empty in Montreal. They had to have drivers and there's a good chance they were locals who knew the area." Motioning to Ben and Kate, Squires added, "Let's take a look at some of the people we suspect are involved."

"But," Steve Day started to interrupt.

"Sorry Sergeant," said Squires, holding up his hand. "We're here to conduct an investigation and I plan to make sure we check out every lead. If the rangers here thinks they might have information pertinent to the case, I want to hear it."

"Park wardens," said Kate, trying to set the record straight. "We're not rangers, we're park wardens."

"Fair enough," said Squires. "So tell me, park wardens, do you recognize any of these faces?"

Ben and Kate carefully examined each of the photographs as Squires provided some details.

"This is the guy we think is in charge," said the detective, handing them a picture of a dark-complexioned man with an intense stare. "His name is Abdul Malawi. He's Algerian and has links to a North African drug cartel. Most of those involved are from the Middle East."

Squires pointed to another photograph.

"This is one of the Frenchmen we suspect of being involved."

"I don't recognize him," said Ben.

"Neither do I," said Kate.

"His name is Louis Desaultiers," said Squires. "He used to be a salvager and explored much of the Cape Breton coast so would know it well."

Ben shook his head. "The name sounds familiar but I've never seen him before."

"We think the boat may have come out of the Magdalen Islands," said Squires.

"We just dealt with a bunch of guys from the Magdalens this summer," said Yvan. "They were involved in a single vehicle accident at Big Intervale. They ran right into the bridge abutment. It happened at night and everyone walked away. When we checked it out in the morning, I remember looking to see if there was any sign of alcohol. There wasn't, but there was a pretty strong stench of weed."

Squires' interest was piqued. "So what became of them?"

"I don't know," said Yvan. "I think Ingonish RCMP dealt with it. As far as I know, there were no charges laid, but if you talk to the corporal over there, I'm sure you could get access to the file."

"Interesting," said Squires, not looking up from his files. "We'll follow up on it."

CHAPTER 40

"SO WHAT DID the detectives have to say?" Michel asked, as Kate and Ben walked into the warden office.

"Not a hell of a lot," said Ben.

"They were interested and showed us a bit of what they know but we're not sure where it will lead," said Kate.

"There might be a connection on a couple of things though," said Ben.

"Like what?" said Michel.

"Well, there's something about the suspects they've identified. Something is clicking for me but I can't put my finger on it."

"Where are they from?" said Michel.

"Mostly North African and Middle Eastern," said Ben. "There were a couple of Frenchmen, but the rest have Arab names. One of the French guys was named Desaultiers, I believe."

Michel looked quizzically at Ben. "Desaultiers? Louis Desaultiers?"

Ben looked at Michel. "Yah, Louis Desaultiers. Why? How do you know that name?"

"There was a Desaultiers involved with the *Cape Enrage* salvage," said Michel.

"You mean the wreck Dickson was supposed to have found?" said Kate.

"Yes," said Michel. "Louis Desaultiers is actually a French Canadian, or at least he has dual citizenship. He was involved with the salvage of a number of seventeenth century wrecks including the *Cape Enrage*."

"Well, how does Dickson come into the picture?" queried Kate.

"It was Dickson who actually found the *Cape Enrage* during a dive. He researched its history and when he found out that it was a French pay ship, he started to investigate how to salvage it. Desaultiers was involved with a couple of the wrecks at Louisbourg when Dickson was superintendent there. They apparently knew each other quite well. Old drinking buddies."

"Then Desaultiers would know the Cape Breton coast quite well," said Ben. "He would have been a good resource for the drug smugglers to tap into."

"Exactly. But I can't see Dickson into this. It must just be coincidence."

Ben shook his head.

"No way, Michel. I'm not a believer in coincidence. There's a connection. You just pointed it out yourself, and it's no coincidence."

"What else did you find out?" said Michel.

"Well, they think the seiner came from the Magdalen Islands," said Kate. "Yvan mentioned the accident this summer with the guys from the Magdalens and that made the detective's ears perk up."

"Another coincidence," said Michel, knowing Ben would bite.

"No such thing," Ben said, looking up to catch the smirk on Michel's face. "Good one, Michel," he added with a smile. "There are a bunch of these niggling little coincidences that I think will ultimately tie a few of our friends into this—including Maurice and John Donald."

"Seems like too big a deal for those guys to have been involved," said Michel.

"Not another one," said Ben, frustrated at not being able to convince people there was more to John Donald than poaching. "Hey, you've already uncovered a possible link that pulls in the park superintendent. Who knows how many others might be connected, including John Donald."

"Well, I would believe John Donald is involved before I would stake my reputation on Arnold Dickson," said Michel. "That one just doesn't compute."

"Not right away, maybe." Ben grinned. "But that's one angle I plan to follow. I'm going to dig into this one a little deeper and let him see what it feels like when the shoe is on the other foot."

CHAPTER 41

SUPERINTENDENT DICKSON WAS just wrapping things up for the day when a knock came on his door. Before he could respond, Ben walked in, much to Dickson's dismay. Without a word, the superintendent shook his head and got up to leave, only to have Ben stand in his way.

"Excuse me, young man," Dickson said curtly.

"I have to talk to you," Ben replied, equally as curt.

"I have nothing to say to you," said the superintendent, sitting back down in his chair.

"Fine." Ben didn't move. "Then you can listen. I just found out that you have a good friend, Louis Desaultiers, a diver and a salvage expert."

"So what?" said Dickson.

"The so what is that Desaultiers is a suspect in the big drug shipment that just came into Chéticamp. I know the two of you were old partners."

"What are you trying to say, Matthews?"

"I'm just saying it seems like too much of a coincidence."

"Are you saying I'm involved in this in some way?"

"Not directly maybe. But there's a connection and I plan to figure it out."

Dickson sat fuming, losing his patience with Ben. "You better watch what you're saying, Matthews, or you will be shipped out of Chéticamp before you can blink an eye. Not only that, you'll be facing libel charges so fast you won't know what hit you."

Ben was unrepentant. "I want to know what your association is with Desaultiers."

"That's none of your business," said Dickson.

"Well, it is my business when it ties back to this park, my

201

wardens and their safety. I think once the RCMP are through with their investigation, they are going to link Desaultiers with Maurice Chiasson, and through him to John Donald Moores. We deal with those two all the time and while you may think they are just poachers, they have been implicated in a lot more serious offences. I want to deal with this before someone gets hurt."

"Listen, Matthews," said Dickson, "I haven't been in contact with Louis Desaultiers for almost twenty years. We were friends and colleagues once but he means nothing to me anymore. Now get out of my way and let me get on with my work."

Ben stayed put. "Well, if it's not Desaultiers, there's some other connection," he said. "And I intend to find out what it is."

"Go right ahead," Dickson moved to step around Ben.

"And if it leads right back here," said Ben, grabbing Dickson's arm and looking him in the eyes, "I'll be the first to step forward and say that you knew about it all along. You've been pressuring the wardens to back off on John Donald Moores and Maurice Chiasson for some reason and I intend to find out why."

"You know, Matthews, you have no jurisdiction in this drug case," said the superintendent. "You continually try to poke your nose in where it doesn't belong. Some day you are going to get yourself or one of your staff hurt or killed. You are park wardens, for Christ's sake, not the cops."

Ben was getting wound up and knew he had better back off but refused to let Dickson go just yet. "So where would you like us to draw the line? Do you just want us to do campground patrols and babysit your salmon fishing pals? Or would you rather the likes of John Donald Moores be allowed to do whatever they want in the park, poaching deer and salmon?"

"No, I want you to deal with the poaching," said Dickson.

"But stop chasing them when they cross back over the Chéticamp River bridge?" asked Ben.

"Exactly. That's where your jurisdiction ends."

"Bullshit."

The superintendent had had enough. Pulling Ben's arm away, he walked to his office door and opened it. Turning back to Ben, he said, "you know, you think you've got to fight all the battles by yourself. I know you don't think I care, but you should let some sleeping dogs lie before they bite you in the ass."

He walked out, leaving Ben alone in the office.

CHAPTER 42

BEN SAT IN the bush along the Rigwash, the cold fall air sending chills through his body. They had been out here for weeks and hadn't come up with anything. Ben knew they were close to catching someone, but deer were still being taken and the wardens had nothing to show for it.

Norm had been right. There had been lots of jacklighting and it all seemed to be happening on the short stretch of coastline from the Rigwash Valley to Trout Brook. But the wardens had decided not to chase the perpetrators down unless they actually took a shot. They didn't want a circumstantial case that could go either way. They wanted to nail someone in the act. That would send a clear message to everyone and maybe put a stop to things once and for all. It was wishful thinking if nothing else.

Only this morning Kate had found a casing and a bloodstain in the Rigwash Valley. When she followed the blood trail, she found the spot where a deer had been shot but there was no gut pile. The poachers obviously knew the wardens were on to them and not wasting time cleaning the deer, opting instead to get the deer out of the park as fast as possible.

So, here he was, again, the fourth night this week that he and Kate had taken turns being dropped off. They figured it was easier to do the stakeouts themselves because they could easily slip into the park without letting the whole community know that the wardens were up to something. There were always people watching their activities. Everyone was related. Everyone talked.

Besides, they had gotten a message to the Big Intervale and Grande Anse warden stations and knew that Norm would find a way to sneak over later in the evening and bring Cole along with him. Because the poachers often checked to see if Cole's personal truck was around the station, Ben had asked him to put it in the garage and leave the warden truck out to give the impression that he and his wife were away. Cole had gone one better by suggesting his wife take a shopping trip to Sydney with her girlfriends, leaving the warden station in total darkness.

After Kate had dropped Ben off in the Rigwash she headed back to Ben's house to monitor the park radio. If anything happened she would get in touch with Joe, Michel or the RCMP to help her block the highway at the bridge. Not wanting to trust the radio system any more than they had to, everyone had agreed to stay close to their phones and to be ready to go at a moment's notice.

Earlier in the evening she sat in the living room with the curtains drawn, making an effort to watch television, but clinging to every sound from the radio. It was now four in the morning and she sat in the darkness with mixed emotions. It would be great to snag someone but she was tense with worry.

Ben always had to do it on his own. But what if he tries to take someone on himself? These radios never work when we need them and he's not like some of the others. He'll never carry a sidearm like Joe or Norm. Christ, even John has a shoulder holster and packs a .357. The rest of us sit out there with a flashlight! Even the RCMP think we're crazy.

Occasionally vehicles would pass and Kate would draw back the curtain ever so slightly, trying to figure out who was on the move at this late hour. On one occasion a small car headed into the park but came back out a few minutes later.

Someone out for a cruise.

Ben sized up the evening and decided to move out of the Rigwash. It was damp and he was cooling down. There wasn't much happening so he decided to walk along the highway toward the Grande Falaise and continue on to Presqu'ile. At least then he would have a view toward French Mountain as well.

Pulling his pack together, he walked down the grassy hillside and onto the road. The foghorn droned monotonously as a fog moved in off the Gulf, hanging stationary over Chéticamp Island.

He had made it as far as the Grande Falaise when he realized that a vehicle was approaching from town, its lights shining on the cliff as it followed the slight grade up and out of the valley.

Ben scrambled into the ditch and pressed himself against the gravel as a small car drove by, moving quickly up around the turn and out of sight. Brushing the dirt from his jacket and pants, Ben climbed up out of the ditch but was no sooner back on the roadway when the lights reappeared around the curve, the car gaining speed as it came off the hill and cruised back towards the Rigwash. Ben again threw himself into the ditch, barely ahead of the car's headlights. He lay there as it cruised past, this time giving himself a few minutes to catch his breath.

Back on the roadway he climbed the grade to the top of the curve overlooking Presqu'ile. He could see the fog rolling in along the coast, a kilometre or so offshore.

Ben walked to the guardrail and peered out into the inky blackness. He drew in a deep breath of cold salt air, allowing its refreshing bite to penetrate his body and drive off the urge to sleep.

Continuing down the roadway, he came to a small embankment that he often used to get a clear view up and down the coast. Strategically, this was a better stakeout location as it was out of the main valley and far enough into the park to give Kate and the others time to get to the Chéticamp River bridge and block the exit from the park.

There were also a lot of deer along this stretch of coast, which increased the odds of an animal being taken.

Ben scrambled up the bank and sat on the edge, pulling his pack off and rolling it into the bushes alongside. He was about to pull his sleeping bag out when he thought he heard a vehicle approaching. He glanced toward French Mountain but couldn't see the reflection of any headlights.

He was about to continue with his preparations when a vehicle suddenly raced around the curve with its headlights off.

The vehicle barrelled past as Ben scrambled to find cover.

It was a pickup and the loud rumble was easy to decipher.

John Donald.

The truck sped out of sight but Ben followed the whine of the engine as it streaked toward Trout Brook.

He pulled himself up onto the bank and grabbed his radio from his pack, intending to let Kate know that John Donald was in the park.

Turning on the radio, he was surprised to hear Norm's voice booming in loud and clear.

"8-5-2. Did you see that truck, Ben?"

"Absolutely. Where are you?"

"Trout Brook. Cole is with me."

"Good timing. It looks like he's on the move this evening. Can you still see him?"

"I can hear him, but I think he's down in the valley by Corney Brook," Norm explained, squinting to try and pick up the outline of the vehicle as it climbed French Mountain. "Got him!"

The pickup was heading up the mountain but its brake lights suddenly lit up as the truck pulled into the lookoff.

The wardens knew to stay off the radio as much as possible, suspecting that John Donald was scanning both the coastline and the airwaves.

Seeing the brake lights, Ben waited with bated breath for John Donald to make his next move.

Norm could no longer hear the truck, but using binoculars he was able to see its silhouette whenever the moon reappeared through the clouds. Sitting back against a large ash tree over-hanging the highway, Norm coolly worked a piece of grass through his teeth.

Cole stood patiently outside the warden truck at the Trout Brook picnic shelter, focused intently on the French Mountain lookoff. He knew Norm would be back in a hurry if John Donald came back down the mountain.

Ben stood on the embankment at Presqu'ile, tense with anticipation. *This is it.*

He was hoping that John Donald would make his move somewhere between Trout Brook and his location, essentially preventing him from getting away.

They waited for what seemed like forever, but Ben's watch confirmed it had only been a few minutes since John Donald had gone by.

CHAPTER 43

JOHN DONALD WAS in no hurry. Sitting in the warmth of the truck, he casually glassed the coastline with his binoculars. Gerald sat quietly in the passenger seat, sipping coffee from a Styrofoam cup.

The two had been at the bar all evening before John Donald decided it was a good night to try for a deer in the park. He was determined to stay out until they found something. They had begun to light the Rigwash but an approaching vehicle caused them to hightail it up French Mountain.

"Can't see a thing," John Donald muttered, scanning the Trout Brook meadows.

"Here, you try," he said, throwing the binoculars to Gerald and spilling coffee on his cousin's pants. Gerald howled a lengthy curse. Rolling down his window, he dumped the cup and contents onto the ground.

"Jesus, smarten up will you," he said, glowering at John Donald, who just smiled back at him.

Gerald raised the binoculars, letting his eyes adjust to the dim light. Trout Brook looked serene as a wave of moonlight passed over the coastline. Without realizing it, Gerald looked directly at the warden truck hidden in the low canopy of spruce trees in the Trout Brook picnic areas but didn't distinguish it from its surroundings.

Tugging at his shirt pocket, John Donald extracted a small plastic bag, containing a single joint of marijuana.

"Last one," he said to himself, unnoticed by Gerald.

He pushed in the truck lighter and holding the wisp of paper to his lips, inhaled as he cupped the lighter's red disk in his other hand.

Smelling the marijuana, Gerald glanced at John Donald. "You've gone through the whole bag tonight."

John Donald glared at Gerald through the haze. He offered the joint to his cousin but Gerald shook his head.

John Donald rolled down the window and threw the bag onto the ground, providing welcome ventilation to Gerald, who gagged at the stench. John Donald sucked hard on the joint until it singed his fingertips then flicked it into the night air.

"Time to go get a little meat," he said, turning the key and patting the rifle lying between them.

CHAPTER 44

NORM AND COLE both heard the engine start and expected to see the vehicle come out at any minute.

Ben stood on the embankment at Presqu'ile, unaware that John Donald was on the move. He strained through the binoculars and finally caught a glimpse of the truck as it wheeled around in the moonlight and moved back onto the highway.

It's heading this way!

Norm ran down through the bushes, crashing through the barrier of spruce surrounding the truck. Cole got in behind the wheel and rolled his window down to listen for the truck as it moved along the coast.

The pickup wound its way slowly down the mountain to Corney Brook. For a moment it seemed to stop and then slowly crested the hill as it passed the entrance to Trout Brook.

Immediately the meadows were lit up as Gerald shone a huge searchlight over the fields, focusing its beam along the edge then sweeping across the area in broad arcs. The light shot over the warden truck as Norm and Cole held their breath, hoping they were hidden well enough to prevent the Moores from seeing them.

"Nothing," Gerald said.

John Donald drove slowly along the guardrail as Gerald lit the fields, stopping from time to time to check for the reflection of any oncoming headlights.

"There should be lots out tonight," said John Donald.

"I don't see anything yet," said Gerald.

Occasionally Ben could see the reflection of the powerful beam along the hillsides and realized John Donald was working his way along the coast toward him. He thought about

211

giving Norm and Cole a call but decided against it, at least until he could clearly see the approaching vehicle.

Norm and Cole waited until John Donald had passed Trout Brook and then made their way up to the gate and out onto the highway, closing the gate behind them.

"He won't head back this way," Norm assured Cole, who drove slowly along the highway, feeling his way in the dark. "Let's get to the top of the hill and stop. We can see all the way to Presqu'ile from there."

Cole nodded and drove the warden truck slowly up the hill, pulling over onto the shoulder as he crested the top.

In the distance they could see the pickup silhouetted by the light sweeping across the fields on both sides of the road.

"I wonder where Ben is, exactly?" said Cole.

"Likely across from the pond," said Norm, referring to the small body of water that contributed to Presqu'ile's local name.

Ben was well aware of the approaching vehicle and started to position himself for its impending arrival. There was a good field off to his left, which would surely be checked, although he wasn't sure how visible it was from the road. He had found a gut pile there a few weeks back and figured it had been shot from the edge of the bush as opposed to the highway.

John Donald worked the truck down the hill from Trout Brook then sped along the coast toward the fields at Presqu'ile. Approaching Ben's hiding place, John Donald slowed the vehicle and Gerald resumed lighting the parts of the fields visible from the road.

John Donald's head was pounding from the mix of booze and weed and he was becoming impatient. Frustrated at his cousin, who was trying to light the small field adjacent to Ben, he caught Gerald off guard by pressing the gas pedal and speeding down the highway.

Just as quickly, he wheeled the truck around and turned back toward Presqu'ile.

"Give me that friggin' thing," he shouted, grabbing the light from Gerald.

Ben had been pressed into the grass at the top of the bank with the pickup immediately below him. Whoever was in the passenger seat was busy lighting the entire stretch of highway.

Unexpectedly, the truck sped off toward the Grande Falaise and Ben's heart sank. He was about to get up and call Norm on the radio when the truck swerved across the road and turned around.

Ben dug himself into the grass and waited.

The pickup moved back toward him, the driver now operating the searchlight and systematically checking the hillsides on Ben's side of the road. It passed by Ben then quickly swerved across the road aiming its headlights towards the fields. Ben could now see the driver working the searchlight out of the side window.

Christ. These guys are not too worried about anyone coming along, Ben thought.

The pickup remained stationary, sitting sideways across the road as the driver scanned the field, focusing the beam back against the hillside. From his vantage point Ben couldn't see what they were looking at.

Slowly the truck backed up and parked on the side of the road immediately across from Ben, who sank deeper into the grass to prevent being seen. Peering over the top of the bank, he could feel adrenaline pulsing through his body. Nervously he moved closer to the edge, parting the grasses and small shrubs to get a better look at the men in the truck.

Ben assumed it was John Donald and Gerald Moores but couldn't tell for sure.

They were moving around in the cab then slowly got out, each carrying a rifle. Slowly they walked across the road and into the bushes, out of sight.

A chill drove straight down Ben's back as he pulled himself

to his knees and wondered what his next move would be, not ever expecting the poachers would end up so close to him.

Ben could hear them talking, then a loud whistle pierced the stillness. Suddenly a shot rang out and the two men were shouting.

Ben scrambled for his radio.

Keying the mike, he spoke in a low voice that could not hide his excitement. "Did you hear that 8-5-4?"

"10-4," Norm replied.

"Where are you guys?"

"We're slowly rolling down the hill from Trout Brook."

"Hang back a bit," said Ben "and see what happens."

"10-4, we're holding back."

Ben could still hear the men in the woods and wondered about the best way to handle this situation.

He could call Kate now and have the two men trapped between the road and the shoreline, or he could wait until they got back to their truck with the deer. He knew John Donald had a reputation for running and his experience on the river with him confirmed this. For a second Ben pondered getting right into the back of John Donald's truck.

That would scare the shit out of them.

He also figured John Donald might just start the truck up and drive off, and then he'd be holding on for dear life.

It would be a hell of a story, if I ever got the chance to tell it! But this is no time for heroes.

He could hear the poachers in the bush off to his left and figured they must have been successful. Either way they could run, with or without the vehicle, but he decided to hold off calling Kate, opting instead to get in touch with Norm and Cole.

"Move in, and come right up to the truck. We'll have to see if these guys come out of the bush, but at least we will have their vehicle."

"We're on our way."

"Don't hit the red and blues until you're at their truck," Ben suggested.

"10-4."

Ben could hear the warden truck approaching with its lights out. He could also still hear the men in the bush, but as the warden truck pulled in and the emergency lights came on, the two men fell silent.

The strobe effect of the red and blues was exaggerated in the mist hanging over the hillside as Ben scrambled down the bank and scurried across the road to meet with his comrades, feeling some safety in numbers.

"They're still in the bush," he said to Norm and Cole, who were exiting the warden truck.

Ben walked to the edge of the pavement and shouted. "Park wardens. Come on out."

There was silence, except for the whir of the emergency lights.

"Park wardens, come on out, John Donald," Ben repeated.

Silence.

Ben turned to Cole.

"Give Yvan a call and see if he can rustle up a dog. We may need it."

Cole got on the radio and contacted Yvan, who was at the detachment and indicated he would head out to assist them.

Thirty minutes passed before the RCMP four-by-four pulled up. Yvan got out, curious as to what exactly was going down.

"We've got John Donald and Gerald in the bush here somewhere," Ben explained. "They were jacklighting and fired shots but didn't respond when we called out to them."

"Well," said Yvan, "you've got the truck so they'll be back."

No sooner were the words out his mouth than Norm pointed down the highway.

"Well, would you look at what just came out of the mountains."

John Donald and Gerald Moores were walking out of the darkness toward the entourage of officers standing by their truck.

Brazenly, John Donald walked up to Ben and shoved his face into Ben's.

"What the hell are you doing around my truck?"

Before Ben could say anything, Yvan grabbed John Donald and twisted his arm, throwing him up against the RCMP four-by-four.

Following his example, Norm grabbed Gerald from behind and held him in an arm lock.

"Shut up and spread your legs," Yvan ordered, quickly searching John Donald, holding him with a simple finger lock.

Finding nothing, he applied a little pressure to John Donald's fingers, immobilizing him long enough to put on a pair of handcuffs. Without a word, he swung John Donald around and using one hand to open the back door of the RCMP vehicle, pushed him inside and slammed the door shut.

"What the fuck do you think you're doing?" John Donald yelled through the closed window.

Yvan said nothing but followed through with the same procedure on Gerald, who was trapped in Norm's iron grip.

"Now get in there and shut the fuck up or you'll be walking back to town," Yvan ordered as he levered Gerald into the cramped rear seat of the four-by-four.

John Donald started to protest but Yvan repeated his threat.

Norm, Cole and Ben were laughing to themselves at how Yvan had handled the Moores.

With John Donald and Gerald watching from the back of the police vehicle, Ben turned to Norm.

"I'll go to the detachment with Yvan. Do you want to take John Donald's truck back to town and put it in the fire shed?"

Norm smiled. "Sure thing," he winked at Ben. Walking to the pickup, he opened the driver side door and checked inside.

The keys were still in the ignition where John Donald had left them. Norm got in and started the truck. Slowly he wheeled it around, then floored the accelerator. The pickup spun on the dirt then caught the pavement, fishtailing across the highway, tires squealing.

John Donald was beside himself. "You'll pay for this, you fucking pigs," he screamed.

Yvan, Ben and Cole stood on the road, watching the taillights disappear, roaring with laughter.

CHAPTER 45

JUDGE MCINTOSH PEERED over his glasses at John Donald Moores.

"Have you ever heard of the three strikes rule, Mr. Moores?"

"No, sir," said John Donald.

"Well, it's popular in the U.S. and I'm thinking about adopting it in my courtroom."

John Donald looked confused and glanced at his lawyer.

Christopher Irons just looked away.

Judge McIntosh continued, "This is the second time in as many years I've had to deal with you. If I see you a third time, that's three strikes, and I'd be tempted to throw you in jail and throw away the key. Three strikes, you're out. Do you understand?"

"Yah."

"What was that?"

"Yes, Your Honour."

John Donald did not like being made a spectacle of and he could see the wardens snickering to themselves.

For his part, Gerald Moores stood silently.

Judge McIntosh sensed John Donald's uneasiness and wouldn't let go. "Mr. Moores, it seems that the wardens have sorted you out. You might well consider taking your activities out of the park in the future."

John Donald was fuming inside as Judge McIntosh continued.

"At least this time you knew when you were caught," the judge continued. "Pleading guilty makes it much easier."

This rubbed John Donald the wrong way. He had fought with Irons over the plea but his lawyer had convinced him that it was the least painful way to go. They had been caught red-handed. Irons had talked to the Crown prosecutor and they had worked out a deal so the Moores would stay out of jail. The prosecutor had indicated the wardens wanted the truck forfeited but Irons had convinced him otherwise. Gerald and John Donald would each end up with a hefty fine, but that would be it. John Donald did not want to see the wardens get his truck.

John Donald glared at McIntosh and cursed to himself, remaining silent as the judge berated him.

Judge McIntosh asked Sean McIsaac if he had anything to say before sentencing.

Sean stood up and glanced back at Ben, who was now paying full attention. This was the part he had waited for.

"Yes, Your Honour. We have one request. The Crown would like to remind the judge of the seriousness of this offence, the fact that it occurred in a national park, and the fact that we are dealing with two men who do not seem to get the message that parks are different than other places. We would also like to remind Your Honour that the maximum fine for this offence in a national park is only five hundred dollars, much less than in most provinces, where there is also a provision to forfeit chattels seized."

Sean McIsaac paused momentarily for effect, looking down at his notes. He lifted his head and spoke clearly to Judge McIntosh.

"We therefore request, Your Honour, that the maximum fine be applied and we also request forfeiture of the vehicle."

This last request caught Irons off guard. He had talked to McIsaac prior to court and insisted that forfeiture not be requested. Obviously McIsaac had gone back on his word.

The judge turned to Christopher Irons and put him on the spot, peering over his glasses at the lawyer.

"Mr. Irons, do you have any objection to the request by the Crown?" he demanded, leaving Irons with the impression that an objection would not be appreciated.

Irons stammered an inaudible reply.

"What was that?" Judge McIntosh asked pointedly.

Irons was not sure how to take McIntosh and offered no resistance, thinking the judge would surely not levy the highest fine plus forfeit the truck.

"No objection, Your Honour."

John Donald was beside himself and shot a dirty look at his lawyer.

"Well then," the judge continued, barely trying to hide a smirk, "I wasn't really planning to forfeit the vehicle but I will grant the Crown's request for forfeiture."

Irons knew that he'd been had and slumped back into his seat.

John Donald started to mouth something but Judge McIntosh cut him off. "Mr. Moores, the Crown prosecutor is right. You have to learn the difference between a national park and the rest of the country. In addition to the forfeiture of your vehicle, I hereby fine you and your cousin five hundred dollars, the maximum allowed under the National Parks Act."

John Donald was seething but Judge McIntosh quickly called the next case, not allowing Christopher Irons time to rethink the situation and launch a protest.

As Irons stood to make a motion, Judge McIntosh cut him off.

"Next case, constable," he said, directing Yvan to pass along the next file on the docket.

Irons motioned for John Donald and Gerald to move out of the way and they sat together in the first row behind the defence table.

There was a clamour of activity in the courtroom as all eyes focused on John Donald Moores. No one expected the conviction, but many thought that he finally got what he deserved. Despite the outward lack of support from the community of onlookers, Ben felt vindicated and sensed a change of face with the locals.

Ben leaned against Kate and whispered, "When we started down this road, they were pretty well all against us, except for a few holdouts like Emile. But look at them now." He nodded toward the crowd gathering near the exit.

Kate looked around then over at the Moores, catching John Donald's icy stare.

She knew this wouldn't sit well with him.

Ben noticed John Donald as well and knew better than to count him out.

It was only a matter of time, but the wardens would be ready for him.

CHAPTER 46

THE NEXT DAY Ben was back in the compound, intending to check out John Donald's truck, which they had stored there for safekeeping. The workmen were standing around in small groups having lively discussions about the previous day's events.

Ben walked confidently past the men, nodding his head, acutely aware of their stares. He was inclined to gloat a little about their prize, but kept it to himself.

Maurice Chiasson stood off by himself, leaning against the side of a building. He had barely managed to keep his job after the salmon poaching incident and had reputedly pulled some strings to keep from being fired. No one knew what influence he had with park management but he was obviously connected in some way. As Ben walked by, Maurice intercepted him, standing in his way to make his point. Ben started to walk around but Maurice stared coldly into his eyes. He was about to say something when Emile, the carpenter, broke away from the small group of men he was standing with and walked out to Ben, a look of contempt on his face.

All eyes were on the three men.

"You know?" Emile spoke loudly, his Acadian accent stronger from the emotions in his voice.

Ben remained silent.

"When you came here I thought you were a cocky young man," he said, turning to look at Maurice as he spoke. "But catching scum like John Donald Moores, who comes into this park and destroys wildlife," Emile hesitated before continuing, "takes a great deal of persistence and dedication." He put his hand on Ben's shoulder. "You and your wardens have done a good job, young man."

"Thank you, Emile," Ben replied, realizing how much courage it took for Emile to stand up for him in front of the men.

Emile turned and walked toward the carpentry shop, impervious to Maurice's stare.

Ben shouldered his way past Maurice and continued to the shed where John Donald's truck was stored. The truck barely fit inside, but it was the only secure building they had access to. Opening the driver's door, he squeezed inside the truck and slid into the driver's seat. The truck still smelled new, its plush seats unmarked. The cardboard dealer mats were still on the floor, covering the clean carpeting beneath. This time John Donald had paid dearly for poaching in the park and Ben knew that losing this truck was going to drive his nemesis mad.

As he sat there, Ben examined the interior of the truck, going through the contents of the glove compartment and under the seats to find any personal items that would have to be turned over to John Donald. There were a few tapes in the glove compartment along with a pair of driving glasses, and some loose change lay in the console between the seats. Looking under the passenger seat, Ben found a science-fiction novel, which he recognized as being on the bestseller's list. A bill from a Sydney bookshop was stuck in the middle pages.

Other than these few items, the truck was empty. Ben slid the items into an evidence bag and squeezed back out the door, locking the truck and leaving the shed.

On his way back to the office, he thought about Emile's comment. He knew it took courage to speak out in support of the wardens. Most of the compound crew were intimidated by Maurice, talking tough when he was not around. When he was, they kept their mouths shut, or more often than not, openly agreed with him. Ben knew there was little he could do to change that other than to demonstrate to them that the park was worth caring for.

Things were quiet as Ben made his way through the empty

compound. All of the men had headed out to their worksites scattered around the Cabot Trail and would not be back until later in the afternoon. Making his way to the office, he climbed the back stairs to avoid the visitors at the front desk of the information centre.

The warden office was empty, dark and damp. Outside, a light drizzle had begun to wet things down. Ben closed the window and turned up the thermostat. He sat down at his desk, leaving his patrol jacket on until the place warmed up. Putting his head down, he thought about just how tired he was. He knew the others were just as tired.

After the long stint of night shifts, Ben had suggested that they take it easy for a while. He had assigned everyone to day shifts, but given most of them time off in lieu of all the overtime hours so they could get rested and spend some time away from the park. Everyone needed a break.

He was happy with the turn of events. In a short period of time they had made significant headway with the poaching problem. He knew it wasn't over, but Ben felt confident they had probably put an end to the worst of it for this year. It was significant, he thought, that in both the salmon case and now the deer poaching, John Donald Moores had been the common denominator. He began to wonder how many others were bold enough to come into the park to poach.

Maybe John Donald was the only one they had to sort out. Maybe there was some modest amount of respect for the park—or at least recognition that if you were caught there, the fines were more significant. Only time would tell.

Ben recorded the items from John Donald's truck in his notebook then placed them back in the envelope. Locking the envelope in an evidence locker, Ben returned to his chair and began to thumb through a selection of files from the summer. They were ready to be closed so he signed them off and threw them in his basket. He was about to leave, but decided to review the statements they had taken from John Donald and Gerald one more time to get a better sense of what made them tick. As he read through the statements, the phone rang.

"Chéticamp warden office." He pressed the speaker so he could stay focused on reading the file.

"Sean McIsaac here, Ben. I just got a call from Christopher Irons," said the Crown prosecutor.

"What's up?" said Ben.

"Not much really but I wanted to run something by you. Moores is interested in getting his personal effects out of his truck. He says there are a few items there that are of no use to us and he'd like them back. I don't really see any problem with this, but I told them I would talk to you first to see if you had any objections."

Ben thought about it for a moment. "I don't have a problem with that. We got what we wanted."

"Fine," said Sean. "I'll call Irons back and tell him that John Donald can contact you to set up a time to pick up the items."

"That's fine. I'll wait to hear from him."

Hanging up the phone, he returned to his files, continuing to read the statement from where he had left off. He shook his head as he read the details. He could not believe how cocky John Donald sounded, which was in stark contrast to the statement they had taken from Gerald.

Ben figured if he had to do it over again, he would have been able to get Gerald to spill the beans pretty easily. He was obviously just a patsy for John Donald and probably scared to death of him, but he was reluctant to divulge anything of value for fear of retribution from his cousin.

John Donald's statement, on the other hand, was obviously well planned and deftly executed. He was so smooth. Everything he said was for a purpose. He didn't waste words. It had been a challenge to interview him, but Ben knew the statement was not critical anyway. They had caught them in the act so it was pretty hard for John Donald to turn it around, especially against Judge McIntosh.

Ben read on, recalling the minute details of the night and how John Donald and Gerald had reacted. John Donald certainly had his own version and related it quite convincingly.

Ben was immersed in the statement and didn't hear the outside door open.

Footsteps slowly climbed the stairs and moved down the hall. Ben looked up from his desk.

John Donald Moores was standing in the doorway. He peered at Ben through tinted, wire-rimmed glasses, hesitating momentarily before he entered the office. He was wearing an ankle-length oilskin coat and cowboy boots and was clean-shaven. His long dark hair had been trimmed, the wisps of grey neatly clipped to just over his ears.

Ben was somewhat taken aback by the man in front of him. He had envisioned John Donald as a big man, a perception that seemed to be confirmed the night they arrested him, but for some reason, he seemed shorter than he remembered. Even in court he had appeared larger in stature.

Based on John Donald's demeanour the day of the search, Ben thought of him as mean- spirited and ruthless, yet the man in the doorway appeared somewhat humble and remorseful, the touch of grey hair giving away his age. Now it seemed that all the intensity had disappeared from his face.

The only features detracting from this contrasting image were his eyes. Even behind the amber lenses, Ben could feel the small black pupils drilling into him. As Ben stirred uncomfortably in his chair, he could detect a slight grin on John Donald's face, and realized Moores was getting some satisfaction from putting Ben on edge.

John Donald's grin broadened. He knew how to manipulate and steer people where he wanted them to go, getting them to agree to his terms just to escape the intensity of his eyes.

It gave him immense satisfaction to see that he could have the same effect on Ben. In the end, Ben was no different than Dickson or any of the other wardens, or even Day and the rest of the Mounties. People were people. You just had to find their weaknesses and use that to your advantage.

John Donald was aware the wardens were taking some satisfaction in this latest encounter with him, but he was a patient man. He would find Matthews' soft spot and wait until his guard was down before he struck. This warden was like all the rest. He would be here for a few years, try to make his mark, then leave. John Donald knew he had all the time in the world and could wait it out if he wanted. But that wasn't his style. When the park warden finally left town, John Donald Moores would make sure Ben knew what he was leaving behind.

Remaining seated, Ben slowly closed the file and motioned for John Donald to come in. He knew John Donald was trying to toy with him and had to remind himself that he was dealing with the man behind the glasses and not someone who had learned his lesson.

"How can I help you?" he asked curtly, wanting to show John Donald that two could play the game.

"I came to get my things. How about giving me my truck back too?" He smiled as he looked down at Ben.

Ben feigned a smile. "I don't think so. It will go to Crown Assets and be turned over to a government department. Who knows, maybe we'll repaint it, put some lights on it and keep it for the Warden Service."

John Donald glared at Ben. "Just give me my things and I'll get out of here."

Ben got up and went to a large filing cabinet. Slowly taking out his keys, he selected one and opened the cabinet, pulling out the small cardboard box.

He laid it on his desk in front of John Donald.

"This is everything," Ben said, offering John Donald a look inside the box.

Moores picked through its contents to see if everything was there. He pulled out a couple of cassettes and held them up to Ben.

"I don't know why you had to keep these?"

"You could have had them anytime. All you had to do was ask."

John Donald pocketed his belongings as Ben looked on in silence.

He hated being humiliated, even if there were no other witnesses to this, and desperately wanted to wipe the grin off of Ben's smug face. He picked up the box and emptied the remaining contents into his hand, putting them in one of the large outside pockets of his jacket.

He glared at Ben. "Thanks a lot," he said as he turned for the door.

"One second," said Ben. "You have to sign a receipt, to show you got your things."

John Donald pivoted back toward Ben.

Before he could say anything, Ben pushed the receipt book in front of him and offered a pen.

Looking steadily at the warden, John Donald reached inside his jacket and pulled out a gold-plated pen. He leaned over the desk and quickly scribbled his name; his signature was almost illegible. Barely discernable between John Donald's thumb and index finger, Ben could see the outline of a cross.

"Thank you." Ben reached for the book and tore off the top copy. "This one is yours," he said, passing it to John Donald.

John Donald took the piece of paper, crumpled it, and threw it on the floor.

"Fuck you too," he said as he stormed out the door and headed down the stairs.

Ben could hear the outside door open and close. From the

window, he watched John Donald hurry to his car, the tails of his slicker dragging in the rainwater pooled on the sidewalk. Ben smiled as John Donald walked around the car, casting one last glance up at Ben in the window before jumping behind the wheel and roaring out of the parking lot.

Ben walked back to his desk and pulled out the other copies of the receipt and placed one in the exhibit ledger. Placing the remaining copies of the receipt inside John Donald's file, he noted the time and date in the occurrence report.

Closing the folder, he skimmed through the information on the front cover and ticked the "Closed File" box at the bottom.

Another one put to bed, he thought.

CHAPTER 47

MICHEL SAT BACK in his chair, watching Lucille float around the kitchen, putting the supper dishes back in the cupboards and rearranging things. They bantered back and forth in French, recounting for each other the details of their days. They always spoke French at home. They wanted to maintain as much of an Acadian atmosphere in their house as possible, especially for Jean Marc. He was exposed to enough English with his friends at school. They had never been restrictive with him, realizing he needed a solid grounding in English for his future, but they preferred to surround him with Acadian culture and traditions at home, hoping he would develop a strong sense of his roots.

"You know, something's bothering me," said Michel.

"I know," Lucille replied, not missing a beat.

"You always know." Michel smiled.

"Yes. I can read you like a book."

Michel laughed. He never had much luck keeping things from her, not that there were any secrets. She was a good sounding board and he felt comfortable divulging his thoughts to her, no matter how silly they seemed. Lucille always offered support and good advice. Despite her petite frame, she was as solid as a rock.

"I've been thinking about Desaultiers and the superintendent," said Michel. "You know, Ben is right. There is too much to this for it to be a coincidence."

"What do you mean?"

"Well, I have heard that Desaultiers moves in dangerous circles. He has always been a gambler and some people say that he got himself in deep with the biker gangs from Montreal. After he and Dickson found the *Cape Enrage*, they say he squandered his share of the money. Dickson supposedly put some of his into the stock market but banked most of it. I can see Desaultiers being linked to the drug shipment, but I still can't figure the superintendent, except for one thing."

"What is that? I always found Mr. Dickson to be a good man."

"I'm not so sure anymore," said Michel. "Since the Moores were caught poaching, the superintendent has been threatening John with closing the Grande Anse Warden Station and getting rid of Cole's position. Cole was so choked he's taken time off and gone west to see if there are any positions open that he can transfer to."

"That's too bad," said Lucille.

"And Dickson's been very uncooperative with Ben," Michel added.

"I wonder why?" said Lucille.

"I don't know," said Michel, "but the one thing I keep thinking of is that the superintendent does have a nephew who used to peddle dope between Ingonish and Chéticamp. He was a grade behind me in school. Jimmy Dickson is his name but they call him 'JD'."

"So how would he fit into this?" Lucille was intrigued.

"That's what I don't know. But if he is still involved with drugs maybe there is a connection with John Donald. Maybe John Donald has something on the superintendent."

Lucille sat facing Michel at the table. "You mean like blackmail?"

"Sort of. I know it sounds farfetched but it makes sense. I don't see why the superintendent would be involved otherwise."

"Have you told Ben about this?"

"Well, I told him about Desaultiers, but I was still trying to figure the rest of it out," he replied. "One obvious thing that I never told him was that I stopped Gerald Moores a couple of weeks back. He happened to be driving a cube van."

Michel hesitated.

Lucille was giving him the look.

"Like the ones used in the drug shipment. I was parked at French Mountain when it went by. I never really thought much of it but decided to check it anyway." He realized Lucille would not be impressed he was stopping suspicious vehicles late at night by himself.

"Michel," she implored.

"I know, I know, I probably shouldn't have checked it out but I figured it was no big deal. I have to admit I was caught off guard when I found Gerald Moores at the wheel. The one thing I never picked up on at the time, but is bothering me now, is that Jimmy Dickson was in the van with Gerald. First I thought it was odd but then I figured it sort of made sense. Jimmy is obviously still in cahoots with the Moores."

"I think you should tell Ben. There *is* something funny about all of this."

Michel nodded. "I'll tell him in the morning. The other wardens are headed to Ingonish tomorrow for a general meeting and it's my turn to hang back. I'll tell him before they leave."

Lucille smiled and got up from the table. She bent down and kissed Michel. "I love you," she whispered.

"I love you too," said Michel. "By the way, I told Ben I would keep an eye on things tomorrow night so I might stay at his place for the evening. I'll be home as soon as they get back."

CHAPTER 48

IT WAS STILL early when Michel got to the office. He had lain awake almost all night, thinking about his discussion with Lucille. As he walked in the door one of the ladies who worked the front desk saw him.

"Hey Michel. Haven't seen you for a while," she said.

"I know," Michel replied. "We've been working lots of nights."

"I figured that," she said. "By the way, one of the RCMP, Luc I believe, dropped off some information for you awhile back. He said it probably wasn't important but I have it at the front desk. I'll go get it for you."

"Oh yes, I completely forgot about that," said Michel as he followed her and retrieved a brown envelope and took it back up to the warden office.

Joe was just coming in as Michel read the note from Luc.

"You're in early," said Joe as he walked into the office and saw Michel sitting at Ben's desk. "You piss the bed or something?"

"No." Michel laughed. "I just wanted to make sure I didn't miss Ben before you guys went to Ingonish."

"Well, you should have come in earlier. Ben and Kate left at first light to take the other truck over for servicing. Ben is probably going to come back with me in the four-by-four later tonight. Kate may stay over and get Norm to drive her back tomorrow."

"Shit," said Michel, as he read Luc's note about Louis Desaultiers and the rental van and realized that the missing piece to the puzzle linking the Moores, Desaultiers and Dickson might be sitting in his hand.

"What's the big deal?" said Joe. "I can pass on whatever it is you want to tell him."

"No, that's okay, Joe," said Michel, sliding the envelope in his desk. "I can tell him when he gets back."

"It's your call," said Joe. "Hey, Ben was wondering if you would mind working a split shift today. He wanted me to ask you. He didn't want to bother you at home last night."

"I don't mind."

"Good, I'll tell him." Joe walked out of the office. Then he turned around and added, "He was wondering if you could keep an eye around the houses. Rose is gone up to her sister's and after the court case Ben didn't want to leave the place with no one around. He figures John Donald will not waste any time getting back into the park."

"I'm one step ahead of you, Joe," Michel replied. "I already told Ben I would camp out at his place until you guys get back."

"You're a good man, Aucoin," Joe grinned.

"Get outta here. You'll be late for the meeting, you old fart."

After everyone left, Michel spent the morning in the office then decided to take a drive out along the coast and hike one of the park trails. It was a beautiful fall day and the leaves were just starting to come off the trees. Pulling into the Corney Brook trailhead, he grabbed his daypack and headed off down the forested path.

As he wound his way through the trees, he came to an open meadow overlooking the Cabot Trail, the heat from the sun rising in waves off the tall grass.

Taking off his pack, Michel sat back against a large rock and relaxed, pulling his Stetson over his eyes to shield him from the sun's rays.

As the surf pounded on the distant shoreline, chickadees skittered through the bushes beside him. He closed his eyes and drew in a heavy breath of cold ocean air. He loved the sights, sounds and smells of autumn, his favourite time of year. Listening intently, he tried to decipher the calls of songbirds flitting through the forest canopy. The fall migration was well underway and the calls of resident birds merged with those making their way south from other parts of the coast. A drone-like sound in the distance caught his attention and as he tried to figure out its origin he realized that it was a vehicle approaching from French Mountain.

He lay back, half hidden in the grass, and waited. The sound increased in tempo as the approaching vehicle raced down the knoll toward Corney Brook. As it rounded the turn Michel could see that it was John Donald's black Mustang. He saw the driver for an instant and thought he recognized Gerald Moores.

The Mustang raced past and disappeared over the hill. Michel could hear it winding its way along the coast, the sound of the engine gradually disappearing.

Michel was in no rush to get up. He lay back, soaking up the rays and the smell of autumn air. He thought of Lucille and Jean Marc and ached to share this moment with them.

"This is why I do it," he was explaining to them. *"This is what it's all about."*

He closed his eyes and imagined them with him.

"This is what it's all about," Michel repeated.

Lucille and Jean Marc were sitting with him, basking in the fall colours. Slowly they got up and made their way to the edge of the meadow, then disappeared into the bushes.

At that moment a raven landed on a branch above Michel and gurgled.

Opening his eyes, Michel nodded to the large black bird.

"Une belle journée," he said. "Just beautiful."

CHAPTER 49

Later that night

MICHEL LAY MOTIONLESS on the sofa in Ben's living room. He closed his eyes and listened to the sound of the approaching vehicle.

Sitting up, he pushed the bottom corner of the curtain aside just in time to catch a glimpse of John Donald's Mustang as it headed toward Chéticamp.

At least he's not in the park, Michel thought.

Earlier in the evening, Ben had called and said it was unlikely that they would make it back, so Michel had decided to stay the night. Lucille promised she'd be fine at home by herself with Jean Marc. Her mom and dad were just next door if she needed anything. She assured Michel that no one would harass her at home. It was almost midnight and he thought about calling her but decided it was too late.

Turning out the lights, Michel lay back down and had just started to doze off again when the rumble of the Mustang roused him. This time the car was headed for the park.

Ben had warned him that John Donald often drove by late at night, only to turn around again and head back to town. He figured it was John Donald's way of psyching him out. Ben said that at first he would bite and get up at whatever hour to follow the car, only to see it drive back just as he was about to leave the house. Once he was back in bed, the car would go by again in the opposite direction. As much as he wanted to go after him, Ben said he would often just pull the pillow over his head to drown out the sound and force himself to go to sleep. He advised Michel to do the same.

Michel waited for the car to return, listening intently for the drone of the engine. Watching the clock slowly tick off the minutes, he finally concluded the car wasn't coming back.

For all he knew, John Donald could be heading back to Pleasant Bay and there was nothing to worry about, but he decided to take a drive into the Rigwash and see if he could spot the car along the coast. He wouldn't stop it, but at least he could show the flag.

He threw his gear into his pack and headed outside, locking the door behind him.

The night was crystal clear and starlit as he backed the warden truck out of the garage and there was enough ambient light to drive without headlights. As he pulled out of the driveway and onto the road, the only sign of life was an upstairs light in the house across the road.

Michel drove into the Rigwash and past the Grande Falaise but couldn't see any sign of a vehicle. As he passed Presqu'ile and headed toward Trout Brook, he caught a glimpse of taillights heading up French Mountain and figured John Donald was probably on his way to Pleasant Bay.

Michel continued along the coast, keeping his lights out and straining to see any deer along the edge of the road that might decide to commit suicide on this particular evening. Pulling into the first lookoff on French Mountain, he wheeled the pickup around and stopped, taking time to scan the Trail back toward town.

Unable to see anything suspicious, Michel decided to return to Presqu'ile. They had been seeing deer there regularly and if John Donald came back, he would be ready. He didn't feel entirely comfortable about being out on his own without backup but he dismissed any notion there would be trouble tonight and wrote it off as worrying too much.

Hiding the truck in the old gravel pit, Michel hiked back to the gate and latched it to give the impression it was locked. Quickly he made his way to a steep embankment across from Presqu'ile Pond. From what Ben had told him, this was the same spot where they had caught John Donald and Gerald earlier. The small clearing used by deer was a short distance away. Scrambling up the steep bank, he pulled his backpack over the top and sat down to catch his breath. From this vantage point, Michel could see most of the highway along this section of coast.

As Michel sat on the bank, the cold air tugged at him. A slight breeze pushed waves up the cobble beaches beyond Presqu'ile, gently rustling the leaves overhead. Pulling his winter jacket and wind pants out of his pack, he slid into them and donned a wool cap and gloves.

It could be a long night.

The Highlands stood out in stark contrast to the clear sky as moonlight washed over the hillsides, illuminating some slopes while casting others in shadow.

It was a spectacular place and the type of night he wished he could share with Lucille. She sometimes accompanied him on evening patrols before Jean Marc came along. It was a nice break from working with the same people day in and day out.

Things were a little quieter back then.

Michel smiled.

Now Lucille would be lying in their warm bed with the wood stove stoked for the night, radiating its warmth throughout the house. Michel wished he were snuggled up next to her.

His thoughts drifted and for a moment he was at home.

Michel had almost nodded off when the glare of approaching headlights brought him back to reality. He lay back against the grass as the light passed over him, brushing across his chest. Turning over, he crawled to the top of the bank, pulling his backpack to his side. As he moved into a better position to view the road, a car drove slowly past. It was John Donald's Mustang, but sounded much quieter as it crept down the highway.

The car travelled about a hundred metres past his position when it turned around and came back toward him. Michel pressed himself down into the wet grass and peered through his binoculars as it stopped a stone's throw away.

Without warning, he was suddenly caught in the glare of the high beams.

Pulling the binoculars away from his face, he sunk down into the grass.

The high beams went out as quickly as they had come on and the car began to move forward.

Michel wondered if his binoculars would reflect light like the eyes of a deer and decided against using them while John Donald was jacklighting. He didn't want to be seen, much less shot.

The car rumbled slowly along the road before pulling over to the shoulder directly opposite Michel.

Michel crawled to the edge of the bank to get a better view.

God, this is way too close for comfort.

The car's interior light was on and Michel could clearly see Gerald pulling a rifle out of a gun case. The driver had his back to Michel and although he could not identify him, Michel was certain it was John Donald.

Michel decided to call someone for backup but wasn't sure who he might be able to raise. Pulling his radio out of his pack, he turned it on and triggered the repeater, careful to keep the volume low.

"8-5-2, 8-5-2, this is 8-5-3, do you read me?" Michel spoke slowly, maintaining his composure.

As he watched the two men, he tried calling Ben again, but again there was no response.

Ben and the others will never hear me if they are still on the other side of the park. I might as well try Yvan in town.

"RCMP Portable One from 8-5-3, do you read me?"

The seconds ground away but finally a voice crackled over the radio.

"Go ahead 8-5-3, this is Portable One. How can I help you?"

John Donald and Gerald were just getting out of the car.

With adrenalin pumping through his body, the waver in Michel's voice was unmistakeable.

"I've got something going down at Presqu'ile and will probably need some backup. What's your 10-20?"

"I'm quite a ways from there, on my way back toward Chéticamp from Margaree Forks. I'll head right there but it'll take me the better part of thirty minutes."

Jesus, I don't know if I can wait that long, Michel worried.

"10-4. I'd appreciate it if you could head this way as fast as possible," he whispered into the radio.

John Donald and Gerald crossed the road just to Michel's left and were moving down into the ditch.

He continued with Yvan, "I have two suspects in view and they are heading into the bush. It looks like John Donald and Gerald Moores."

Michel could sense the caution in Yvan's response. ·

"Take it easy and don't make a move until I get there, Michel. I'll put on the afterburners. Portable One, clear."

"8-5-3 clear." Michel turned his radio off and fumbled to put it back in his pack. His hands were shaking and he could feel a surge of cold air invade his body as he lifted himself off the damp grass and knelt down to take stock of his situation.

He could hear movement in the bush off to his left then without warning there was a loud yell from one of the men and a rifle shot shattered the night air.

Michel flung himself face first into the grass.

Christ, they've got something already.

Despite the cold, a bead of sweat trickled down Michel's forehead as he lay on the bank wondering what to do.

CHAPTER 50

THE BUCK HAD been taken down with a single shot between the eyes and lay in a thicket at the edge of the clearing.

"Nice shooting," said John Donald.

"Thanks," said Gerald, eager to get the animal out of the bush and into the car. "Grab an antler and let's haul this thing out of here."

Gerald tried to speed things along by suggesting they deal with the deer back at John Donald's, but his cousin would have no part of it.

"Why the hurry, cousin?"

"It'll save making a mess in the car if we don't gut it here," Gerald suggested.

"There's no rush," said John Donald.

"What about the wardens and the cops?"

"We've been scanning their frequencies all night. Matthews and all of the wardens are over in Ingonish."

"But you don't know when they'll be back."

"Later," said John Donald, getting frustrated. "They won't be back until later."

"But the cops are always out this way as well," said Gerald, trying to build an argument for not sticking around too long.

"The cops are down the coast. The sergeant's around town but he's too fucking lazy to get out of the office."

"I still don't like dogging it like this," said Gerald.

"The coast is clear," John Donald reiterated with a grin.

"But," said Gerald.

"The coast is clear," John Donald repeated as he pulled out his skinning knife.

CHAPTER 51

TRYING TO REMAIN calm and maintain his composure, Michel thought about his options. Ben and the others weren't around to help and Yvan wouldn't get there in time. The chances of this happening were small, but it had—and he was on his own.

I am the only one who can stop them.

Michel struggled with the decision to confront them alone. *They're caught red-handed. Surely they wouldn't resist?*

Fumbling with his pack, Michel crawled away from the edge of the bank and turned to get his bearings. He could hear the two men talking and from time to time caught glimpses of a light in the bush.

Crawling on his knees, Michel pulled himself through the tangle of alder and spruce separating him from the small field. As he got closer he could see the outline of John Donald and Gerald bent over something on the ground. No doubt it was a deer.

Michel tried to determine the best way to approach the two men.

If I walk right up on them, I might startle them and get shot. It isn't worth that. But if I stay back, they might get past me and make it to the car.

He decided to position himself at the edge of the field and announce his presence. That seemed to make the most sense.

For a moment he thought about pulling out altogether, but decided it was now or never. Crawling to the edge of the opening, he stood up, prepared to dive back into the bush if either man reacted suddenly.

"Good evening, gentlemen." He spoke loudly but clearly. "Park wardens."

Gerald turned to run but John Donald grabbed him by the

arm to prevent him from bolting. John Donald casually looked up, the light from their flashlights illuminating his face.

"Park wardens," Michel repeated. "Put your guns down. You're under arrest."

Gerald started to move toward the road but John Donald stopped him.

John Donald shone his light towards Michel and started to move toward him, blocking his view of the deer lying in the grass.

"Put down that gun and move back," Michel ordered.

John Donald walked a few feet closer, trying to get a good look at Michel, then stopped.

"What the fuck do you want, Aucoin? We aren't doing anything that you should be concerned with."

"Just put the gun down, John Donald. You and Gerald are under arrest for poaching."

John Donald would not back off.

As Michel moved closer, Gerald edged in behind his cousin.

"Doesn't look like a good night for you to be out here on your own, Aucoin, what with that prick Matthews over on the other side of the park," John Donald threatened.

Michel started to tense up. He hadn't really counted on John Donald giving him a hard time and realized the desperation of his situation. John Donald shone his flashlight in Michel's face.

"John Donald, you and Gerald have been caught red-handed, so put down the guns and we'll head out to the road."

"Like fuck we are. You came right out of the bush and surprised us. We just thought you were a deer."

Unsure of what John Donald and Gerald were up to, Michel shielded his eyes from the light but was unable to see what either man was doing.

"We just thought you were a fucking deer," John Donald yelled.

Michel could see some movement and thought he saw the silhouette of a gun being raised.

He didn't have a chance after he heard the rifle bolt slam a cartridge into the chamber. He was about to hit the dirt when a blast to the chest drove him into the air as the sound of the gunshot cascaded through the Highlands.

"Oh my Jesus," Michel cried out as he crashed backwards into the bushes.

Reaching across his chest, Michel could feel the warmth of his blood as it seeped from his body. His back felt like it had been blasted apart. He knew immediately he was seriously injured. He was drifting into shock, but could hear footsteps in the grass, moving closer. "Goddamn, goddamn," he said, as he heard the bolt of the rifle one more time. A light shone in his eyes and he could sense John Donald hovering over him.

"Just thought you were a fucking deer," said John Donald as he levered another cartridge into the rifle.

Gerald stood behind John Donald and Michel could hear him plead with his cousin to get the hell out of there.

John Donald waved him off and leaned over Michel, placing the barrel of his rifle between Michel's eyes.

"Don't like to leave a job half done," he muttered.

Gerald saw what he was about to do and moved forward into plain view. He looked down at Michel's chest and then stared into his eyes.

"He's finished, John Donald. Let's get the fuck out of here."

"Yeah, I guess you're right, Gerald. If I shoot him between the eyes people might get a little suspicious."

John Donald pointed the barrel into the grass next to Michel's head and squeezed the trigger.

The blast jolted Michel one last time.

"Oh Lucille, please forgive me, please forgive me," Michel murmured, his voice fading into the cool night air as John Donald and Gerald dragged the deer past him and made their way to the road.

CHAPTER 52

YVAN GUNNED HIS patrol car down the Rigwash Valley and past the Grande Falaise. He had been trying to contact Michel on the radio but had no luck. As he crested the hill approaching Presqu'ile, he met another vehicle heading toward Chéticamp but it was there and gone again before he could get a good look. He slowed down for a moment, wondering if he should turn around and stop it, but decided against it. Figuring Michel was still waiting for him, he thought it was better to continue on and find out what had taken place.

Driving past Presqu'ile, Yvan slowed down as he approached the spot he thought Michel had been referring to on the radio, half expecting Michel to come up out of the ditch at any time. Seeing nothing, he turned the car around, stopped and tried to raise Michel on the radio.

"8-5-3, Portable One, come in Michel."

Nothing.

He tried again but again there was no response.

"8-5-3, Portable One, come in."

The radio crackled.

"Go ahead Portable One."

Thank Christ.

"Good to hear your voice, Michel," said Yvan.

"Sorry, this is 8-5-2, Yvan. I thought you were calling me. What's up over there?"

Yvan slumped into his seat, wondering where the hell Michel was.

"Ben, you guys better get back over here pronto. I got a call from Michel about twenty minutes ago, asking for assistance. He said he was at Presqu'ile. I'm there now but I can't raise him."

"10-4, Yvan. Joe and I are just on top of French Mountain

headed your way. Michel should be okay. He may just be having radio problems. You know how our system works."

"10-4, but something just doesn't seem right. Just get back here."

Yvan continued driving slowly along the highway looking for something that might lead him to Michel, but nothing seemed obvious. He drove back and forth along the stretch of road by Presqu'ile then decided to keep going toward Trout Brook. As he headed toward French Mountain a set of headlights came into view so he quickly pulled into the Trout Brook entrance and waited for the vehicle to pass. Realizing it was a warden truck, he pulled back onto the highway and raced after the pickup, flashing his headlights to get them to stop.

The warden truck pulled over and both Ben and Joe got out.

Yvan pulled up alongside and jumped out of the car.

"Did you find him?" Ben asked.

"No," said Yvan. "I can't figure out where he is."

"Well, we usually park in the old pit just above Presqu'ile," said Ben.

"Fine, I'll go take a look," said Yvan, turning to get back in the police car. "You guys head to Presqu'ile and see if you can find him."

"Hey Yvan," said Ben. "What was up anyway? Why did Michel say that he needed help?"

Yvan looked hopelessly into the night sky.

"He called me and said John Donald and Gerald were on the move and most likely hunting."

With that, Yvan got into his car and sped off down the road.

Joe looked at Ben, a crease of worry etched across his face.

"Jesus, this doesn't look good," said Joe. "Why the hell did Michel come out here by himself?"

"Calm down, Joe. We won't know what's up until we find him. Come on. Let's see if we can figure out where he is."

They jumped into the truck and headed toward Presqu'ile, driving slowly along the road looking for any clue that might lead them to Michel.

Suddenly, Joe raised a hand for Ben to stop the vehicle.

"Pull over, I saw something."

"What was it?"

"I'm not sure," said Joe. "It looked like a track back there on the other side of the road."

The two wardens methodically searched the opposite shoulder of the road, shining their flashlights along the gravel at the edge of the pavement.

"There it is." Joe pointed to a drag mark. "It looks like they crossed the road here."

Following Joe across the road, Ben knelt down and ran his finger through the gravel.

"What is it?" asked Joe.

Ben shone his flashlight into the red ooze staining his finger. "Blood."

Carefully, he walked down into the ditch, staying to the side of the blood-stained path. "They dragged a deer out of here tonight," said Ben. "There's deer hair all over these bushes."

Ben turned around to address Joe, who stood back at the road, hesitant to accompany Ben beyond the edge of the bushes.

Ben sensed his discomfort.

"Get on the radio and tell Yvan to come back here," said Ben. "I'll check this out."

Joe headed for the truck as Ben continued to follow the trail of blood into the bush, uneasy about what he might find. The fact that Michel had not shown up was cause for concern.

Joe called out to him from the road to say that Yvan had found the truck at the pit and was heading back to help. The words were no sooner out of his mouth when Yvan's patrol car pulled in alongside, its alley lights illuminating the narrow path into the bush.

Getting out of the car, Yvan asked Joe what they'd found but before he could reply they heard Ben yell.

"Get in here."

Yvan bolted into the trees following the sound of Ben's voice, the rose bushes tearing at his legs as he made his way to the opening in the forest.

Fearing the worst, Joe followed slowly behind, staying off the trail and picking his way through the alders instead.

As Yvan walked into the clearing, he found Ben standing over the body with tears rolling down his face.

Yvan stared in disbelief at the contorted figure sprawled out, half hidden, in the grass at Ben's feet.

He knelt down and felt for a pulse in Michel's neck.

Looking up at Ben, he shook his head.

Joe was just making his way to the edge of the clearing.

"You better stay there, Joe," said Ben.

Joe didn't need a second offer.

"Go call an ambulance, please," said Ben.

"What's up, Ben?" Joe was barely able to get the words out. "Is he…"

"Yes. It looks like he didn't have a chance."

Joe hung his head, turned and headed back to the truck.

Realizing he should go with him, Ben put his hand on Yvan's shoulder. "I'm going out with Joe to call for an ambulance. We should get a camera and record the scene before it gets mucked up."

Yvan nodded his head but said nothing.

"You going to be okay?" said Ben.

"I don't know," said Yvan. "I can't fucking believe this."

"I can't either," said Ben. "But we have to deal with it. And we should get the sarge to pick up John Donald and Gerald Moores."

Yvan looked up at him, barely able to control his rage.

"Those bastards are going to regret this night," he said, fighting to hold back tears. "You've got that right," said Ben patting Yvan on the shoulder. "But right now I've got to get out there with Joe."

Turning away from Yvan, Ben continued on to the truck.

He found Joe sitting in the driver's seat, crumpled over the steering wheel, head buried in his hands.

"It's all right, Joe," said Ben. "Let it out. It's just you and me, buddy."

"I can't believe those fuckers would do this. How are we going to tell Lucille and her folks?"

"I don't know," Ben replied.

"Christ, this is way more than poaching," said Joe, tears rolling down his face.

"It always has been," said Ben. "It always has been."

Ben reached across for the radio and tripped the repeater for the mobile operator.

When she responded he identified himself and asked her to notify the Chéticamp hospital to send an ambulance. "Is everything all right?" she asked.

"Things are okay," Ben said. He advised her of the location and signed off.

Yvan was just coming out of the bush in his shirtsleeves.

"I covered Michel with my jacket."

Reaching into the warden truck, Ben pulled out a spare patrol jacket he kept behind the seat. He passed it to Yvan, who forced his arms down the sleeves and struggled to zip it up across his broad chest.

With his head hanging low, Yvan slumped back to the patrol car and contacted Steve Day. When the sergeant asked why Yvan wanted him to check on the whereabouts of John Donald and Gerald Moores, Yvan lost it.

"Just pick those fuckers up and I'll talk to you when I get back to the detachment," he yelled, slamming the mike into its holder.

"I'll track them down," the sergeant replied. "Over and out."

Yvan returned to the warden truck to wait for the ambulance with Ben and Joe.

"I'll get some photos before the ambulance arrives, but I just want to remind you that we should try to stay away from the body. This is now a crime scene," he said. "We'll have to search the place for evidence in the daylight and I don't want to track it up tonight any more than we have to. You know, right now we've got nothing that ties John Donald and Gerald Moores to this other than the radio call from Michel."

Ben and Joe nodded.

"I'll go to the pit and get the warden truck," said Ben. "Yvan, why don't you do a preliminary search and whatever else you need to do to secure the scene? Joe can stay here and monitor the radio until the ambulance arrives."

Both agreed and Ben started off down the road.

"I can give you a ride," Joe offered.

"Thanks, but I need the walk." Ben moved into the shadows away from the vehicle lights, overwhelmed by the turn of events.

We've been on the edge of this kind of thing for quite a while. It was only a matter of time before John Donald lost it. I decided to play hardball and painted him into a corner. Kate was right. I should have known better. Now Michel is dead. God, what have I done?

Arriving at the pit road, Ben unlatched the gate and swung it open. Walking up and around the dogleg turn, he found Michel's unlocked truck.

Climbing inside, he sat behind the wheel and turned on the dome light. A picture of Lucille and Jean Marc hung from the mirror.

Michel must have hung it there when he took the truck this evening. Christ!

Taking the key from the ashtray, Ben put it in the ignition and turned it on. The tape deck kicked in automatically and a traditional Acadian fiddle tune flowed smoothly out of the speakers.

Suddenly feeling hot, Ben rolled down the window and sat for a moment, clenching the steering wheel. The picture hanging from the mirror swayed slowly in the breeze.

Ben hung his head and sobbed.

How the hell do I tell Lucille? This is not how it's supposed to be.

CHAPTER 53

STEVE DAY DIDN'T know why he was picking up John Donald and Gerald Moores as he combed the back roads behind Chéticamp but assumed it had something to do with poaching in the park. Whatever was up, he figured he would find out when Yvan got back to the office. Day had been monitoring his radio and picked up calls between the hospital and ambulance so he knew someone was in need of medical attention. He didn't know the details but John Donald and his cousin must have been involved in some way.

Day checked both men's homes but found no sign of their vehicles. He knew they usually travelled in John Donald's truck, but since he lost it in court he was stuck using his Mustang.

Checking all of the back roads, Steve Day was unable to find the car anywhere.

One last place he knew he could check was the home of John Donald's father-in-law. The old man had a garage and they often used it to clean up deer. The garage was away from the house, down an old lane that was growing in with overhanging birch trees.

Day passed by the house and turned into the lane, turning off his headlights and working his way slowly towards the garage. Sure enough, there were lights on, even though it was now two in the morning. He stopped several hundred feet back from the garage and turned off his vehicle. He would normally call in to Telecom in Sydney but he had been getting lax of late and decided to forego this routine procedure. Working in such a small detachment, maintaining regular contact with Sydney Telecom while on patrol was usually their only assurance that someone would know where they were if anything went down.

Steve Day found the cool night air tugging at him. It had

been so warm inside the cruiser. He walked to the rear of the car and opened the trunk. He pulled out his flak jacket and put it on, then pulled on his heavier patrol coat, making sure he had quick access to his Smith and Wesson service pistol. He didn't really expect problems, but he had heard too many stories about John Donald to take chances.

He quietly closed the trunk and retrieved his portable radio, sliding it into the big pocket of his coat. He left his vehicle unlocked in case he had to get back in quickly, and then walked toward the garage, staying to the side of the road where he was concealed in the shadows of the birch trees. As he approached the garage, he could hear voices. He crept up to a window and peered inside. A deer hung from the rafters, a fresh kill by the looks of it.

So that was it. The boys got a deer from the park tonight.

John Donald and Gerald Moores were standing on the other side of John Donald's car near a large freezer, but he was unable to tell what they were doing.

Day strained to hear what they were talking about, keeping out of sight to the side of the window. Gerald sounded quite agitated as he watched John Donald, who was bent over and only occasionally visible to Day.

"I told you they would be expecting us," Gerald said.

John Donald's reply was barely audible, making reference to the fact that there wasn't supposed to be anyone around.

"But there was," continued Gerald, "and we should have just fucked off out of there when we saw him. What was he going to do?"

Again, Day was unable to hear most of John Donald's response.

"How was I supposed to know? Could have been anything in the bush... the goddamn wardens."

So the wardens must have been on to them. I'm not sure why Yvan would have been involved though. I've told him time and again that we don't have any business in the park when we've got the whole coast to look after.

John Donald came into view and Day could see he was trying to avoid Gerald's questioning, continuing about his business, whatever it was he was doing. He appeared to be placing packages of meat in the freezer.

Steve Day decided to make his entrance, still unsure as to what exactly he would do, but he had John Donald and Gerald together with a fresh deer so he figured he could bluff them into admitting it was taken from the park. He had enough to bring them in.

Moving around the back of the garage to the side door, he turned the knob and pushed, but it was latched on the inside. He stood back and hauled out his pistol, making sure the safety was off. He was a little nervous, trying this on his own, but thought *to hell with it.*

Day raised his boot and kicked, aiming straight for the edge of the door by the latch. The door flew inwards and Day burst into the garage. John Donald and Gerald were both caught off guard. They were standing toward the back of the garage, next to the freezer, both in Day's line of sight. Before they could move he yelled at them to stay put, aiming his service pistol directly at John Donald.

"RCMP, stand back and don't move a muscle."

"I fucking told you," Gerald screamed at John Donald.

Coolly, John Donald reached out and closed the lid to the freezer.

"Shut the fuck up." He glared at Gerald.

John Donald stood stock still, but Steve Day could sense that Gerald was thinking about making a break toward the front door. Stepping forward quickly, the sergeant blocked any chance of Gerald getting away.

"Don't think about it, Gerald. I've got an itchy finger tonight and this baby leaves a big fucking hole in things."

Day looked at the deer hanging next to him then looked at John Donald.

"Looks like you guys got lucky in the park tonight," he said, studying John Donald's face for a reaction.

John Donald seemed unfazed.

"What the fuck do you mean?" said John Donald, scowling at Day.

"C'mon, John Donald. You have a freshly killed deer and I know you just came out of the park with it."

John Donald and Gerald immediately picked up on the fact that Day had not mentioned Michel. They looked at each other and John Donald nodded to Gerald as if to tell him not to say a word.

"We weren't in the park and what if we were? We got this deer up back of Belle Cote today. I've got a licence. It's perfectly legal."

"Right," said Day. "Like everything else you do, perfectly fucking legal."

The sergeant began to point things out.

"Let's see what we've got here. Fresh blood, plastic lining the trunk and by the looks of those pails, you were just about ready to clean things up. You'd have had it done if you shot the deer this afternoon."

John Donald started to protest but Day cut him off.

"Shut the fuck up, John Donald. You boys get your jackets and come with me. I'm taking you to the detachment in Chéticamp."

The Moores picked up their jackets that were lying on a table next to the freezer. Holstering his gun, Day escorted the two men to the patrol car and put them both in the back seat. As the sergeant got in the car, John Donald leaned over and mumbled something to Gerald then straightened up and looked forward as the sergeant settled in behind the steering wheel.

"Getting the story straight, are you?" said Day.

John Donald and Gerald remained silent.

"Fine by me," the sergeant continued. "This is pretty straightforward shit." He backed the police cruiser down the lane and wheeled the car onto the roadway.

Arriving back at the RCMP detachment, he pulled into the driveway, and after pressing the automatic door opener for the garage, drove straight in, closing the door behind them. Getting out of the car, he opened the rear door and directed the Moores into the office.

With no one being held in the cells, the sergeant would have to call in one of the part-time guards for the night but first he needed to deal with his prisoners, directing John Donald and Gerald to empty their pockets onto the desk and take a seat.

Handcuffing John Donald to a chair, Day escorted Gerald to the cells and searched him before locking him inside.

"You're next," he said to John Donald, as he returned to the front office. Escorting him to the back of the detachment, Day felt John Donald tense up as he was about to search him.

"This is routine, John Donald. You've been here before so don't fuck with me or I'll have to get you to strip down in front of my pal," he said, patting his holster.

John Donald complied, allowing Day to finish the body search.

The sergeant escorted John Donald to Gerald's cell and directed him inside with his cousin.

"Guess you boys can't do too much harm together," he said as he closed the cell door and locked it.

The Moores were silent.

Back in the front office, Day glanced at the personal effects on his desk and grabbed a couple of plastic evidence bags. Sitting down at the desk, he started to record and bag each item. *Pretty standard stuff,* he thought. *Lighters, keys, watches.*

Collecting everything on the desk, he opened a nearby evidence locker and placed the items inside, then remembered that he hadn't yet called a guard to keep an eye on the Moores overnight.

Checking the duty roster, he reached for the phone.

Jean Yves is next on the list. He'll be a good one for these two.

Jean Yves was a vet and although he had turned sixty-five a few months back, he was powerfully built and not a man to be reckoned with.

Day picked up the phone and dialled his number. Jean Yves picked it up right away.

"Whoa," Day said, "that was fast. I thought you'd be dead to the world at three in the morning. Your wife keeping you up?"

"Goddamn, no, Sarge. I've been up for a while since we heard the news," Jean Yves blurted into the phone. "It's terrible."

Day was perplexed.

"What news, Jean Yves, what's up?"

"Goddamn, Sarge, you didn't hear?"

"Hear what?" said Day, barely catching Jean Yves' next statement as he saw the other RCMP patrol car pull into the driveway and Yvan jump out.

"My son-in-law works on the ambulance and he called and told us that Michel Aucoin was killed tonight," said Jean Yves. "They say John Donald gunned him down in cold blood out by Presqu'ile."

Day stared into space and dropped the phone as Yvan burst through the door.

"Did you pick them up?" Yvan demanded, his eyes on fire.

Before he could get his answer, Day raced to the back room with Yvan on his heels. Opening the cell door, he pulled Gerald into the hallway by his shoulder.

"Come with me," he said sternly.

Gerald cowered and gave no resistance.

Day opened a side door and unlocked one of the cells used to isolate prisoners.

"Get the fuck in," he told Gerald, who scurried inside.

Day slammed the cell shut behind him and returned to the

main cells only to find Yvan inside, with John Donald pushed up against the wall.

"You fucker, this time you've gone too far," he screamed at John Donald. "I'm gonna see you fuckin' roast for this."

John Donald just stood there and took it in, barely restraining a smirk.

Rushing into the cell, the sergeant separated the two and pushed John Donald up against the bunk.

"Stay the fuck there or I'll kick the shit out of you myself."

Turning to Yvan, the sergeant spoke angrily.

"Get the fuck out so I can lock this fucking cell."

Yvan hesitated, then moved back and allowed Day to close the cell door and lock it. He continued to look at John Donald.

"Don't fucking think you are going to get away with this."

John Donald just stared at him, cursing Yvan under his breath.

Day pulled his constable into the front office but before he could speak Yvan ripped a strip off of him.

"What the fuck were they doing in the same cell?"

"I didn't know what happened," said the sergeant, realizing he had given John Donald and Gerald time to sort out their stories. "I thought we were dealing with a poaching. I had them dead to rights so I didn't figure it was a big deal."

"Well, it is a big deal—a big fucking deal," said Yvan. "They blew the guts out of Michel Aucoin tonight and left him in the bush to die like a fucking animal."

Tears rolled down Yvan's face. He was in shock and started to shake uncontrollably as he faced Day and tried to relate what had happened.

Day listened intently, realizing he had made a major faux pas keeping the two suspects together for such a long period of time. The Crown prosecutor would rake him over the coals for such a basic mistake.

As Yvan described what happened, the sergeant realized important evidence was probably sitting back at the garage.

"Did you find anything out there that would put these two at the scene?" he asked Yvan.

"Not a hell of a lot, but we've got the scene secured and we can take a good look around in the morning. We better get the dog in from Sydney."

"Good idea, but we should also take a quick run back to the garage where I picked these two up. I think I walked in on them in the middle of cleaning things up but I didn't have time to search the place. We'll just wait until Jean Yves gets here before we can head out."

Day no sooner had the words out of his mouth when the old guard walked through the door. Day started to pull on his patrol coat.

"Thanks for getting here so fast, Jean Yves. We can't talk right now. We'll be on the radio if you need us. Otherwise, just sit tight and we'll be back as soon as we can."

Yvan and the sergeant whisked through the door and jumped in the patrol car.

"We'll have to sort out a warrant in the morning," Day pointed out, "but as far as tonight goes, we're not taking any chance that someone might get rid of evidence crucial to this case."

Yvan nodded in agreement and stared ahead. Pretty soon it would be daybreak. He couldn't help thinking about how Ben had broken the news to Lucille.

It must have been so difficult. I wouldn't have been able to do it.

The sergeant glanced over at Yvan and noticed he was drifting.

Leave him alone. He looks terrible, he thought as he pulled into the lane past the old house and drove right up to the garage, using the takedown lights to illuminate the front of the building. As they got out, the sergeant went to the back of the car and pulled the investigator's kit from the trunk.

"Keep your eyes peeled for anything unusual," he said. "We don't want to miss anything."

CHAPTER 54

IT WAS NEARLY six in the morning before Ben got away from the Aucoin house. Despite the early hour, Lucille and Michel's house was already jammed with people arriving by the minute, shocked by the news of Michel's death.

It had been so difficult telling her.

He knew that as soon as he woke her, she would be suspicious something had happened to Michel. Driving past his house, he considered waking Kate to tell her the news and pondered waiting until later in the morning to go to Lucille, but knew he could not put it off. He thought about getting Kate to come with him, but he knew it was important to do it himself. One way or the other, Lucille had to find out and everyone deserved to be told as soon as possible. He did not want her to discover the truth inadvertently.

Approaching the small village, Michel and Lucille's home sat in total darkness with the exception of a small light over the back door. Lucille always left the light on when Michel worked night shifts. At her father's house next door, the light was a signal Michel was still not home. From time to time, Louis Gouthro would get out of bed and go to the upstairs hallway window and check to see if the light was finally out. He fretted over his daughter and grandson, and often worried about his son-in-law's choice of career. When he saw that the light was out, he would breathe a sigh of relief and go back to bed, telling his wife that Michel must be home.

Pulling into their driveway, Ben parked close to the highway then turned off the headlights and sat quietly in the darkness, wondering what he would say. He knew he had to keep it together and didn't want to upset Lucille with the details. Collecting himself, he got out of the warden truck then proceeded to the back door, a habit developed in his earlier years at home but reinforced by Michel's comment to him on that first visit. The front door was reserved for clergy, special guests and the mailman.

The back door was for friends.

Taking his time, Ben walked quietly up the wooden steps, cognisant of the hour and not wanting to be any more obvious than was necessary.

How do I tell Lucille? How will she react? Will she blame me for all of this?

Ben raised his hand slowly to the door and knocked lightly. He rapped again, this time a little harder. Almost immediately an upstairs light came on, as if Lucille had been poised waiting for Michel's return.

Ben could hear the shuffling of feet and then the hall light came on as Lucille walked down the stairs. She turned off the light when she reached the landing. Ben could see her wrapping her housecoat around her as she approached the back door. She peered out through the window, a look of concern on her face as she recognized Ben. She opened the door, a draft of cool morning air ruffling her long, dark hair.

Ben could feel the warmth of the kitchen, the sweet smell of wood smoke wafting from the stove as he stood beneath the light over the door, taking off his Stetson as Lucille invited him in.

Louis Gouthro, looking at the man at the back door of his daughter's house, realized he was not his son-in-law. His first thought had been that Michel was bringing the park truck home, as he was accustomed to do on some late shifts, but this was not a person familiar to Louis Gouthro. He knew something was wrong and went to wake Lucille's mother.

Ben stepped inside the back porch, pulling the door closed behind him. He turned to face Lucille, who shared the same instinct as her father. Clenching her hands together in front of her, she tried desperately to control the shaking that had already started.

Michel always called to let her know if he would be late. He knew she worried about the night patrols and would lay awake until he finally got home, whatever hour in the morning. If for some reason Michel had been unable to contact her, he would get one of the other wardens to call her. Often it was Rose who would phone after receiving a radio call from Joe or Ben.

"What's the matter, Ben?" she finally managed to ask, not able to say Michel's name.

Ben forced himself to look at her, tears starting to form in the corners of his eyes.

"I'm sorry, Lucille," was all he could manage to say as he reached out for her.

She grabbed his arms and he pulled her in, holding her trembling body tightly to his chest. Realizing the news would not be good, she could no longer hold back the flood of tears.

"Michel is dead, Lucille," Ben said, finally managing to force out the words he desperately wanted to leave unspoken.

"How?" Lucille was trying to maintain her composure and spoke through her tears.

"We think he was shot by John Donald Moores," said Ben, leaving out the details of how they had found Michel.

"Why?" Lucille asked, pulling away for a moment to look up into Ben's face.

Ben looked down at her and could see why Michel raved about this woman. Even under the circumstances, her strength was obvious. Smoothing back her hair, she pulled a tissue from the billowy pockets of her housecoat and patted the tears on her cheeks.

"We're not sure," Ben replied. "We think that Michel must have caught them red-handed, poaching deer near Presqu'ile."

Lucille moved backwards into the kitchen and sat down on a chair.

"For a deer?" she said, shaking her head as her hair fell down around her face. "For a deer? John Donald Moores shot my Michel, for a deer?"

Ben hung his head. He knew it had to do with more than just a deer. They had pushed John Donald Moores, humiliated him in court; he was out to seek revenge from the people who were upsetting his plans. This was a calculated act, but Ben could not bring himself to discuss that with Lucille. For all intents and purposes, Michel Aucoin had been murdered for a deer.

It was that simple.

Behind Ben, the back door opened up and Louis Gouthro, dressed in wool pants and suspenders with a plaid shirt partially tucked in at the waist, stepped inside the porch followed by his wife. She was fussing with a button on the front of her blouse, sputtering something in French that Ben could not make out.

Louis Gouthro saw immediately that Lucille was upset and went to her side, resting his hand on her shoulder. Caressing the back of her neck, he looked at Ben as his wife moved to her daughter's side.

"What has happened to Michel?" Louis Gouthro asked Ben.

Ben raised his head to look Lucille's father squarely in the face. "He's been killed. We found him at Presqu'ile. He had been shot." He started to tell Lucille's parents the details but held back. There was still so much they didn't know.

Mrs. Gouthro knelt down in front of her daughter, held Lucille's head in her hands and began to cry. Lucille comforted her, her strength taking over from raw emotion. She had to be strong for her parents, for Michel's parents. She had to be strong for Jean Marc and herself.

As word started to spread along the coast, an onslaught of family crowded into Lucille's home. She was amazingly strong but finally succumbed to the constant retelling of the story.

Yes, it was true. Yes, Michel had been killed. No, they weren't sure but word was that John Donald Moores had shot him near Presqu'ile.

As the parade of people continued, Ben slid out the back door as the sun was finally making its way above the Highlands.

Walking past the vehicles lining the long driveway, Ben was glad he had parked closer to the road. Just as he got into the warden truck, another car turned off the highway and pulled up alongside. Realizing it was Yvan and the sergeant, Ben rolled down his window.

"How was it, Ben? How is Lucille doing?" asked Yvan.

Ben motioned toward the house. "Well, as you can see there are lots of people coming over to lend support."

Steve Day looked past Yvan to Ben. "Christ, Ben, I'm sorry about what happened."

"So am I," said Ben.

"I hate to drag you out of here," the sergeant continued, "but would you mind coming with us to search the place where I picked up John Donald and Gerald Moores?"

"They had a fresh deer," said Yvan, "and we found a .308 rifle. But because poaching is your area of expertise, we thought it would be good to get you over there to make sure we haven't missed anything."

"Sure, Yvan. Do you want me to follow you?"

"No," said the sergeant. "It would probably be better if we all went in the car. Why don't you park at the detachment and we'll go from there?"

Ben nodded and drove to the detachment, pulling in in front of the patrol car. Getting out of the warden truck, Ben leaned into the window of the car.

"Have you got the Moores inside?" he asked the sergeant.

"Yeah, Jean Yves is guarding them."

"Why don't you tell Jean Yves to give me a minute with them, then we wouldn't have to worry about a court case."

"I hear you, Ben, but you better get in the car. We've still got lots to do to tie these two to what happened tonight. Yvan and I think we've found something that might help but we still have work to do."

Ben opened the back door and squeezed into the cramped rear seat, his knees pressed against the reinforced Silent Patrolman, a Plexiglas and steel frame that prevented prisoners from reaching the driver.

"There's not a lot of room in here," he said as they backed out onto the road. "So what did you find, anyway?"

"Let's wait until we get there and you can see for yourself. We want you to tell us what you think before we give anything away. We need an objective viewpoint for this one."

Ben shrugged and settled back in the seat. Something was digging into his back and he felt around and pulled an object from the seam between the seat backs.

"Pull over for a second, Steve," said Ben.

The sergeant pulled the car off the road and looked into the rear view mirror at Ben.

"What's up?"

"I'm not sure. What do you make of this?" he said as he passed an object to Day through the portal in the Silent Patrolman. "Have you guys been leaving live ammo lying around?"

Day held a bullet up to the light.

"Jesus Christ, this is hollow point ammo. How the hell did that get in here?"

Yvan looked at Day sternly. "It's not the same as the ammo we found in the garage," he said. "This is .270 calibre, hollow point."

"What? What are you thinking?" said the sergeant.

"The same thing as I am," said Ben.

"Exactly," said Yvan. "Dollars to doughnuts, Moores had this on him. I thought Michel had run into a cannon by the size of the hole in him. This must be the shit John Donald was firing. They must have had two guns."

"Christ," said Ben. "If that's what he's using for deer, there'd be a lot of damage."

Ben thought for a moment then continued, "unless he wasn't aiming for deer."

"What are you thinking, Ben?" Day inquired.

Ben poked his head through the portal, his voice rising. "I'm thinking John Donald set Michel up. He knew goddamn well we were in Ingonish and he probably knew you guys were down the coast."

"Are you suggesting John Donald and Gerald planned this all along to draw Michel into the park alone?" said Yvan.

"Damn right."

Day turned and stared at Ben. "If what you're saying is right, John Donald is looking at first degree murder instead of manslaughter. I've been thinking about this one and John Donald is probably cooking up a story to say that Michel surprised them and they thought he was a deer or something. That could buy him a manslaughter charge or less, but if we can show that it was premeditated, even Irons won't be able to save his ass."

Ben was fuming in the back seat. "Surer than shit, John Donald had this planned all the way."

"So we've got to make sure we cover off all of the bases," said Yvan. "Right now we don't have a fuck of a lot to even put him at the scene."

Without speaking, Day turned the car on to the road.

"And if there is a second gun," said Ben, "we've got to find it."

CHAPTER 55

THE CRUISER PULLED in the lane leading to the garage. Ben sat up, taking note of the scene as Steve Day parked along the side of the lane where he had parked earlier.

"I just want you to approach the place as I did last night."

Ben waited for Yvan to let him out of the back of the car.

"Keep your eyes open," Yvan advised. "And let us know what you think."

Ben scanned the road as he slowly led the way toward the garage.

He walked to the door and gave it a slight push. It swung open easily, hanging loosely from its hinges. Peering inside, everything was as the sergeant had said. A four point buck hung from the rafters, a pool of blood lying underneath. John Donald's car was parked inside with the trunk open. A large freezer occupied one corner of the back wall.

Ben stepped inside the garage and looked around, followed by the two Mounties. He looked in the back of John Donald's car. Although the Moores' had tried to clean it, Ben could still see traces of deer blood and hair above the rear bumper.

"I wish it was possible to trace DNA to an individual animal," said Ben as he continued to search for clues. "That would put them at the scene."

"I thought they could trace DNA to individual animals," said Day.

"Someday maybe, but no. Right now, only human DNA can be traced back to the individual," said Ben. "For wildlife work, DNA will only tell you what species you're dealing with."

Ben looked at the deer hanging from the rafters and pulled up the head to inspect it.

"Here's where the bullet went in," he said, pointing to a

small mottled dot of blood. "And here's where it came out," he added, pointing to an exit wound on the back of the head.

"Most likely shot with the .308 you found. If John Donald was using the stuff that hit Michel, the entire head would be blown apart."

"Two guns for sure," said Yvan.

"For sure," Ben nodded.

He carried on to the front of the car and opened the driver's door. Reaching across the seat, he opened the glove compartment and a single bullet fell onto the floor.

Picking up the round, Ben checked the calibre. "Another .308," he said. "This is what they would have used for the deer. No sign of any .270 calibre ammo."

He closed the door and walked to the back of the garage. There was the usual array of tools along with a couple of skinning knives.

Turning to the freezer, he moved the jacket lying on top and lifted the lid.

Steve Day walked over and picked up the jacket.

Ben continued to check out the freezer contents. It was full of packages and some unwrapped fish. Slowly he sorted through the top layer but before he could dig deeper the sergeant interrupted him.

"I don't remember this jacket," said Steve Day, turning to Ben.

Lowering the lid, Ben took the jacket from the sergeant. "What do you mean?"

"Well, I told John Donald and Gerald to get their jackets and come with me. They both had their coats on when they got to the detachment."

"I think it was here when we came back to search the place," Yvan said to the sergeant. "But I didn't think anything of it."

Ben held the coat up to his chest. "It looks quite small for either of the Moores."

Yvan stepped forward and tried to put it on. "I guess!" he

said, barely able to get his arm half way down the sleeve. He checked the collar and label.

"It's got John Donald's initials on it though," he said, pointing to "J.D." marked in blue ink on the tag.

"It must have been something John Donald had lying around here for years," said Day.

"No way," replied Yvan, emptying the pockets to reveal some loose change. He held up two quarters for inspection. "These coins are only a year old."

"Well, we should take this jacket with us," said Ben. "I don't see anything else right now, but we should secure this place and have your Ident guys check it out."

"They've already been called and should be here later this morning," said Day. "They'll give the car a good going-over."

Turning to the sergeant, Ben asked, "so what were you expecting me to find?"

"I was wondering about the bullets mainly. I figured that we could tie the deer back to the scene at Presqu'ile," Day explained.

"Well, the bullets are definitely a curiosity but the DNA is a no go. We still need to find a .270 rifle to tie John Donald to Michel. We should get Ident to check John Donald's clothing, too. If he shot Michel at close range there could be blood spattered on him that the labs could run DNA tests on."

Day nodded in agreement.

"I wonder where the other gun is?" said Yvan.

"I don't know," said Ben. "That's always bothered me about John Donald. The last time we caught him we never found his gun either but it was probably the .308 you found here. I always wondered if he had it stashed somewhere, but never figured out where. The other gun is probably standing up against some tree out there, just wrapped in a plastic bag."

"Well, it would sure help to get something to tie him to this," Day commented. "Without solid evidence, this case could go either way."

CHAPTER 56
The following week

A COOL BREEZE drifted in off the Gulf as a snow squall fought its way along Chéticamp's main street. Sunlight momentarily caught the front of the large stone church where a crowd had assembled outside, waiting for the service to begin.

As the black hearse moved slowly toward the cathedral, Cole's two horses came into view. They were decked out in gleaming national park tack flown in from Riding Mountain National Park for the occasion, and ridden by park wardens in ceremonial uniforms. An army of uniformed officers marched slowly behind the horses, led by a contingent of wardens from national parks across Canada.

The crowd outside the cathedral watched the procession work its way along the car-lined roadway. Uniformed police officers standing at attention on both sides of the lane saluted as the first limousine carrying Lucille Aucoin and her family passed. As the hearse pulled up to the front of the church, the people standing outside filed inside to their seats.

As the second limousine pulled to a stop, Ben Matthews got out with Norm, Cole and John Kerry along with two other park wardens from the Ingonish side of Cape Breton Highlands. As they made their way forward to the lead car, Ben opened the passenger door for Lucille and helped her out. Dressed in a pale blue outfit, she smiled at Ben as she fought back the tears.

"Too much black and grey today," she said. "Michel would have preferred some colour."

Ben nodded and led her up the stairs, where her father took her arm and brought her into the cathedral. Walking back to the hearse, Ben joined the other pallbearers who had begun to slide the casket from the car.

On cue, they took the weight and shouldered the coffin up the steps, where they lowered it onto the handcart. Adjusting their uniforms, they lined up on either side and started into the cathedral.

Just inside the porch, Joe waited with a hand-carved wooden box. He opened it to reveal Michel's Stetson.

Two of the local fisheries officers draped the coffin with Acadian and Canadian flags and Joe laid the Stetson on top, squarely in the centre. Tears were rolling down his cheeks.

On command, the park wardens wheeled the casket through the inside doors and made their way slowly to the front of the cathedral. As they positioned the casket lengthwise across the church, Kate and Gerard played a slow Acadian melody from their positions high in the balcony, their fiddles synchronized perfectly. As the pallbearers took their seats behind the family the remainder of the uniformed officers filled the cathedral.

Father Camus, dressed in white robes, lit the candles on either side of the altar and walked back to the microphone positioned in front of the casket.

Raising his hands for quiet, he began.

"Chers amis, dear friends. Nous sommes ici aujourd'hui... We are here today to pay our respects to a dear friend, husband, father, brother, neighbour and comrade. This is a difficult occasion, not only because we have lost Michel Pierre Aucoin, a gentle man, but also because of the tragic circumstances involved."

Father Camus paused, collecting his thoughts.

"It is especially tough for me as Michel and I were friends from the beginning. We grew up next door to each other, were classmates throughout our school years, and until the time that I left Chéticamp for seemingly greener pastures, we were frequent visitors to each other's houses."

"But Michel never left to find his greener pastures. He always knew they were right here. After finishing university with a science degree, he had an opportunity to work for the national park and he soon realized his true calling."

"I remember him telling me about one day when he was working on a salmon survey along the Chéticamp River. He had caught a large salmon in the salmon trap and when he lifted it out of the water it was struck by a ray of sunlight that reflected its colourful scales. He was amazed by its beauty."

Father Camus paused again.

"After he had taken measurements and gently placed the fish back in the river, Michel released his grip on its tail and the fish bolted forward, heading farther upstream to spawn."

The congregation was silent.

"That was a turning point for Michel," Father Camus continued.

"The national park and the Warden Service provided him an opportunity to follow his two passions. For not only was he a dyed-in-the-wool Acadian, a true believer in the cause, he was very much dyed in the green. He was a preservationist, committed to preserving not only his people's culture and identity, but also committed to the ideals of national parks. He knew this place like the back of his hand, every trail and track. His dream was to live and work here, and he fully expected to die here."

Ben and the congregation listened intently to every word but the expression "dyed in the green" stuck in Ben's mind.

Yes, he thought. *It is a calling. Low pay, long hours, the works. But I wouldn't do anything else and neither would most of the other men and women here today.*

Father Camus continued for a few more moments before beginning the formal service. He knew this was tearing Lucille apart and did not want to linger.

On signal, the organist began to play the selection of hymns Lucille had chosen for the service. Meant to be uplifting, they were no match for the weight of sorrow settling over the cathedral. Father Camus, with as much sensitivity as he could muster, rallied through the funeral ceremony, fighting back the tears he so easily could have shed. He had lost a true friend and was still overwhelmed by the violence of Michel's death. He dearly wanted to vent, to get it off his chest, but knew that Lucille and her family were struggling just to get through the day. He paused before the final benediction, drew a heavy breath, then proceeded to finish his sermon in French.

Nodding to Ben, he walked down the stairs leading from the altar and met the pallbearers, now assembled on either side of Michel. Father Camus stood over the casket; raising his right hand, he made the sign of the cross, whispering a final farewell to Michel.

On cue, Ben and the other pallbearers positioned the coffin in the centre of the aisle as the funeral march reverberated from the massive organ. Slowly they wheeled Michel's coffin toward the front doors. It was the first chance Ben had to see the crowd that had packed the cathedral, the pews bulging with friends and family. There was not a dry eye in the place.

Row upon row of uniformed officers of all stripes completed the picture.

The pallbearers proceeded into the front porch and under the direction of the undertaker, shouldered the casket off the trolley. Walking slowly out into the ocean air, a light flurry of snow floated down from the heavy clouds covering the coastline. After placing the casket in the hearse, they lined both sides of the steps, forming an honour guard as the family came out of the cathedral.

Lucille was holding up, but just barely. She walked slowly down the steps and as she passed Ben, held out her hand to him. He grasped it, bent over and kissed her on the cheek. Fighting back the tears, she reluctantly let go and walked back to the waiting limousine.

Lucille had decided that Michel's body would be taken to

a crematorium and his ashes spread over the Highlands at French Mountain but today there would be a private ceremony with the family.

Slowly, the hearse and limo moved onto the main road and drove away as a crowd of onlookers gathered outside the cathedral.

The local Royal Canadian Legion had graciously offered its facility to the funeral-goers so the throng of people gradually made their way back to their vehicles and proceeded toward Chéticamp.

When Kate, Ben and the other park wardens arrived at the Legion, it was packed to overflowing. While the others jostled their way to the bar, Kate and Ben claimed standing room next to an open window at the back of the hall and stood silently with their thoughts, relishing the breeze blowing in from the ocean.

The snow was melting as it hit the pavement, but the wind had shifted to the northeast and Ben knew colder weather was on its way.

The last few days had been a blur for them, what with getting the funeral details organized amongst the myriad of service organizations that had wanted to be a part of the farewell to Michel. The local officers had been their salvation, arranging lodging and meals for more than two hundred fellow officers who had travelled from as far away as British Columbia and Montana.

Michel was one of their own and his violent death had attracted attention from comrades in conservation, protection and police organizations across the country. The outpouring of sympathy was staggering.

Now, as he stood there, a fresh breeze blowing in his face, Ben had a chance to look back and consider the magnitude of events leading up to this. The din of chatter faded as he focused his thoughts. He scrolled through the bullets of information, second-guessed his actions, but was still convinced Michel had been set up. No matter what he might have done, John Donald was playing a wild card that Ben never, in his wildest dreams, could have imagined. He had seriously underestimated the vengeance seething in John Donald.

Kate knew Ben was tearing himself apart but there was nothing she could say to help the situation. Every time she tried, he lashed back at her. She knew it was something he had to deal with alone, even though she felt it was tearing everyone else up as well. There would be some benefit if all of the wardens supported each other but Ben was too proud, *or too stubborn*, to share his feelings.

Seeing Joe, Norm and Cole standing in a corner, Kate pointed them out to Ben.

"Do you want to join them?" she suggested.

"Not now," he said. "You can go if you want."

Kate shook her head and turned to leave.

"Hey," said Ben, touching her arm. "I know I haven't been easy to live with these past few days. Just give me some time."

Kate nodded and made her way over to the others.

As the crowd in the Legion recounted their stories, Ben made his way silently toward the exit. He planned to go back to the warden office but not having seen Yvan at the Legion, he decided to take a detour and drop into the RCMP detachment. As he walked into the office, Yvan was just getting off the phone. He looked devastated.

"What's up?" said Ben. "You look like shit."

"That was the lab in Halifax," Yvan started. "They've been trying to run the DNA sample of the blood on John Donald's clothes, but are having complications."

"What do you mean by complications?"

"Well, it looks like they won't be able to get anything conclusive from the samples we brought in."

"What?" Ben shouted. "Without that connection to tie John Donald to the crime scene, we'll lose the case."

"Well, there's still other circumstantial evidence," said Yvan, not lost on the fact this was a major blow to their case.

"Fuck!" Ben slammed the office counter. "We're going to lose this." He turned and stormed out of the office.

Yvan watched through the window as Ben drove away. Yvan was as furious with himself as he was with the news from the crime lab. He knew the Crown prosecutor would want to drop the charges unless they came up with more evidence, but they had been unable to extract statements from either Gerald or John Donald Moores, and they had not found the murder weapon. He knew the circumstantial evidence was probably not enough to convict the two men of murder and at most, the Crown would propose reducing the charges to manslaughter.

Ben drove through town with tears streaming down his face. As he crossed the Chéticamp River bridge, he slammed the gas pedal to the floor and the truck roared through the Rigwash.

He was tearing himself apart, thinking of how to connect the Moores to Michel's death, but was coming up empty. He drove as far as French Mountain then pulled off near the Veteran's monument.

Sitting alone in the truck, he felt the weight of the world on his shoulders.

He knew Kate felt he had to rein in his emotions, but Michel's death had to be avenged. They had to figure out a way to bring the Moores to justice.

He owed it to Michel and he owed it to Lucille and her family.

Getting out of the truck, Ben walked over to the veteran's monument.

He and Kate had always liked this location, particularly the inscription on the monument dedicated to the veterans who had died overseas.

"They will never know the beauty of this place,
See the seasons change, enjoy nature's chorus.
All we enjoy we owe to them, men and women who
Lie buried in the earth of foreign lands and in
the seven seas. Dedicated to the memory of
Canadians who died overseas in the service of their
country and so preserved our heritage."

Ben stood in silence as he recited the lines from memory, the wind cutting into his face, forming tears in the corners of his eyes.

All we enjoy we owe to them.

Walking back to the truck, he sat motionless in the cab.

We owe it to them.

CHAPTER 57

MUCH TO THE chagrin of the people of northern Cape Breton, Judge McIntosh's courtroom in Chéticamp was off limits to the general public. The preliminary hearing to assess the evidence against John Donald and Gerald Moores would only be open to Michel's family and the officers involved in the case. But that did not dispel the eagerness of the locals to make their presence felt in an overwhelming show of contempt for the Moores. Their apathy had transformed into rage over the death of one of their own. Despite the fact that he was a park warden, Michel Aucoin was an Acadian, a local boy who may have crossed the line to work for the park, but someone who also crossed back every day of his working life to help build the community he had grown up in.

Traffic was lined up along both sides of the road leading to the temporary courthouse, once again set up in the local community centre. The parking lot exploded with activity as the RCMP van carrying John Donald and Gerald Moores inched its way toward the rear doors of the building.

Inside, Christopher Irons was concerned about the safety of his clients, but not as much as he was concerned about his own. He had underestimated the volatility of the Acadian community and the basic mistrust of the English that lurked beneath the surface. For as much as this was an attack on a local, it was soon contorted into just another example of the conflict between the French and English. Even the crowd was somewhat physically split along linguistic and ethnic lines, with the Acadians on one side of the road and the predominantly English-speaking fishermen from Pleasant Bay lining the opposite side of the street.

Today, however, their strongest commonality was the

outright contempt for John Donald and Gerald Moores. They had had to contend with these two hooligans long enough and no one appreciated the bad name they were giving to their communities. As the van carrying the Moores passed by, a few people in the crowd starting pelting rocks at the vehicle.

John Donald and Gerald Moores sat in the back, facing each other, their backs to the wall. John Donald barely reacted when the rocks smashed against the truck but Gerald almost jumped out of his skin. John Donald looked across at him with silent contempt.

"Don't worry about it," he said to Gerald, seeing his cousin for the first time as a liability.

"Stick together. We're family."

"Some family," said Gerald. He could sense the loathing in John Donald and looked away, focusing on the rear door of the van. He thought they were in way over their heads and he saw no way out of the predicament. Gerald was convinced that John Donald would do him in if he so much as hinted at pleading guilty, which is what he thought they probably should do if they wanted to live to see the outside again. Already he was convincing himself that he wouldn't walk the Cape Breton beaches with his girlfriend for a long, long time. It was so stupid, just pure fluke that Aucoin had caught them. And what of it? They could have run, hell they could have just swallowed a poaching charge. It wasn't as if they had never been in that boat before.

But that night, something was different.

Gerald couldn't understand why John Donald was so intent on hunting at Presqu'ile when they knew it was a regular stakeout spot for the wardens. Sure, Matthews and the other wardens were over in Ingonish, but John Donald had to know that Aucoin would follow them into the park.

The RCMP van wheeled around and backed toward the doors of the courthouse, surrounded by eight Mounties on foot. While the other officers stood guard, one of the Mounties opened the rear doors and pulled the shackled suspects into the daylight.

For a moment there was silence as the crowd caught their first glimpse of the pair, then the stillness was broken by a yell from one of the local fisherman.

"The two of you will roast for this," he shouted at the top of his lungs, starting a cascade of catcalls.

The locals had converged after the van had gone by, English and Acadian mixing to form a wave of onlookers, unanimous in their heckling. No one dared to show any sign of support, and John Donald's few accomplices who were interspersed in the crowd didn't dare breathe a word. Maurice Chiasson moved with the flow, casting his eyes downward whenever anyone noticed and pointed him out to companions.

Hauling Gerald and John Donald from the back of the van, the Mounties pushed the Moores in through the doors of the courthouse as the throng swarmed around the rear of the building. Luc, who was court officer for the day, met them in the porch, his eyes burning through John Donald. He approached him, his chest pushing up against John Donald's, his face looking straight down into his unwavering eyes. Christopher Irons was trying to reach his clients, but was momentarily blocked by two giant constables.

Luc pushed his face into John Donald's to emphasize his contempt. "We should throw you two fuckers out to the pack," he said in a low voice, inaudible to Irons, who was now almost directly behind him.

John Donald was unmoved, but Gerald, now in the lion's den, was looking to Irons for some relief. Irons tried to push past the Mounties to talk to the Moores, but Luc turned, blocking his passage, and with undiminished contempt looked at Irons.

"And you too," he said, the inference not lost on Irons.

Not taking his eyes off the lawyer, Luc pushed past and back into the main courtroom.

Irons looked at the Moores and waved them forward past the Mounties and into a side room, a makeshift counsel chamber, its windows covered inside and out with plywood. A single light dimly lit the interior.

As Irons closed the door behind them, John Donald was on him immediately.

"What the fuck do I pay you for? Did you see the way they brought us into this shithole? Are you gonna let them do whatever the hell they want with us or are you going to speak up for our rights?"

His voice was rising nearly to the point of breaking. This was a different situation than the other times he'd been here. His intensity only added to the strain as Gerald, now sitting in a plain metal chair against the wall, started to shake.

Irons tried to calm John Donald down. "This is a different kettle of fish, John Donald," said Irons in a calm, almost cocky tone. "And yes, this is what you pay me for. And you can keep shooting off your face or, for once, you can shut up and let me do my job. Because if I don't do it well, damn well," he emphasized, "you won't have to worry about getting a lawyer in the future."

The points were sinking in and for once, John Donald was silent and Gerald was starting to calm down.

"Besides," Irons continued, "I think they've lost the use of the DNA evidence."

This got John Donald's attention. "What do you mean?"

Irons shifted over and stared John Donald in the eyes. "I mean I know someone at the crime lab and they appear to have screwed up the DNA sampling. They have nothing to tie you directly to Aucoin."

Gerald Moores finally comprehended this last piece of detail and perked up. "You mean, we've won the case?"

"Not yet," Irons replied, "but it's damn close."

John Donald was curious and pressed on. "What do you mean, you know someone at the lab?"

"Never mind," said Irons. "Let's just say I was owed a favour."

"Some favour," said Gerald.

John Donald was waiting for the other shoe to drop. He had dealt with lawyers, and Irons in particular, long enough to know there was a catch.

"So what's in this for you?"

"I get to keep a client who gives me lots of business."

"Go on," said John Donald, realizing Irons was up to something.

"And," said Irons, "a partner."

"What do you mean a partner?"

"I mean it's common practice to archive DNA samples. You never know when they might surface again. And murder charges don't fall under the statute of limitations. This is just a preliminary hearing to assess whether or not the Crown has enough evidence to proceed to trial. If you get off with this today, they could recharge you tomorrow."

John Donald got up and walked behind Irons. He was cool to the notion of being a partner with Irons. He didn't trust lawyers and now he was even more suspicious.

"So what do you want?" he challenged Irons.

The lawyer didn't flinch and was about to lay out his conditions to John Donald when the door opened and a Mountie informed Irons that the judge had called for them. They filed from the room amid the din of voices.

Irons took his seat at the front table and motioned for the Moores to sit next to him.

Yvan stared across the courtroom at the trio. He had a bad feeling about what was coming and couldn't bring himself to look at Kate, Ben and the other wardens sitting in the first row.

Judge McIntosh entered and walked up to the front as Yvan went through the formalities.

"All rise. This preliminary hearing is now in session, Judge Stewart McIntosh presiding."

The court clerk passed the dossier to the judge, and McIntosh opened it and studied the contents.

The courtroom fell silent.

"We are here today," said the judge, "to conduct a preliminary hearing into the charges proposed by the Crown."

Pulling the information off the top, Judge McIntosh cleared his throat and began to read, looking with disdain at the Moores.

"John Donald and Gerald Moores," he began. "You are charged with the first degree murder of Michel Joseph Aucoin, a park warden and a peace officer of Cape Breton Highlands National Park."

Judge McIntosh hesitated to let the significance of the charges sink in. While not everyone would know that park wardens were peace officers under the law, the consequences of murdering a peace officer were not lost on anyone present.

"Do you understand the charges?" he asked.

Christopher Irons stood up.

"We do, Your Honour."

"And how do your clients plead, Mr. Irons?"

Christopher Irons slowly adjusted his braces before answering, giving an impression of indifference to the matter at hand.

"Not guilty, Your Honour." His voice was tainted by a smugness that betrayed his contempt for the judge.

Irons sat down and whispered something to John Donald Moores, who nodded and smiled at the defence lawyer. Irons glanced around the courtroom, his grin fading as he caught the stolid looks of the officers. Quickly he turned around and brushed his hand through his long hair, preening himself for the event.

Judge McIntosh sighed heavily, exasperated that nothing came easy anymore. The guiltiest men would never admit to petty theft, let alone murder. In this day and age there was no honesty or honour. Everything was a battle. Yet this was one battle he was prepared to wage to the bitter end.

Through his years, he had watched Michel Aucoin evolve as an officer of the law. He had taken care to encourage him in subtle ways that could not be construed as a conflict of interest. He gently nudged him through his first cases, patiently listening to the evidence he presented. Although he didn't know him personally, Stewart McIntosh had a sense that Michel was a man of honesty and honour, the type of young man he would have wanted for a son.

From time to time, when the court docket demanded he carry proceedings over into a second day, he would choose to stay overnight instead of making the long drive back to Sydney. Sometimes, sitting near the window at his favourite restaurant, he would see Michel Aucoin and his family strolling hand in hand along the harbour. His wife, dressed in a pretty flowered pattern, always seemed to have a smile on her face.

He would sit there and reminisce, turning his face away from the other patrons, tears creeping to the corners of his eyes. He was separated from his own wife of twenty-five years, still unable to believe a marriage that had endured for so long could suddenly dissolve into nothing. But deep down, he knew it was not a sudden gesture, but rather one that had evolved with his frequent absences from home. Being a circuit judge, he had paid the price for levelling out justice to the people.

Margaret had been exceptionally tolerant of the lifestyle, but rebelled when his desire for the bottle seemed to outgrow his desire to be home with her. They had no children, for which he was thankful in light of the divorce, yet as he watched Michel and his family walking through town, he was determined that having children would have made the difference and kept them together.

He would watch Michel, Lucille and Jean Marc until he couldn't do it any longer, excusing himself and hurrying to the washroom where, he was forced to face his own reflection in the mirror. It was a face he wasn't always proud of, a face of aging less than gracefully, wrinkled and gnarled from soul-searching and tough decisions, a face of punishment rendered severely. It was also a face of growing intolerance for serious abuses of basic human values.

But Stewart McIntosh had to frequently remind himself that his was also a face of compassion, of discretion when appropriate, a face of fairness and equity, and most importantly, a face of justice delivered.

In that regard, he was different from lawyers like Christopher Irons, a man who manipulated the system to suit his own ends, gaining the freedom of clients who should be locked away. The two of them represented opposite ends of the spectrum and despite Iron's apparent affluence, Stewart McIntosh knew in his heart that he had followed the nobler path. Despite his own shortcomings, he could still look at himself in the mirror and find more than a glimmer of respect for the man he saw. He wondered if criminal lawyers like Christopher Irons could say the same.

Looking up from his files at John Donald and Gerald Moores, he cast his eyes around the courtroom at the people he had spent his life serving, and finally focused on Lucille Aucoin, surrounded by her family. McIntosh was convinced he would indeed deliver justice.

Turning to the Crown prosecutor, he nodded.

"You may proceed, Mr. McIsaac."

"Thank you, Your Honour," said Sean, getting up from his seat to address the court.

This was new ground for the Crown prosecutor. He had never dealt with anything so serious, but he was determined to conduct a thorough and precise prosecution, confident that as long as the DNA evidence held up to scrutiny, he could get these charges past the preliminary hearing and into the criminal courts.

As a matter of formality, Sean McIsaac had chosen to wear his black robe for the preliminary hearing. Neatly pressed and spotless, it rolled off his shoulders, only his feet and calves visible beneath its length. His demeanour was professional and he carried himself with an air of seriousness. In his opening remarks, he was sensitive to the gathering of family surrounding Lucille Aucoin, and indeed sensitive to her need for compassion. He was not about to sensationalize a brutal murder that needed no additional media attention.

He explained the circumstances of the case, pointing out the Crown's intention to prove, beyond a reasonable doubt, that Michel Aucoin had been murdered by John Donald Moores, and that Gerald Moores had been a co-conspirator. He provided a synopsis of what the Crown witnesses were prepared to attest to, and the significance of the circumstantial and direct evidence that would show a clear link between the deceased and the accused men.

As he listened, Gerald Moores began to fully comprehend the gravity of his predicament. Ashen-faced, he stared at the floor, looking up occasionally to catch the snarling frown of his cousin. He knew he just didn't have it in him to go the distance; he knew John Donald could easily sense that failing. It was a trait that John Donald had exploited in him from the beginning and he was only now admitting to it as his options to avoid the rest of his life behind bars were becoming increasing clear.

Gerald's most logical choice would have been to confess to being an accomplice to murder and hope for a plea bargain. Surely, Irons could work out a deal. The repercussions of that choice would be a life of looking over his shoulder and waiting for John Donald, but he would have a clearer conscience. But his silence had led him to this moment and his fate was now in the hands of Christopher Irons.

As Sean McIsaac finished his introductory statements, Christopher Irons sat with a matter-of-fact expression on his face. He appeared to be waiting for something else to happen, a predetermined event that was lost on everyone else in the courtroom.

Judge McIntosh waited briefly for the defence lawyer to make his case then asked, "Mr. Irons, are you planning to make an introductory statement?"

"Yes, Your Honour," said Irons. Raising his hand, he added, "a moment please." He turned and grinned as Giselle hurried into the court and made her way to Yvan, seated at the end of the Crown prosecutor's table. Passing him an envelope, she leaned down and whispered in his ear. Yvan pulled a paper from the envelope, quickly scanning its contents, his mouth dropping as he did so.

Sean McIsaac looked toward him and nodded as if to ask what was up. Yvan passed him the paper, which he read carefully. The defence lawyer was about to stand up again when the Crown prosecutor interrupted.

"Your Honour, may I approach the bench?" said Sean.

"Yes, you may."

Turning to the defence lawyer, Judge McIntosh added, "Mr. Irons?"

Christopher Irons slowly rose to his feet and also approached the judge.

Sean McIsaac spoke softly. "Your Honour, I would like to ask for a brief adjournment."

Judge McIntosh sensed that something serious was transpiring.

"What's happened, Sean?" asked Stewart McIntosh.

The Crown prosecutor had a look of alarm in his eyes.

"The forensics lab has somehow corrupted the DNA evidence. We're lost without it."

"How could that be?" said McIntosh, noticing the defence lawyer casting a quick glance at John Donald Moores.

"Counsellor?" he said to Irons. "Pay attention. This is a serious matter."

Christopher Irons turned to face Stewart McIntosh's growing scowl.

"We're not sure," said Sean. "We will have to talk to the lab and see what's happened."

"Well, if we continue with the preliminaries and cannot move these proceedings to a criminal trial, John Donald Moores is a free man," said the judge, confirming McIsaac's worst fears.

"What are our options?" Sean asked.

"You could request a stay of proceedings," the judge advised, contemplating the situation. "Sort this out with the RCMP and reinstitute proceedings when you are confident with your case against the Moores. Right now, without the DNA, you may forfeit this case."

Judge McIntosh directed his attention to Christopher Irons.

"Sir, were you aware of the information from the crime lab?"

Caught off guard by the judge's insinuation, Irons stammered a response then regained his composure. "No," he said emphatically. "No, Your Honour. I'm not sure what you're referring to."

Judge McIntosh waved off Iron's comment and turned back to the Crown prosecutor.

"Let's resume proceedings," said the judge.

Sean returned to his table and quickly considered his options. Despite his disappointment at the notion of letting John Donald and Gerald Moores walk away, he knew that he needed a solid case to get a conviction.

"Your Honour, it is my duty to inform you that the Crown is not prepared to proceed with the charges at this point in time and we are requesting a stay of proceedings."

A gasp spread throughout the courtroom.

"It has just come to our attention," he continued in a solemn voice, "that a key piece of evidence will not be forthcoming, specifically the DNA evidence that was to be provided by the RCMP crime laboratory in Halifax."

Lucille Aucoin crumpled as she heard the news.

McIntosh stumbled for words then slammed the dossier closed, scattering papers across the floor of the courtroom, much to the amusement of Christopher Irons.

"Mr. McIsaac. How long will you need to clarify this situation and make a decision with respect to a continuation?"

"At this point, I really don't know, Your Honour."

"Very well, Mr. McIsaac," said the judge, frustrated at the turn of events. "I will see you back here once the Crown has got its act together. Mr. Irons, do you have any objections?"

"No, Your Honour," said Irons smugly. "But I do request that my clients be released at this time."

"Very well, Counsellor," said Judge McIntosh, realizing he had limited grounds to keep John Donald and Gerald Moores in jail. "Make arrangements with the clerk. They are released until this case resumes."

The small group in the courtroom erupted in a barrage of chatter as Ben, Kate and the other park wardens gathered around Lucille Aucoin.

Turning to the crowd, Judge McIntosh held up his hand.

"Before anyone leaves this court," he said, his voice booming through the hall. "I want to state clearly, for the record, there has been a terrible crime committed here. This community has lost a respected and committed citizen."

Looking directly at John Donald, who looked straight back at the judge, McIntosh continued. "In the fullness of time, I expect the perpetrators of this act to be brought before me and dealt with in the eyes of the law." With that, he got up from his chair and stormed out of the courtroom.

The crowd outside was chaotic as word of what happened inside spilled into the street. Christopher Irons and the Moores remained in their seats, nervously waiting for the crowd to dissipate, but it didn't happen.

The heckling started almost immediately and it took all of the RCMP to keep the crowd at bay while Irons dealt with the clerk and his clients scurried for the back door.

CHAPTER 58

IT WAS A typically windy day on French Mountain. A small group of close family and friends stood around Lucille Aucoin, who was holding a small container tight to her chest. Michel's parents stood next to her clinging to a small wreath bearing a photograph of Michel.

Emile Aucoin stood behind them, holding the family Bible. Bound in heavy black leather and emblazoned with the family name, it had been passed down through the generations for more than two centuries.

Lucille's parents held back their tears as they looked down at Jean Marc.

The sun was sinking lower in the western sky, turning the Highlands into a blaze of orange hues.

A piper in kilt and knitted sweater fought off the cold long enough to fill the pipes and work the bellows, playing a traditional Scottish air. Joe, Rose and Kate, standing back by the cars, held each other's hands.

Ben approached Lucille and held out his hand. Taking it, she followed him past the Veteran's monument onto the grassy slopes overlooking the Gulf. Jean Marc walked along behind, hand in hand with Michel's father. Michel's mother, looking years older, grasped Emile's hand as they followed along behind, stopping momentarily to place the small wreath at the base of the monument. Emile opened the Bible briefly to remind himself of the few lines he was to recite.

Ben stopped near the crest of the slope and took the urn from Lucille. Carefully he removed the lid and passed the container back to her. She turned to Jean Marc, who joined her in reciting the first line of the Acadian anthem. Slowly they held Michel's ashes aloft and poured. The ashes swirled in the breeze and floated seaward before an updraft scattered them skyward.

They were caught momentarily in a ray of sunlight, dancing along the ragged coast, before disappearing into the salt air.

Lucille spoke a few words in French, barely audible to the small group of onlookers. Emile quoted the Scripture, his deep voice challenging the wind to whip its meaning away. Jean Marc watched, teary-eyed. Lucille took his hand and, turning him around, walked him back to the waiting arms of his grandfather. Together they hugged and kissed, holding on to the memories, then walked arm in arm back to the waiting vehicles.

Joe held the car door for Lucille and Jean Marc. Michel's father sat in the driver's seat. Ben walked Kate, Rose and Joe back to their vehicle and opened the door for Kate to get in. As she did, Ben could hear a car approaching and looked up to see a black Mustang fly past. John Donald was at the wheel.

You ignorant bastard, he thought. *You have no shame.*

Joe caught Ben's stare as he got into the car and shook his head.

"He'll get his," said Joe.

"You're damn right," Ben vowed, getting into the car with the others.

They were about to drive away when Emile pulled up alongside and motioned to Ben to roll down his window. Emile looked serious and Ben wondered what was up.

"I have to talk to you," said Emile, biting his lip to hold back the tears. "Alone."

"Right now?" said Ben, glancing across the seat at Kate.

"No, not here," said Emile, "but as soon as we get back to town."

Ben looked to Kate.

"I'll go visit Lucille," she said. "I haven't really spoken to her much since all of this happened."

"Thanks," said Ben.

Turning back to Emile, Ben said, "We can talk at my house. Kate is going to see Lucille so we'll be alone."

CHAPTER 59

KATE GAVE LUCILLE'S family time to disperse before she made her way to the Aucoin house. Getting out of her car, she was looking forward to speaking with Lucille and finding out how she was doing. They were kindred spirits in a way, both strong, independent women who didn't take a backseat to anyone. They had instantly taken to each other and although they rarely found time to get together, when they did, their similar feelings on a number of issues strengthened their relationship.

Lucille was happy to see Kate at the door and welcomed her in with a huge embrace.

"Thanks so much for dropping by," she said. "I've had my fill of family. God love them but I need my space."

"I can come back later if you want," said Kate.

"No, no, I want to talk to you. I need to talk to you."

Lucille grabbed Kate's hand and led her to the kitchen table. "Sit. Please."

Kate sat down while Lucille filled the kettle and placed it on the stove.

"I need to keep busy," said Lucille, getting tea and cups out of the cupboard, methodically going through the motions as she spoke. "Jean Marc is next door, which is great, but the silence is overwhelming. I don't know if I will ever get used to this."

"Give it time," said Kate.

"Time? I seem to have plenty of that. But what I wanted was more time with Michel." She filled the teapot then placed it on the table to steep.

"I still can't believe what happened," said Kate. "And to Michel of all people."

"I don't know," said Lucille as she poured two cups of tea

and slid one across to Kate. "I had a bad feeling that night. I never liked it when Michel worked on his own but that was when he seemed to be in his element."

Kate raised her eyebrows.

"I think it's a common trait in the Warden Service," she said. "At least with the men."

Lucille smiled as she lost herself in the teacup.

"God, men can be so stubborn."

"Don't I know it," said Kate.

"I really didn't want him to go out that night. It was fine that he was staying at Ben's house but I didn't expect him to do any more patrols on his own after the last one he told me about."

Kate's interest was piqued.

"What do you mean, the last one?" she asked.

"Oh, there was a night when he was telling me about his thoughts on how the superintendent might be tied in to the big drug shipment that happened. Neither one of us thought Mr. Dickson was that type of a man but Michel wondered if John Donald was somehow using the superintendent's nephew to blackmail him."

"This is the first I've heard of all this," said Kate. "Go on."

"Well, Michel said he stopped Gerald Moores on the mountains one night. He was driving a van like the ones the drug smugglers used and the superintendent's nephew, JD, Jimmy Dickson, was in the van. Michel didn't think it was odd because Jimmy used to peddle dope back when they were in school together, so for Jimmy to be hanging out with Gerald Moores wasn't necessarily a surprise."

"I believe he mentioned stopping Gerald one night but I never heard the details," said Kate, pressing Lucille for more. "I do remember him saying something about the RCMP having some information for him that he forgot to pick up. I wonder what it was about?"

"I don't know," said Lucille. "I don't recall him mentioning it."

"Do you know if he mentioned Jimmy Dickson to Ben?" said Kate.

"I think so," said Lucille, trying to recall what Michel had said to her. "He was going to talk to Ben the day he stayed back, when you all went to Ingonish. Before he was..."
Lucille stumbled on the words.

"But we left early that day," said Kate. "I know they never spoke."

"Then I don't know," said Lucille, feeling distressed. "It's all just a blur right now."

"But it might be critical information, Lucille. Michel probably wrote it down in his notes. Do you know if he keeps his notebook at home?"

"Usually, but of course I don't know what happened to it after..." Tears were rolling down her cheek.

Realizing what she was doing, Kate stopped and reached across to Lucille.

"God, I'm sorry Lucille," she said, holding her hand. "I didn't mean to get you upset. That's not what I came here for."

Lucille stood to get a box of tissues on the counter as Kate gave her a big hug.

"I'm sorry. That's so not what I came here for," she said, holding on to Lucille as they both broke into tears.

"I know," said Lucille. "I know."

CHAPTER 60

KATE DROVE RIGHT past Ben's house when she saw Emile's vehicle was still in the driveway. She knew what she was looking for and probably knew where to find it.

Michel's personal effects had been returned to Lucille but Ben had stored Michel's files and notes in an evidence locker for safekeeping.

Sitting at Michel's desk, Kate carefully went through his notebooks and found the most recent entries. On the night he stopped Gerald Moores, Jimmy Dickson was indeed recorded as a passenger in the van. Michel had also been in contact with Luc and requested a timer. It was standard procedure when they were working alone.

Luc had apparently run a check on the vehicle but Michel had noted that he was unable to hear the complete radio transmission from the RCMP officer. The details of the vehicle check were missing from the notes but Michel had flagged the page with a reminder that Luc was planning to drop off the information the next day.

Kate scoured the remaining pages of the notebook but could find no further reference to the vehicle check.

Turning to Michel's files, she wondered aloud about where he would keep the information and whether or not he had ever received it. Kate thoroughly checked each file folder but found nothing.

It has to be here somewhere.

Opening the top drawer of Michel's desk, Kate thumbed through the contents then smiled as she noticed an envelope bearing the RCMP insignia.

Yes!

Inside was a CPIC report detailing the information about a

rental van bearing Nova Scotia licence R46392. The date and time of the report coincided with Michel's notes.

The van had been rented by one Louis Desaultiers, with Gerald Moores listed as an alternate driver. Kate wasn't entirely certain of the significance of the information but knew she had to talk with Ben.

Taking the CPIC report, Kate returned Michel's files to the evidence locker and left.

CHAPTER 61

BEN WAS BARELY in the door when Emile arrived. The house was dark and cold as it was buffeted by a suête spilling out of the Highlands.

Ben flicked the light switch but there was no response.

"It's a good thing Kate is going back to her cabin for the night," he said. "Power's off."

"Happens all the time in these winds," said Emile.

"I better get a fire started." Ben went into the living room. Kneeling down by the woodstove, he opened the draft and front door of the stove. Grabbing a newspaper, he pulled it apart, balled it up and threw it on the old coals. Carefully he placed kindling on top and struck a match. The fire caught quickly, pulled up the flue by the howling winds outside.

Ben placed a large piece of rock maple on the pile then shut the doors, the flame reflecting through the glass plates casting an orange glow over the walls. The snapping of the kindling soon died down as the hardwood log blazed brightly.

Ben turned to his visitor, offering Emile the seat next to the stove.

Emile looked weary and weather-beaten. His hair was windblown and his suit was dishevelled. He had lost the infectious smile and had an air of apathy about him, finally resigned to the fact that Michel was dead and considering the very real possibility that no one would pay for what had happened.

Ben waited for him to speak, curious as to what Emile had on his mind.

"I have some information for you," Emile offered. "I'm hoping it will help sort this thing out."

Ben listened intently.

"I heard that the blood samples had been tampered with."

Ben was caught off guard.

"What do you mean, 'tampered with'?"

Emile waved him off. "That doesn't matter, in the great scheme of things. You are dealing with very corrupt people and you should not be surprised to find that the corruption permeates the justice system as well as the police force."

Ben wanted to interject but let Emile say his piece.

"That scoundrel, John Donald Moores, will get off unless you tie him to Michel's death. You need someone to give evidence against him, but the whole community is scared, despite the fact everyone believes he alone is responsible for what happened to Michel."

Emile's face glowed in the firelight, his eyes gaining intensity as he slowly unravelled the details. Outside, the suête growled through the eaves and pummelled the bungalow, forcing its way down the chimney, churning the fire's fury. The grit and gravel carried by the gale-force winds etched grooves into the cedar siding, sand-blasting the house layer by layer, the sound accentuating the agony on Emile's face as he started to peel back the layers of a story he desperately wanted to erase from his memory.

"You remember this?" he asked Ben, showing him the tattoo on his right hand.

Ben nodded.

"I got this in Dorchester," Emile said. "I can still feel the stinging of the needle as one of the prison guards held my hand flat against a block of concrete."

Ben winced at the thought.

"Dorchester was everything it was rumoured to be," Emile continued. "There were fourteen other men with me on the bus the day they took us there. We were all handcuffed to the seats in front of us and our legs were shackled to the seat posts. The others talked boldly about doing time and laughed when the driver and guards joked about how we would soon be crying the prison blues.

"Me, I was scared shitless.

"I was a kid, caught up in a small drug deal, and thought for a first offence I'd end up with a suspended sentence. Instead I got ratted out in a plea bargain and took the rap for the whole thing.

"My mother was shocked to think that her son was a drug dealer and wept throughout the trial. I was devastated about letting her down. I was always her pride and joy. The only consolation was that my father wasn't alive to see me chained up like a dog."

"So who ratted you out?" said Ben.

"It was John Donald and Gerald Moores," said Emile. "I pleaded with the legal aid lawyer to let me tell my version of events, but he told me I couldn't testify in my own defence. He said he requested the judge to sentence me to two years less a day to keep me out of the federal penitentiary because I was just a kid, but the judge rejected the request. I was looking at doing time in a maximum-security prison and the Moores were going to walk free.

"I had hoped to be sent to Sydney, an easy day's drive for my mother, but now I might as well have been across an ocean. I had never been off the island. In my worst nightmares I never expected to end up in Dorchester."

Emile looked haggard, as if he had revealed the depths of his soul in the retelling of the story. Beads of sweat dotted his forehead, dripping down into his bloodshot eyes. Mechanically, he pulled at his left hand, the sensation of his missing fingers still guiding his brain.

Emile continued to recount the details.

"I couldn't figure out initially how John Donald and Gerald were involved, but it turns out they didn't get off entirely scot free. At least John Donald didn't. He and Gerald got pulled in for some other things, even more serious than mine. I don't know exactly what happened but Gerald and I crossed paths when I was close to getting out on parole. One day, we were left on our own in the prison yard. I was ready to stick a knife into him but he swore that John Donald was the one who turned me in.

"Turns out, Gerald was released on good behaviour not long after I got out, and John Donald somehow managed to get sprung before he did much time. Still, he supposedly blamed Gerald for it all.

"Anyway, I had lots of time to think in prison and there were lots of stories. I heard them all and finally started to connect the dots. Of course, there was John Donald and Gerald, a guy named Louis Desaultiers, who became a famous salvager but somehow later got tied into the Montreal drug scene, and a young legal aid lawyer, Christopher Irons, who just happened to be the legal aid lawyer assigned to my case. I know there are others but I'm not sure who they all are. To this day, it drives me crazy."

Emile looked up into Ben's face.

"I swore when I got the chance I would make them pay for what happened to me. If I did this might never have happened to Michel."

"That was a long time ago, Emile," said Ben. "Not much can be done about it now."

"I know. There's nothing I can do to get back the time I lost in Dorchester. But I don't intend to let them get away with murder," said Emile.

"So what can we do?" said Ben.

"I was hoping we might help each other."

"In what way?"

"Well, I think we both know some of the pieces but it might take two of us to put the puzzle together."

Ben pondered the situation. He knew he had to sort out a few more details before they would be in a position to go after John Donald. Inwardly he felt he could trust Emile but he sensed there was still something the carpenter was holding back. This wasn't just a case of a vendetta from years past. Emile had made peace with himself on that score.

"I think I know where you are coming from, Emile, but you could be getting in way over your head and I'd hate to see you drawn into this any further."

"I'm already in further than you know, Ben, and after what happened with Michel, there is no turning back for me. Either with you or without you, there will be payback. I'll see to that."

"I understand. But promise me that if we share information, you will leave it up to the RCMP and the wardens to deal with this?"

"Fair enough. But if John Donald Moores walks away from this, I will be waiting for him. And I am a man of my word." He held out his hand.

"What I can't figure is who is running the show?" said Ben, grasping the carpenter's gnarled palm. He started to relate what he knew about the people involved.

"Irons and the Moores are obviously in cahoots along with Maurice. The drug angle pulls in Desaultiers, and somehow Dickson is connected. But what's the connection? How do we draw it out in the open?"

"Well, first off, these guys are all about the same age," said Emile. "If you think about it, they are all in their early forties, even Irons. Maurice and John Donald were all in school together at roughly the same time. Gerald Moores is maybe a bit younger, about Michel's age actually."

"Maybe that's it then," said Ben. "Maybe Michel knew something or maybe there's some legacy of bad blood from those earlier years."

"Knowing John Donald," said Emile, "it could just be payback for catching him poaching deer and embarrassing him in court. Or perhaps Michel was in the wrong place at the wrong time."

"I don't buy that," said Ben. "This was no coincidence. Moores set him up and got him out there. He knew we were gone to Ingonish and would have suspected Michel was working alone. He probably figured there was a pretty good chance that Michel would be holed up at my place for the night. I'm sure he had it planned."

Emile nodded.

"I wouldn't put it past him, but either way, he's going to pay for this."

"So is there anything else you haven't told me?" said Ben.

Emile looked down at his hands.

"I haven't told you that I intended to use you," he said, hesitating as he picked his words carefully. "From the moment I met you, I could tell you were going to set this place on fire. We needed an outsider's perspective, a fresh set of eyes. I knew that a persistent person could soon uncover the real John Donald Moores. It wasn't rocket science, but no one ever really tried."

Emile pointed at Ben with his good hand. "I knew you would. I could tell you cared," he said. "And P'tit Pierre knew too, but everyone was so used to turning a blind eye. It took the strength of my niece to show him it had to start somewhere."

Ben looked up, surprised at this admission.

"Marielle?"

"Yes," said Emile.

"To be honest," said Ben, "I was never sure if she was watching out for us or keeping an eye on us for someone else."

"Oh, she was watching out for you," Emile offered. "But I told her to be careful. I couldn't let them hurt her."

"Emile? Was it you who took out Maurice at the fish plant?"

"I had to. Maurice is a dangerous man. He would have followed through on his threat. There was no way I would let that happen."

"But did he know it was you? Weren't you scared of what he might do?"

"Oh, he knows it was me. I made it clear in no uncertain terms that if he touched a hair on Marielle or ever came near anyone in my family again, it would be the last thing he ever did. I stopped being scared of people like Maurice Chiasson and John Donald Moores a long time ago. Most people along the coast would make away with them as soon as look at them. It's because of people like them that I ended up in that godforsaken place."

Emile smirked and held up his hand. "Besides, I didn't hurt him as bad as they hurt me."

Ben nodded. "So we know that Maurice, John Donald and Irons are all somehow tangled up in this. How do we tie them to Michel so they don't get away with murder?"

He looked into the fire before continuing.

"The RCMP figured Gerald might be the one who would break under pressure and give us what we needed. But he's so scared of John Donald, they don't figure he'll ever talk."

"I don't know," said Emile. "There might be a way to get to him. But we shouldn't put all of our eggs in one basket. I think our best bet is to work more than one angle."

"What do you mean?"

"Maybe I can turn the screws a little tighter on Gerald to get him to talk. You could focus on the connection with the superintendent. I don't understand that one."

"I've been wondering about that too," said Ben. "What's the connection?"

"I'm not sure. He and Desaultiers go back a long way, but I think they parted company long ago. The only thread that may be linking him to John Donald Moores is his nephew."

Ben looked at Emile. "Dickson's nephew? Who is that?"

"His name is Jimmy Dickson but everyone calls him JD. He's just a little fart of a guy, a few years younger than the rest of them. I believe he would also have been about Michel's age."

"So why do you think he's involved?"

"I don't know for sure but I've heard he peddles dope over on the Ingonish side. I just have a nagging feeling that he's somehow in the loop with the Moores and Maurice Chiasson."

Ben realized there was something familiar about the name.

"At John Donald's place, when we searched his garage, there was a jacket on the freezer," he recalled. "It had the initials JD on the collar. We assumed it was John Donald's but it was small, too small for either John Donald or Gerald. If your hunch is right, maybe it belonged to Jimmy Dickson. Maybe he is the connection and John Donald is using him in some way. I'll see if Yvan has any leads on how to find him, or I might have to go see the superintendent again. Either way, we have to get to him and see if we can pressure him into talking."

"You go see the superintendent," said Emile, getting up from his seat by the stove. "And I'll pay a visit to my old acquaintance."

CHAPTER 62

BEN WAS IN the superintendent's office early the next morning. He had been awake all night thinking about Emile's visit and the information Kate had discovered. Together they speculated that Jimmy Dickson was indeed the lynch pin that connected the Moores to Arnold Dickson, but they still had to find him.

Ben decided to get up early to drive to Ingonish. It was still dark when he rolled out of Petit Étang and made his way along the coast to French Mountain. The wind was out of the northeast, carrying a hint of snow with it. On the lee side of French Mountain, a solitary fishing boat was heading back toward Chéticamp, hugging the cliffs to avoid the sudden squalls.

The top of French Mountain already had its first dusting of snow and the little lakes had caught over with a thin layer of ice. Ben observed a single moose on a small bog near Benjie's Lake, but saw no other signs of wildlife. The moose was a large bull and Ben stopped for a few minutes to watch it as it browsed along the edge of the forest, effortlessly raising and lowering its huge rack as it fed on willow buds.

Pleasant Bay was just coming to life as Ben descended Mackenzie Mountain and the Grande Anse Valley provided a momentary reprieve before heading up North Mountain and the reminder that winter was on its way.

Ben desperately wanted to resolve things before the impending winter storms put a damper on their chances of bringing John Donald and Gerald to justice. Everything would slow down on the coast as soon as the Highlands were buried under snow and he did not want to lose any momentum or let people forget what happened to Michel. If Dickson had information that could tie things together, he wanted to know it and he wanted to know it now. He hadn't called ahead because he thought Dickson might avoid him, even though Ben knew he was taking his chances walking into the superintendent's office unannounced again.

Dickson wasn't entirely surprised to see him, and he already seemed out of sorts, as if he had other things on his mind.

"Good morning, Matthews," he said. "That was terrible news about the court case. I hope the Mounties can pull this thing back on track."

"That's what I'm here about." Ben looked directly at Dickson. "I know what you've been holding back."

"I'm not holding anything back." Dickson was insulted by the insinuation.

"I know about your nephew Jimmy." Ben was pushing the truth to gauge Dickson's reaction. "I know he's involved with John Donald Moores."

The superintendent paused for a moment to collect himself, a pause that told Ben he had struck a nerve. Before Dickson could respond, Ben launched into his argument.

"I don't know all the details, but John Donald is somehow using Jimmy to get to you. I think what he's really been after is the connection to Louis Desaultiers and a bigger prize, but on the way he's intimated that you should keep us off his trail. To him, we're just flies in the ointment and a pain in his ass. We distract him from his real objective, and you're just the right person in the right place for him. You were or are an associate of Desaultiers, and Jimmy provides leverage to get to you."

Ben was stretching it, taking a shotgun approach and hoping something would hit the mark, but the superintendent was unrepentant.

"I told you, I haven't seen Louis Desaultiers for years. As for Jimmy, he's my sister's problem and has nothing to do with me. I really don't care who he hangs with or what happens to him as long as he leaves me out it."

Ben wasn't quite sure where to take the argument and was clutching at straws. He had nothing to confirm his theory that

Jimmy Dickson was in cahoots with the Moores, just a jacket with a set of initials that matched Jimmy's, or John Donald's. He hated to say it, but it could all just be a coincidence.

Ben's pause gave the superintendent ammunition for his own comeback. With the experience of an old warrior, he went in for the kill.

"Matthews, you are so far out of line I should fire you right on the spot, but you know what? I'm going to give you another chance. I know you've been under terrible pressure and Michel's death is no doubt weighing on your mind. I shouldn't have to remind you that you were warned about pushing people too far. Now look what's happened. One of your wardens is dead and you have no one to blame but yourself."

Ben could feel his anger rising but he knew Dickson was partly right, and he bit his lip. It took every bit of self-control he could muster to keep from launching at Dickson.

"You..." he said, stepping toward the superintendent. "When I'm finished with this, you'll regret those words. And if I find out you've been lying, I'll make sure everyone knows your role in this whole mess."

Ben stormed out, leaving Arnold Dickson alone in the office, a bead of sweat trickling down his back. His nephew had landed him in a bad spot, and now with Michel Aucoin's death, he could be dragged into the whole mess. Collateral damage, John Donald would say. If Jimmy knew what happened and talked about it, he could implicate them all. Jimmy never knew when to keep his mouth shut and would probably be dead right now if it weren't for Gerald Moores, who had apparently stepped in before to save him. John Donald would go berserk and do God knows what, if he thought Jimmy was shooting off his mouth again.

Somehow, Arnold Dickson had to get a message to Jimmy to keep quiet, but it wasn't going to be easy to do on this coast, without someone knowing about it.

Gerald Moores was probably his only option.

CHAPTER 63

GERALD MOORES WAS trying to lay low but time only seemed to make his situation worse. John Donald had not exactly endeared himself to the locals, and now he had brought an even greater amount of shame to the community. Most people realized that Gerald was guilty more by association than anything else, but he had lumped himself in with his cousin and was meted out the same social punishment and shunned at every turn.

Gerald's solution was to stay inside during the day and only venture out at night after most of the locals had gone home. He knew it meant that any retribution they might want to visit on him could happen without the benefit of daylight and potential witnesses, but he opted for the better odds that darkness offered.

Travelling was risky so he stayed close to home, relying on the few friends he had left to pick up supplies and any morsels of news that might let him know where he stood. He needed to put some time between the murder of Michel Aucoin and the collective memories of people along the coast.

John Donald's plan to use Jimmy Dickson had become more of a liability than anything else; while he served as leverage to pressure Dickson to connect them to Louis Desaultiers, the loss of the third van had not been something the bikers from Montreal were likely to turn a blind eye to. And Jimmy had a nasty habit of speaking up at the wrong time and could take them all down with him.

Although Gerald and John Donald's relative isolation on the Cape Breton coast was a reprieve from retribution at this point, he knew that the distance between them wouldn't make much difference in the long run. Gerald was convinced it was only a matter of time before someone from the bike gang paid them a visit. Waiting for the other shoe to drop kept him on edge, not knowing what or who to expect, or when it might happen.

Gerald drove his old pickup into the darkened carport and got out, disgusted that the light had burnt out again. He needed supplies and his short list of allies had dwindled to zero as anybody who helped him also bore the brunt of the community's anger. Getting things on his own increased his vulnerability but it was do or die, and he had to eat.

Walking around the truck, he opened the passenger door and pulled out two bags of groceries. Turning around, he was caught off guard when the carport light came on and he was face to face with John Donald.

His cousin did not look impressed.

"What the hell do you want?" Gerald asked.

"Now, Gerald," said John Donald. "That's no way to treat family. I just thought I should pay you a little visit to remind you where your allegiances lie."

"Allegiances? Right."

"Right. I shouldn't have to remind you that we're both in this together. If I go down, you go down."

"You think I don't know that? Down is the only direction we're heading anyway."

"This will blow over," John Donald reassured him. "With Jimmy out of the way and Irons taking care of the DNA samples, you and I are the only ones that matter. As long as you don't spill your guts, we'll be fine."

"Fine? I don't think so. At this point I'm just happy to be alive."

"And you will stay that way, as long as we keep this to ourselves. Remember, we're family. Blood is thicker than water, as they say. No one will get hurt."

"Like Jimmy?" said Gerald. "Christ, he was on our side."

"That was different. Jimmy screwed up."

"But Jimmy gave you the connection to Dickson and Desaultiers. You never would have made that on your own."

"That doesn't matter now. That's water under the bridge. What matters now is that, unlike Jimmy, you keep your mouth shut. Over time, this will blow over and things will get back to normal."

"Right," said Gerald. "I doubt things will ever get back to normal."

Turning to open the door to his house, Gerald fumbled for his keys. When he turned back around, John Donald was nowhere to be seen.

"Good riddance," said Gerald, unlocking the door and stepping inside.

Reaching for the light switch, he was surprised when it also didn't turn on.

"Great," he said, walking into the darkened kitchen and striking a match to a candle on the windowsill. As his eyes adjusted to the dim light, he placed the grocery bags on the counter and began to put things away before noticing the candle flame flicker. Sensing a light breeze moving through the kitchen, Gerald walked over to the sliding glass door leading to an outside deck. It was slightly ajar so he pushed it shut, certain he had locked the latch before leaving the house earlier in the evening.

When he turned around, Emile was waiting for him.

Displaying an agility that belied his age, Emile swiftly put Gerald in a powerful headlock that forced him to his knees. Gerald was no match for the wiry carpenter and deprived of air, started to collapse in Emile's arms. Feeling no resistance, Emile loosened his grip, allowing Gerald to look at his attacker.

"I'm not going to hurt you," Emile said, relaxing his grip slightly, but still maintaining control of Gerald. "If you listen to me, this will be easier on you. Do you understand?"

Pulling air into his lungs, Gerald managed a weak "Yes."

"That's better," said Emile. "Now pay careful attention to what I have to say."

CHAPTER 64

BEN WAS TEARING himself apart as he drove back to Chéticamp. He knew that if he couldn't make the connection between Jimmy Dickson and John Donald, his only options were to find the second gun or set Moores up again and catch him red-handed with the weapon. He knew John Donald wouldn't take the chance of having the gun with him and Ben was convinced it was stashed somewhere along the highway.

But where?

As he made his way across French Mountain, the sun was just beginning to set.

Pulling into the Veteran's monument lookoff, he parked the truck and contemplated his options.

Above the treeline he could see three black dots working their way across the few bare patches left on the open slopes. Taking out his binoculars to get a better look, he focused on a large female black bear accompanied by twin cubs, likely born this past spring and now looking for a place to hibernate for the winter. He watched them for a few minutes as they foraged, then he continued scanning the slopes falling away to the Trail.

Closer to the highway he noticed a pair of snowshoe hares chasing one another before disappearing into the bush. A moment later they resurfaced on the opposite side of the road. Ben stared aimlessly at the rabbits, his mind focused on finding the gun.

Pulling out of the lookoff, he took his foot off the gas pedal, put the truck in neutral and let gravity pull the pickup downslope toward Corney Brook.

Suddenly he pulled over.

That's it.

Jumping out of the truck, he ran into the ditch and pulled

aside some dead grass and small bushes to reveal the opening to a culvert that crossed the highway. Getting down on his hands and knees, he peered inside.

Running back to the truck, he continued along the coast toward Chéticamp. At Presqu'ile he pulled off the road and parked. Carefully, he checked every culvert opening on both sides of the road, but found nothing.

Frustrated, he made his way back to the truck, sorting out the possibilities in his mind.

John Donald would have had the gun when he stopped, so he either picked it up on his way to Presqu'ile or somewhere else along the coast. He always seemed to go as far as French Mountain before turning around.

Ben smiled to himself as he started the truck and headed to French Mountain. Stopping at the lookoff by the Veteran's monument, he got out and walked to the edge of the highway, then followed the guardrail a few yards south. At the closest culvert, he jumped the guardrail and made his way down into the bushes. Pulling back the grass, he peered inside.

Nothing.

Climbing back up to the highway, he crossed to the other end of the pipe.

This must have been where those rabbits crossed.

Bending down, he pulled back the grass from the opening and looked inside.

Nothing. Damn, where would he hide it?

Then Ben recalled the night Kate was staked out in the Rigwash Valley and her story about the man who had walked past her hiding spot on the side hill. Kate had been convinced at the time it was John Donald and she had mentioned him waiting in the ditch to be picked up.

Maybe he was getting his gun that night.

Making his way back to the valley, Ben located the culvert closest to where he had dropped Kate off that night.

Pulling back the grass, he peered into the opening.

Bingo!

Lying in the bottom of the culvert was a heavy black plastic bag. Smiling to himself, Ben pulled a small camera from his jacket and took a picture. Reaching into the culvert, he pulled the bag out and cautiously looked around.

He carefully untied the bag and pulled out a nylon gun case. Opening the case, he found what he was looking for: a Browning .270 rifle and a box of hollow point ammunition. Ben looked for the rifle's serial number to record it in his notes, but it had been filed off the barrel.

He thought about taking the gun to have it checked for fingerprints but figured John Donald would have been smart enough to wear gloves.

Somehow he would have to tie the gun directly to Moores.

Ben knew he would be taking a chance, but he carefully placed the rifle back in the case then slid it into the plastic bag and retied it. Pulling aside the grass, he placed the bag back in the culvert, being careful not to disturb the area any more than necessary.

He knew this might be their only opportunity to connect John Donald to Michel's murder. It was a risk to leave the gun behind but it was one he had to take.

Climbing out of the ditch, Ben made his way back to the warden truck and jumped in. Turning the key and starting the truck, the radio crackled to life.

"8-5-2, 8-5-2, Portable One. Come in."

"Go ahead," said Ben, pulling the radio mike from its holder.

"Hey, can you drop by the detachment as soon as you can? We've got something we thought you would want to know."

"10-4. I'm on my way." Ben pulled the truck onto the highway and headed for Chéticamp.

As he drove up to the detachment, Ben was surprised to see a vehicle parked in the driveway with the words "Provincial

Coroner" on the door. Walking into the office, Yvan, Giselle and Steve Day were just finishing some paperwork as the coroner prepared to leave. Nodding to the man, Ben waited until he had closed the outside door before speaking.

"What's up?" he asked.

"I thought you would want to know that Jimmy Dickson's body was discovered by a tourist today," said Yvan. "It washed up on the beach at Chéticamp Island. The guy who found it was pretty distraught so after we interviewed him we sent him on his way back to Halifax. Word hasn't got out around town yet."

"Drowned?" said Ben.

"Not likely. There will have to be an autopsy, but the coroner's initial thoughts are that he was dead for quite a while before he was thrown in the ocean. The way he was folded up looks like he was stored in a fish crate or something like that."

"Or a freezer?" said Ben.

"Jesus, Ben, maybe you're right," said Yvan.

"And that would explain the jacket," said Ben.

"His body was probably there the night we searched the garage," Yvan said, sitting down on the edge of Giselle's desk.

"But we never did get into searching the contents of the freezer," said Ben.

"That's true," said Yvan. "I guess we weren't thinking straight that night, what with everything else that happened. Anyway, I knew you'd want to know about Jimmy."

"We're just about to notify next of kin," said Steve Day. "I was just going to call his mother in Ingonish."

Ben thought for a moment about all of the disparate pieces of this puzzle.

"Any chance you can hold off letting anyone know about this?" said Ben. "At least until tomorrow."

"What are you thinking?" said Yvan.

"I just need to speak to someone before they find out about Jimmy. It might be the lynch pin to this whole deal."

"What do you think, Sarge?" said Yvan.

"I guess one night won't make that much difference. How long do you need, Ben?"

"Give me until noon tomorrow at the latest. If what I'm thinking is right, I should have something before then."

"Noon tomorrow it is," said the sergeant as Ben turned to leave.

"Where are you going?" said Yvan.

"To make a repeat visit," said Ben.

CHAPTER 65

BEN WAS SITTING in the superintendent's office early the following morning when Arnold Dickson walked in.

"What the?" said the superintendent as he turned on the lights and saw Ben sitting at his desk. "Matthews, how did you get in here?"

"Let's just say a little bird let me in," said Ben, getting up from the superintendent's chair as Arnold Dickson made his way over to his desk.

"I thought I told you yesterday I had nothing to say," said Dickson, who seemed to have aged considerably since the previous morning's blow-up.

"But that was yesterday," said Ben. "I thought you might have a different tune this morning considering the news."

"News?" said the superintendent. "What news?"

"You know as well as I do, Arnold. Do you mind if I call you Arnold? Because after the news gets out, I suspect I won't be calling you Superintendent Dickson any longer."

"I have no idea what you're talking about, Matthews," said the superintendent, desperately trying to avoid eye contact.

"I'm talking about Jimmy Dickson's body washing up on Chéticamp Island yesterday."

"Oh that," said Dickson, slumping into his chair. "He had it coming. It was an inevitable ending considering the company he kept."

"Inevitable, or convenient," said Ben.

"What do you mean?"

"Dead men tell no tales," said Ben. "And Jimmy was known to have loose lips. Getting rid of him ties up one loose end that John Donald Moores won't have to worry about anymore. Or you either."

"Matthews, if you are implying I had anything to do with Jimmy's death, then once again, you are skating on thin ice. I know nothing about what he's been up to."

"Then how did you know he was dead?" said Ben.

"Figure it out, Matthews. It's Cape Breton. Everyone knows everyone. Everyone knows everything."

"But no one knew about Jimmy except the RCMP, the provincial coroner and the tourist who found him. It's unlikely he told anyone around town because he shipped back to Halifax right away, and the RCMP and coroner were sworn to secrecy for the time being."

"Bullshit," said the superintendent.

"Not bullshit," said Ben. "You found out because you talked to Gerald Moores last night."

"Who told you that?"

"Let's just say that same little bird who knows how to pick locks also knows how to get information out of someone when it's needed. And I bet if the RCMP got a warrant, they could get records of your phone calls to Gerald Moores."

This last comment seemed to take the wind out of Arnold Dickson's sails.

Ben wasn't expecting him to roll over but the threat of being implicated in murders he had no part in seemed to be more than enough to get Arnold Dickson to spill his guts. Reluctantly, Arnold Dickson explained how he had been blackmailed to put John Donald and Maurice in touch with Louis Desaultiers, his old salvage partner, who had actually tried to screw him out of part of the treasure recovered from the *Cape Enrage*. There was no love lost between the two men and keeping Jimmy alive to save his sister further anguish was Arnold Dickson's only reason for giving John Donald what he wanted.

The wardens hadn't made it any easier by tackling John Donald's poaching activities, and the superintendent was under pressure to have them back off. He never expected Michel would end up dead in the ensuing battle.

There was little he could do now but to come forward to help bring John Donald to justice. As far as Dickson could tell, Gerald might be the only loose end that was left for John Donald to worry about but the superintendent doubted Gerald would speak, considering the potential for retribution from his older cousin.

Barring that, Ben knew they would have to focus their efforts on drawing John Donald out one last time. Ben suspected John Donald would be wary but figured his ego would get the better of him and he would soon be back to his old tricks.

The wardens would have to come up with some way to draw him out, but on their terms.

CHAPTER 66

THE MUSTANG WOUND its way along the Trail, working easily around the curves as it slid effortlessly up North Mountain. The full moon cast its light over the highlands as John Donald wove the car through the shadows cast by the forest lining both sides of the road. Gerald clung on for dear life, hoping they wouldn't run into a deer, or something larger.

In many ways, John Donald had wanted tonight to be his alone.

Gerald had told him earlier that he had things to do in Ingonish, but John Donald figured he was probably just too chicken-shit to take on the wardens anyway. Well, that was fine. Gerald was a handicap. He wasn't up to the tough stuff and he had just about lost it at the pre-trial hearing.

But Gerald knew better than to shoot his mouth off. If he lost his nerve and ratted them out, John Donald had let him know in no uncertain terms that he would end up feeding the lobsters off of Chéticamp Island, like Jimmy before him.

Gerald must have had second thoughts since in the end he had shown up at John Donald's mother's place and said he would go along.

Tonight John Donald had planned some payback. He was free and he was taking the opportunity to rub it in the wardens' faces. He'd leave them burning with a message of his own. They would never be looking for him to come out of Pleasant Bay and head east toward Big Intervale. His routine was to always work the area between the Rigwash Valley and French Mountain on the Chéticamp side.

But tonight he would slide into the Intervale and get that big buck he'd been seeing. He doubted the wardens were on the move anyway.

They figure I'll be laying low.

He laughed.

The .270 Browning lay across his lap, uncased and ready for action. Leaving it in the culvert had worked well once again.

As they crested the top of North Mountain, John Donald turned off the headlights, cruising along in the moonlight at top speed. With tires squealing, he rounded the first turn heading down into Big Intervale. Instead of throttling back, he kept the pedal to the floor and banked into the series of turns leading to the Aspy River bridge. On the last turn before the river, he let off the gas just enough to allow himself a margin of error. The Mustang bottomed out as it hit the bridge deck, forcing John Donald to slam on the brakes and causing the car to fishtail.

"Jesus," yelled Gerald. "Take it easy, for fuck sake. I don't want to die tonight."

John Donald slowed down to stop the rocking. When he was within sight of the campground entrance, he slammed on the parking brake and spun the steering wheel hard to the left. Pressed up against the door, Gerald muttered a few more oaths as the car turned a full one hundred and eighty degrees and came to a screeching stop in the middle of the highway, directly in line with the campground.

"Excellent," said John Donald, following the beam of headlights shining through the trees to the river.

A pair of eyes glared at them though the blackness.

"That would be him." John Donald manoeuvred the car down toward the campground and into the grass alongside the Aspy River as it babbled along under the canopy, barely audible in the crisp fall air.

John Donald slid out of the car and looked up toward the warden's residence. There were no lights on and no other sign of life. His information had been correct.

Pulling the rifle from the seat, he held it up to his eye, spying through the scope toward the distant warden house.

Perfect.

Lining up the crosshairs with a bedroom window then delving into the dark shadows around the house, the night-vision scope cast a green hue, picking up details lost to the naked eye. Lowering the gun, he let his eyes adjust to the darkness then motioned for Gerald to get out of the car.

"C'mon. Let's do this."

Walking slowly into the campground, John Donald could make out the silhouette of the deer off to his right. Motioning for Gerald to stay behind him, he pulled the rifle to his shoulder once again and scoped the area. The big buck stood staring at him twenty metres away.

"This is too easy," John Donald said under his breath as he lined up the crosshairs with the buck's white throat.

"This guy will look good hanging on my wall," he added, pausing as the deer bent down to continue feeding on the manicured grass.

Suddenly, John Donald pursed his lips and sent a shrill whistle into the night air. As the deer snapped to attention, John Donald squeezed the trigger and the deer dropped in its tracks, its spinal cord severed by the single shot, which reverberated through the valley.

A few kilometres away, on top of North Mountain, Ben keyed his mike.

"Did you hear that, Norm?"

"Sure did," Norm replied. "Looks like we're gonna nail that shitrat tonight."

"He'll likely be back this way in fifteen minutes or so," said Ben. "How is the moose calling going?"

"Too good," said Norm, looking over at Joe. "If I keep this up, I might get laid tonight."

Ben turned to Kate and smiled.

"Well, hold off till we think they're on the way back. We only need that bull to cross the road once. If that doesn't work,

Kate and I will head him off before he gets back home with whatever he's bringing back from your yard."

"10-4. I'm glad I sent the family over to Ingonish for the night. I just hope he didn't shoot the dog."

Back in the campground, John Donald laid the deer's head on a plastic sheet in the rear of the Mustang. Pulling out a piece of nylon trawl line he laid the rope across the trunk and closed the lid.

"Tie this to the deer," he said to Gerald, handing him the end of the rope.

Gerald looped the nylon trawl line around the deer's hind legs.

"Get in," said John Donald, motioning to Gerald.

Getting back into the driver's seat, John Donald hit the gas and the car spun across the grass, dragging the deer along behind. The car careened across the highway and up into the drive leading to the small bungalow. John Donald wheeled the car around to the front of the house, grass flying as it fishtailed across the lawn and into the back yard. He stopped just short of the garage, jumped out, and ran back to the deer. Using his skinning knife, he cut the rope from the animal's legs and pulled the legs apart before he slit the deer open, spewing its stomach onto the concrete walk.

Tossing the rope into the car, John Donald jumped back in behind the wheel and sped off down the driveway. Once on the highway, he turned back toward North Mountain and Pleasant Bay, laughing out loud as the Mustang started the long climb to the top of the Highlands.

"That'll teach those bastards," said John Donald, grinning at Gerald and pressing the accelerator to the floor. "That'll teach them to fuck around with John Donald Moores."

"You should slow down," said Gerald, clinging to the door as the car flew into the curves.

John Donald was unrepentant and kept the pedal to the floor but as the car rounded the last turn and crested the top of the mountain, he looked up just in time to see the outline of a large moose coming out of the ditch. The lanky bull towered over the car and at the last second John Donald swerved to avoid hitting him, brushing the animal's flank as it panicked, hooves slipping on the asphalt. The car screeched to a halt and John Donald flew out in a rage.

"Jesus, Jesus, Jesus," he screamed, stomping the pavement. He reached back inside the car and pulled the rifle from its partly-zippered case. Pointing it up in the air, he jerked back on the trigger and sent a blast skyward. Spying a park information sign a hundred metres down the highway, he sighted through the scope and blasted a gaping hole in the middle.

Splinters of plywood rained down on the two wardens crouched in the bushes below the sign.

"Holy shit," said Norm. "I'd like to drive that fucker into next week if I get my hands on him tonight."

"Keep it down," said Joe, shaking from the suddenness of the shot.

"I'll give another call and we'll see if we can't get this fucker to really commit himself," Norm said as he brushed paint and wood chips from his fur hat.

Slithering up by the side of the sign and cupping his hands over his mouth, he let out a guttural call that drifted across the Highlands.

John Donald, still standing in the middle of the highway, perked up and strained to pinpoint the location of the call.

"Give him another one," said Joe, as he looked through his binoculars. "He's starting to walk this way."

Norm repeated the call, but quickly dropped to his knees. He didn't want to be standing in the line of fire if John Donald decided to take another whack at the sign.

John Donald hesitated, suspicious about the moose call. He wondered if it was the bull he had just missed hitting, but it seemed to be coming from farther down the road. Not wanting to get too far from the Mustang, he went back to the car, jumped in and started to pull ahead. Figuring John Donald was about to hightail it, Norm rose for one last try to pull the big bull moose back across the highway. John Donald, oblivious to the loud bawl, drove a hundred metres down the road and stopped the car.

Turning off the ignition, he got out and pulled the gun along just as a monstrous bull moose crashed through the bushes at the edge of the ditch.

Without hesitating, John Donald raised the rifle and fired. The big bull lurched forward but regained its footing and ran across the road and down along the ditch, following the edge of the bushes.

"Fuck." John Donald swore at himself, certain that the bullet had hit the mark.

The bull stopped just short of the large sign and started to move into the woods along an old cutline. John Donald raised the scope to his eyes and scanned the trees, hoping to get off one last shot.

This will really put the icing on the cake for those wardens.

He could see the outline of the moose standing behind a small clump of fir but didn't have a clear shot.

Come on. Move forward just a hair.

The bull made two steps forward.

John Donald sighted in on the bull's head, but something in the background caught his attention. Focusing the scope, he could see the outline of a truck hidden in the trees. Scanning with the scope again, he could just pick out a person standing next to the highway sign.

John Donald's chin dropped in disbelief.

"You fuckers," he screamed.

Without thinking, he sighted in on the person standing by the sign and squeezed the trigger.

Norm dropped to the ground as the blast splintered the sign post.

"That was way too close," said Norm to a wide-eyed Joe, as the moose crashed headlong past them into the trees.

"No kidding," said Joe.

"Let's get to the truck," said Norm, pushing past his partner.

John Donald ran back to the Mustang, threw his rifle across the seat to Gerald and jumped in behind the steering wheel. As he turned the key, a warden truck came bursting out of the cutline, its red and blue emergency lights cutting through the darkness. The truck bottomed out in the ditch and screeched onto the highway just ahead of John Donald, who immediately dropped his foot to the floor and wheeled the sports car around the truck and headed toward Pleasant Bay.

"He got by us," Joe screamed into the mike.

"I'll try to take out his tires," said Ben, wheeling the second truck out of the bushes and onto the highway just as John Donald came over a slight rise in the road. As Kate clung to the door handle, Ben spun the truck broadside, blocking the roadway and turned on the red and blue emergency lights.

"Hopefully this works. Take the wheel," he said to Kate, who slid over into the driver's seat.

Pulling the Winchester Defender from its rack, he jumped out and lay across the hood, snapping a slug into the pump action shotgun.

The Mustang raced toward the warden truck as Ben sighted down the gun barrel.

"Stop, you bastard or I'm gonna drop you in your tracks," he yelled.

Furious at being trapped by the wardens, John Donald kept coming, slowing down just long enough to notice the other warden truck moving in from behind then hitting the gas and driving straight at Ben and Kate.

Ben stood his ground, figuring there was no way John Donald would make it around them.

"He's got to stop," Ben yelled as he pushed off the shotgun's safety.

When he realized John Donald was not going to stop, he prepared to jump clear of the truck.

"Watch out," he yelled to Kate as he levelled a blast toward the front right wheel of the Mustang.

John Donald braked as the car fishtailed out of control. He was metres away from the warden truck when he managed to spin the wheel hard to the left, pulling the car onto the shoulder and down into the ditch. The Mustang hit the dirt with a heavy thud, then with tires screaming pulled itself out and back onto the highway.

Ben ran out of the opposite ditch and fired a second blast as the car started down the mountain. This time the slug found its mark as the rear window exploded in on John Donald and Gerald.

With his cousin in a blind rage, Gerald hung on as John Donald slammed on the brakes, preparing to turn around and do battle.

Seeing the brake lights come on, Ben jumped back into the passenger side of the truck just as Joe and Norm crested the hill.

"Let's go," he said to Kate.

The Mustang moved forward as John Donald reconsidered his options, then, with a squeal of rubber, raced down North Mountain, the two warden trucks in hot pursuit, sirens blaring.

John Donald knew he could outrace them to Pleasant Bay, but decided against heading into town as the three vehicles screamed off the mountain and through the Grande Anse Valley.

Ben was prepared to chase John Donald into Pleasant Bay but as they approached the turnoff, he realized John Donald was going to keep heading towards Mackenzie Mountain and Chéticamp.

"We'll never catch him this way," Ben called into the mike, yelling above the sound of the siren's wail as Kate tried to stay as close to John Donald as possible.

"And we'll never get anyone in Chéticamp on these radios," Joe replied.

Realizing the perfect setup may not work after all, Ben pounded his fist on the dashboard.

"Shit, shit, shit," he yelled, urging Kate to press the gas pedal as far as it would go, as the engine howled in protest.

The Mustang and warden trucks crossed the Mackenzie River bridge within seconds of each other but as they began the climb up Mackenzie Mountain, the second warden truck fell well behind while Kate worked the curves to stay within range of the Mustang.

"Great driving," Ben said to Kate as she focussed on the turns.

"We'll be behind you," Joe radioed, resigned to the fact that they could never keep up. "Don't do anything stupid. That guy is likely psycho over this whole deal."

"I read you," Ben responded, realizing they were also going to have a hard time keeping up to the faster Mustang.

As they climbed the switchback turns of MacKenzie Mountain, John Donald could clearly see the second warden truck falling back and assumed Ben and Kate were in the lead truck. Finally calming down, he plotted his next move.

Soon it would be just them and the two park wardens alone on top of the mountain.

Slowing down slightly, John Donald took time to assess the damage and realized that the back of his neck was coated with dried blood and shattered glass. The interior of the car was also covered with small shards of glass but Gerald somehow managed to wipe most of it off the seats while John Donald focused on driving.

The car was also handling differently and John Donald suspected the car's steering and undercarriage had been damaged during his escape.

He relished the thought of revenge.

As the two vehicles reached the plateau and sped across the Highlands in the moonlight, Ben was surprised that Kate was able to keep pace with the Mustang. He suspected that John Donald was either toying with them or the car had been damaged by the two shotgun blasts and John Donald's detour through the ditch.

Suddenly the car's running lights went out, but Kate and Ben were still able to see it clearly as it sped away in the moonlight.

"They won't be so easy to spot in the shadows," Kate said as they headed over the first small rise on top of the plateau.

The words were barely out of her mouth when the silhouette of the Mustang loomed up in front of them.

"What the hell?" she yelled as she pulled the steering wheel hard to the left to avoid hitting the car.

The warden truck swerved past the Mustang, turned broadside in the road and stalled. Looking behind him, Ben could see the outline of John Donald raising his rifle.

"Get down," Ben yelled.

Scrambling to get the truck started again, Kate quickly managed to turn the vehicle away from John Donald just as the rifle blast took out the rear window.

"He's fucking crazy," Ben yelled as John Donald stood on the road, laughing.

"Now we're even," John Donald muttered under his breath.

Passing the gun to Gerald and jumping in the car, John Donald raced after the warden truck.

"They won't run too far," he said.

Gerald sat dumbfounded. Realizing this would not end well, he just grunted as John Donald sped down the highway, searching for the warden truck in the distance.

John Donald felt the car handle a little sluggishly, but not wanting to be stranded in the middle of the park, he kept racing after the taillights disappearing over the crest of the next hill.

"We're just about at the Skyline," he said to Gerald, realizing that once they got on the downhill side of French Mountain, the park wardens could potentially stay ahead of him if they decided to make a run for Chéticamp. John Donald desperately wanted to stop them before they made it down French Mountain.

CHAPTER 67

BEN HAD BEEN frantically trying to contact the RCMP in Chéticamp while Kate navigated the turns, and miraculously the radio worked for once. Managing to raise Yvan, he quickly let him know what was going on.

"Where are you exactly?" said Ben.

"Just on the other side of town," Yvan replied.

"Well, turn around and get out here as fast as you can."

"Will do, Ben. Just see if you guys can coax John Donald and Gerald as close to Chéticamp as possible and I'll intercept them."

"10-4," said Ben. "He's pretty well committed himself and with Norm and Joe coming along behind, we should have him hemmed in. After what happened on North Mountain, Norm won't be too keen on letting him get away."

"I hear you, but watch yourselves. It sounds like John Donald is close to the edge."

"10-4. We'll see you somewhere between here and the Rigwash." Ben placed the mike in its holder on the dash.

If he figured correctly, the Mustang wouldn't be far behind.

John Donald bore down on the Skyline, keeping his headlights off to avoid warning the wardens of his approach. As he crested the hill and started down French Mountain, he kept his foot to the floor and the Mustang screeched around the first corner. When he rounded the first turn he had a clear look at the next three curves hugging the inside of the mountain, but there was no sign of a vehicle.

He cursed and was about to backtrack to see if the park wardens had slipped into the Skyline when the warden truck roared up behind him. Kate turned on the takedown lights, blinding John Donald momentarily.

John Donald pressed the gas pedal. The Mustang shot ahead with the pickup tight to its tail.

Crouching low against the steering wheel, John Donald laughed hysterically as the two vehicles careened down French Mountain. He knew this road intimately and efficiently used its every nuance. Hugging the inside turns, tires squealing, John Donald was in his element, but he had underestimated Kate's driving abilities.

She had done her share of high-speed driving along the Trail and managed to stay within a couple of car lengths of the Mustang, but John Donald was not about to let a warden get the better of him.

Maintaining pressure, Kate approached each turn cautiously as Ben kept an eye out for oncoming vehicles. Powering through the S curves, they continued to push an unsuspecting John Donald toward Yvan, who had already made it to Corney Brook and the last straightaway before the climb up French Mountain.

John Donald was being played like a salmon on a line as Kate and Ben gave him some slack then reeled him back in.

The warden's strategy was not lost on John Donald, who glared in the rear view mirror through bloodshot eyes.

"There's no fucking way they're going to take me down this mountain," he swore to Gerald.

"Whatever you say," Gerald said through clenched teeth, doubtful that they would make it down the mountain alive.

"Fuck you," said John Donald, planning to put some distance between himself and the warden truck so he could slow down enough to power turn and catch the inside lane without broadsiding into the cliffs at the edge of the road.

Wise to the plan, Kate hugged the turns, staying close to the Mustang's bumper and taking away any opportunity for John Donald to manoeuvre the car.

"He's going all the way," said Ben as Kate pressed the gas

pedal to the floorboards, determined not to give John Donald any room to escape.

"If he tries anything, he'll go off the road," said Kate.

John Donald was furious, realizing there were only one or two places left he could make his move. He had to do something before the last hairpin turn, which he knew would be impossible to navigate at high speed.

Kate read John Donald's intentions perfectly and, staying close on his tail, prevented any manoeuvre to turn the car around.

Realizing that he had been outsmarted, John Donald was livid.

"You fucking wardens," he screamed through the broken rear window.

Ben could see John Donald looking back at them, momentarily distracted from driving around the twists and turns in the road.

"Try something, you fucker, and we'll send you out into the bay," Ben shouted, his voice drowned out by the scream of tires cascading off the mountain walls.

As they approached the last curve on the mountain, John Donald geared down to take the turn on the inside.

Copying their quarry's tactic, Kate was prepared to not let up until the last moment.

The vehicles passed the final pull-off before the last curve and John Donald, blinded with rage, touched his brake slightly.

There was no response.

Pumping the brake harder, his foot slammed into the floor. Frantically he shifted down into fourth and then third gear, hoping the motor would slow the Mustang's momentum.

The engine screamed in response.

In desperation, he tried to move to the inside lane just as Yvan came racing around the corner in the RCMP cruiser.

"Watch out," Kate yelled as she saw the impending collision.

John Donald saw Yvan at the last moment and spontaneously turned the wheel hard to the right to avoid a head-on collision, clipping the front left fender of the police car.

Reacting at the last second, Yvan turned the police car hard into the curve, careening into the narrow ditch and sliding along the rock wall in a shower of sparks and screaming metal.

John Donald let out a wild scream as the Mustang swerved broadside, crossing the narrow road and slamming through the guardrail, losing enough momentum to prevent it from catapulting through the air toward the ocean, but leaving it cantilevered perilously on the cliff edge.

"Hang on," Kate yelled, slamming on the brakes to try and avoid a collision.

The warden truck fishtailed out of control, spinning around in the road before smashing into the side of the RCMP cruiser, pinning Yvan in the vehicle and tossing Kate and Ben into the passenger side door of the warden truck.

John Donald sat trapped in the Mustang, clawing at the dashboard as he tried to work his legs out from under the steering wheel and pull himself onto the hood of the ill-fated car. Miraculously unscathed except for a cut across his forehead, Gerald scrambled through the broken windshield and over the hood of the car to solid ground, causing the Mustang to list even more precariously on its perch above the ocean.

Sensing that the car might plunge backwards into the abyss at any moment, John Donald managed to free his legs and use the steering wheel to pull himself onto the hood.

"I think my leg is broken," he said to Gerald, holding on for dear life with one hand and reaching for his cousin with the other.

Gerald stood silently assessing the situation, looking over his shoulder toward the entangled vehicles pressed into the rock cut.

"Gerald, for fuck's sake, give me your hand," John Donald commanded.

Gerald hesitated, then, leaning against the hood of the Mustang, reached for his cousin's hand.

"You were going to kill us both," he said in a low voice, barely touching John Donald's outstretched fingers.

He could feel the car teetering on the brink.

"For Christ's sake, Gerald, help me," said John Donald.

Gerald wavered.

"Help me," John Donald screamed, the fear in his voice rising.

Gerald looked back over his shoulder.

There was movement in the warden truck as Ben and Kate checked out the damage to themselves and their vehicle.

"You okay?" Ben said to Kate.

"Yah. I think so. You?"

"Yah, but we've got to help Yvan," said Ben.

Ben looked into the police cruiser and could see Yvan's shoulders move.

"I think he's okay," Ben said as he rolled down the window and called to Yvan, who raised his head and managed a grin.

"We'll get you out in a minute," Ben yelled.

Sliding past Kate, he tried to force his weight against the driver's door. It had jammed from the impact and his shoulder screamed with pain as he tried to wedge it open. He could see Gerald standing next to the Mustang with John Donald splayed out across the hood, fighting to hold on. The car looked like it could go over the side at any moment.

John Donald's pleading brought Gerald back to the reality of their situation.

"We're screwed," said Gerald. "This is the end."

"No," John Donald pleaded. "Help me and we'll get out of this."

"I don't think so," Gerald countered, remembering Emile's visit.

"For fuck's sake, help me, Gerald. We're family." John Donald was almost begging. "Remember."

The words stung as Gerald remembered a night when John Donald had indoctrinated him into the shady world of petty theft, poaching and drug trafficking. He had wanted nothing to do with it. He wanted out of Pleasant Bay and off Cape Breton Island. It was home; some day when his cousin was gone, he would come back to the good things it offered. But John Donald had forced his hand in more ways than one and he couldn't escape.

Looking at John Donald, Gerald's emotions were mixed. His cousin's life hadn't been a joyride, but Gerald had only one chance to turn things around for himself, and he wasn't about to screw it up.

"Gerald," said John Donald. "We're family."

For a moment, Gerald thought perhaps there was a way he and John Donald could work things out, but he also remembered what Emile had said. There was only one way out and he knew what he had to do. Under different circumstances maybe he would be able to make another choice.

But not tonight.

Leaning against the car, he could feel it move slightly backwards with the least amount of effort as gravity fought for control.

"What are you doing?" John Donald screamed at Gerald, sensing the slight shift in balance as his own weight tipped the odds against him.

Gerald looked over his shoulder as Ben struggled to get out of the warden truck, his face and shoulder pressed against the truck door. Looking up, the warden seemed to be yelling something to him but it was lost to the sound of an approaching vehicle, speeding down the mountainside.

Gerald nudged his legs forward, pressing against the front bumper of the Mustang.

"Gerald, no," John Donald yelled. "Stop."

But there was no stopping him.

With a final, almost imperceptible movement, Gerald gave gravity the edge it needed as the car slowly slid backwards past the point of no return.

Unable to hold himself, John Donald screamed as he fell back through the broken windshield, his weight tipping the balance and sending the Mustang somersaulting off the mountain into the surf below.

Finally managing to get out of the warden truck, Ben stood in disbelief as the car slid backwards in slow motion just as Norm and Joe pulled up in the second warden truck, its emergency lights pulsing over the scene of Gerald standing by himself in front of a gaping hole in the guardrail.

Helping Kate, the pair hobbled over to the warden truck as Norm jumped out.

"Did he go over?" Norm asked, surveying the scene.

"Like a rock," Ben responded.

"Good riddance," said Norm. "If I had gotten my hands on him, he would have been in worse shape."

Joe jumped out of the truck and strode over to the trio.

"Christ, that was some piece of driving," he said, putting an arm around Kate and wiping the sweat from his brow. "How the hell did you ever keep up to him?"

"I don't know, Joe," said Kate. "I figured he could have easily outrun us, but Ben must have damaged something when he shot at the car back on North Mountain. I think it was losing power."

"You never know with John Donald," said Ben. "I had a sense he was going to end it for one of us tonight."

"Well, that he did," Joe replied.

Ben laid his hand on Joe's shoulder. "Let's get Yvan out of his car," he said, pointing to the cruiser trapped between the rock wall and the warden truck.

"Where the hell did he come from?" said Joe.

"I managed to raise him on the radio," said Ben.

"Must have been a miracle," Norm said with a grin.

Turning to Norm, Ben pointed at Gerald, who was standing like a deer in the headlights. "Check him out, Norm. He seems to be lost."

Norm approached Gerald and placed him in handcuffs while Ben, Kate and Joe made their way to the RCMP cruiser to find Yvan sitting with his head on the steering wheel. As they approached, he looked up and breathed a heavy sigh.

"Christ, Yvan, are you okay?" said Kate.

Yvan closed his eyes momentarily then he looked into Kate's face and smiled. "That was too close for comfort," he said. "I thought one of us was heading over the cliff."

"You're lucky it wasn't you," Ben said as the three park wardens forced the door open and helped Yvan out of the car.

CHAPTER 68

"I UNDERSTAND YOU have some preliminary matters, Mr. Irons," said Judge McIntosh.

The Chéticamp courtroom, now open to the public, was once again packed to the rafters with Ben and Kate and the full contingent of Cape Breton Highland's park wardens sitting alongside Lucille Aucoin and her family.

Christopher Irons was seated next to Gerald Moores, an empty chair sitting auspiciously between them. Irons rose and faced the judge.

"Your Honour, as you may be aware, one of my clients, John Donald Moores, was recently killed in a high-speed vehicle chase in the national park."

"Yes, I am aware of that," said Judge McIntosh without any sign of emotion.

"Therefore, Your Honour, I would like to ask that the charges against John Donald Moores, relating to the death of Warden Aucoin, be dropped posthumously."

Judge McIntosh looked down at his notes, pondering the request.

"Before I render my decision on that request, Mr. Irons, are there other matters you wish to speak to?"

"I have one other matter, Your Honour. Regarding charges against my other client, Mr. Gerald Moores, I have been advised by Mr. Moores that he wishes to change his plea. On that basis, we propose to waive the preliminary hearing and proceed to sentencing."

"Very well, Mr. Irons, is that all?"

"Yes, Your Honour."

Judge McIntosh stopped briefly to gather his thoughts.

"With respect to the first item, Mr. Irons, I do not have to deliberate long to deny your request regarding John Donald Moores. I have no sympathy for the man and it is my understanding that if he had been taken into custody on Saturday night, he would have faced additional charges, just as serious as those we are currently discussing."

"But, Your Honour."

"No buts, Mr. Irons. In my books, John Donald Moores was not just a criminal. He was a murderer. I only wish I could have put him behind bars for what he's done to this community.

Regarding the second matter, I would first like to reread the charge against Gerald Moores. Please rise, Mr. Moores."

With his head held low, Gerald Moores slowly got to his feet.

Taking his time, Judge McIntosh read from the docket, emphasizing the seriousness of the offence.

"Mr. Moores, you are charged with being an accessory to the murder of Park Warden Michel Pierre Aucoin. How do you plead?"

Christopher Irons stood up to enter his client's plea.

"Your Honour," he started, but Judge McIntosh cut him off.

"Mr. Irons. I want to hear it from Gerald Moores' own lips, so please sit down."

Gerald Moores waited painstakingly as the charge was read, then looked into the eyes of Judge McIntosh. He could detect no sympathy, just contempt. He looked down at the floor and sealed his fate in the eyes of the law.

"Guilty, Your Honour."

The courtroom was alive as Judge McIntosh looked at Gerald Moores, then fell silent as he was about to speak. Lucille Aucoin, surrounded by friends and family, fought back the tears. Ben caught a glance from Joe, who nodded and mouthed the words "Good job."

Ben wanted to feel a sense of satisfaction but the guilty plea could never replace the loss of Michel. It could never make up for the hole left in Michel's family, or the Park family. But at least this time, Gerald and John Donald Moores would not walk away from their actions.

"Gerald Moores," said Judge McIntosh, "I must now render a sentence directed by the Criminal Code of Canada. Trust me when I say that you are lucky I cannot attach my own conditions. You are sentenced to 25 years in the maximum-security prison at Dorchester, New Brunswick. I am obliged to tell you that you may be eligible for parole in ten years."

Gerald Moores stood by his chair, shaking as the judge continued.

"Mr. Moores," said Judge McIntosh, pausing again to collect his thoughts. "I have one question of you before you are taken into custody. This may seem a little unorthodox, but considering that John Donald Moores is no longer with us, what I would like to know, and I'm sure all of the people here in this courtroom would also like to know, is this: in the matter of Jimmy Dickson, whose body was recently found washed up on Chéticamp Island, was John Donald Moores responsible for his death?"

Christopher Irons stood up to object to the question, but Gerald Moores waved him off. He had nothing to lose from answering. He would not be eligible for parole until he was almost fifty and likely wouldn't see the outside until he was in his sixties. He had been haunted by the murders and coming clean might serve him some good, now and perhaps down the road.

Looking up at Judge McIntosh, Gerald Moores cleared his throat.

"He was, Your Honour."

John Donald Moores' mother sat in the courtroom behind Christopher Irons. The words from Gerald's lips hit her hard. She never wanted to believe her son was capable of one murder, let alone two. Hanging her head in her hands, she sobbed quietly.

A buzz went through the crowd as Judge McIntosh closed the court. Gerald Moores was handcuffed and leg-shackled, then led to the rear doors where the RCMP had secured a small area.

Ben followed Gerald to the door where Yvan was waiting to release him into the custody of a guard. Yvan and Ben took one last look as Gerald struggled through the door in half steps and was shoved into the rear of the waiting van. As the guard stepped in behind Gerald, Yvan and Ben quickly closed the van's rear doors. Two Mounties stood at the opposite side of the courtroom, preventing people from exiting before Gerald Moores was driven away. As the van pulled onto the highway, people poured from the courthouse.

CHAPTER 69

THE WIND WAS out of the southwest, a warm breeze pushing the small boat down the coast.

Kate sat in front, leaning back against the bags of diving gear. The breeze blew over her as she lay in the calm beneath the gunwales.

Ben was at the tiller, the outboard churning through the blue water. The sky was clear with the sun beating down from directly overhead.

As they made their way to Fishing Cove, they couldn't help but marvel at the view of the Highlands from this ocean perspective, a dark grey mass pushing out of the sea.

At Fishing Cove, they decided to dive from the boat, providing a deeper dive for the first part of the day. Later they would take a break before doing a second dive in shallower water.

Following the anchor rope down, Kate regularly adjusted her buoyancy compensator, taking time to give her ears a chance to equalize to the increasing pressure. She was an experienced diver and the stronger of the two when it came to the marine environment.

Ben was right behind Kate and followed her lead. They reached the end of the rope and checked the anchor, ensuring it would not drag.

Slowly they worked their way along the bottom. At this depth there was little colour as most of the light was absorbed, but the water was still crystal clear. They swam in the grey depths, stopping to check the occasional wrecked lobster pot.

Kate noticed a round object lying in the muddy bottom that seemed out of place. Pulling it from the sediment, a mushroom cloud of fine silts spiralled upward, enveloping her. As she peered at the object in her hand Kate's tank alarm suddenly went off and she thought she could hear her scuba tank free flowing, discharging its full load of air.

She looked around for Ben.

He was swimming toward her.

Panicking, Kate reached down and undid her weight belt, letting it drop into the silt. She started to ascend rapidly, but Ben suddenly appeared through the grey ooze and grabbed her leg, pulling her back down toward him.

Startled, Kate pushed him away and kicked furiously for the surface.

Ben tried to grab her leg again but missed. With a strong kick, he tried to catch up, finally grabbing Kate's leg to slow her down. She kicked vigorously, but he somehow managed to hold her back long enough to get his arms around her chest.

He had never seen her so scared.

As he tried to calm Kate down and slow their ascent, Ben quickly looked around them for the anchor line and boat, which he realized was just a short distance away. Struggling to get in the boat they managed to pull themselves over the side. Ben pulled off his gear and helped Kate undo her tank. She was shaking uncontrollably.

"Put this on." He wrapped a fleece jacket around her shoulders. "We'll go to shore and get a fire going."

Kate nodded, unable to speak.

Ben pulled the anchor, started the motor and headed for shore. Hauling the plank boat up onto the cobble beach, he helped Kate out. She was showing signs of hypothermia.

He collected driftwood and started a fire on the beach next to Kate.

"You've got to get out of your wetsuit." He started to unzip her jacket. She managed to get it off, then pulled the Farmer Jane bottoms off as well. Ben wrapped her in towels and dried her off.

Kate was starting to feel a little better and managed a smile.

"Thanks, Ben."

Ben threw a few more pieces of driftwood on the blazing fire and sat down beside Kate. Pulling a thermos of hot tea from his pack, he poured a cup and passed it to her. She held it tightly between her knees as a noticeable tremor shook her whole body.

The tea brightened her spirits and she gradually began feeling warmer. Kate laid her head on Ben's shoulder and stared at the fire. Ben put his arm around her, pulling her close.

"What happened down there?" he said.

"I don't know," said Kate, handing Ben the object she retrieved from the bottom. "I pulled this from the silt then it sounded like my tank was free-flowing. I had to get to the surface."

"But I checked and there's lots of air in the tank," said Ben, rubbing the object with his thumb and forefinger to clean off some of the grime.

"I don't know then," said Kate. "It was more of a feeling that came over me than anything else. I'm not sure what it is about this place. It's so beautiful yet it scares the hell out of me sometimes."

"I know what you mean."

Kate looked up at him. "Right. You sure don't seem scared."

"Maybe not on the surface, but just below the surface, I'm scared to death."

"Of what?"

"Of everything. I can't stop thinking about the night we were chasing John Donald and Gerald. We could have both ended up like Michel."

"I think about that too and it scares the hell out of me," said Kate. "I think about Lucille and what she must be going through. Is it worth it?"

"No. No one should lose their life over something like this" said Ben. "But you just never know who you're dealing with or what they're capable of. It's what got Michel killed and I'll never forgive myself for that."

"So why do we do it?"

"I'm not sure. I think it's because they're out there every night, taking salmon and deer out of the park. If we let it go unchecked, they'll ruin this place."

Ben hung his head and continued.

"But then, sometimes I think it's about egos. Mine at least."

"What do you mean?"

"Well, I let people like John Donald Moores eat me up."

"I can see that," said Kate. "I don't mean to ride you, but you were more than a little preoccupied with him. You know it's just a game to these guys."

Ben was about to object, but thought a moment about the way John Donald consumed him.

"Maybe you're right," he conceded. "I can't let go and he knew it. He was probably laughing at how easy it was to get us going. To get me going, at least."

"So what are you going to do about it? You can't get up every night you hear a vehicle go into the park. You'll run yourself into the ground."

Ben thought for a second.

"I think we're going to have to get out of here."

"What do you mean, 'we'?" said Kate.

"I mean you and me. I think we should get married and get out of here."

Kate was taken aback.

"Married? You think so?"

"I know so. All I ever wanted was for us to be together. But I didn't know how to deal with you as a warden. I used to think it was because I didn't want to see you get hurt, but maybe it was more than that."

Kate listened intently.

"I think I needed to separate work and my home life. That's hard to do when you're going out with another warden."

"That's not going to change," Kate said honestly.

"I know," said Ben.

"But I think we could make it work," said Ben, taking a closer look at the object in his hand.

"What is that thing anyway?" said Kate.

"If I didn't know any better," said Ben, "I'd say it was a French coin. A very old French coin."

"And who do we know that would have had an old French coin," said Kate.

Ben smiled and nodded.

"Another coincidence?" said Kate.

"Yah, right," said Ben.

CHAPTER 70

A WARM AUTUMN breeze blew in off the Gulf as the small group of park staff and their families gathered around the large table of food in the Trout Brook picnic area. Behind them, the Highlands were illuminated in a blaze of colour as the sun slowly made its way toward the horizon. Having already said their good-byes, Lucille and Jean Marc had departed along with some of the other younger families, leaving those remaining to take over the space around the large fire pit. As the wardens and their wives huddled with Kate and Ben around the fire, several of the work crew pulled out their musical instruments and began playing a medley of Acadian tunes, with Emile leading on guitar.

"I can't believe you're moving, Kate," said Joe.

"Neither can I," Kate replied. "But permanent jobs don't come by every day. And Keji has always been a place I've wanted to work."

"And you, Ben," said Rose. "It seems like you only just got here."

"Seems that way," said Ben. "But time has flown by. It's been almost a year since Michel..."

"And chances to go North don't come up all the time, either," Kate interjected.

"That's right," said Ben. "I've always wanted to go to Wood Buffalo so I had to jump at this opportunity."

"We just thought you'd be leaving together," said Rose.

Kate looked at Ben and smiled.

"We kind of thought the same thing," said Kate, "but I'd like to get a permanent position nailed down first. Then I'll have more flexibility. We'll see what the future has in store for us."

"And we've got another summer under our belt," Ben added. "So it's probably time for us both to move on anyway."

"Hell, I thought for sure I'd be out of here before you," said Joe.

"We were all hoping," said Norm, grinning from ear to ear.

"Funny thing, that," said Joe, ignoring Norm's comment. "The superintendent changed his mind at the last minute and is going to let me finish out my last year."

"We're glad for you, Joe," Ben replied. "You deserve to go out in style."

Joe held out his hand, gripping Ben's hand firmly. "You wouldn't have had anything to do with all this?"

"Not a chance," said Ben, smiling. "Hell, if it was up to me, you'd be walking," he lied.

"And Norm will be taking over here so you're in good hands," said Kate.

"Actually, I wanted to talk to you about that," said Joe, turning to Ben.

"Touché," said Norm.

"Enough of that, you two," said Rose, giving Joe and Norm a stern look before turning back to Kate. "We're going to miss you both."

"Same here," said Ben.

Rose gathered Kate in her arms.

"You take care of yourself, girl," said Rose.

"I will," said Kate, as tears rolled down her face. "I'm going to miss this place."

Joe's eyes were watering as he threw his arms around Kate, not wanting to let her go. They both cried silently. Ben looked at Rose. She sensed his hesitation and held out her hand. He fell into her arms and held her close, unable to speak.

Joe collected himself and stood back, wiping his eyes with a handkerchief, as Norm gave Kate a bear hug.

"Enough of that," said Joe, tapping Rose on the shoulder. "We'll look like hell if we keep this up." Turning to Ben, Joe inquired, "Where to from here?"

"We're off to Canso this afternoon then on to Kate's folks' place. We'll stay there for a few days then I was going to give Kate a hand to get her stuff to the Valley. I fly North in a few weeks."

"But hey," said Kate, "it's not like we won't be back this way."

"We sure hope you both come back," Rose said, holding Kate's hand. "Together."

"Wild horses couldn't keep us away," said Kate, looking at Ben, who nodded in agreement.

"Wild Horses?" said Emile, overhearing the conversation and motioning for the other musicians to be quiet. "That's not what we're going to sing, eh Gerard?" he added, as he nodded to the fiddler.

Walking into the middle of the gathering Emile held a small piece of firewood firmly in one hand. Turning to face the group, he pointed the "microphone" at Ben and Kate. Not knowing what to expect, everyone stood in a hushed silence. Slowly Emile began to sing as Gerard lightly pulled the rosined bow across the strings.

Immediately, the crowd recognized Kenzie MacNeil's now-famous "anthem" and remained quiet as Emile led off with the chorus, speaking the words slowly as he looked straight at Kate and Ben.

"We are an island, a rock in the stream
We are a people, as proud as there's been
In soft summer breeze, or in wild winter winds
The home of our hearts, Cape Breton"

With that, they all joined in for the first verse as those remaining settled in for a long night.

Closing her eyes, Kate rested her head against Ben's shoulder and moved slowly to the music. As a slight breeze pushed the flames around the fire pit, she imagined the fiddle tune drifting slowly through the cool autumn air. Drowned out from time to time by the chorus of voices and clinking beer bottles, it floated away from the small group, high above the trees, toward a little valley along the Trail.

No matter where we end up, she thought, *this will always be a special place.*

CHAPTER 71

THE HOUSE STOOD empty by the edge of the road, its windows bared to the world, the front rooms bathed in moonlight. The silence would be momentary, for in a few weeks the new warden would take up residence. In that time, the house would get a new coat of paint and carpet throughout.

But tonight, it was the lone sentinel at the entrance to the park.

Across the road, the two-storey saltbox sat in total darkness except for one small light in an upstairs bedroom.

Down the road, a truck started up and backed onto the Trail, an open gun scabbard sitting between the driver and his passenger. Alternating between clutch and accelerator, the driver shifted gears and headed toward the park.

As he approached the warden residence, the driver glanced at the house and smiled, then pressed the gas pedal to the floor.

Rounding the curve heading toward the Chéticamp River, the taillights disappeared into the night.

POSTSCRIPT

FOR MORE THAN 100 years, Canada's National Park Warden Service performed law enforcement, public safety and resource management duties, employing almost five hundred park wardens in recent decades to manage these programs in our national parks.

All of that changed in 2008, when the Warden Service was restructured, creating an armed group of one hundred park wardens to provide law enforcement for more than half a million square kilometres of park land spread across the country. The remaining former park wardens were reassigned to natural and cultural resource management and public safety duties, and lost the "Park Warden" title. Their numbers were subsequently reduced in 2012 by federal government cuts that left Canada's national parks seriously understaffed and underfunded.

Poaching continues to be a serious issue in some of Canada's national parks, and is especially prevalent in other national parks around the world, notably in many African countries, where illegal activities threaten the existence of some species.

You can support the protectors of wild species and spaces by contributing to the efforts of The North American Wildlife Enforcement Officers Association (http://naweoa.org), The Thin Green Line Foundation (http://www.thingreenline.org.au/) and the International Ranger Federation (http://internationalrangers.org/).

A portion of the proceeds from the sale of this book will be donated to these organizations.

George Mercer
July, 2014

Read the opening chapters of the next book in
the *Dyed In The Green* series …

Wood Buffalo

PROLOGUE

THE WILLOWS LASHED at his face as Charlie struggled through the deep snow, weighted down by the ice quickly encasing his tattered snow boots. Despite the thirty below temperature, a steady stream of sweat stung the blood-encrusted lacerations creasing across his weathered face.

Out on the delta's snow-covered expanse, the occasional howl of the pack could still be heard, buffeted by the steady drone of the snowmobiles working their way toward him.

The wolves' focus had been shifted only momentarily by the movement of people along one of their well-used travel routes, the pangs of hunger quickly re-establishing priority over a passing curiosity. Regrouping in the willows bordering the large frozen lake, their objective was now foundering in its attempt to get away.

The band of willows seemed impenetrable but a survival instinct continued to propel Charlie toward the small creek winding its way into the forest of white spruce and the possibility of escape. The small cabin, sheltered by a thick canopy of evergreens and known only to him, offered the sole advantage over his pursuers. The rusted 12-gauge stored under the mattress might be his only defence.

Their advantage was that he was breaking trail, making their pursuit that much easier.

But first they would have to find the opening.

Charlie hoped the slight lead he gained on his pursuers might have been enough, giving him time to put some distance between them before backtracking and jumping off the trail unnoticed. He had landed a couple of good blows and both men were struggling back to their feet when he pulled the keys from their machines and tossed them into the wind. He knew they would be able to quickly bypass the ignition switch and start the snowmobiles without the keys. Still, it might be all the time he needed.

When they caught up, he hoped the view down the barrel of a shotgun might be enough for them to reconsider their options and leave him alone. Back in town, cooler heads might prevail, hopefully reducing the likelihood they would do something stupid. Either way, he knew they had a score to settle and wouldn't give up easily. Staying in the bush might be in his best interest for a while, at least until things settled down, but only time would tell.

The snap of a willow branch somewhere behind him reminded Charlie that his focus right now was just making it to the creek.

Pushing forward, he crawled the remaining distance through the spider web of crisscrossed branches, completing the final few feet by grabbing the stem of a thick willow and pulling himself through the tangled mess to the top of the creek bank.

As he lay in the snow catching his breath Charlie's attention was distracted by the yipping of wolves. They were closing in for the kill and seemed much closer than he had previously thought.

Desperate to find the cabin, Charlie willed his waning energy into one last push to rise to his feet but slipped and rolled headlong down the bank, snowballing into a heap on an open patch of ice. Remaining facedown, the cold against his cheek provided a brief respite from the sweat and stench engulfing his body, as he took a much-needed rest before struggling to his knees.

At that moment, the rising crescendo of wolf yips suddenly went silent as a young cow bison came crashing through the willow thickets and plowed its way down the creek bank, streaming a trail of blood from a series of gashes shredding her hindquarters.

Standing less than a dozen metres away, Charlie's presence barely registered with the animal as she stood motionless on the ice, staring over her shoulder at the large whitish wolf regarding her from the top of the rise. Sporting a blood-matted coat of yellowing fur, the alpha male sat for a moment before being joined by six other members of the pack. Taking their cue from the large male's teeth-bared snarl, the younger wolves lay panting on the snowbank on either side of their leader, awaiting his next move.

Wary of the wolves but deciding that they were more interested in the bison than himself, Charlie rose slowly to his feet just as his pursuers waded through the willows and stopped on the creek bank above him.

Realizing they had landed in the middle of a standoff, the two men quickly assessed the situation and exchanged comments that were barely audible to Charlie. The larger of the two, sporting a swollen right eye that reinforced the meanness in his stare, reluctantly nodded to the other man, took one last look at their quarry and turned back toward the willows.

The smaller man looked down at Charlie as his scowl morphed into a smile that didn't escape the older trapper's gaze.

"See you in town, Quentin," Charlie called out, as he sidestepped slowly toward the other side of the creek, keeping one eye on the wolves while simultaneously searching the far bank for a route into the forest.

His movement seemed to trigger the alpha male into action as the large white wolf rose slowly and led his charges down the steep bank and onto the ice, encircling the young bison and the old trapper.

Quentin's smile broadened as he pulled the flaps of his fur hat down around his ears. Saluting to Charlie, he took one final look at the scene unfolding on the creek then disappeared into the willows behind his partner.

CHAPTER 1

LIKELY NO ONE else on the jet was paying attention to the changing landscape below them but since leaving Edmonton, Johnson Bourque had watched the slow transformation from prairie farmland to poplar forest to boreal plains. Before they reached Fort Smith there would be one more shift as the granite knobs of Canadian Shield protruded from the earth, adding an element of relief to what might seem to others a relatively flat topography. With the exception of the massive deconstruction of the northern landscape that was the Athabasca tar sands, the seamless transition would challenge even the most astute ecologist to define where one biome ended and the other began.

Fort Mac, for all its size, was just an aberration, but the massive oil and gas operations were of such a magnitude it was impossible to ignore their impact on what appeared from the air to be an otherwise untrammeled wilderness.

Johnson looked down upon the tar sands and shook his head, preferring to wipe them from his memory. He viewed them as an insidious assault on Mother Earth, creeping steadily northward toward the traditional territory of his people. But for others they were a mixed blessing, paying high wages to the members of his community that worked the long shifts on a two week rotation, stealing away a cohort of young people who had been expected to follow on with the traditional pursuits of their parents and grandparents. The aboriginal cultures of the Cree, Chipewyan and Dene were quickly eroding as they gave in to the lure of western technology and the pressures of a consumer driven economy.

Johnson knew he was fighting a losing battle. Like his father before him, he accepted that change would happen but he wanted it to happen on their terms and at their pace. Looking around him at the half-empty plane, he knew that many of the familiar faces did not share his perspective on northern development but he wondered what side of the coin some of the new faces were on.

Sitting across the aisle, Ben Matthews thumbed through the weekend edition of the Edmonton Journal, his attention captured briefly by a story about the disappearance of a local trapper from the Wood Buffalo area. Somewhere north of here the man had seemingly vanished into thin air, the recent heavy snowfalls all but obliterating any hope of tracking him in a subarctic landscape that would become Ben's new territory for the foreseeable future.

Ben was anxious to get to Fort Smith and settle in but for the moment his attention was diverted from the story as he looked out the window of the plane. Mesmerized by the view below, Ben could barely grasp the extent of the tar sand's open pits and tailings ponds, their earthen berms seemingly metres from the Athabasca River, threatening to empty their toxic contents into the massive waterway. It was his first glimpse of what was fast becoming the internal combustion engine of the country's economy, revving up to make Canada an "energy superpower", supplying the United States' insatiable thirst for oil.

"They're massive aren't they?" said the passenger from across the aisle who now settled into the seat next to Ben and pointed his nose toward the window.

"I'd heard they were big," said Ben, "but never thought they were that big."

"Johnson Bourque," said the stranger, extending a hand callused by years of work in the bush. "You're new here."

"Ben Matthews. Yes, I'm coming north to work in Wood Buffalo."

"I had you pegged for a government guy," said Johnson. "What are you? A park warden?"

"Good guess," said Ben, smiling. "Or are we that easy to spot?"

"No, it's just that you white guys all look alike and park wardens in particular, they all have that little moustache thing happening and take things way too serious."

Before Ben could respond, Johnson let out a massive laugh that rocked the insides of the aircraft.

"I'm only screwing with you," he said, rolling his shoulder into Ben's then motioning for the stewardess. "Can I buy you a drink before we get to Smith?"

"What would you like," said the young flight attendant, making her way to their seat.

"I'll have a ginger ale," said Johnson. "And this young man will have."

"A ginger ale as well," said Ben.

"A man after my own heart," said Johnson. "I like you already."

Leaning across Ben and looking out the window, Johnson could see they were almost over the delta.

"Take a look," he said, motioning to Ben. "You can even see them from thirty thousand feet."

"What am I looking at exactly?" said Ben.

"Those are the lakes that make up the delta," said Johnson. "And if you look on the north side of the largest lake you can see the corrals of Sweetgrass. They were used for the bison roundups when the park was still dealing with TB and brucellosis in the park herds."

Once they had been pointed out, Ben could see the outline of the large corral system and the kilometres of wing fences fanning out into the forests of white spruce and poplar.

"Those fences were used to direct bison back into the corrals. Initially they used horses to drive the bison but they shifted to helicopters around twenty years ago. The north isn't a great place to keep horses because the flies and mosquitoes drive them nuts. They say most of the horses had to be put down."

"I can only imagine," said Ben. "I've never been North before but I've heard all about the bugs."

"Well, hearing about them and hearing them are two different things," said Johnson, smiling. "The sound alone has been known to drive some people over the edge. Most of those folks leave and only the ones who are already crazy stay in the North. I seen it so bad you had to duct tape the kids mouths shut when they played outside."

With this last comment Johnson leaned back and searched Ben's eyes for a response, a twinkle glistening in his own deep brown orbs before he burst out laughing again.

"I'm only shittin' ya," he said, stifling another laugh. "We don't even let the kids out when it gets bad. Scared they'll be carried off."

"You don't miss a beat, do you?" said Ben, with a huge grin.

"Ah, hell," said Johnson. "People are too serious. Living up here you need a sense of humour to get you through the long winter nights. You'll see."

"I'm actually really looking forward to it," said Ben. "It will be a whole new chapter in our lives."

"Our lives?" said Johnson.

"Hopefully my girlfriend will be joining me," said Ben.

"Smart man," said Johnson. "Bringing a woman up here will make it easier. If she likes it. If she does, you're in like Flint. If not, well need I say more?"

Ben laughed and nodded in agreement with Johnson.

Hopefully Kate would be keen to stay, as long as she could get work. The outfit was pretty good at finding jobs for couples but it sometimes meant that one of them had to pretty well start again at square one, not something anyone was keen on.

Looking out the window he wondered how she was doing and let his mind wander back to Cape Breton.

It was night-time and he was following a trail into the bush. Joe was telling him to wait up but something was drawing him into the darkness. He had to find Michel. Rushing into the clearing he almost stumbled over the body, partially hidden in the bushes.

It was a recurring nightmare and he wondered if he would ever be able to shake it, waking up in a cold sweat when he saw Michel's empty stare searching the night sky.

Hopefully time and distance would erase the image but he knew he would never forget what happened.

A noise from the aisle brought Ben around as a small man in a beaded moose hide jacket muscled his way rudely around the flight attendant's drink cart to stand opposite them.

"Hey Johnson," said the man, brusquely. "You out spending the band's money again?"

"What's it to you, Quentin?" said Johnson, looking up from his seat. "You've been bellied up to the government's pork barrel for so long your nose is flat."

"Fuck you too," said Quentin, glaring at Johnson and mouthing the words so they were barely audible, then pushing his way further down the aisle to take a seat in the back of the plane.

Johnson looked at Ben and shrugged.

"That's the first time I've seen him when he's not up front flying First Class."

"Who is he?" said Ben.

"Oh, you'll get to know him," said Johnson. "His name is Quentin Spence. He's a local Metis who's spearheading the push to slaughter all of your bison. Or have you heard about that?"

"I've heard. It's one of the reasons I wanted to transfer here."

"To get in on the kill?" said Johnson sarcastically.

"No. To help put an end to the idea."

"Well, good luck with that. It's pretty much a done deal."

"But there's a federal review panel set up to look at it," said

Ben. "They don't make their decision for another six months or more."

Johnson shook his head and grinned at Ben.

"I hate to say this young man, but you've got a lot to learn. The panel is a formality and the back door deal has already been made. It'll take something pretty serious to stop it. Likely something more than you or I could muster."

Stifling a response, Ben turned and looked out the window, following the path of the river northward toward the horizon. Settling back in his seat, he closed his eyes and tried to force his thoughts away from the Highlands and into the new frontier he was about to enter.